Contradictions

SEVeith

I0640346

Chapter One

A hooded figure wandered through the bustling marketplace, his hands buried in the sleeves folded in front of him. From within the shadows he watched the people move about, buyers buying, sellers selling, beggars begging, children playing. Women walked by with their children in tow, each one carrying a load appropriate to their age and strength. The men sat in small groups discussing the jousting championship that had just ended.

He walked past them all, his eyes seeing them without any real purpose except to watch with a detached interest in human behavior. That was his passion, the study of the behavior of the people around him. It was always interesting to watch how people would change their stance and posture when someone important would walk by. Those with confidence would straighten up, standing tall and proud, respectful of the importance of the person passing by. While on the other hand those without confidence, or whose confidence had been beaten out of them, would shrink away, hiding themselves as best they could from the person of seeming importance.

It was that type of person that held his interest. The ones who shrank away, hiding their face with a bowed head, they were the ones that he studied with the most enjoyment. The working classes, the poor, the serfs, those people who weren't confined to the laws and rule of behavior the rich were forced to abide by. Life had taught them to stay away from, if not fear, the members of the upper class. But when there was none of that distant class present, or at least none to their knowledge, they were free to live and act as they pleased. Laughter could fill the air, music pulsing through each soul until their feet were lifted to dance.

But he knew there were other sounds that filled the air, especially the night air, when the silence of the world around them seemed to amplify those other sounds. The sound of a child plagued by a fit of coughing. The noise made by a woman crying as she sent her children to bed with little more than a bite in their stomachs, her own aching one empty. The silence of a tortured man who watches his family suffer the lack of necessities they simply cannot obtain; necessities he cannot provide. The frustrated sigh of the brightest student who must abandon his studies to learn a trade to help feed his family.

Those sounds served as a reminder to him that as difficult as his life may be, as frustrating as it sometimes became, there were people worse off than he ever was.

Sitting down at the water fountain he listened in on the conversation of the two women gathering water for their family, the antics of a comedic performer who had performed in the street last night still lifting their voices in laughter. Smiling in the shadow of his hood he tilted his head to hear the men on the other side as they discussed the rise in the price of meat, shocked at how much the lords were trying to make the peasants pay for the sustenance they needed to survive. He listened to them debate the prices from five years ago, until a sight across the street caught his attention.

Outside a small pub, a serf was clearing a plate from before her master, the portly man having had his fill while those around him went hungry, when she saw a small child eyeing the scraps sitting on the plate she held in her hands. Glancing quickly at her master the woman slipped a portion of the scraps into her hand, giving it to the child as she passed him on her way away from the table. The little boy scurried away, the food quickly disappearing into his mouth.

"Stop!" the master commanded, ordering her to come back to the table.

Watching with curiosity he could see the calmness in the serf's eyes as she turned around. Moving back toward the table she stood before her master with a steady stance. Saying nothing she stood before the glowering man, plate still held in her hands. She didn't flinch as he began to yell at her, scolding and berating her for giving a scrap she hadn't paid for to an insignificant child. The woman took the verbal abuse without flinching, her back straight and her eyes meeting the masters with a steady gaze that was uncommon among the serf class. He wondered why her spirit hadn't been beaten down like the others she worked with.

Listening to the pompous windbag berate the woman he was about to turn away when he saw the Lord raise his ringed fist and hit the woman who had stood peacefully before him. His jeweled rings catching the sleeve of her shirt, tearing both cloth and skin, and the white material began to turn crimson with the blood drawn by her master. He watched the woman turn away, cradling her arm, covering the wound with her hand and pressing against it to stop the bleeding.

Another serf came to her aid but found herself under attack for doing so. His attention riveted the man watched the scene from the shadows of his cloak as the first woman, the injured serf, came between the master and the woman who had tried to help her, giving the second woman a chance to escape the blows. Seeing the serf stand up to him the master became even more infuriated but before he could do anything his manservant approached, whispering in his ear and gesturing toward the end of the street. Following the gesture, he realized that the Lord had been warned that there was royalty in the area, the guardsmen standing at the carriage carrying the royal crest on their tunic.

Ignoring everyone else the Lord straightened his clothes and headed down the way to the carriage to offer his greetings to the royal waiting in the carriage. Watching him walk away for a moment the man turned his attention back to the serf only to find her gone, the half empty plate sitting on the ground where it had been dropped. Glancing around he couldn't see her anywhere and wondered where the intriguing serf had gone.

Seeing the servants approaching the man stood up from his seat by the fountain and headed away from them, towards the inn they had stopped at to rest. Entering the small building he made his way up the stairs to the room they had taken for the night and shut the door behind him. Removing his cloak, he laid it over a chair before sitting down by the fire to warm his chilled hands. As he watched the flames dance he couldn't help but think of the serf who had stood up to her master. Under the light of the sun her hair had been the same shade of red as the flames that licked the wood and brick of the fireplace.

How strange it had been to see a serf, a slave, stand up to her master the way she had. Had any of the serfs serving his family done it he knew his fathers' manservant would have killed them. It simply was not the place of a serf to be so bold. But even still he couldn't help but respect a woman who would risk that kind of abuse to feed a starving child or defend a fellow serf. She intrigued him, not only as a bold serf, but also as a person. What inner strength she must possess to have not let the life of a serf beat her down and wear away any boldness and courage she had left. And yet, despite all that, she had stood respectfully before her master, not defiant or rebellious.

The woman was a puzzle that he wondered if he would ever have the chance to solve.

Pulled from his thought the man looked up to see that the door to the room had opened and a young woman had entered, her dress practically shimmering against the firelight. Smiling at him she crossed the room to kiss his cheek. "Good day, brother," she greeted him before sitting down across from him.

Watching her sit down he shook his head with a slight scowl. "How did you find me?"

"Mother has one of her spies keeping an eye on you. He informed us of where you were."

"And you came out to make sure he told the truth?"

"To welcome you home," she smiled back, ignoring his black mood. "You have been gone for too many months, we miss you."

"It's only been five months."

"Are you not happy to see me?" she asked with a small frown.

Realizing he had hurt his sisters feeling he leaned forward and took her small hands in his. "Of course, I am happy to see you. Forgive me, it has been a strange day," he told her, bringing her hands to his lips to kiss them gently.

"Tell me what bothers you and I shall set it right."

Shaking his head, he smiled for the first time all day. "Enough about me. Tell me how you have been keeping yourself these past five months."

Sitting back, he listened to his sister detail the events of the last few months, the visits, the balls, the tea's; all the frivolous details of her life that she loved so much. Watching his sister come alive with her laughter he hoped that their father would give her some time to truly live before forcing her into a marriage she wasn't ready for.

Rianne was his last sister, the youngest in the family, and he knew it wouldn't be long until their father began to search for a proper match for her, a husband to bed the young woman and produce heirs. His older sister, Victoria, had been fortunate enough to fall in love with the man their father had chosen for her. But Elizabeth, his first younger sister, had been married to an ogre of a man. As mean as he was ugly it wasn't long until she had begun spending more time at her childhood home than she did at the home of her husband.

Their father had taken no note until it was too late. Sadly, it took the death of his first granddaughter for the older man to realize the monster he had married his daughter to. Bound by the laws of both God and country their father had been unable to break the marriage he had given her to but he had brought his daughter home to live away from her husband, while keeping the agreement between the two men.

He hoped that experience would be foremost on his father's mind as he searched for a husband for his youngest daughter.

"Are you listening to me?"

Lifting his eyes from the fire to his sister he realized she had been trying to get his attention. "I'm sorry, you were saying?"

"Where had your thoughts taken you?" Rianne inquired; a curious look on her face.

Smiling he shook his head and stood. "Somewhere far less pleasant than being here with you. Are you hungry? Perhaps I should call for the servants and we can take our meal together."

Waiting for her to agree he opened the door and stepped into the hallway, motioning to one of the servants in the hall that they were ready for their meal. Closing the door, he turned around to see his sister standing by the window, about to open the curtain. Hurrying to the window he stopped her before she could pull the curtain back, telling her he wanted it to stay closed.

"But why?"

Pausing for a moment he replied, "Because I wish it to remain that way."

Confused Rianne opened her mouth to ask a question but was silenced by a knock on the door. Moments later they were seated at the table that was filled with food, the savory aroma of roasted meat and vegetables filling the air and making his mouth water with anticipation. Waiting for the servant to finish dishing out the food he sat still until Rianne had begun eating before beginning his own meal. Occupied by their meal the room was silent as they ate, a reprieve from the curiosity he had seen in his sister's eyes.

They had been traveling for only a few days when it had happened the first time, the arrows flying through the air faster than they could move. He'd already lost one man to them; several more had been injured, and he knew better than to take a foolish risk like opening a curtain. Someone was trying to kill him and it angered him that his men had paid the price.

Chapter Two

Sitting on a small ledge she pulled the strip of cloth tighter around her arm, putting the necessary pressure on the open wound on her upper arm from the many rings the man who claimed to own her wore on his meaty hands. Grimacing at the pain she wrapped the strip around once more before tucking the edge of it under the fold so it was secure. It had been a stupid risk to give away the scraps while he was still there to see but the boy had been eyeing the food on the table all morning, his ribs visible through his threadbare shirt. A stupid risk, yes, but one she would take again if she were given the opportunity.

Sighing she stood up and moved across the room to gather the plates that needed washing. Lord Byron of Pirtonshire had left their area some time ago to greet the royalty that had arrived in the carriage after Alec, his manservant, had informed him of their presence. No sooner had the man left the table than she had darted into the pub, hurrying to the kitchen, knowing better than to stick around in case he came back to deliver some more of his heavy-handed punishment.

As she gathered the dishes to wash she heard the sound of bare feet on the stones outside and lifted her eyes to see Beatrice enter the kitchen, a bruise forming on her cheek from where the master had hit her. With soft hands, she brushed away the tears that lingered on her bruised cheek. Forcing a smile onto her face she thanked her friend for what she had done. Hugging her for a moment they got to work, side by side at the wash buckets, to clean the kitchen before the master returned.

She was just finishing drying the last dish when she heard a sound from the doorway. There in the arch of the doorway, a pained expression upon his face, stood Alec. Frowning she watched him come into the room and stop a few feet away from her. Reaching out she touched his shoulder and asked what was wrong.

"The master has just informed me that we will be selling a few of the serfs tomorrow in the market."

"Who?" Beatrice asked fearfully.

"Both of you," he admitted with difficulty. "I'm so sorry, if there were any way to stop him I would,
but..."

Placing her hand on his arm she stopped him. "There is nothing you could have done."

Resigned to the truth Alec nodded and turned to leave. A teary Beatrice turned back to her chore of scrubbing the floor. Standing still for a moment she finished drying the last dish and dropped the rag into the wash bucket to wet it. Wringing out the excess water she turned and went outside to wash the table. Her hands moving automatically, she wiped off the dry crumbs and the used the wet rag to wash off the rest. As her hands moved in rhythmic circles, she couldn't stop the anger that was building in her, bubbling up over the wall she had built around her heart. For more years than she cared to remember she had been working for the Lord Byron in the role of a serf. It was a humiliation she had been forced to bear since the day her father had been lost in service to the King.

The day she had been stolen from her bed.

It had also been the last day that she had seen her mother. She remembered that day as though it was only yesterday even though it had been over fifteen years ago. As a child of barely eight years she had woken up to find a man she didn't know coming into her bedroom in the middle of the night. She had managed to scream once before the man raised his fist and brought it crashing down to her face, knocking her into a black oblivion. When she had come to her beautiful nightclothes had been exchanged for the roughly woven skirt and shirt of a serf, her beautiful long red hair chopped short and jagged, her feet and hands bound as she had laid on the cold stone floor of a cellar.

Thus, had begun a nightmare that continued for the last ten years of her life.

She had been alone and scared, terrified really. The others shied away from her at first until one older woman took her under her wing and taught her what she needed to do to stay alive as a serf. It was that woman who had shown her how to keep her own sense of pride while serving as a slave to a man who cared more for the lives of his dogs than of his serfs. She had soaked in the knowledge the older woman had given her, taking it all in like a parched ground does water, until the work was second nature to her.

As the years had passed she'd found that she remembered less and less of her childhood days, 'the before' time as she had dubbed it. All she had left were a few of her memories. A child's memories as seen by an adult. She could remember picnicking with her mother while her father had fished in a nearby pond. At night, when she dreamed, she saw herself sitting on her fathers' lap by the fireplace and listening to him tell a tale of far off lands; places like Spain, France, and England with their different clothing and traditions. But the memories seemed as distant as the sun and as pale as the moon.

Years passed, as they always did, and she had come to accept her new place in the world. But even through all the trials, the pain and the sadness, she never forgot who she was and where she came from. Her goal hung before her like a carrot dangled before a horse.

Finished with the table she gathered the rag and went back inside to the kitchen. With no other work needing to be done she crossed the kitchen to the fireplace and sat down in a small chair by the hearth. Staring at the flames she let herself drift off to sleep, not realizing she had done so until Beatrice was shaking her awake the next morning.

Getting to her feet, stretching out the slight knot in her back from such an awkward sleeping position, she hurried with the rest of the kitchen serfs to get the morning meal ready for the master when he emerged. An old habit from his childhood days the master always took his morning meal at the pub. His midday meal as well if he were in the area. But his evening meal was always taken at the manor with his wife, a reprieve for the serfs that had been serving him all day.

As he ate the serfs stood nearby, ready to come if he called. No sooner had he finished than Lord Byron stood and motioned to the two men standing by the awning of the pub. Almost immediately the two men rushed forward, locking their hands around the two women's shoulder with viselike grips. Propelled forward they stopped before the master and were held in place as he looked them over one by one. With a sneer, he ordered the men to take them to the main square to be sold to the highest bidder.

Carried away neither woman could stop what was happening and mere moments later they found themselves standing on a platform with the others in the middle of the square, an auctioneer calling out prices as the serfs were sold one by one. When it came time for Beatrice to be sold she forced herself to be strong for the woman, the teary-eyed serf already emotional enough without adding her own pain and frustration to it.

Listening to the prices being called out, various men bidding for their Lords as though Beatrice were little more than a side of beef, she felt her frustration begin to turn to anger. Biting her cheek, she watched as her friend was bought and paid for by the kitchen servant for a Lord she had never heard of. Watching her being taken away she fought the urge to scream at the injustice of it all. They were still humans, God's creatures just like the Lords and Ladies that were buying them, why could they not be given the same decency as the lowest of farm animals?

Pulled forward she was brought to the edge of the stage and the auctioneer began to call out her past masters, the strength and skills she possessed and her health. Refusing to allow them to demean her she held her head high, watching from the corner of her eyes as one man after another passed her over as being headstrong and stubborn, too much of a problem to bother with. Why buy a headstrong serf when they could buy a broken one for less?

After some time, she heard the auctioneer begin to lower the price and she bit back a smile of satisfaction. There would be less money for Lord Byron to prosper from the sale of her to another master. Suddenly there was a bid. Seeing his opportunity, the auctioneer declared her sold to the man, the only one who had dared to bid on such a headstrong serf. Pushed off the stage she was pulled through the crowd to the man who had placed the one and only bid. Money changed hands and suddenly she found herself facing an older man dressed in fine clothes, finer than even Lord Byron could wear.

"This way," the man said, his voice carefully neutral, neither harsh nor kind.

Following behind him she wondered just what kind of man had purchased her. Was he the servant or the master? If he was the master, why did he attend the sale himself? But if he is the servant dressed in finer clothes than a Lord, who was his master? Questions filled her head as she followed the man through the street. Glancing around her she realized they had stopped in front of a dress shop, the wares finer than any serf would be dressed in. Was this where she was to work?

Motioning for her to go inside she did as he asked, surprised that he didn't follow her in. Before she could question her presence in the shop the attending matron was at her side directing her to the back of the shop. There, waiting with smiling faces, were two other women standing around a copper tub filled with steaming water. Without a chance to protest she was stripped of her clothes and told to climb into the tub of water where one of the women began to scrub her body while the other scrubbed her hair. While the other two engaged in their work the third woman gathered the rags they had taken from her and crossed the room to toss them into the fire that burned against one wall, the clothing catching fire and burning quickly until they were little more than ash.

Silenced every time she tried to speak there was nothing she could do except to let the three women do their work, her mind filled with questions. What kind of man had bought her? What did he want with her? Why was she being treated this way?

The washing completes she was lifted from the tub and told to stand on a mat near the fire. Given a large bath sheet with which to remain decent she huddled near the fire to stay warm while watching the three women bustle around the room. Pulling things from cupboards and drawers the three women hurried around, pulling this and that from everywhere until they stood before her, showing her the complete product of their labors.

Her eyes widened in awe as she saw them approach her, gown in hand, and remove the bath sheet, drying her off before lowering the gown over her head and fitting it to her body. Sitting her down in a chair one of the women began to fit a pair of slippers to her feet while the second worked to remove the tangles and snarls from her hair. Unable to watch the other two she turned her attention to the third woman as she began to pull even more items from various trunks and drawers around the room and putting them into an empty one in the middle.

Before she had time to contemplate the change in her life the right sized slippers adorned her feet and her hair had been brushed out and braided into a plait running down her back. Getting up from the chair she stood before a full-length mirror and stared at her reflection. It was a face she saw in her dreams, the face of a mother so long removed from her life that her dreams were all she had left.

An unbidden tear came to her eye and she hurriedly brushed it away before it could fall and ruin the gown she was wearing. The powder blue material, soft as a flower petal against her skin, flowed down from her shoulders to the floor, tucked in to show off her figure, a figure that had been built by years of hard work. At her waist rested a belt, tied loosely and hanging down almost to the floor. Staring at her image questions began to fill her mind all over again. Why was she dressed like this? What did this new master want of her?

Not given the chance to contemplate her questions the three women escorted her out of the room to the street where the man stood waiting. Nodding his approval, he handed the shopkeeper a small bag of coin and motioned for two men to carry the trunk that the woman had filled. Motioning for her to follow him the man began to walk down the street again, heading away from the shop and toward the inn at the end of the street. Up the stairs to the top floor the man opened a door and motioned for her to enter the room.

Entering the empty room, she turned to see him closing the door, telling her to stay there.

Left alone she looked around her in silence. The room was one of the more expensive ones, she could tell by the size and the furniture that filled it. Her new master was obviously a very rich man but that fact didn't tell her anything else about him or the reason she had been purchased. Forcing herself to silence her question filled mind she chose to sit on the window ledge after pushing back the curtain, the warmth of the sun's rays warming her against the chill of a cold hearth. She had almost succeeded in silencing her mind when the door opened and a man she had never seen before entered.

Chapter Three

Sitting at the table, an empty plate pushed to the side, he watched Rianne finish her own morning meal while going over the list of things she needed to get before leaving for their return trip home. Listening to her list the things she needed he wondered why it was a woman needed so many things with her for what was, hopefully, going to be a simple journey home. When she had finished, he took the list and, kissing her cheek as they always did, he left the inn, his hooded cloak shadowing his face from the view of any that might recognize him.

As he emerged from the inn to the street he smiled when his manservant joined him in his trek down the street. From his childhood days Edward had been by his side as his manservant. Edward was the one man whose loyalty he had never doubted, trusting the man implicitly with his very life. He was closer to him than he was to his own father. Sharing the list of items needing to be purchased he listened as Edward advised which places to go first, having already checked each shop for the quality of their products. They both knew that it wasn't his place to be shopping for their wares but he didn't care.

Letting Edward take the lead he was walking toward the square when he heard the call of an auctioneer. Curious he moved forward to get a better look. Stopping in an archway at the edge of the square he watched as a man pointed out the finer qualities of the serf standing on the platform next to him. Frowning he watched for a moment before turning to leave only to stop at the flash of red hair that caught his attention from somewhere in the crowd. Focusing he scanned the people before him, wondering if she had come to watch a fellow serf be sold. Not seeing her, knowing he had pressing business to attend to, he was about to continue on his way when he saw her again.

Raising his eyes to the stage he saw her, standing tall above the crowd, her head held high with pride instead of cowering before the man who was yelling at her. She kept her eyes forward, refusing to allow herself to stoop under the pressure he was piling upon her. Listening as the man called out bids trying to entice the crowd to buy her; he watched as one man after another looked her over and turned away. No man wanted a proud serf, it would entail too much work to try and break her of her willful spirit.

After several moments, listening as the auctioneer dropped the price in a last-ditch effort to entice a buyer, he turned to Edward and handed him a small sack of coin. "Take her. Have her ready to travel with Rianne by the midday meal."

Leaving Edward in the crowd he moved on to place the orders he needed to make so that they could begin their travels this afternoon. Having ordered everything on the list Rianne had written for him he turned back toward the inn, wanting to get a few moments of peace before Rianne returned from her morning tea. Climbing the steps to the room they were using he opened the door and entered the room only to see a woman sitting in the window, her face gazing out with a longing look in her eyes.

It was her.

~~*~*~*~*~*~*~*

"Milord," she said as she stood from her seat to bow with a respectful grace.

"Do not let me disturb your viewing," he told her, waving his hand toward the window she had been sitting in. "Was it something of interest that caught your attention?"

"No, milord," she replied. "It was nothing important."

Nodding he sat down in a chair in the corner, watching her. "What is your name, woman?"

"I am called Da'Leth."

He raised an eyebrow; curious as to why she would phrase the answer in such a way. Keeping his curiosity to himself he watched her for a moment. She stood tall and proud yet at the same time respectful of the authority of the man that had purchased her from Lord Byron. He could feel his earlier curiosity returning to him. Stamping it down, for now at least, he focused in on her last answer.

"A unique name, how did you come to have it?"

"It was given to me by an old woman who took me into her care as a child." His questions were beginning to enter a personal area of her life and Da'Leth hoped he would stop asking her such personal questions.

"What name were you given at birth?" he asked.

"Josephine." It was a common enough name and she was sure he would not be able to associate it to her family.

"But you prefer to be called Da'Leth?" She nodded. "Very well. What has become of your family?"

"I do not know, milord," she replied, watching him take in the knowledge. She could see that he assumed their master had sold her family and Da'Leth was content to let him continue to believe it.

Watching her for a moment he wondered if there was more to what she was telling him. Choosing to let it go he stood up from his chair and began to pace the floor, an old habit that annoyed him as much as it helped him think. "You will be accompanying my party on our journey. My sister has joined us without the escort of her ladies' maids and I cannot have her traveling among a large group of men without one."

Understanding dawned in Da'Leth's eyes. She was to be a ladies' maid to the Lords sister; hence the superior quality garments.

"You will begin your duties tomorrow morning and there are several rules you will adhere to. I will not have my sister listening to anything less than proper speech or witnessing any improper etiquette. If you do not know what you need to do or say, then do or say nothing."

"Yes milord," she replied with a soft tone and a small curtsey. Inwardly she smiled, knowing what the Lord before her was thinking of her, a serf with no education could never speak properly to a Lady.

"Very well. If you have anyone you need to say a farewell to before we leave in the morning, please do so now. You will be left alone until tomorrow morning," he advised her as he moved toward the doorway that led to the bedroom. "We leave at first light."

Shocked, Da'Leth raised her eyes to meet his. "Thank you, milord," she said after a moment of silence.

Nodding he shut the door behind him as he left the main room, heading over to the window to look out from behind the safety of the curtain, pulling it back just enough to see out. As Nicholas had expected he saw her, walking away from the inn towards the heart of the square. Watching until he could see her no more he wondered what she was thinking of this strange man who would let a serf run free. Would the temptation to run away prove to be too strong? He hoped not, as the guard that was following her would bring her back if she did try to escape and he was sure to do it none to gently.

Passing his eyes over the crowd of people he saw two men sitting at the table outside the inn across the way and something about them made him linger for a moment. He didn't recognize them but there was something he couldn't quite put his finger on that made him question their being there. Before he could think of what it was one of the men raised his eyes to the window only to lower them quickly and reach for his tankard of ale.

"The sooner we leave, the better," he whispered to the empty room.

~~*~*~*~*~*~*~*

Standing outside the building Da'Leth stared at it, trying to force herself to go in but unable to take that first step. Staring up at the stone building that stood before her she could hear the man that had made her life a waking nightmare, she could hear his verbal attacks in her mind, feel his fists on her skin as it tingled with memory. From the moment she had come to this place she had hated him for the things he did, not only to her but also to the people she had quickly come to care for as though they were her family. But the Lady of Pirtonshire held a different place in her life. Looking off to the left she saw the stone fence that marked the time she had first met the Lady Jane.

Forcing herself to climb the stairs and enter the manor her mind drifted back to that day nearly twelve years ago, when she had been ordered to take a sack of flour to the kitchen in the manor for the cook there had run out. She had been walking along the footpath between the two kitchens when she'd heard a muffled scream coming from around the corner of the building. Dropping the sack of flour, she had run with all her might to find the source of the noise and saw a beautiful woman cornered by a snarling dog, the woman backed up against the stone fence with nowhere to go.

Stopping only long enough to gather several decently sized stones she had run towards the dog, hurling the rocks at it and yelling until it ran off to get away from this strange little girl who had dared to attack it. Making sure the dog wasn't going to come back Da'Leth turned to look at the woman and found that she had fainted; slumped down into the corner of the stone wall she had been backed up against. Remembering that her mother had always kept a small vial of smelling salts in her purse she had opened the delicate purse the woman was carrying with her and waved the small vial quickly under her nose until she had startled awake.

"Miss?"

Glancing about, pulled from her thoughts by the small voice that intruded into her memory, Da'Leth saw a small little girl in a maid's dress waiting nearby, a small pitcher of water in her hands. "I am looking to speak with the Lady of Pirtonshire."

"One moment, miss," the little girl replied, hurrying off with the pitcher in her hand. A few moments later she reappeared, her hands empty this time, and motioned for her to come. Down the hall and through an outer room Da'Leth followed the little girl until she stopped outside another door and motioned for her to continue on her own. Thanking the girl, she opened one of the doors and slipped into the room.

"Who's there?" a voice called out from the bed, the curtains preventing her from seeing who had entered the bedroom. "Come closer."

Slowly Da'Leth approached the bed and gently pulled one of the curtains back so that the woman lying on the bed could see her. Da'Leth was shocked at the woman she saw lying on the bed. The young beautiful woman she had remembered from eleven years ago, had aged. Though she still held her grace and traces of her beauty the woman she saw now seemed only a withered copy of the woman she had known back then. "Lady Jane?"

"Yes," she replied, squinting to see clearly. "Who are you? You look familiar to me."

"I am Josephine, milady."

"Little Josephine?" Lady Jane repeated, shock entering her eyes as she examined Da'Leth closely. "The same little girl who scared off the wild animal that was going to kill me? You have grown into a beautiful young woman, child. But this costume you wear, it is hardly the dress of a serf owned by my husband."

"I have been sold to another Lord, milady."

"I see," Jane said with knowing eyes. "What will you be to this man for him to have dressed you in such a way?"

"I am to escort his sister as ladies' maid among a group of men that they travel with," she told her. "We
leave at first light."

"And you have come as I had asked you to do that day so long ago."

"Yes, milady."

Lady Jane smiled a soft sad smile. "Go to the bureau child and find the trinket box with a jeweled rose on its lid. Bring that box to me." Getting up from the bed Da'Leth did as she was told and, after a moment of looking, found the box the older woman had described. Bringing it back to the bed she set it down on Lady Jane's lap and stood up to wait. "Sit down, girl," she was told. "I am too ill to raise my head to look at you."

Sitting on the edge of the bed she looked at the woman closely. "You do not look well," she said gently.

"I'm not. I had to send my guests home early as well. It was most embarrassing to have to ask her Majesty the Princess to leave my company before she was ready."

"Perhaps, if I may be so bold as to say, it was better to have had her leave before she was ready than to
have had her witness your illness and perhaps become ill herself?"

Despite her embarrassment at the memory Lady Jane smiled. "I believe you may be right, girl." Patting the spot next to her on the bed she invited Da'Leth to move closer. "There is something that I have been keeping hidden for a very long time. I promised myself that before we parted our ways I would make sure that it was passed on to you." Opening the box Lady Jane withdrew a small velvet bag tied shut with ribbon and set it to the side. Closing the box, she set it on the bed and picked up the small bag, stroking it gently as she allowed her mind to drift away.

"The day you were brought to my husband there was a large chest that came with you, a bribe and payment to my husband for keeping silent about what had really happened that night. I didn't know any of the details about what had happened only that he had taken a free girl and made her a serf. To keep me from asking too many questions he gave me the chest and he hoped it would keep me from speaking about what he had done. I am ashamed to admit that I let it."

Looking up at Da'Leth Lady Jane took the young girls' hands into her own and squeezed it gently, pressing the small velvet bag into her hands. Looking down Da'Leth saw the bag in her hands and frowned, unsure of what Lady Jane was trying to tell her.

"Over the years, the various items from that chest were sold or given away or stolen. This is the only thing that remained. I have hidden it since the day I realized who you were." Lady Jane smiled at her. "You look too much like your mother to have been anyone else's daughter."

Da'Leth lifted her head to stare at the Lady leaning back against her pillows. "You knew my mother?"

"I would not dare to presume that I knew her. Passing acquaintances, I'm afraid, I only knew her by her reputation as one of the most beautiful women in the kingdom. It was a beauty that she has passed on to you. Be careful how you go, child. Any who knew your mother will see her in you, take care that you are not seen by any of your Uncles' friends lest they report it to him. As a serf, you had no reason to be recognized but now that you travel with a Lady and a Lord you must take care."

"I will, Lady Jane," Da'Leth answered her. Opening the small bag, she turned it upside down and watched as a long gold chain fell into her palm. Lifting it she saw a pendant at the end, a blacker than black onyx surrounded by gold engraved with the words 'Whispering Winds'. "I remember this," she whispered after a moment. "My father had this made for me when I told him how much I loved the name of our home. I'd forgotten what it was called but sometimes when I sleep I remember the sound of the wind blowing in through the trees."

Placing the chain around her neck Da'Leth slipped the pendant under her dress. "Guard it closely, Josephine. I wish there was more but that is all I have left to give you."

"It is enough, Lady Jane. I thank you for giving it back to me."

"Go now child, and let an old woman sleep away her illness."

Smiling softly at her Da'Leth stood, taking the box away to return to its place. Pausing for a moment before leaving Da'Leth wished the older woman well, unable to hold any ill will against the Lady that her life had gone as it had. The blame was to be held by one man, her uncle. Though she felt no love for Lord Byron and though she knew he had played a part in the nightmare her life had become she placed sole responsibility upon the shoulders of her uncle for the crime he had committed against her family.

Having nowhere else to go Da'Leth headed back to the Inn, walking at a leisurely pace through the lanes, the reality that she was leaving beginning to sink in. This would be the last time that she would see the walls of Pirtonshire. A smile dawned on Da'Leth's face, shining brightly. No matter who this Lord was, no matter what she had to endure from here on, she would serve with loyalty for the man that had rescued her from the black nightmare of her adolescence.

Chapter Four

Hearing the early morning call of a bird she allowed herself a moment to wake before mentally reviewing the chores she would need to do before helping Beatrice to ready the meal for Lord Byron.

Slowly stretching out her limbs Da'Leth opened her eyes and saw the brown wooden planks over her head and reality came back to her in the blink of an eye. She was no longer a cook in Lord Byron's kitchen, she was a lady's maid.

Rising from her bed she reached for a gown from the trunk she had been given yesterday, a simple deep green one, as she knew they would be traveling today, and dressed quickly. Brushing her hair, she braided it into a single plait and reached for her shoes, putting them on as she hurried for the door. Down the stairs, she slipped quietly to the kitchen where she knew the servants would be preparing the morning meal for the guests. Requesting a kettle of boiling water along with a cup and saucer for tea she went outside to the water pump to ready a pitcher of water for the Lady to wash with before she dressed.

Silently slipping up the stairs she entered the main room of the space the Lord had rented and placed everything onto the table. Bending low to stoke the fire she straightened up and stepped back in surprise at the sight of the Lord standing in the doorway to his sleeping quarters. His attire was incomplete, as though he hadn't finished dressing yet. Though his shirt was tucked into his breeches he wore no jacket over it and the flowing material shifted as he approached the fire to warm himself against the morning chill.

Apologizing for waking him she turned to place the poker back against the wall when he spoke. "We shall breakfast after we have traveled. See to it that my sister is ready within the hour," he told her.

"Yes, milord," Da'Leth replied, curtseying before she reached for the pitcher and bowl to take into the other room. When she returned for the tea tray he was gone; his door shut as he, no doubt, finished dressing himself. Curious, but knowing she had to get to work, Da'Leth hurried into her Lady's room, setting the tray down onto a table and shutting the door so the Lady could dress in privacy.

When all was ready for the woman Da'Leth approached her bedside, pulled back one of the curtains and let the early morning light to gently wake her, calling out just as softly, "Milady, it is time to wake," until the woman had opened her eyes. Pulling off the covers she readied a robe for her to wear while the still sleepy woman climbed out of the bed.

Seated at the table, sipping her tea while she slowly awoke, Rianne watched the stranger bustle about the room, pulling undergarments from her smaller trunks and choosing a dress from the large trunk in the corner. As her mind began to wake she looked up at the titan haired woman and asked, "Who are you?"

Stopping in her work Da'Leth turned to face her and gave a low curtsey. "Your brother has taken me on to serve as a lady's maid during the journey ahead." Knowing she was being evasive Da'Leth couldn't bring herself to say that she had been bought, no matter how generous or kind the Lord was.

"I see."

Assuming she had been dismissed to return to her work Da'Leth turned, finishing the task of gathering the Lady's clothes as quickly as she could. Turning back to face the woman at the table she lowered her head in a respectful stance. "I beg your pardon milady, but your brother was quite specific in his wishes. We must have you ready for travel within the hour."

"Then I suppose I should dress," Rianne said with a nod. "I would not want to keep my brother waiting any longer than he already has."

Working with Rianne to don her clothes and style her hair she was able to emerge into the main room with a few moments to spare. Standing by the fire Nicholas looked at his sister and nodded his approval. The dress was neither too flashy nor too noticeable; perfect for travel and being inconspicuous. When he complimented her on her choice she smiled at him. "I did not pick it; you may thank my new maid for the garment choice."

Raising an eyebrow, he lifted his gaze to Da'Leth as she ordered the servants as to what was to be taken first. His curiosity beginning to bubble forth again but Nicholas stopped it for now, knowing he would have plenty of time to consider it once they were traveling on the road. Giving an order to his men Nicolas watched as the Captain held out his hand to Rianne and escorted her down to the waiting carriage.

Reaching out to gather her Lady's wrap and her satchel Da'Leth hurried out the door after the Captain, helping Rianne to get settled into the carriage comfortably for the long journey ahead. As she was laying the wrap over her legs Da'Leth heard the Captain mutter to his men the need to keep a sharp eye out. Getting into the carriage she shut the door firmly and set the satchel on the seat by her side. Through the window, she could see a man emerge from within the inn and hurry into an alleyway, his cloak gathered around him to keep it from blowing in the wind.

Curious about where this man was going, wondering what was taking the Lord so long to come down from their room Da'Leth questions doubled when the carriage suddenly began to roll through the street. She could see that the Lady was just as curious though she refrained from peering out the window. Settling herself back into her seat Da'Leth forced her questions out of her mind, succeeding after several hours of concentrated effort.

"If we are to spend several long days together I fear I may go mad if we do not speak."

Glancing up Da'Leth saw the Lady smiling at her with a kind smile. "If you wish it milady," she said, unsure of what she wanted to talk about. "I am called Da'Leth."

"What a unique name."

"It was given to me by an old woman who took me under her wing when I was a child."

Feeling the carriage begin to slow down Da'Leth looked out the window to see a small inn on the side of the road, a stable across the way. When one of the men traveling with them disappeared into the inn only to reemerge with a sack Da'Leth realized they have stopped to breakfast. "A bit of food, milady," he says, handing the sack to Da'Leth through the window. "We cannot stop but for a moment to water the horses. Do you wish to walk for a moment?"

"Yes," Rianne replied.

Lifting the wrap from her legs Da'Leth set it aside while the man opened the door to the carriage, helping Rianne to step down. When the Lady was safely settled on the ground he turned back to help Da'Leth only to find that she too was standing on her own next to the carriage. Nodding he pointed toward the fields that the Captain had already scoured for any possible threat to the women.

Following behind the woman Da'Leth walked with her as Rianne slowly stretched out her legs after being confined to the carriage for several hours. Hearing a noise in the woods Da'Leth turned a sharp eye towards it, a feeling of being watched starting to sink over her. Glad when the Captain came to ask them to return to the carriage she waited until Rianne was settled into the carriage to turn to the Captain and whisper, "Might I have a dagger, Captain Krausley?"

Looking down at the serf he saw the seriousness in her eyes. "Why?"

"For the same reason you keep scanning the woods around us." Da'Leth knew she was taking a risk with her request but something in her very bones was telling her something was amiss. If she had been purchased to protect Lady Rianne, then she would do so with everything she had in her.

Eyeing her for a moment Captain Krausley suddenly nodded and pulled a sheathed dagger from within his tunic. "Take care that your Lady does not suspect," he ordered her.

Nodding Da'Leth tucked the sheath into the fold of her dress, hanging it from a loop in her belt. Climbing into the carriage she took her place across from Rianne and set about draping the wrap over her legs. As the carriage began to roll again Da'Leth pulled some of the bread and cheese, placing it on a cloth before handing it to Rianne for her meal. "Would milady enjoy some wine?" holding up the skin of wine for her to choose.

"Thank you," she replied. "It will go well with the cheese." Nodding Da'Leth put the wine away and began to close the sack when Rianne stopped her. "Are you not hungry? Take some bread and cheese for yourself. I'll not have you fainting from a lack of nourishment."

Thanking her Da'Leth tore off a piece of the bread and a small piece of cheese, putting the rest away before settling down to eat. Lulled into a peaceful daze by the wine Rianne began to drift off to sleep, her head nodding to one side. Watching her Lady fall asleep Da'Leth couldn't stop her curiosity from rising to the surface again. Who was this woman? And who was her brother, a Lord who took a lowly serf and elevated her to the status of a lady's maid over night?

Unable to find an answer, unsure where to even begin to look for one, she turned her gaze out the window of the carriage to watch the greenery as it passed by. From somewhere in the deepest chambers of her heart Da'Leth felt the tug of a memory, a dream from so long ago that only the barest of images remained. Closing her eyes, she could see herself, her long red hair flying out behind her as she ran, dodging the trees and shrubs. There was someone with her, a tall man, who he was she wasn't sure, but she felt safe with him so she assumed he was a friend.

Jolted, her eyes flew open when the carriage ground to a halt suddenly. Looking out the window she was shocked to see that the men who had been traveling behind the carriage were suddenly surrounding it, their eyes alert, hands ready to grab their weapons at the slightest movement.

"What is going on?" Rianne began, tossed from her slumber when the carriage had jolted to a stop. Seeing Da'Leth hold up a hand for her to be quiet Rianne did as she instructed, unsure of what was going on but scared by the look of concern and worry she saw in her new maids' eyes. When she saw Da'Leth brandish a dagger from her side Rianne began to realize just how dangerous their situation could be.

Straining, Da'Leth heard the whispered command from the Captain to the men to be ready. Her hair stood on end when she saw Captain Krausley place his hand on the hilt of his sword. The silence was thick as it settled over the group of travelers, each one waiting with alert senses. Suddenly the silence was broken by the whistling of a shooting arrow, the whistle ending with a resounding thunk as the arrow sunk its head into the wall of the carriage just inches from Rianne's head.

Too frightened to even scream Rianne allowed Da'Leth to pull her down to the ground, cowering behind the safety of the sturdy wooden doors of the carriage. All around them they could hear the sounds of battle, men fighting with each other, their swords clanging together time and again. The sounds of the blades passing through the men's protection to the precious skin beneath, the screams of death and the moans of pain filled the air.

Trembling in the bottom of the carriage Rianne dared to glance up and what she saw was a soothing balm to her frightened nerves. Da'Leth, her face void of expression, stared out at the battle raging before them, dagger in her hand, eyes filled with a concentration Rianne had seen in the faces of many men as they battled for sport. Crouched down low, her body protecting her Lady, Da'Leth's free hand lay comfortingly on Rianne's shoulder, a silent promise that all would be well.

Suddenly the door to the carriage was opened, a man reaching in to grab Rianne and drag her out. Quicker than she could think, her instincts taking over, Da'Leth stabbed the dagger into the man's hand, the man withdrawing his hand with a howl of rage and pain. Using the moment to make sure her Lady was unharmed Da'Leth was about to go after the man when the other door opened and Captain Krausley fell into the carriage, an arrow sticking out from his shoulder, buried several inches deep.

One of the attackers followed the Captain as he fell into the carriage, his eyes raking the inside before turning away in disgust. "He's not in there, check the woods! Find him!"

"What is going on?" Rianne demanded as the sounds of the battle began to move farther away.

"They are searching for your brother, milady," the Captain advised, his voice filled with pain.

"Nicholas? But why?"

"To kill him!" a man growled from behind Rianne.

Screaming when she felt herself being grabbed from behind Rianne struggled as best she could but it was no use, her limited strength no match for his. Seeing that her Lady was in trouble Da'Leth grabbed the sword from Captain Krausley's hand and leapt from the carriage. Glancing around she saw the man trying to drag Rianne away from the carriage.

Hefting the heavy sword in her hands she brought it down onto the man's shoulder, the metal shielding echoing when metal hit metal. Staggering he let go of Rianne in favor of protecting himself. "You're too puny to be lifting such a heavy sword, wench. Give it here and I'll take your burden."

With a firm grip Da'Leth pulled Rianne away from the man's side, making sure her Lady was a safe distance away before turning her attention to the man that had tried to take her. "If you want this sword you'll have to pry it from my lifeless hands."

"Milady," the Captain called, struggling to get to her side. "Come away from there. You'll be hurt."

Going to his side, helping him back to the safety of the carriage Rianne, glanced worriedly back to Da'Leth. "But she'll be killed!"

Seeing the skill with which the woman defended herself against the blow from the rebel's sword he replied, "I dare say she may do well enough without our help."

Knowing that Rianne was safe with the Captain Da'Leth focused her complete attention on the man before her. His blows were heavy but unskilled, chopping at her instead of skillfully attacking. Studying his movements for a moment the way she had been taught Da'Leth found his weakness and used it the next time it presented herself. Kicking his legs out from under him she forced him to fall, using the handle of the sword she carried to render him unconscious.

Sure that he wouldn't rise, she turned to verify that Rianne was safe with the Captain before heading off to find the men who still fought. Running as fast as she could, the sword heavier than she was used to, Da'Leth hurried down the path to stop the group of attackers she saw disappearing around the bend. "Stop right there," she ordered. "You carry what does not belong to you. Return it at once."

Looking at the woman standing before them the men laughed. Setting the treasure they carried with them down, one man standing back to watch, two of the men moved forward to teach the woman a lesson. Watching them advance Da'Leth gave them a moment to get closer before she lifted her sword to defend herself.

Chapter Five

"What happened here?"

Reining his horse to a stop Nicholas looked down at the sight waiting for him. His men were wounded, some mortally, and the carriage had more than one arrow sticking out of it.

"An attack milord," Captain Krausley advised him from his seat on the floor of the carriage, an arrow still stuck out from his shoulder. "The rebels attacked and then ran off with the chest, milord."

"What of my sister?" he demanded; his concern for her outweighing his concern for the money chest.

"I am well enough," Rianne answered for herself as she rounded the corner of the carriage and came into his view, a scrap of cloth in her hands that she handed to the Captain. Seeing that one of his men was about to pull the arrow from his shoulder she turned away, putting her hand over her mouth when she heard the sickening slurp as the arrow was pulled.

"You're hurt!" he cried. Jumping down from his horse he hurried to her side, his heart pounding at the sight of the blood on her bodice.

"No, 'tis not my blood!" she assured him. "It must be from the man who attacked the carriage. Da'Leth
stabbed him with her dagger."

Suddenly realizing that Da'Leth was among the missing he frowned. "Where is she?"

"Probably run off to freedom," one of the men muttered under his breath as he wrapped the Captains
shoulder with a temporary bandage. "Ungrateful serf."

"No!" Rianne cried when she heard him, the Captain agreeing with her. "She didn't run away."

"Then where is she?" Nicholas asked. Unable to answer him they were silent. "The lure of freedom is too much to resist, the moment an opportune one to escape. Get ready to travel. We must make good time to the next inn for safety if they attack again."

"Nicholas," Rianne said softly, her eyes worried. "I fear for her."

"If she is anything she is strong, Rianne. I am sure she will be fine."

Turning away Nicholas worked with his men to ready their group for travel. As he mounted his horse again he couldn't help but wonder at the twinge of disappointment that filled him. He had thought this one to be different, perhaps one that would be as loyal as the servants he had grown up with. It saddened him that he had been so mistaken as to trust the woman with the life of his sister, a mistake he did not intend to repeat again. From this moment on he was the only one he would entrust his sisters' life to.

The group ready to travel they began again, heading down the path, rounding the bend of it only to stop suddenly at the sight that lay before them. There, lying in the middle of the road lay two men, both dead. The chest of gold coin that had been taken from the carriage sat off to the side, open and some of the gold gone. A trail of blood littered the dirt path off in the direction of the woods, disappearing into forest.

But the most shocking aspect of the sight before them was the woman in a deeply colored green gown lying in the middle of the road, her pale face streaked with blood. A bloody sword that Nicholas recognized as Captain Krausley's lay a few inches from the fallen woman's hand. Dismounting he hurried to her side, removing his glove and placing his hand over her mouth and nose to feel for the breath he hoped would assure him she was still alive.

"She lives," he announced. "Bring her to the carriage," motioning for two of the men to move forward to help. One picked up the chest while the other lifted Da'Leth from the ground, carrying her to the carriage and laying her on the bench as best he could.

Seeing the wounded woman Rianne reached into the satchel that had been stored in the carriage and pulled out a small skin of water, wetting a scrap of cloth thoroughly to wipe the blood from her face with gentle strokes. Satisfied that she had removed as much of the blood as she could, and that the wound had stopped bleeding, she looked up to see Nicholas watching them through the window. "Now do you have faith in her, brother?" she asked softly so none of the men around them could hear.

Nicholas nodded. "Let me know when she wakes."

Mounting up again the group continued down the road, traveling slowly so that the many that had been wounded could keep up. Keeping a sharp eye out for any sign of danger Nicholas allowed his thoughts to stray once more to the woman who was lying unconscious in the carriage with his sister. While he had been traveling a few miles behind his party, to maintain secrecy as a shield to any danger, he had given thought to her as well.

Where had she gone when she had left the room the previous afternoon? Who had she said her goodbyes to? He found it difficult to believe that she would have said goodbye to the Lord or Lady of Pirtonshire, one of his men advising him that she had gone to the manor. Though it was feasible that she had gone to wish a farewell to the fellow serfs he wondered if she would truly miss her life in Pirtonshire.

Then, when he had seen her lying on the ground, blood streaming down her face, his mind was filled with questions all over again. What had happened? How had she ended up with Krausley's sword? Why had she gotten separated from the others and how had she gotten hurt? Nicholas had resigned himself to having to wait for the answers but there was a part of him that wondered if he would ever get them.

"Milord."

Looking to his right Nicholas smiled at his old friend. "Edward," he nodded. "You are unharmed?"

"Yes Milord, thank you for your concern." The two men rode in silence for a moment. Nicholas could tell that his loyal friend was mulling something over in his mind and he waited for the man to speak. "I know that you have yet to decide your thoughts of this woman that you have brought with us, and you are wise to keep your final decision until you have gathered some more information. I would ask that you allow me to tell you the scene I witnessed during the attack."

Nicholas nodded for him to continue.

"They came at us from the woods, hidden among the brush. When they had searched the entire group and not found you they decided to steal what we had and make do with that. Alone in the carriage your sister had been pushed to the floor by the woman and she was crouched over her, defending her. I saw the man approaching the carriage but I could not get to him in time to stop him from attacking."

"Your sister was grabbed and about to be taken away but Da'Leth stopped him with a dagger that the Captain had given her. Only after she made sure her Lady was safe did the woman pick up a sword and attack the man who had attacked her Lady. Milord, her skill with the sword was not that of an untrained serf."

Glancing quickly at his old friend with surprise Nicholas quickly schooled his face and looked over his shoulder towards the carriage. "How skilled is she?"

"I would be so bold as to say that her training is extensive though her skills are rusty. With proper instruction I do not doubt she would be skilled enough to hold her own against many of your own men."

"How is this possible?" Nicholas wondered aloud. "A serf with knowledge of the sword?"

"And a woman, milord," Edward added before he was called away by the Captain.

"And a woman," Nicholas repeated to himself, his list of questions growing larger with every thought.

~~*~*~*~*~*~*~*

One by one her senses became aware of the world around her. The sound of the crowd from somewhere farther away; the smell of pig flesh roasting over a fire; the feel of a warm blanket covering her body from shoulder to toe. Slowly she opened her eyes to see an old woman bending over her.

"Well it's about time you woke up, love," she said, her voice cracked with age. "You got's some o'them men out there fearing for you like you was gonna die. O'course it ain't my place to be saying you being a Lady an' all," she smiled.

"I'm a serf," Da'Leth answered, pushing herself up onto her elbows to look around, trying desperately to ignore the pain pounding in her head. "Where am I?"

"Lie still, you been hurt. I don't know what kind of man would attack a woman anyway, he weren't no man if you ask me, but it ain't my place to be saying..."

"Attack?" Closing her eyes, she sat up, swinging her legs off the side of the bed and trying to remember the events that had led up to her waking in a strange bed. Images flew into her mind as she gasped. "Milady!"

Getting to her feet, concern for Rianne outweighing the pounding pain in her head, Da'Leth hurried out the door of the little room and into a narrow hall. Hearing the clanging of dishes and the voices of the guards she headed down the hall until it ended in a large main room, the men seated at various tables while Rianne and Nicholas sat closer to the fire at a table of their own. Letting go of the wall that had been supporting her Da'Leth crossed the room, falling to her knees at Rianne's feet.

"Milady, are you well?" she inquired hastily, fear filling her eyes that the woman had in anyway been hurt.

"Da'Leth!" Rianne cried, her hands automatically reaching out to steady the pale woman. "What are you doing out of bed? You should be resting."

"Please, Milady. Please tell me you are well," Da'Leth asked again.

"Yes, I am well; but you are not." Looking up Rianne spoke to her brother. "Please have one of the men help her back to the bed Nicholas; she should not be up yet."

Several of the men stood but he motioned for them to sit down. "I will do it; I wish to speak with her."

Helping the weakened woman to her feet Nicholas could see that she was straining herself to give the appearance of strength. Letting her do so until they were out of sight he stopped and, hooking one arm under her knees, lifted her into his arms, carrying her the remaining way. When she was safely in the bed he sat down in a chair across the room for a moment while Da'Leth tried to get rid of the pulsing pain in her head.

"Milord," she said after some time. "Was there something you wanted from me?" curious as to why he was still in the room for her.

Raising an eyebrow Nicholas was silent for a moment, surprised that she knew he was still there. He'd been silent and unmoving the entire time; her eyes were shut and yet she knew he had remained in the room. "You are a mystery to me woman, and it is intriguing."

Furrowing her brow Da'Leth opened her eyes and looked at her master. "I do not understand."

"No, I suppose you don't." Seeing the pain in her eyes Nicholas chose to let his questions go for now, knowing she would need to rest for the long journey tomorrow. "Rest for now. We shall speak again tomorrow."

"Milord?"

"Rest, woman."

Leaving the room, he shut the door tightly, muting the sounds from the main room. Curious about the strangeness of the few words he had said to her Da'Leth found herself unable to concentrate on them, her exhaustion lulling her back to sleep.

~~*~*~*~*~*~*~*

Dressed and ready for the day Nicholas opened the door to his room and stopped in the doorway to watch as Da'Leth walked down the hall, her arms holding a carefully balanced tray stacked high with dishes. Wondering how she was going to open the door with both of her hands occupied he smiled to himself when he saw her carefully balance on one foot, using the other to move the door latch. When she had slipped inside and shut the door behind her he stepped out of his room, shaking his head with a small smile at the scene he had just witnessed.

Sitting down at the table with Krausley he reached for a tankard, pouring himself a drink from the pitcher that sat between them. Drinking in silence for a moment Nicholas looked up to see his old friend watching him, waiting for the right moment to speak what had been weighing on his mind. "Say the words that are burning your tongue, Richard."

Smiling quickly the seriousness never left his eyes. "That woman, Da'Leth, how much do we know about her?"

"Very little," Nicholas replied without hesitation. "And less with every passing moment it seems," he finished, staring at the flames of the fire burning low in the hearth.

"I would dare to say it might be worth the effort to learn what we can. The secrets she keeps seem to be plentiful. Secrets such as how a woman of her station would have the skill with a sword to defeat the soldiers of our enemy. Though the one I find most curious is why a serf would have such a deep loyalty to her master in such a short amount of time."

Curious Nicholas looked up. "What do you mean?"

"After I was wounded I fell into the carriage. I saw Da'Leth hovering over your sister, her dagger ready for an attack. Then, when she knew that the Lady was safe with me she went after the men that had stolen from her master. We don't know exactly what happened in that battle but the evidence is strong towards one conclusion."

Nicholas nodded. The evidence was pointed clearly to the fact that she had killed two of the men, a third knocking her unconscious before running of to safety with the others.

"There were three men," a soft voice said from behind the men. Turning sharply, they looked up to see Da'Leth entering the room. Watching as she moved about the room, gathering the bread and cheese and bringing it to their table along with some of the gruel she had picked up from the kitchen. "I'm sorry the meal is meager, Milord, the inn keeper is a poor one but he gives you the best he has."

"This will do," he replied to her. "What of the three men?"

Meeting his eyes for the briefest of moments Da'Leth moved to the fire to stoke it to life. "They were stealing the money chest that the men had been carrying. When I saw that my Lady was safe with Captain Krausley I went after them to try and stop them. I was able to kill two of them before the third knocked me on the head with his hilt. I do not remember anything else until waking here at the inn."

"How is your head?" Richard asked as she stood, the fire sufficiently stoked. Before she could speak a loud clatter of crashing pots rang out from the kitchen. Wincing she put her hand to her head, trying to rub away the pain that had suddenly sprung to life like the stoked fire. "As I suspected," he smiled.

"It is tolerable, Captain. It will not keep me from my work."

Turning away from them she grabbed several more of the tankards, placing them on the table. Curious, Nicholas was about to ask why she had done that when the room suddenly filled with the rest of his men, each one ready for food and drink. "You there, serf," one of the men called out to Da'Leth. "Fetch me some food."

Pausing for the briefest of moments, gritting her teeth against the anger that rose in her heart, Da'Leth turned and reached for some more bread and cheese, placing it on the table before the man that had requested it. Turning to walk away she stopped when she felt something grab her arm. Looking behind her, she saw that the man had grabbed her arm and was glaring at her.

"You would dare to call this food?"

"It is the best that they can provide," she replied honestly.

"Go and attend to my sister," Nicholas said from his seat.

With a small curtsey, grateful to have been given an escape Da'Leth fled the main room, down the hall to her Lady's room. Entering the room quietly she quickly poured a cup of the tea that had been brewing and set it down to cool for Rianne to drink once she awoke. The breakfast tray ready Da'Leth turned to wake the Lady only to find that she was already awake. "Your tea and breakfast are ready Milady," she said, helping to remove the covers so Rianne could sit up.

"Thank you, Da'Leth," she said, standing while Da'Leth put the robe over her nightclothes. Sitting down at the table she was midway through her meal when she realized Da'Leth had been silent, inactive for the last few minutes. Looking up she saw the young woman sitting in a chair near the fire, a hand gently rubbing her temple while the other held a gown and undergarments ready and waiting for Rianne to dress.

Why she felt such a feeling of friendship toward this woman Rianne didn't know other than to accept that it was there. Reasoning that it was because Da'Leth had saved her life she focused on making sure that she would do what she could in return for such an unpayable debt.

"Are you unwell?"

Starting in her seat Da'Leth dropped her hand to her lap and raised her eyes to meet Rianne's. "Well enough, Milady," she replied.

"You do not need to hide your pain if you have it," Rianne told her, putting her cup down onto its saucer.

"'Tis merely a headache, Milady. Nothing I cannot manage while I work."

Getting up Da'Leth laid the gown down gently, the underclothes next to it, and began to make the bed that Rianne had spent the night in. "Did you eat?"

"Not yet, Milady. When my work is done, I shall take my meal."

Silent for a moment Rianne looked up at Da'Leth and asked her to sit down at the table. When the woman had done so, confused as to why, she regarded her silently for a moment longer.

"From this moment on you shall take your meal when I do. Unless you wish time alone you will join me when I travel to spend time with others," she said.

"Milady," Da'Leth said after a moment. "I am a serf. My position is one of servitude, it is what I do."

Locking her gaze with Da'Leth's Rianne advised, "Then you may consider it a command. You saved my life, Da'Leth, the least I can do is to make sure you are cared for as best I can."

~~*~*~*~*~*~*~*~*

Riding in the carriage, her eyes passively scanning the scenery passing them by, Da'Leth let her mind wander over the last few days she had spent in the company of her new master. The fairness with which she had been treated was almost too good to be true and she expected to wake up at any moment under the roof of the pub on Pirtonshire lands.

A small sigh caught her attention and she looked across the carriage to see the Rianne was shifting in her sleep, leaning slightly to rest her head upon her brothers' shoulder. When she was settled again Da'Leth brought her gaze back to the scenery passing by. Her mind still reeled at the command the Lady had given her only that morning. A serf was not to mix with a Lady; the fact that she was sitting in the carriage now was enough to have been put to death. Closing her eyes for a moment against the sting of emotion that pricked at her eyes Da'Leth turned her mind back to the changes she had been through in the last few days.

"What ails you?"

Glancing toward the man that had spoken the words Da'Leth looked up to see Captain Krausley watching her intently. The injured man had been ordered to ride with them and his horse had been tied to the carriage. Sitting next to him Da'Leth knew he had been watching her but had been content that he wasn't going to speak.

"I am well, milord."

"I did not mean your health, madam. What ails your mind?" he said with an amused gleam in his eye.

For the briefest moment Da'Leth considered not answering him but knew she couldn't do that. "I have been thinking on the change my road has taken milord."

"I do not understand your meaning," he frowned.

"The direction my life has taken has changed and I only meant to think upon where it might go from here."

"Have you come to a conclusion yet?" Nicholas inquired, curious about the deepness of her thoughts.

"Not yet milord, I am still too confused about recent events to reach a conclusion."

"What confuses you?"

Pausing for a moment Da'Leth wondered if she had the freedom to say what was truly on her mind. As if reading her thoughts, he told her to speak her mind freely.

"Why would milord choose a serf to accompany his sister, a woman he obviously cares very much for? Especially when he knew there was the possibility of an attack from an enemy."

"What makes you think they were nothing more than common thieves?" Nicholas asked, ignoring the first question, one that even he did not have an answer for.

"Common thieves would have taken the entire chest of gold, not just a small portion. And why would a common thief be intent upon finding you, milord?" she asked Nicholas.

"All very good questions; what do you believe the answers are?"

"I believe," she said, meeting his eyes with all seriousness. "That milord has made some enemies in his travels."

"We approach an inn," a man announced from the road. "Shall we stop to water the horses?"

Giving the order to stop silence fell as the carriage pulled off to the side, the horses being led to a watering trough to drink. Wakened by the sudden stillness Rianne decided to stretch her legs and both women emerged from the carriage to wander the fields across from the inn. Standing in the yard, tankards in hand, the two men watched the women.

"She is smarter than she appears," Richard said aloud.

Nicholas nodded. He would have to speak to her tonight. There were too many questions surrounding this woman he'd taken on their journey.

~~*~*~*~*~*~*~*

Looking up from her work by the fire Da'Leth frowned when she saw Nicholas enter the empty room, an equally empty tankard in his hands. She watched as he sat down in the chair across from her, his eyes meeting hers as he toyed with the tankard. Unsure of what to say she dropped her eyes back to her darning and went back to work repairing her Lady's stocking.

"You had been a serf for Lord Byron for how many years?"

Da'Leth paused for the briefest of moments but quickly resumed her work. "Many years, milord."

"Do you know how many?"

"Since I was a child."

"Whom did you serve before that?"

Looking up at him she wasn't sure she understood his question but gave the only answer she could think of. "Only his Majesty the King."

"You were not born into serfdom?"

Understanding dawned in her eyes and Nicholas saw her stiffen in her chair. "No milord I was not."

"How did you come to be a serf to Lord Byron?"

"I do not know all of the details, milord. Only that I was."

Watching her intently for a moment he could tell she was keeping something back. "Tell me."

Slowly raising her eyes to meet his she paused. "Milord?"

"Tell me what you know about how you came to be a serf to Lord Byron," he told her. Seeing the stiffness in her posture he added, "And leave nothing out."

Da'Leth set the darning in her lap, stilling her hands atop it, and looked up at her new master. "I was taken from my bed in the middle of the night by a man I did not know. He hit me and I fell to sleep. When I woke I was dressed as a serf and being held against my will by Lord Byron. What else is there that you wish to know milord?"

Silent for a moment he didn't know what to say. "What of your parents?"

"My father is dead and I do not know what became of my mother."

Her tone was terse and cold; a smaller man would have shuddered at hearing it. "Were you taken in exchange for money?"

Her first instinct was to say that she did not know but then Da'Leth remembered the story Lady Jane had told her and she knew it wasn't the truth. "Yes milord, I was exchanged for money. The man who took me was paid by my uncle to take me away."

Nicholas could taste the bitterness in her tone. This wound was fresh, of that much he was certain. 'Perhaps she did not know about the money?' he reasoned to himself. Aloud he asked, "How do you know how to use a sword?"

A hint of a smile tugged at her lips. "My father was a man of modern ideas. He felt it important that all his children be given a proper knowledge of the sword. As I was his only child he felt it only fair that I be given the best tutelage he could give."

Setting his tankard down on a table Nicholas leaned forward and stared at her. "Who taught you? My men tell me your skill with a sword is as good as any of my officers, if a bit unused."

Her eyes widened for a moment before a blush spread over her cheeks. Dropping her eyes to her darning she picked it up again shaking her head. "My father taught me, milord."

Leaning back in his chair he studied the blushing woman for a moment. It had been a simple compliment, nothing he had expected a woman to blush over and yet she had. True she was a serf but surely even among the other serfs she had received a compliment before? Had the years spent in such a hard life made her unable to accept even a small nicety? Questions still rang out in his head but there was one that rang louder than the rest.

"Why are you loyal to my sister?"

Frowning she raised her eyes to meet his with a confused look. "Milord, I do not understand. Would you have me not be loyal to her?"

"No, your loyalty is appreciated and welcome. I simply wish to inquire as to why it came so quickly."

Thinking for a moment, unsure of how to respond Da'Leth chose to simply tell him what was in her heart and hope that he understood.

"Milord removed me from a nightmare that I have lived since the night I was taken away from my family. In the beginning my loyalty lay with milord for his kindness to me. When I began to serve your sister, I began to see that same kindness in her as well. It is a feeling I have not known for quite some time, one that I have missed almost as much as the childhood I lost. As a child growing up under the direction of my mother and father I was taught that kindness is one way in which we may imitate our Lord God. To feel such kindness again has given my loyalty to you and your family with an unbreakable bond."

Nicholas was silent as he listened, hearing the pain in her voice, a voice that was usually carefully neutral in its tone. "Thank you," he said when she was finished. "I am pleased to know that my trust in you was not misplaced."

~~*~*~*~*~*~*~*

Watching the scenery pass by Da'Leth listened as Rianne, sitting next to her, kept up a steady stream of excited chatter as they neared her home. Across from her she could see that Captain

Krausley had relaxed a little bit, as had Nicholas. The nearer the caravan got to their home the more relaxed both men became. As the carriage rounded a bend in the road Rianne looked out the window and smiled brightly.

"There it is," she laughed. "We're home at last."

Leaning over to look out the window Da'Leth's eyes grew wide. As she sat back in her seat she stared at Nicholas sitting across from her. Meeting her gaze with his own he saw the questions in her eyes and nodded once. Averting her gaze out the window Da'Leth closed her eyes for a moment.

Royalty.

Nicholas and Rianne were royalty.

Opening her eyes, she saw the palace towering in the distance and her heart skipped a beat. All this time she had thought she was serving a Lord and his sister when she had been serving the Prince and Princess of her country.

Chapter Six

Queen Winifred Anne, wife to his Majesty King Liam Philip, sat in her chair, speaking with her daughter, the Princess Elizabeth, when she saw a sight that lifted her heart. "Nicholas!" she called out, raising her voice to greet her son with the joy she felt in her heart at the sight of him. "You have been too long gone from my side."

Smiling at her he bowed low before stepping forward to kiss her cheek. "I leave so that you may appreciate the time while I am here."

Swatting his arm, she couldn't stop a smile from pulling at her lips. "Wicked boy," she chastised lightly. "Rianne," greeting her daughter with a smile as she approached. "Did you not tell him I wanted him back sooner?"

"I did, Mother, but he was insistent on taking his time."

"I travel to enjoy the scenery, not to fly down the lane as though I were a bird in flight."

Winifred laughed at his antics. Turning to speak to Elizabeth she paused at the sight of a woman standing, half hidden, in the doorway. "Who is this titan figure lurking at the entrance?"

Turning to look Rianne smiled. Motioning for her to come forward, Rianne waited until Da'Leth was closer to face her mother again. "Mother, this brave woman is my savior. Her name is Da'Leth."

"Savior? Rianne, what do you mean?"

"Our caravan was attacked while traveling, mother. Da'Leth fought off one of the men that tried to hurt Rianne. She also managed to save our money chest from being taken by the thieves," Nicholas answered for Rianne, giving out the details he wanted made known and keeping the others to himself.

Winifred's eyes widened. "Are you well?"

"We are well however two of my men were killed."

"I'm so sorry," she said, gently touching his hand. Winifred knew the importance Nicholas placed on his men, caring for them as though they were part of his family rather than his guard. Turning to look at Da'Leth she examined the young woman. "Da'Leth, you say? A strange name for such a beautiful young woman."

Bowing low, her knees skimming the floor beneath her skirt, she didn't reply, unsure of what to say. Standing again she kept her eyes low, staring at the hem of her skirt.

"Have you nothing to say, girl?" Winifred wondered at the silence.

"I know not how to reply to your words, my Queen."

"Then tell me what you think of them and that will be enough."

"Da'Leth is a strange name, but it bears sentimental value to me as I was given the name by a woman who took me into her care and loved me as a grandmother. I shall love her with all my heart until it beats no more."

"And of your beauty?" she asked, wondering if the girl was vain or humble.

"I am an image of my mother, my Queen. God could have given me no better gift."

Winifred smiled. "Very well spoken, child. Sit, you shall join us for tea."

Hesitating for a moment she saw that the older woman was sincere in her command and Da'Leth sat down next to Rianne. Accepting the cup of tea that was handed to her she sipped the hot liquid and listened as the family reunited. Against her will her thoughts drifted back to her own family, the mother she had been separated from for far too long and the father she missed dearly.

"Da'Leth?"

Startled by the gentle touch on her hand Da'Leth looked up at Rianne, a puzzled expression on the Princesses' face. "I'm so sorry," she apologized. "My mind was elsewhere. Did you say something to me?" "No, but mother did."

Da'Leth was horrified. "My Queen, I..."

"Do not fret, girl," she said, holding up a hand to stop the apologies. "I simply inquired what it was that you planned on doing while you were here."

"I will do as is commanded of me, my Queen," Da'Leth answered simply.

Winifred frowned. "A curious answer. What does she mean by it?" she asked, looking to Rianne.

Unsure, Rianne looked to Nicholas. "Da'Leth is a serf, mother," he answered. "While we were in Pirtonshire she joined us so Rianne would not be alone with the men as we traveled home."

Staring at her tea Da'Leth found that she was grateful he hadn't used the word 'bought', though she wondered why he hadn't.

"I see," Winifred replied. "What shall you do now that you are home?"

Whether the question was directed at Nicholas or Da'Leth wasn't clear but it was Nicholas who answered. "I shall find a place for her here at the palace mother, I'm sure you can think of a place where she would do well."

"What was your place in Pirtonshire child?"

"I worked in the pub, Majesty."

"And what did you do?"

"Whatever was required," Da'Leth replied. "Cleaning mostly; some cooking, though it was not my strongest skill."

"Oh mother, you cannot put her in the kitchen," Rianne interrupted. "She saved my life! Surely we can do better."

"Have you any patience for children?" Winifred asked after thinking for a moment. Da'Leth assured her she had worked with children before. "Then you shall assist with Tome while Elizabeth travels to visit her cousin. Does that suit you?"

"It would be an honor to serve her Majesty," Da'Leth said, nodding her head.

"Very well then. As she does not leave for three days still you shall enjoy the palace as our guest."

Da'Leth was speechless. "Your kindness is too much, my Queen. Perhaps I might find another chore to occupy my time until I am to care for the child?"

"Nonsense. You saved my daughter's life, it is the least we can do."

~~*~*~*~*~*~*~*

Standing in the corridor Da'Leth was motionless as she stared at the doors. Beyond them she could hear the laughter and noise of the dining hall and the people enjoying their meal within. Her hands clasped behind her back she fought to force herself to move, to open the doors and enter the room as she had been instructed to do. Neither foot would move, rooted to the floor she wondered what type of tree she might be considered, standing as still as she was.

"The doors shall not open themselves."

His tone was teasing and she recognized it at once. Turning to look she saw Captain Krausley walking towards her. Smiling at him she waited until he was closer to speak.

"I fear my feet have become as one with the floor," she tried to laugh.

Richard smiled. "There is no need to fear, the will not bite you unless you bite them first," he teased some more. Taking her arm, he opened the door and led her into the dining hall. As he propelled her towards an empty seat, calling out greetings to the various people that he saw, Richard's smile was bright. "There," he said once they were seated. "Now, have some wine, and there are specialty dishes, meat, cheese, and fruit; as much as you wish."

Taking the initiative to cut herself a small piece of cheese Da'Leth opened her mouth to protest when Richard cut a bigger piece and placed it on her plate along with a hunk of bread and a bunch of grapes from a platter on the table. "Milord, that is too much!" she protested.

"Nonsense," he replied, filling his own plate. "You will need your strength for the morrow."

Giving in she pulled a grape from the plate and asked, "What is so important that my day has been filled?" before she put the small fruit in her mouth.

"Me."

Coughing gently in shock she swallowed. "Beg pardon, milord?"

Richard smiled at her. "I am interested to see the extent of your skill with the blade. As I cannot spar with you myself I have arranged for one of my apprentices to spar with you so that I may observe."

"Why?" she asked, her tone filled with confusion and distrust. Realizing what she had said, and who she had said it to, she tried to correct her meaning but he stopped her.

"I am curious as to how well a serf could possibly be trained in the art of swordsman-ship. I intend to have my answer one way or the other. Since I am too busy a man to follow you around in hopes of seeing you engaged in battle again I have created an opportunity to witness your skill, though from what I have already seen I am sure it is extensive."

"As milord wishes," she said after a moment of embarrassed silence.

"Captain Krausley, I must say I am shocked at you."

Looking up with innocence Richard looked across the room to Rianne. "How have I shocked you, highness?" he called back.

"Your words, good Captain, have caused poor Da'Leth's face to color as though it were on fire. What have you been saying to her? I demand that you tell me what you have said to my friend."

Glancing down at Da'Leth he smiled, her face an even brighter shade of pink than it had been. "I fear you have heightened the color of her face, Princess. My words were to merely advise the woman that her skill would be tested in the morrow against one of my apprentices."

"What skill?" the King demanded. "What skill could this young thing possibly have that would call for such a test?"

"The long blade, milord," Richard answered.

"That little creature has skill with the long blade? This I cannot believe."

"I assure you your Majesty; it is true, I have seen her skill with mine own eyes."

King Liam eyed Da'Leth intensely for a moment, the young woman forcing herself not to squirm under his gaze. After several tense moments, the older man sat back in his chair and smiled. "I believe it may be possible after all, Captain. You will report back to me after you have tested her."

"As you wish it my King."

Seeing his nod Richard advised that he would report back to the King when the test was complete. With a grin of triumph at Da'Leth Richard turned his attention back to eating, missing the uncertainty in Da'Leth's face.

Sitting in his chair across the way Nicholas watched Da'Leth chew on a piece of bread. Her eyes were on the plate before her but it was obvious to anyone paying attention that her mind was somewhere else entirely. Questions still rang in his head about the many mysteries that surrounded this woman. He knew she hadn't lied to him at all but there were things she was keeping to herself, he was certain of it. Setting his questions aside for now he leaned back in his chair and brought an apple to his lips, examining Da'Leth closely.

Her hair was red, not too bright but enough to never be mistaken for any other color. It was long, judging by the length of the braid she kept it in, and he remembered the way the tip of it curled slightly. The wisps that escaped around her face had a slight curl to them and he wondered if her hair was simply wavy or curled of its own accord. He found it hard to believe that she would take the time to curl her hair the way he knew other women did, as a serf it would have been the last thing on her mind no doubt.

But Da'Leth's most intriguing feature was her eyes. Blue, the color of a sparkling river, was rare to see on a redhead. It made him wonder where she had gotten the color from. In those eyes, he could see so much and yet, at times, it seemed so little. When she wasn't guarding her face, her emotions shone through as rays of sunshine through a cloudless sky. He knew what she was feeling just by looking at her eyes. But when her guard was up her eyes were as blank as a schoolroom slate. Void of any expression, any glimmer of what she was thinking or feeling, it was impossible to know anything more than what she was willing to say.

Wondering how she had managed to keep her hurt and anger about the past from infecting the present, Nicholas smiled when he saw Richard piling even more food on her plate each time he helped himself to another helping.

"What are you smiling at?"

Turning to see his older brother Nicholas shook his head. "Nothing to worry about, Philip."

Following his younger brothers line of sight Philip suddenly smiled. "Who's that?"

"A good woman," Nicholas warned; his tone clear.

Philip, the Crown Prince, was notorious for his handling of the servants but especially of the serfs. Too many times he'd seen a shamed woman avoiding his eyes as he passed by, knowing he wouldn't approve of what had happened. No matter what he said to his brother Philip refused to stop, using his authority as heir to the throne to get him whatever he wanted. "What are you trying to say?"

"I'm not trying to say anything, Philip, I'm saying it. Leave her alone."

Philip challenged him with his gaze and Nicholas met it without letting up. Shrugging he turned his attention back to his meal, letting the challenge drop. A bad feeling came over Nicholas and he knew this would not be the end of it with his brother. He wasn't sure why he felt so protective of this woman he had just met, reasoning with himself that it was because of her loyalty to his family. All he knew was that Da'Leth was a beautiful woman and Philip was not going to let her go without a fight.

~~*~*~*~*~*~*~*

Waking in the warmth Da'Leth thought for a moment that perhaps she had lain too close to the fire the night before but when she felt the pleasant pressure of a heavy cloth covering her she remembered where she was sleeping. Opening her eyes, the young woman saw a dark brown canopy over her head, stretched out over the poles and hanging down to the floor, the thick material blocking almost all of the sunlight. Shocked that she had slept as long as she had Da'Leth thought over the events from the night before.

It had been a long time since she'd had a night of such unbridled fun, not having to worry about catching the unwanted attention of Lord Byron, and she had thoroughly enjoyed herself. Smiling at the memory of Tome, Elizabeth's adventurous daughter, climbing all over her Uncle Nicholas she pushed the drape aside and blinked as the sunlight poured into the bed. Knowing she should rise and begin her day Da'Leth forced herself to abandon the warmth of the bed and stood. Crossing the room, large to the serf though it was no doubt small when compared to the others; she peered out the window and saw the serfs and servants readying the palace for when the royal family awakened to the day.

Hearing a noise behind her Da'Leth turned and saw a young girl, barely older than thirteen, carrying in a tray of food. Her thin arms trembled with fatigue as she carefully set the tray on the small table near the window. With a small bow the young girl turned to leave but stopped when Da'Leth called after her.

"Please, sit down," Da'Leth invited her as she herself sat down at the table. After a moment, the girl slowly moved toward the table, refusing to meet Da'Leth's eyes though she could read the curiosity in them. "Are you hungry? I cannot possibly eat all of this food and I would hate to insult their Majesties by returning the tray still full."

At her insistence, the young girl reached out and took a small morsel of the bread, no more than a mouthful. Smiling at the reminder of how Captain Krausley had responded to her own actions like that Da'Leth reached out and tore off a piece of the bread, handing it to the girl along with a piece of cheese and some of the fruit. Her eyes wide the girl's stomach would not let her refuse and she began to eat.

"I am called Da'Leth," she said, pouring tea for herself. "What is your name child?"

"My name is Jennifer, milady," came a hushed reply.

"Jennifer, what a beautiful name."

The girl smiled, small but genuine, at Da'Leth, encouraged by the praise. "Are you a real Lady?"

Da'Leth's smile was frozen on her face as she thought about how to reply to the innocent question. "I am a servant to the King, just like you are."

"I'm a serf," she said, shaking her head.

"But whom do you serve?"

Thinking about it for a moment Jennifer's smile grew a little brighter. "The King."

"Then you, too, are a servant to the King just as I am."

Smiling at her Da'Leth gave the girl some tea to warm herself with before settling back to eat a slice of cheese she had cut off from the whole. Eating in silence she listened as Jennifer told her about her life here in the palace as a kitchen serf. By the time they were finished Da'Leth knew that the King and Queen governed over their serfs with a fair hand and it warmed her heart that she would be able to serve under their rule as well. Wishing Jennifer well she paused in the doorway to watch her walk away before turning to get dressed.

Dressed in a gown that would be simple enough to fight in Da'Leth left the room she had been given and headed down to the courtyard to find the Captain. After several moments, she was directed toward the training area. Though still far enough away to go unnoticed Da'Leth could see the men practicing against each other. Stepping closer she waited for Krausley to notice her. When he did, the Captain smiled, motioning for her to come forward.

"Come Da'Leth, you must choose your blade."

Walking with her to a small array of blades hanging from a wall, Richard waited while Da'Leth looked them over, handing them to her one by one to test their weight. "Why have you put me in such a state, milord?" she whispered. "I have no skill that would match an apprentice to the Captain of the Guard."

"I disagree."

"But..."

"I saw you fighting in the woods. I know how well you use the blade. If my faith in your skill is misplaced I would rather know it now than in the heat of battle."

Resigned Da'Leth moved to look over the swords and after examining them all, chose one. It was lighter than the rest and would help her to move more quickly. Turning around she saw a man standing in the center of the ring. Tall, sandy haired and young he was in his prime and Da'Leth felt herself shrinking from him. Pushing her toward the center of the ring Richard introduced the two sparring contenders before claiming his seat off to one side

"A woman?" James said, his shock clear.

Despite her apprehension Da'Leth felt her spine stiffen. "Yes," she replied. "A woman."

Shaking his head, he grinned. "An easy victory," he sneered.

Staring at him as he readied his sword Da'Leth's embarrassment melted away. She had been taught by the best and she was not going to let anyone tell her otherwise. Pulling the sword from its sheath she leaned the leather sleeve against the rail and turned to face her opponent, her face set in a mask of indifference.

From his seat Krausley watched Da'Leth with interest. He was eager to see her skill with a long blade in action again. Watching as she had chosen a sword he had seen that she was picky about it, a sign that told him she knew something about what she was getting ready to do. With keen interest he watched as she turned to face the young man and, hearing the words exchanged between them, Krausley wondered at the sudden change in her demeanor. Gone was the deep blush that tinged her cheeks, the embarrassed shuffle of her hands and feet. The woman that stood before them now was a woman that seemed to have no Achilles heel.

"Are you ready wench?" James taunted.

"You will call me Da'Leth," was her only reply.

"I will call you beaten when this test is finished."

Da'Leth didn't bother replying to him, merely readying herself for his first move. Waiting for it she mentally reviewed the last lesson her father had given her before riding off with the other knights to fight in the King's war.

'Steady, little one, be patient. Wait. Do not be anxious, when the time is right the victory will reveal itself. Watch your opponent carefully. Within the first ten moves he will have revealed his weakness to you. Count the moves he repeats, these are his favorites and he will know how to block them well. Above all, remember that good will always triumph because the heart is pure.'

"Are you waiting for someone to come and fight this battle for you, wench?"

Removing her mind from the past Da'Leth met his gaze. "I am simply waiting for you go bathe, the smell of you makes me ill."

The men around them guffawed at her insult. Outraged that he had been embarrassed James attacked, showing her no restraint as a woman. Doing her best to keep safe she watched and waited, counting the moves he made. Then she saw it, relief flooding through her as his tenth move revealed his weakness. Suddenly the cowering woman straightened her stance and gripped her sword, taking the offensive against him. He frowned at the sight of her resolve but felt confidence in his skill. Defending himself against her blows he kept his ground. Stepping back one step he reasoned it was only to gain a better grip with his feet in the dirt. On his second step back, he reasoned the same way again, the ground slippery from the morning dew. When she forced him to take a third step backward he realized she wasn't going to be an easy victory but on the fourth step James began to realize he could very well lose this match.

"Stop!" Both fighters stopped, their swords stilling at Krausley's command. Entering the ring again he moved to Da'Leth's side, taking the sword from her hands. "I was right," he gloated with a smile. "You do have skill. It is still rusty, James would have beaten you, but with work it can be developed."

"You want to help me?"

Richard nodded. "Yes. I have no doubt you will be of use when it comes time to protect her Majesty the Queen and the royal daughters of the throne."

"How do you mean?"

"Anyone who would attack would think nothing more of you than a lady in waiting or a servant. They would not be able to comprehend that you are as skilled with a blade as any knight."

Chapter Seven

Sitting on the ledge of an upper balcony Da'Leth peered out over the grounds below her. From up here she could see the palace garden and the people who were walking in it. Resisting the urge to pinch herself she watched them walk about, smiling, and talking, completely oblivious to the woman who was watching them. It was how she wanted it to be, how it needed to be. Being at the palace was dangerous for her. She had spoken truthfully when she had told the Queen she was an image of her mother. Though she had her fathers red hair her face and body were her mothers. At one time the two women had been close, her mother and the Queen. If she were to be recognized by anyone, be it serf, servant, or lady, she would be shamed beyond any hope of ever regaining her family's name.

Protecting her family's name meant more to Da'Leth than her own life did. For a daughter of a Lord and a Lady to be sold as a serf...

Da'Leth shook her head; it did no good to dwell on what, for the moment at least, could not be changed. One day she would right the wrong that had been done to her but until that day she could never let anyone know who she really was.

"Da'Leth?"

Startled she turned quickly to see Nicholas standing a few feet away. Seeing him standing there Da'Leth waited for him to approach, smiling to let him know he wasn't interrupting anything.

"I called you but you didn't respond."

"I'm sorry, milord, I was thinking. Was there something you needed?" she asked.

"No, I was walking below and saw you sitting here. It's such an odd place to be I thought I would come and talk to you so that I may find out why you are up here."

Thinking over his words Da'Leth frowned. "Why is it an odd place to be?"

Moving a little closer Nicholas leaned against the stone ledge. "This is the tallest tower in the palace. To most such height would be terrifying."

Shaking her head, she replied, "The height does not bother me, highness."

"What draws you to this place?"

Looking out at the world before her Da'Leth motioned toward it with her hand. "The view." Silence fell for a moment and she saw from the corner of her eyes that Nicholas was looking out at the view. After several moments she spoke gain. "After spending so long within the walls of Pirtonshire it's nice to see that the world goes on farther than the eyes can see. The stars were the only expanse I could see and as beautiful as they are the greenery of the ground holds much more interest to me."

Looking down at Da'Leth Nicholas frowned. "You are a mystery, and I admit I am having trouble solving it."

"Milord?"

Sitting on the ledge he focused his attention on Da'Leth. "You are a serf, but not always. Though you are more than familiar with a long blade you have a woman's frailty in everything you do. You're a beautiful woman but you're shy, almost to a fault. You walk with pride but you are humble and self-conscious. I have never heard you lie and yet at the same time you manage to keep everything about you a secret. Woman, you are a mixture of opposites that leave nothing but questions in their wake."

Despite herself Da'Leth could feel a smile tugging on her lips. "I'm sorry if I have confused you, highness, it was not intended."

Watching her closely Nicholas grinned at the sight of her twitching lips. "You don't smile very often Da'Leth. Why is that?"

"I used to," she shrugged. Unbidden a memory came to her mind of running through the forest alongside a giant of a man. His red hair fell to his shoulders and blew in the wind as he ran with her, his gate easy while she struggled to keep up. Suddenly he had picked her up and swung her up onto his shoulders, emerging from the woods to see a large garden, a young woman waiting for them with a smiling face. "My favorite thing in the world was to laugh," Da'Leth whispered.

Standing beside her Nicholas heard the sadness in her voice. Unsure what it was that had caused it he could see the change in her,

her face veiling over so he was unable to see her emotions anymore. Frowning Nicholas stood still, unsure of what he could do or say to make the sadness go away. After a moment of silence, she stood up from her perch and curtsied, moving away from him and out of sight. Letting her go he shook his head and stared out at the world before him.

A loud crash drew his attention from down below and he looked down to see a billow of dust blowing up into the air. He heard the shouts of men and the cries of women and he raced for the stairs, taking them two and three at a time until he had reached the hall. Running as fast as he could he passed Da'Leth and from the corner of his eyes saw her frown. Moments later he heard someone running a few steps behind him and glanced over his shoulder to see Da'Leth a few steps behind. Confusion filled her face but as they passed a window she glanced out and her eyes widened at the sight of the dust filling the air. Quickening her pace, she reached the doorway just before Nicholas and pulled it open as quickly as she could.

Outside they coughed as the dust flew into their lungs but didn't stop until they had reached the fallen building. One of the stables had collapsed, horses and men trapped inside. Reaching for the first hand she saw in the rubble Da'Leth gripped it firmly for a moment before she began to pull away as much of the wood and stone that she could. See what she was doing one of the serfs, a woman she didn't know, stepped forward to help her. Working together they were able to clear the man from the debris and pulled him to safety.

"Rest here," Da'Leth told the man. "Stay with him please," she asked the woman, waiting to see her nod before heading back to the rubble.

A few of the horses came streaming out, led by several men and Da'Leth skirted around them. Looking around for anyone who still needed help she saw Nicholas struggling to soothe a frightened horse at the same time as free the reins from the pole they were twisted around. Moving quickly, she kept her distance from the horse and tackled the reins to try and free them so Nicholas could lead the horse to safety. Once they were free he shoved the leather into her hands and ordered her to lead the horse out of the destruction. Wide eyed she stared at the giant creature before turning her back to it and stumbling her way out, leading the horse to safety before hurriedly handing the reins to a waiting woman and stepping away from it. Turning to head back to help the men again she saw that they had finished saving everyone that needed to be saved.

"What happened here?" Nicholas demanded of one of the men, his face filled with a mixture of anger and concern.

"The support beam gave out, milord," one of the men answered, pointing to one of the large pieces of wood.

Looking down at it Da'Leth tuned out of the conversation and examined it closely. Frowning she ran her fingers over one of the edges and shook her head. Kneeling down to get a closer look she saw that half of the break was jagged but the other was smooth. "This was not an accident," she whispered.

"What?" Nicholas turned to face her suddenly. He had seen her examining the pile of debris but had let it go until he heard her whisper to herself. "What did you say?"

Looking up she stood up straight and faced the Prince. "This was no accident, Highness." Asking her to explain she knelt again, pointing to the wood. "This section of the beam has been sawed through. When the pressure became too much the rest of the beam gave out. This was done on purpose."

Raising her eyes Da'Leth saw the realization dawn in his eyes. Without a word Nicholas turned on his heel and left, Krausley following after him until they had both disappeared from sight.

Standing up again she was about to leave the crowd when she felt something nudge her shoulder. With a twinge of fear, she turned around, afraid of what she was going to see and stepping back quickly when she saw it. "You stay away from me," she whispered at the horse that had nudged her shoulder.

Walking away, forcing herself not to walk too quickly, Da'Leth headed to the training ring on the other side of the castle. Stopping some little ways away she was surprised to see Nicholas and Krausley standing in the middle of the ring, deep in conversation. Not wanting to interrupt she sat on a nearby stump, waiting for them to finish. Krausley was gesturing as he spoke and she could tell he wasn't happy about something. Standing with him Nicholas had a contemplative look on his face, as though his mind were weighed down heavily by their discussion. She wondered what it was that made him worry so and the answer came to her mind almost immediately.

His enemies had followed him home.

Da'Leth was glad she was sitting, the wind knocked out of her by the realization of what had happened. The entire royal family was now in trouble. 'Then why destroy the stable?' she wondered to herself. 'None of the royalty would have been there, only the servants or serfs.'

Thinking back over the attack while they had been traveling she thought over what had happened. They had attacked, searching for Nicholas even as they fought with the guard. Only after they realized he wasn't there did they try to take Rianne. 'Somehow this all centers on him,' Da'Leth mused. 'But why? It can't be for the throne; Prince Philip is next in line.'

"Da'Leth?"

Startled out of her thinking she looked up, surprised to see Richard standing over her, Nicholas beside him, both men watching her with a frown. "Milord?"

"What are you doing?" he asked her, holding out a hand to help her to her feet. "You look positively pale, did the collapse frighten you?"

Meeting his eyes, she glanced to Nicholas and then back to Richard. "Not the collapse, milord," she said honestly. "The realization of what it meant."

She saw both of the men stiffen slightly but it was Richard that spoke. "And what do you believe it means?"

Da'Leth was silent for a moment, her station battling with her instincts. Her instincts won this time. "That the men who attacked us on the road have followed us to the palace."

Richard glanced at Nicholas who was staring at Da'Leth with a stony face. "Contradictions," he said softly. Shaking his head, he raised his eyes to the sky with a sigh as though he were searching for something before looking at her again. "Richard, go back and put things in motion. Da'Leth and I are going for a walk."

Nodding once Richard walked away towards the palace, leaving the two of them alone. Standing quietly, unsure of what to expect, Da'Leth waited for Nicholas to do or say something, anything that would tell her what was going on. After watching Richard walk away for a moment he turned and linked her arm in his, turning them to walk away from the rest of the palace and off into a secluded place in the garden. Trying to take her arm away from his, knowing he shouldn't have taken it in the first place, Da'Leth found herself stuck, Nicholas increasing his hold on her the more she tried to escape. Giving in she allowed him to lead her to a small bench and sat down, watching him walk a few steps away before turning to face her.

"I don't know how much you have already guessed or may already know," he began. "So, let me begin at the beginning. Had you met me a several years ago you would not have known me, I was a spoiled child who was only interested in getting what he wanted at the moment he wanted it. As much as it shames me to admit it I was more like my brother than I would have thought possible." Shaking his head, he fell silent, remembering the man he used to be.

"I was studying at the university and drinking every night in a local tavern with a crowd of non- reputable men that would barely pass for scholars. There was a wench who worked there that had taken to serving our table as the night wore on. I drank, too much I now know, and the next morning I woke up in the stable with the livestock. A few of the other men were still passed out around me but when I got to my feet I saw that the leader of the group, John of Cotton Bay, was already up. He was pushing hay around with his foot and when he finished he turned to leave. I called to him but he didn't answer, simply stepped into his carriage and took off at a race."

"I headed out of the barn to watch him leave but stopped when I saw something peeking out from under the hay where he had just been. Moving the hay around I almost lost what little I had in my stomach. The wench from the previous night was buried in the hay, raped and beaten to death."

Da'Leth closed her eyes, putting her hand to her throat.

"I was terrified, Da'Leth," he said after a moment of silence. "I fled the area, came straight home to the palace and didn't leave again for a year. Sometime after that I heard that every man from the group that night that had still been passed out had been killed while they slept in that barn by the girl's father. They were all Lord's sons and the man became a fugitive, running from the law. But he was still seeking revenge against the two men from that group that hadn't been killed that day, myself and the man that had fled in the carriage."

"About two years ago I received a report that John had been found murdered in his carriage hidden away in the middle of the forest. The father was still looking for us; he was still seeking revenge for his daughter's death. I was the only one left. My only saving grace was that no one knew who I was, not even the men from that night. At the time I had just begun to joust in the tournament, under an assumed name of course, and while I was in France the father found me, he tried to kill me and had it not been for Richard I would be dead. From that moment on he has been following me, haunting me, searching for any opportunity with which to take his revenge."

"I had managed to keep my real identity from him, he knew me only as Lord Richmond of Glisten Cove. But when his men found you that day on the road, they surely recognized Rianne as the Princess and had to have known the truth. Now, they are here, at the palace, and no one is safe."

Silence fell as Nicholas contemplated what had happened because of his prior life. Watching him stare at the bush surrounding them Da'Leth wondered a question that she hated to even think. "Milord" she said after several moments, hating that she needed to ask it.

"No, I did not touch that woman," he said, meeting her eyes. "Of that much I am certain."

"What are you going to do?" Da'Leth asked.

Nicholas shook his head. "The only way to protect my family is to leave. He's coming after me, if they are not around me they cannot get hurt."

"Where will you go?"

"I'm going to the jousting tournament under a different name. Richard and I will be leaving in the morning."

"You will need to be careful. Travel lightly, stay at the crowded inns."

"No," he said, gently shaking his head. "There would be too many chances to be recognized. We'll stay at one of the secluded inns."

"Prince Nicholas, please," Da'Leth said, looking up at him with a serious face. "Hear my logic. In a small, empty inn, two men traveling will stand out and be recognized. In a crowded inn, where men of all sort will be, two men can easily become one with the crowd and spend the night unnoticed. You would be safer in a crowd."

Listening to her describe her reasoning Nicholas began to see the logic of it. "You sound as if you've had to do this before."

Da'Leth shrugged. "When the man who tells you what to do does it with his fists you learn to make yourself invisible." Getting to her feet she walked towards him, briefly touching his arm before folding her hands again. "Please be careful."

Nodding his head, he smiled a small smile. "I will. It will be a comfort to know my family has its own protector here to take care of them." Putting his hands on her shoulders Nicholas looked down into Da'Leth's eyes. "You are our hidden blade, Da'Leth," he told her. "No one will know you are there except the ones who will need you should the time come. I know you have not been with my family for long but you have already proven your loyalty to me; I have no doubts about you."

Her cheeks burned and Da'Leth ducked her head, twisting to try and get away from his attention. Nicholas refused to let her go.

"Take care of my family while I am gone, I'm entrusting my role of protector to you for so long as I am gone."

"I will not let you down," she softly replied. Staring at the gold fringe of his jacket for a moment Da'Leth raised her eyes to his and continued, "You have my promise."

"Good." With a gentle squeeze he released her shoulders, folding his hands behind his back. "You should head back to the palace, I'm sure Rianne is looking for you."

Curtseying Da'Leth turned to leave the garden. Standing in place he watched her leave. The grace in her walk was not that of a serf but rather a young woman who was still learning the art of social positioning. He recognized it as the way Rianne used to walk while she was still a little girl, her tutor teaching her the fine art of sitting, walking, standing, eating and drinking; all the graces a young lady would need to know. Furrowing his brow for a moment he continued to watch her leave. Something about this woman just didn't add up but just what it was he couldn't quite put his finger on.

Chapter Eight

"You've been ordered to go and see Prince Philip, Miss Da'Leth."

Looking up from her book she had borrowed from the palace library, Da'Leth nodded. "Of course," she said, getting to her feet.

Leaving the maid to watch Tome, the Princess sleeping during her nap time, she made her way to the Prince's chamber, entering when he motioned for her to come in. "Shut the door," he commanded her.

Doing as she was told Da'Leth stood before the Prince, hands folded behind her. She watched as he stood, a book in his hands, and moved behind her. Listening to him putting the book on her shelf her attention was caught by the display of swords on the wall behind his desk. Waiting for him to speak to her she examined them. The craftsmanship was excellent and she was looking each one over in detail when Da'Leth jumped in her skin from the suddenness of his movements.

From behind her Philip wrapped his arm around her waist, his other reaching around to cup her breast, pinching and squeezing painfully. Moving away she succeeded in taking a single step before he pulled her back to him. "Stay here, serf," he commanded.

"Prince, please," she cried, still trying to get away from his unwanted touch.

Holding her tightly to him Philip refused to release her. Terrified that he would take the only thing she had left to give her husband Da'Leth struggled to get away, tears filling her eyes as her heart and mind battled with each other. Her mind telling her that this man was the Crown Prince and she served the crown her heart was arguing that no man had the right to take what did not belong to him.

She belonged to no one.

The door opened suddenly and a woman gasped. Distracted Philip loosened his hold just slightly but it was all Da'Leth needed to get away. Turning she ran out the door, brushing past the three maids that had come to clean the chamber, Da'Leth ran as fast as she could, going to the one place she knew she would go undisturbed. Up the flight of stairs that led to the tower, slamming the door shut behind her, Da'Leth fell against the solid door, sinking down to the ground.

Alone in her shame she wept, her head laid on her knees, until she had no more tears to shed. What had almost been taken was all she had to give to the man she would one day marry. Da'Leth would do anything the royal family asked of her, she served the crown, but she had finally found a line that she would not, could not, cross.

~~*~*~*~*~*~*~*

Kneeling next to Tome Da'Leth helped her to pull one of the barn kittens into her lap. "Now you sit here and pet the kitten gently, okay?"

"O'tay," Tome smiled, gently running her hand up and down the kittens back. "Sof', Day," she announced, using her own pronunciation of Da'Leth's name. "Sof' kitty."

"It is soft, isn't it?" she agreed, gently rubbing the kittens head. "Does the kitten have a name?" she asked, looking up at the stable boy.

"No, ma'am," he answered shyly. "We don't bother naming them 'round here."

"Do you want to give this one a name, Tome?" Excited at the responsibility the small Princess nodded. "Okay, what name do you want to give this kitten?"

"Nich'las!" she cried, clapping her hands in delight.

Laughing Da'Leth shook her head. "You can't name this kitten Nicholas, this is a girl kitten, and she needs a girl's name."

Tome shook her head defiantly. "Nich'las!" she declared.

"Okay, okay, okay!" Da'Leth said, holding up her hands in defeat. "I hereby dub thee Lady Nicholas." Giggling Tome pulled the kitten tightly to her, hugging it and kissing its head. "Shall we go show the Queen?"

Tome nodded and stood up, holding onto her new friend by the neck. Bending down Da'Leth quickly rescued the kitten and knelt back down to tell Tome why she had taken the kitten. "You need to hold the kitten nicely, Tome," she advised. "Or else you'll hurt it and the kitten won't want to play with you, understand?" She nodded solemnly and Da'Leth smiled in return. "Would you like me to carry the both of you back to the palace?"

A grin split her mouth and Tome held up her arms to be picked up. Holding both the girl and the kitten in her arms Da'Leth headed towards the palace. Walking through the corridors they wove their way through the palace and up the stairs toward the Queens sitting room on the second floor. As they neared the door to the room Da'Leth snuck a free finger into Tome's side, tickling the girl until she giggled, squirming to get away.

"Is that my granddaughter?" Winifred called out. "Bring her in here."

Entering the room Da'Leth curtsied as best she could, still balancing the child and the kitten, and greeted the Queen. "Tome wished to show you her new friend, my Queen."

"A new friend?" she replied. "Who is your new friend, Tome?"

Setting the girl down on her own feet Da'Leth cuddled the kitten into her arms and told her to go show her grandmother. Walking with her to make sure she didn't drop her accidentally, she smiled up at the Queen. "This is Lady Nicholas, Majesty."

Winifred laughed. "Lady Nicholas!" Pulling Tome into her lap she gently rubbed the kittens paw. "I am glad to meet you, madam," she teased. Letting Tome go she watched as Da'Leth knelt down next to her to help the little girl settle the kitten into her lap. As she bent over the long red braid that usually laid down her back fell over her shoulder and brushed Tome's nose resulting in a small giggle and a scrunched face. Taking the tip of it Da'Leth brushed it over her nose again before swinging it back behind her again.

Smiling as she watched Tome playing on the floor with Da'Leth Winifred's heart suddenly stopped in her chest. Her braid in her way Da'Leth had flipped it back over her shoulder, a simple move that would not have caught the attention of most people but Winifred saw more than anyone else could have.

She saw her best friend.

Since they had been children they had played together, first as two little girls learning their lessons together, then as two young women aching to be older. When the day had come for each of them, having found the man they would marry, she for duty and her friend for love, they had celebrated and cried their tears together. Though she had been the first to become pregnant and bear two children the friends had rejoiced when they were pregnant together, crying, laughing, and suffering through the same problems at the same time.

And when her dearest friend had lost both her husband and her child in one blow it was she who went to her, lying in the bed, cradling her broken friend until she could regain the strength to go on.

Her heart aching Winifred stood, waving off the help of her ladies' maid, and left the room. Pausing just before she entered her own chambers she sent her maid to find Da'Leth and bring her to the chamber in one-hour time. When the door had shut she fell into her bed, stunned by the knowledge she had just come to know, staring at the canopy overhead while her mind drifted back through the years. Unsure of how much time had passed she stood up from the bed and crossed her room to the desk by the window. Questions rang in her mind.

'Why had she come here instead of going home? Why hadn't she told them who she really was?'

Pulling out a piece of parchment she was reaching for the ink well when a knock sounded at the door. "Come in," she called out.

"You sent for me, my Queen?"

Motioning for Da'Leth to come in Winifred pointed to a stool by her feet. "Sit down, child. I fear we need to talk." Waiting until Da'Leth was seated she sat still, watching her, seeing her dear friend Chelaine. "Tell me something," she said once Da'Leth was settled. "Who is your mother?"

Her eyes widened in shock. "I... I beg your pardon, my Queen?"

"Tell me who your mother is."

Turning her gaze to the floor she replied, "She is a good woman who loved her family very much."

Raising an eyebrow Winifred stared silently as Da'Leth before shaking her head. "Since the time that you came to our home I have noticed many things about you Da'Leth. One of them is your ability to answer a question without really answering it. I have also learnt however that when you are asked a question directly you will answer it truthfully no matter what the cost to yourself. With that knowledge I will re-word my question to you. What is the name of your mother?"

Da'Leth's heart sank, tears filling her eyes. "You already know," she whispered. "Or else you would not need to ask the question."

"Tell me."

"My mother's name," she said at last, closing her eyes against the pain of her failure, "... is Chelaine."

Seeing the pain in Da'Leth's face Winifred wondered if she had done the right thing by forcing the young girl to tell her; taking advantage of a flaw she had seen in her. Reaching out she placed a gentle hand on her shoulder. "Why did you not tell us who you are?"

"I cannot," she whispered, shaking her head. "So long as I am a serf I can never admit who I am, not even to you."

"I don't understand! You are the daughter of a Lord and a Lady, our good friends no less. Do you expect me to sit still and do nothing when the people I care about and love as my own family are in pain?"

"Yes!"

Her forceful tone stopped Winifred still. Never before had she heard anything more than a soft-spoken word from Da'Leth, even when Tome was misbehaving. Now, with teary eyes fixed on her, she began to realize how like her father the young woman before her really was. "Why?"

"Because if you value my family as much as I do then you will help me to leave their honor intact," Da'Leth replied quickly. Softening her tone, she tried to explain. "Please, my Queen. Try to understand. My father is dead, my mother is alone with the servants and my uncle is controlling Whispering Winds. There is nothing I want more in this life than to save my family from my uncle and restore Whispering Winds to its proper place in this world. But as long as I am a serf that is impossible."

"You knew my father," she reasoned. "You knew his views on owning a human being. How could I possibly let the world know that his only heir is now a serf? My father's honor is all I have left to hold on to. Without him here to defend it therefore it falls to me to do whatever I must to keep his honor, my family's honor, from being besmirched."

"My only consolation in this painful predicament is that my uncle will care for his brother's widow. It was I who was in the way of him having what he wanted. As the only heir there was a possibility that the King would grant to me ownership of Whispering Winds. That is why my uncle got rid of me. However, my mother was no threat and I know she will be safe with my aunt and cousin."

"I beg of you, My Queen, please," Da'Leth pleaded, tears slipping down her cheeks. "Tell no one who I am or who my parents were. The pain that would come from dishonoring them would be too much for me to bear!"

The pain and sadness in her voice tore at Winifred's heart. She longed to heal the wounds done to her friend's daughter but, hearing why Da'Leth refused to make known who and what she was, the Queen knew she would have to grant her wishes and stay silent.

"Tell me everything and I give you my word I will not tell anyone who you are," she said gently. "Though I do not promise to try and convince you to change your mind or to do what I can to make your life here with my family easier."

Relief flooded through Da'Leth. "Thank you, my Queen. This means more to me than you could ever know."

Staring down at her Winifred shook her head sadly. "You look so much like your mother; how could I have not seen?"

"People do not look upon a serf for anything more than to get a task completed. To know that you could have seen a friend in a person that most would over look says more about you than anything I could ever hope to put into words. My mother would be proud."

"Yes," she replied, thinking about a mother's pride for her daughter. "Yes, she would."

~~*~*~*~*~*~*~*

Sitting in the window, Tome sound asleep in her adjoining room, Da'Leth fanned herself, trying to cool herself against the unusually hot night air. Giving up she lay down on the bed, forgoing the blankets, and tried to go to sleep. Her mind refused to turn off, going over and over her conversation with the Queen from the day before. Knowing that there was someone who knew who she really was, who her parents really were, made her feel better, a burden lifted from her shoulders. A smile pulling at her lips she finally fell asleep.

Lying on the bed, asleep, Da'Leth didn't hear the door to her room open, didn't see the man entering her room, or the way he looked at her sleeping form. The material of her gown was light to help stay cool in the heat and it had shifted as she slept, her knees exposed for him to see. A grin pulled at his mouth as he silently approached her, reaching out to touch her calf, sliding his hand up her leg until it disappeared beneath her gown.

Startled out of her sleep, Da'Leth jumped, trying to get out of the bed but pinned to it by the arm that had snaked around her midsection. "Let go of me!" she cried, struggling to get away.

Elbowing her attacker in his side she felt him loosen his hold on her and she took advantage of it to slip out of the bed, away from him. Turning back to see who it was Da'Leth's eyes widened when she saw James lying in her bed. With a low growl he rushed towards her, angry that she had gotten away, hurting him in the process. Reaching for the first thing she could lay her hands on Da'Leth swung it at him when he was close enough, hitting the side of his arm with the silver candle stick, cutting his skin.

Enraged he was coming towards her again when they both heard the cries of Tome, the sleepy little girl standing in the doorway between the two rooms, wakened by the struggle she'd heard. Hurrying to her side Da'Leth picked up the little girl, turning back to face the man that had attacked her.

"Get out of here and leave me alone!" she hissed at him, her voice filled with venom. Without bothering to wait for his response Da'Leth hurried back to Tome's room, locking the door firmly behind her. Loud noises echoed from the other room as Tome clung to Da'Leth. Soothing the scared Princess, she helped her to go back to sleep, spending the rest of the night locked away in Tome's room.

The next morning Da'Leth unlocked the door between their rooms and peered into hers, checking to make sure James was gone, before stepping into it. The room had been attacked, tables overturned, chairs scattered, blankets and curtains torn. Her own personal belongings had been scattered about the room, some of them torn others simply crumpled. Tears came to her eyes as she began to pick everything up.

As she was working her door opened, Jennifer carrying in the morning tray of food for her and Tome to breakfast on. "Miss Da'Leth?" she whispered in shock. "What happened?"

Trying to smile, her tears obvious to the little girl, Da'Leth couldn't say anything. Setting the tray down Jennifer left the room, returning some time later with an older woman by her side. Seeing the destruction, the woman got to work quickly, the three of them working together to fix the room. When it was cleaned up as best they could the woman told Jennifer to gather the torn items and take them to the seamstress to be fixed and returned when they were done. Sitting Da'Leth down at the table she fixed her a cup of tea to help soothe her nerves.

"Who did this, love?" the woman asked at last.

"One of the guards," Da'Leth replied, keeping her eyes on the tea she was holding in her hands. "He came in here last night."

"With the little one right next door?" she asked, shocked that he would have the gall to make such an attempt. Shaking her head, she reached out to touch Da'Leth's hand. "Are you all right, child? Was he able to hurt you?"

Shaking her head Da'Leth took a deep breath. "No, he only touched me a little but it was enough," tears coming to her eyes again. "I feel so dirty and ashamed!"

Gently patting her hand, the old woman let her cry, soothing her as she herself had Tome the night before. "You'll be all right, little one. We will make sure you stay safe from now on." The older woman smiled at Da'Leth. "You are an important woman to us serfs; we protect our own whenever we can."

Frowning, Da'Leth lifted her head. "I don't understand."

"Rumor has it that you saved the Prince and the Princess while they were traveling. There are some who think you put on airs because of it, but I've seen the way you treat the other serfs and servants. You give the same respect to them as you do the King himself." The woman nodded. "My Jenni has told me how you ask her to eat with you and how nicely you treat her. I don't see any airs about you, Miss Da'Leth. None at all."

Humbled by the woman's honesty Da'Leth thanked her. Letting her know she would have her items returned as soon as they were fixed she left. Forcing her mind off the events of last night Da'Leth heard Tome stirring in the other room and stood to go see to her.

Chapter Nine

Tired, exhausted if he was honest with himself, Nicholas and Richard rode through the courtyard toward the stables. "Nicholas!" he heard Da'Leth cry. His brow drawn together in confusion Nicholas looked around for her, unable to see her anywhere. Leaving their horses with one of the stable boys both men headed for the palace, ready for a long to soak to ease their aching muscles. As they entered the long corridor to the palace he heard her again. "Nicholas!" Once more he looked around, unable to find her, wondering aloud why she was calling out to him.

"Why is Da'Leth calling you by your given name?" Krausley wondered when it happened a third time.

Knowing better than to simply go to their rooms the men stopped at the main hall to greet the King and Queen before doing anything else. "Mother, Father," Nicholas smiled as he approached them, Krausley stopping several yards away from the thrones. "It is good to see you again."

"A much shorter journey this time," Winifred noted. Reaching out she motioned for her son to come closer, kissing his cheek warmly when he did. "I'm glad to see you well."

"Well enough, your Majesty," Richard advised.

Liam frowned. "Are you hurt?"

"Only a little," Nicholas glared at Richard. "Soreness mostly. I will be well enough."

"Nicholas!"

Turning, hearing Da'Leth call his name as she entered the room he opened his mouth to ask why she was calling him when he saw Tome toddle in behind her, clutching at her skirts, tears streaming from her eyes. "What is going on here?" he asked.

"Nich'las!" Tome sobbed, letting go of Da'Leth to reach out for her uncle's consolation. Lifting his niece into his arms, wincing at the pain the flared up in his shoulder, Nicholas kissed her cheek.

"Da'Leth, what is going on?"

"We seem to have lost Nicholas, my Queen. I'm afraid Tome is not taking the search very well."

"It's okay, Tome," Nicholas soothed, kissing he cheek again. "I'm right here." The little girl's sobs increased, weeping in her confused uncles' arms.

Hissing at the sudden pain that clawed into his leg King Liam frowned and pulled the small cat off his leg. "Never fear, Da'Leth, it appears Nicholas has simply returned to gnaw on my leg again."

"Father, what are you...?"

Turning to look at his father Nicholas stopped his question when he saw Liam holding a small gray cat out for Da'Leth to take. Hurrying over to him Da'Leth took the cat and cuddled it to her, scolding the thing for running away from them. "There, you see Tome, Lady Nicholas is fine," stroking the girls' hair as she held the cat up for Tome to see. "Do you want to hold her?"

"No!" she cried. "Nich'las bad kitty!"

"Okay," she shrugged, turning away, knowing what was going to happen next.

"No!" Tome cried again, struggling to get down from Nicholas's arms.

Unable to hold her he bent over, releasing her before she did more damage to his already tender shoulder, Nicholas put the little girl down and watched her run to Da'Leth, yanking on her skirt to get her attention. Smiling Da'Leth handed the cat to her and looked up. Her smile dropped from her face when she saw the pain on Nicholas's face. "Milord?" she said, moving a step closer. "Are you hurt?"

"I will be fine," he announced, looking back at his mother for emphasis. "A long hot soak is all I need right now."

Turning on his heel he left, Richard bowing before he followed his friend in leaving the room, both men more than ready for some well-earned relaxation. The jousting tournament had been difficult this year and Nicholas had been hurt too early into the matches to recover the tournament.

Letting them go Winifred motioned for Da'Leth to come closer. "I do hate to ask this of you," she began. "Please, go with him; tend to him with your healing touch."

Nodding Da'Leth turned to leave, motioning for one of the Ladies in waiting to take care of Tome. Making her way to her room she picked up a small basket and left to find the Prince's chamber in the northern wing of the castle. Knocking on his door she waited for one of the servants to open it. "The Prince is soaking in a hot bath at this moment, Miss Da'Leth."

"Good," she smiled. Taking a small vial out of the basket she handed it to the man. "Please put half of this into his water by pouring it over his wounds. Then, when he is ready to come out of the water have him dress only with pants and lie down on the bed with his stomach facing down."

Nodding, the man took the vial and shut the door. Sitting down outside of the door Da'Leth waited until finally the door opened again and the man emerged. "It has been done as you asked, Miss Da'Leth, the Prince is waiting for your next instruction."

Getting up she motioned for him to step aside and entered the room. "All he needs do is lie still and try not to make too much noise," she teased, knowing he could hear her.

"Were I in a better mood I would laugh at that comment, Da'Leth," Nicholas called out from where he was lying on the bed, his head resting on his crossed arms. "Why are you here? And why have I been ordered about like this?"

"Because your mother, the Queen, asked me to tend to your shoulder," Da'Leth answered, setting her basket on the floor by the bed. Leaning over him she saw the redness of the shoulder and knew what had happened. "Someone broke their lance on your shoulder, milord."

"What makes you so certain?" turning his head as far as he could to look at her.

"I have seen this type of wound before. I hope you can at least tell me you won the match."

Smiling he laid his head back down. "Of course, I did."

Barely resisting the urge to roll her eyes she simply set about to work. Pulling a small flask of peppermint oil from her basket she poured a small amount into her hands, rubbing them for a moment before turning to rub the oil into his shoulder. Da'Leth could see him wincing as she worked, though she was being as gentle as she could, and knew the pain was worse than he was letting on. Suddenly he groaned and she stopped for a moment, knowing that she must have touched upon an extremely sore spot. Reaching into her basket again she pulled out another small vial and gave it to the servant waiting nearby.

"Pour this into some hot water and let it steep for several minutes. When it has turned a dark green color pour it into a cup so his highness may drink it."

"Green?" he said weakly, doubt and pain battling for control of his voice.

"Yes, green. Trust in me, milord, I would not do anything to harm you." Seeing the look in his eyes she added, "Permanently."

Despite the pain a small smiled pulled at his lips. "Keep going, I'm all right."

Nodding Da'Leth put her hands to his shoulder and pressed once, stopping when she saw the rest of him tense with pain. "No, we shall wait until you have drunk the tea. Then I shall continue."

Letting him rest for a few moment's Da'Leth took the tea and held it out for him to drink. Making a face at the taste he swallowed it as fast as he could. "That brine is disgusting!"

She shrugged, "But it works wonders."

"What is it supposed to do?" he asked, laying his head back down on his arms.

Da'Leth said nothing, watching as the potion took effect, the Prince's pinched face slowly smoothing out as he fell into a painless sleep. "What have you done?" the servant asked nervously.

"Do not worry," she replied, getting back to work on his shoulder. "It is an herb that pulls the patient into a deep sleep so that they do not feel the pain anymore. The Prince shall wake by the morning and he will feel much better, I assure you."

~~*~*~*~*~*~*~*

Lying still Nicholas listened as the world bustled around him. Servants came and went, fretting over the fact that he still hadn't woken up, the smell of food permeated the room when they brought the tray in but it didn't tempt him, he wasn't hungry for food just yet.

Information.

That was what he hungered for at the moment. What had happened after Da'Leth had come into his room? He remembered her massaging his shoulder with oil as well as drinking a disgusting brew but after that he had no memory other than waking up in his bed. Knowing he wouldn't get any answers so long as he was in bed Nicholas pulled the covers off him and sat up, nursing his shoulder carefully. Dressing himself more causally than usual he left the bedroom chamber and headed down the corridor to find the person who had the answers he sought.

Entering the sitting room, he saw Da'Leth sitting on the floor, Tome in her lap, telling a story to the small girl with a soft voice, her back was to him and he took a moment to watch her. She was always so gentle with Tome, though he had seen her be firm when the need arose, and the child had bonded with her almost instantly. In the three months that he'd been gone Tome had changed quite a bit, 'Heavier than before,' he thought to himself with a small frown.

"Nicholas?"

Looking over at his mother he saw her sitting with Elizabeth and Rianne at the table, a cup of tea before each of them and a plate of pastries on the table. "Good morning mother," he smiled, moving closer to kiss her cheek. "I hope you are all well?"

"Yes, we're fine," Rianne answered. "How are you? Mother said you'd been hurt?"

Shaking his head, he sat down with them. "I'm well enough. Much better now, thanks to Da'Leth. Why did you send her to me?"

Winifred smiled at her son. "Da'Leth has the uncanny ability to make pain go away. She has helped these poor old legs on countless occasions." Nicholas nodded, understanding dawning in his eyes. "Did she make you drink the tea?" Seeing his face at the memory of the taste she laughed. "I can see she did."

"It does what it is supposed to," Da'Leth interjected from her seat on the floor.

"Uncle Nich'las!" Tome laughed when she realized her uncle had joined them. Getting up from Da'Leth's lap she toddled over to him, climbing up into his lap and wrapping her arms around his neck.

Turning to face them Da'Leth stayed where she was; content to watch the family from her seat on the floor. Her focus on Tome as she told Nicholas about recent events she didn't see Philip enter the room until she felt his boot tread over her hand, pressing it into the floor with his full weight. The suddenness of the pain shocked her and a gasp flew out of her mouth. Pulling the wounded hand into her lap she schooled her face, putting her mask on before anyone could see her.

"Da'Leth?" Elizabeth called out, hearing the gasp. "Is something wrong?"

Shaking her head, she smiled. "No, milady, all is well."

Satisfied with her answer the three women went back to talking, Tome still babbling to Nicholas though he was no longer paying attention. Frowning he watched Da'Leth hesitate before looking down at her lap, following her movements with his eyes. Lifting her hand, a little she examined it, the skin already bright red.

He could see a boot print on her hand and looked over at his brother as he stood at the window, realizing why Da'Leth had suddenly gasped.

Narrowing his eyes Nicholas knew that something wasn't right. Philip held no love for any serf, that wasn't unusual, but he had never before been so cruel to them before without provocation. 'What happened while I was gone?' he wondered, hoping his brother hadn't pursued Da'Leth as he did all the other maids. Knowing he couldn't do anything right now he pushed it to the back of his mind, turning his attention back to Tome, smiling when he realized she was talking about her new cat.

"I am honored that you would name your cat after me, Tome," he grinned. "But why is it called Lady Nicholas? Shouldn't it be Lord Nicholas?"

"The cat is a female, milord," Da'Leth smiled at him, dropping her hand back into her lap. "However, Tome was quite insistent that we name it Nicholas."

Chuckling he looked down at his niece. "Thank you, I think I am touched by your loyalty."

"Are you not sure?" Rianne laughed, teasing her older brother.

"It's only a cat," Philip sneered, turning away from the window to leave the room.

As he passed by Da'Leth Nicholas saw her straighten her back, squaring her shoulders as if she were trying to prepare herself. Once Philip was gone she relaxed again, the tension leaving her body, and Nicholas knew his instinct had been correct. Something had happened while he was gone and he intended to find out what it was.

~~*~*~*~*~*~*~*

Listening to the crowds below Da'Leth sat at the edge of the tower quietly, watching the people below dancing to the music of the orchestra King Liam had requested. She had stayed with the crowds until it was time for Tome go to bed, the little girl tired out from all the excitement, falling asleep the moment her head touched the pillow. Her time now her own she had escaped to the one place she knew she would be alone. True to what Nicholas had pointed out very few people journeyed up to this tower as it was the highest in the castle, a steep fall should something go wrong.

Looking down she saw the royal family seated at a table, watching and enjoying the show before them. As she watched them she saw Nicholas suddenly turn his face to the sky, his eyes finding her, and he rose from his seat. Da'Leth saw him disappear and knew he was coming up to the tower.

A part of her wanted to leave, to go where he could not find her, but another part told her to stay, knowing she had nothing to fear from the younger Prince. Staying where she was Da'Leth wondered why he was coming to the tower. "Da'Leth?" she heard come time later, the door shutting behind him with a soft click.

Getting to her feet Da'Leth curtsied. "Milord?"

"I have to admit I thought you would have left when you saw me coming."

"Would you like for me to leave?"

"No," he replied quickly. "I wished to talk to you but haven't had the opportunity to do so."

Sitting down on the ledge he motioned for her to join him. Taking a seat on the ledge as well, keeping a more than respectable distance between them, Da'Leth waited for him to say what was on his mind. "How have you been doing while I was gone? Has my family been treating you well?"

"Oh yes," she agreed. "The family has been too kind to me; I could never find cause to complain against them."

"All of them?" He saw her hesitate and waited to see if she was going to tell the truth or lie to him.

"The royal family has treated me far better than I have known in quite some time."

Shaking his head Nicholas knew he should have been surprised by her evasive answer but had to admit he wasn't. "You always find a way to avoid truly answering a question that you don't want to answer, don't you Da'Leth? Very well, I shall rephrase the question. Has my brother Philip done anything that he oughtn't?"

"He is the Crown Prince, milord, what is there that he is not allowed to do?"

"There are basic human rights that all people are entitled to Da'Leth," Nicholas replied. "Has my brother violated any of them?"

"No."

Though he heard her word Nicholas heard more in her tone. It was too even, too careful; he knew there was something she wasn't saying. "Did he attempt to violate any of them?" he asked.

Silence fell between then and he knew the truth from it. Philip had tried to have his way with Da'Leth and, for reasons he didn't quite know, the knowledge of that boiled within him until his fist clenched with anger. Looking at Da'Leth carefully he could see the shame in her eyes and it hurt his heart. He had taken her from one nightmare only to place her in another.

"I'm sorry," he said gently when she still didn't speak. "I knew the kind of man my brother is and I didn't do enough to protect you."

"It is not your job to protect me, milord," Da'Leth spoke at last. "I am here to serve and protect the royal family."

"You are here because you have proven to me that you are a woman to be trusted and to be held in high regard, not treated as a toy to be tossed about as he pleases."

She could hear the disgust in his voice and the tears she had been holding back filled her eyes. Her skin still crawled from the feel of Philips hands on her chest. The fact that he had gotten as close as he had without her realizing still shocked Da'Leth, used to fighting off the advances of drunken men at the pub, and it shamed her that she had not been paying closer attention.

Seeing her tear-filled eyes Nicholas realized his voice had been harsh and frowned. Moving closer he took her hand in his own, waiting for her to look at him. When her red-rimmed eyes finally looked at him he felt as though his heart had been stabbed with a red-hot poker. He could see the shame in her eyes; it burned into him, but no matter how hard he tried he could not think of anything to say other than the first thing that had popped into his head.

"I'm sorry," he told her from the bottom of his heart. "The blame is mine for leaving you here to face him alone. I knew he had put his sights on you but I thought I had warned him enough to stay away. I swear to you this will not happen again."

Da'Leth shook her head, lowering her eyes. "You've done nothing wrong, milord. I did not hear him coming, I don't know why. Had I heard him I could have left as before."

"This has happened before?" Nicholas repeated, his frown quickly curving into a scowl. "With my brother?"

"Among others," she answered honestly.

"Here in the palace?"

Getting to his feet Nicholas paced the small tower. Watching him Da'Leth's heart was touched by the realization that he was truly upset with the knowledge of what she had been dealing with.

"Who?" he demanded suddenly; turning on his heel to face her. "Who has been trying to get you besides my brother?"

"Mostly the men in the guard," she admitted. "Though, to be fair, almost all of them have stayed away once I made myself clear."

"Almost all," he pressed. "Who hasn't?" Nicholas could see that she was hesitant to give out a name and he pressed her for it. "Tell me who it was, Da'Leth. I trust my men with the life of my family. If one of them would dare to do such things even after you had made yourself clear I must address the situation at once."

Sighing she looked down at her hands again, the black and blue bruise still coming to the surface from the Prince's boot. "It is James, milord," she admitted softly.

"James? The apprentice you fought with in the ring?" Da'Leth nodded. "You shamed him and he's retaliating."

"I did not want to," she began, stopping when he held up a hand to silence her.

"You have done nothing wrong. The blame lies with James. I give you my word he will hear about it."

Chapter Ten

Early the next morning, walking through the yard, trying to find Krausley to warn him about what Nicholas might do, Da'Leth stopped when she saw a small group of men gathered around the Prince. Staying where she was she could still hear what was being said and closed her eyes for a moment when she realized Prince Nicholas was ordering the men to leave her alone. Though a small part of her was embarrassed that she needed help from someone else to handle the situation, another part of her was relieved. Finally, she would be free to walk through the yard without having to worry about anything or think ahead about the quickest way to flee should the need arise.

The men started to disperse but Da'Leth heard him call James back, telling the man to stay while the others left. Silent for some time Nicholas simply looked the apprentice up and down as if measuring him in his mind. Finally, the silence beginning to drag on unendingly, he spoke, his voice eerily calm after the verbal lashing he had just given the group.

"I am a man of honor," he began. "I choose to surround myself with men of the same values and attributes as I do. When I choose people to protect my family I choose the ones that have proven to me they can be trusted, the ones that I know would do whatever they had to in order to protect my family. You lack the necessary skills needed to protect my family and now I am uncertain if I should allow you to continue as an apprentice to the royal guard."

James was startled. "Milord, I am the best guard here, better than those who have already finished their apprenticeship!"

"Your skill is one of the best in the guard, of that there is no doubt, but you have given me proof that you cannot be trusted.

Da'Leth, on the other hand, has proven her loyalty and valor to me and my family from the moment we first set out on the same road."

"How have I proven that I cannot be trusted?" he asked, confused about where this information was coming from.

Nicholas moved a step closer and Da'Leth had to strain to hear him. "You proved your true colors when you tried to force yourself upon a woman that I have brought to the palace to care for my family."

Realization dawned in James eyes. "Milord, I..."

"Silence," Nicholas hissed. "Do not even attempt to speak a defense. I owe that woman the life of my sister and my own health on top of it. When you turned on Da'Leth you turned on me."

Nicholas stepped closer, putting a hard hand on James neck as he pulled the man close, whispering in his ear. Though she couldn't hear him Da'Leth saw James reaction, his eyes widening, a touch of fear creeping into them before Nicholas stepped away. Meeting his eyes with a final unspoken warning Nicholas left the apprentice standing alone in the yard. Watching Nicholas leave for a moment Da'Leth looked back to James and saw him staring at her. Meeting her eyes for only a brief moment James turned on his heel and left the yard, disappearing into the stables.

"When someone gets on Nicholas's bad side they had best stay out of his way."

Looking to her left Da'Leth saw Krausley standing next to her. "Why?"

"Have you ever seen a mother protecting her young? That is how Nicholas is with the people that are within his closest circle of friends and family. Once you are within his protection he will do whatever he needs to make sure you are kept safe."

Listening to Krausley's insight Da'Leth couldn't stop a warm feeling from spreading over her heart. Seeing that she wasn't going to speak Richard walked away, wanting to have a word with his men himself, none too pleased with the things he had heard about their actions while he was gone.

Caught up in her own thoughts Da'Leth didn't notice him leave until sometime later, standing in the yard as still as a statue. Pulling herself together she left the yard, heading to the nursery to check on Tome. Finding the little girl still asleep Da'Leth sat down on the windows ledge, staring out at the garden below, her mind a jumble of confusion. Looking out over the grounds below she saw Nicholas walking with Rianne and her heart skipped a beat at the memory of what he had just done.

Watching him from above Da'Leth wondered why he was so protective of her, a serf. Though the reasons eluded her she couldn't help but smile at the warm feeling that knowledge spread through her, like sitting by a warm fire on a frigid day. Thinking back over her time with him Da'Leth knew he was a good man but the place he had begun to hold in her heart surprised her. Sitting on the ledge Da'Leth had to remind herself that he was a Prince and she, for now, was only a serf. No matter what her heart tried to tell her she had no choice but to silence any feelings other than respect or friendship that were starting to form.

Closing her eyes against the sadness that bubbled up in her heart Da'Leth focused on the reasons she could not allow herself to be distracted. Her family's honor was still at stake and she needed to focus on that, pushing aside any pain that she suffered as a result.

~~*~*~*~*~*~*~*

The family was gathered in the dining hall by the time Nicholas arrived. Making his excuses he sat down, scanning the room to locate Da'Leth. As usual she was sitting next to Tome;

helping the girl with her food, making sure she ate something healthy before allowing her any of the pastries that were on the table before them. He hadn't had the chance to talk with her yet today, though he had seen her sitting in the window of Tome's room early that morning.

Though his face was blank Nicholas's eyes burned at the memory of the discussion he'd had with the men this morning, James still making his fist clench. Before he'd been able to find Philip, Rianne had asked him to walk with her in the gardens, wanting to find out in detail how the jousting tournament had gone. That was when he'd seen Da'Leth sitting in the window, her bright red hair making it impossible to be anyone else. Too far away to see her clearly, he had meant to find her and assure her that she would be left alone but had been sidetracked by his mother and it had taken all morning to slip away again.

By then he discovered that Da'Leth was tied up with Tome, unable to get away and Nicholas had returned to his original intent of finding his brother. Philip, as usual, had been in his study with one of the maids. Ordering her to get out Nicholas had sat down opposite his brother and folded his arms over his chest. Philip, sensing Nicholas's bad mood, had let the woman go and sat down to face his younger brother.

He had kept the conversation short and sweet, detailing, in no uncertain terms, that Philip was to leave Da'Leth alone. His reaction was exactly what Nicholas had expected and he had stood to face his brother. Though they were two years apart in age the two men stood at the same height and Nicholas had met his brother's angry gaze with his own cool one, telling him the same thing he had said to James.

'If I hear that you have so much as looked at Da'Leth in a way as to make her uncomfortable, you will pay in ways you could never imagine.'

Philip had dared Nicholas to try and stop him and it had taken every ounce of his self-control to not hit the man. Now, sitting at the table a few seats away from him he looked over and saw his brother openly staring at Da'Leth, her back to him. Drawing his brow together Nicholas realized that her back had been to him the entire time and he smirked. She was fighting him in her own way, by not allowing Philip to see the effect his unwanted attentions were having on her.

'Good girl,' he thought to himself, pleased that she would stand up for herself against the Crown Prince. 'In her own humble way.'

"What has you so happy?" Krausley asked as he sat down next to the Prince. "This morning you were in a foul mood." Following his line of sight, he nodded. "And rightly so. I gave the men a piece of my mind as well."

Looking at his friend Nicholas raised an eyebrow. "And?"

Krausley smiled. "They don't even want to look at her anymore."

Chuckling Nicholas sat forward, reaching for a piece of fruit, not hungry just yet but knowing he hadn't really eaten all day. The movement shot a stabbing pain up his shoulder and he winced. "Milord?" Krausley asked softly, not wanting to attract anyone's attention. "Your shoulder?"

Nicholas nodded. "Hurts like a bear." As he sat back in the chair, the fruit clutched in his fist, he looked around to see if anyone had noticed. Meeting Da'Leth's gaze he saw the question in her eyes and nodded, acknowledging the pain. She nodded in return before turning her attention back to Tome to help her finish the meal.

"How does she do that?" Krausley wondered aloud.

"What?"

"If I didn't know better I would say she could read a man's mind. Da'Leth always seems to know exactly what is needed, even if I myself don't know what it is yet."

Nicholas smiled through the pain. "I suppose it's from her years as a serf, always serving other people."

He shook his head, "I'm not so sure. There are serfs that have been serving in the palace for years and yet they don't serve the way she does."

Agreeing Nicholas took a bite out of the fruit absently, watching Da'Leth tempt Tome with a piece of apple. His silent contemplation about the many mysteries surrounding her was interrupted when his father stood to gain everyone's attention. "I have decided," he announced, "That we shall travel to the river in one weeks' time."

Rianne clapped with delight. "I was hoping we would go soon!" Her brow furrowed in confusion Da'Leth looked at the Princess and Rianne explained. "Every year we take a holiday in the country. There is a small manor there that you will find very quaint, I'm sure."

Nodding Da'Leth turned back to Tome just in time to catch her from throwing her food to the ground. Traveling to the country side would be nice; she only hoped they would not pass through her family's lands in the process. Realizing Tome had no more interest in her food she wiped off her mouth and hands before releasing her.

"Da'Leth."

Turning her attention to the speaker she saw Renee standing nearby, waiting for her to reply. "Yes, milady?"

"While we are on holiday Betty will not be there to watch over Brian and Giselle. Would you be so kind as to take charge of them while we are in the country?"

"She will do as she is told, Renee," Philip declared, stopping beside his wife. "Do not ask her when she should be told." His tone filled with disgust that his wife should ask a serf instead of commanding it Philip cast a meaningful glance at Da'Leth before walking away.

Waiting until he was out of hearing range Da'Leth smiled warmly at Rene, the nervous little woman wringing her hands. "I would be happy to, milady."

~~*~*~*~*~*~*~*

Riding in the carriage, Tome sleeping in her lap, Giselle sitting next to her holding her doll, and Brian sitting on the bench across from her, Da'Leth prayed that they would arrive soon. Though she had always known him to be a terror to his governess Brian had proven to be on his worst behavior for Da'Leth during the trip to the country. Once she had realized they were traveling in the opposite direction from Whispering Winds Da'Leth had relaxed only to realize that the young Prince was going to do everything he could to make her miserable.

Unlike her brother, however, Giselle was a sweet child. Even tempered and quiet, she was content to simply sit still and play with her dolls or, when she was awake, with Tome. Both of them were blond haired and blue eyed like their mother, very little of their father showing in either one. Brian had picked up his fathers' contempt for anyone beneath him and never failed to remind a person of their position in life. Da'Leth had been called serf more times in the last two days than she had in the last eight months.

"Thirsty," Giselle said softly, tugging on Da'Leth's arm.

Looking down at her she smiled. "We shall be stopping soon, Little One. Can you wait?"

Giselle nodded but Brian knew he had found a new fight to pick. "My sister has told you she is thirsty, serf. Fetch her some water."

Barely resisting the urge to sigh Da'Leth looked at the young boy. "We are on the road traveling, highness. There is no water in the carriage, nor is there a pond or river outside the carriage. How do you suggest that I find the Princess some water?"

Careful to keep her tone even Da'Leth waited for his reply. Seeing that he had none Brian simply glared at her, and she knew he would not hesitate to report her inaction to his father as he had during the last three days. Setting her gaze on the passing scenery Da'Leth ignored the burning glare he was giving her as best she could until the carriage began to slow.

"Look Da'Leth," Giselle announced, reaching for Da'Leth's hand. "We're here!"

Looking out the other side of the carriage Da'Leth saw what had the quiet girl so excited. A large mansion sat partially hidden among the trees and as they made the turn into the drive Da'Leth could see the river sparkling under the sunlight some distance away. "It's beautiful here," she smiled.

As Tome began to stir and wake the carriage slowly came to a stop and the door opened, allowing the passengers to get out and stretch their legs for a moment. Leading the children up into their home for the next two weeks Da'Leth looked around her, taking in this new place.

It was smaller than the palace, less than half the size at most, but it was comfortable enough for the large party. Entering the building she saw the stairwell that led up to the second and third floors. Unsure of where she was going Da'Leth let Giselle lead the way to the nursery. Seeing that their things had already arrived and been unpacked Da'Leth decided she would take the children for a walk around the land.

The group of four was in the middle of the garden when she heard someone calling her. Turning to look Da'Leth saw Nicholas and Rianne strolling towards them. She smiled as Tome and Giselle ran towards their aunt and uncle. "Don't you want to go and say hello?" she asked Brian, standing a few feet away.

"What could I have to say to them?" he declared, turning his back on them.

Shaking her head Da'Leth smiled when the girls brought the two groups together. "Milord, milady," she greeted them with a small bow. "Was your journey pleasant enough?"

"Tolerable," Rianne said. "It would have been better if there had been someone to talk to."

"Could you not talk to your brother?"

"I tried," she grinned. "But he was too tired to be of any use to me."

"And we both know why," Nicholas grumbled.

"I accept the blame, highness," Da'Leth nodded. "It is the tea that makes you sleep."

"A vile brew," he grumbled in good humor. "But as you say it does what it is supposed to."

"Your shoulder is better then?"

"Stiff," he admitted. "But much better than before."

"Must we stand around talking with the serf all day?"

Turning to look at his nephew Nicholas simply watched the young boy for a moment before he spoke. "And how has my nephew been treating you?"

Instead of answering Da'Leth lifted Tome into her arms and took Giselle's hand in hers, leading the way through the garden to a small clearing one of the servants had told her about. There, in the center of the clearing, the servants had set up a small table for them to sit around, a tea setting ready to be used.

Excited to be using the same dishes as the adults Tome and Giselle were the first to be seated; Brian reluctantly being the last. Though he kept silent Da'Leth could see his displeasure over the whole situation and wondered why he was being so silent about it. "He's afraid of me," Nicholas whispered to her. "A few years ago, I caught him doing something he knew he oughtn't and punished him for it. Ever since..."

Letting the thought hang Nicholas simply shrugged. "Well I am grateful for the respite from his tongue."

"Has he been that bad?"

Though their conversation had been in hushed tones Da'Leth said nothing more, simply offering a small shrug in return for his question. Nodding Nicholas didn't need anything else. They had only known each other for a few months he knew enough to understand she would never say anything bad about the royal family, no matter how ill they had treated her. Hearing something from behind him Nicholas turned to see one of the maids coming towards them.

"Pardon the intrusion," she began after bowing to them. "The Queen has asked that Miss Da'Leth come and see her to tend to her legs. After the long carriage ride they are hurting her in the most fearful way. I've been sent to watch over the children."

Nodding Da'Leth stood and asked where she could find the Queen.

"While we are here she spends most of her time in the southern garden," Rianne explained. "It has the prettiest view of the manor."

Thanking Rianne, bowing to them, she said goodbye and left to find the Queen, hurrying to her room first to pick up her basket. As advised she found her in the southern garden, reclining on a small couch with her legs propped up in front of her. Without saying a word, she set about preparing the oils and herbs to help get rid of the pain. Giving her the tea she waited for her to drink it as quickly as possible before setting to work. Kneeling before the Queen she pulled her skirt hem over her knees and began to rub the mixture on, massaging it into her muscles.

Silence reigned for some time. The Queen was asleep when she was finished and Da'Leth looked up to see that she was being watched. King Liam, standing a little way away, had been watching Da'Leth work. When she stood, he approached. "Winifred has told me that your time with her has helped more than anything the doctors had been able to do for her."

"I'm glad to be of help," she replied gently.

"My son calls you a contradiction," Liam advised as he sat down. "You have hidden talents, girl, I can see why he finds you so intriguing."

"I do not mean to draw attention to myself, Majesty, I only wish to serve."

"And you have done so exceedingly well."

Touched by his compliment Da'Leth could feel a blush filling her face as she thanked him, curtsying humbly. Letting her go Liam watched the young woman walk away, wondering why she seemed familiar to him. Shrugging it off he assumed she resembled one of their previous servants.

Chapter Eleven

Sitting by the river Da'Leth wiggled her toes as they soaked in the cool water. She had been waiting all day for this moment and was glad it had finally come. The children were sound asleep, as was the rest of the manor, lord, lady, servant, and serf alike were all asleep and she, "I thought I was the only one awake."

Spinning around where she sat Da'Leth saw Nicholas standing over her. Putting a hand over her heart she took a deep breath. "Milord you scared me!"

Grinning Nicholas sat down next to her. "It was unintentional, I give my word." Taking his boots off he followed Da'Leth's example and dipped his feet into the water. "Is this what brought you out here tonight?" "Mostly," she shrugged. Looking down at the water she saw his feet next to hers and noticed his feet were not white like most others. Instead they had a tanned color to them. "You have revealed a hidden trait," she advised him.

"What do you mean?" Nicholas frowned, trying to think of what she was talking about. "What have I revealed?"

"The color of your feet tell more than if you are healthy or not." Moving her foot a few inches closer to his she compared them.

"Do you see how mine glow brightly under the moonlight while yours simply appear white in color?"

Looking closely, he saw that she was right. "What does that mean?"

"In the light of the moon that which is normally pale appears to glow with an inner light while that which would appear darker simply seems pale. Your feet have told me you prefer to not wear shoes."

Looking again Nicholas saw what she had mentioned and nodded appreciatively. "Very true," he admitted with a smile. "Do you know what else I see?"

"What?"

"I see that you take good care of your feet," he teased. "Your toenails are trimmed and clean."

Embarrassed that he was examining her feet Da'Leth curled her toes and brought her foot back to its place beside the other one. Her face reddened when he called attention to it.

"You seem to embarrass easily," Nicholas noted aloud. "Why is that?"

"It is a personal flaw I can't quite seem to overcome," she admitted to him with a shrug.

"I find it endearing," he admitted honestly. "It reminds me that you are unlike most of the people I know. They pretend embarrassment of course, but it is only to gain favor in my father's eyes. Yours is true and refreshing in its honesty."

"You like that I feel embarrassed?"

"No," shaking his head. "Not that you feel embarrassed but rather that you allow yourself to express it. Da'Leth, you never really show what you feel, it's one of the many things that make you such as mystery to me."

"I don't know what you are talking about, milord."

"I am saying that the moment you look as though you are about to laugh or cry or get angry you shut down your face like blowing out a candle. One moment everything can be seen clearly, the next it is hidden away in darkness. You smile, but you never laugh. I have seen tears in your eyes but you never cry. There have even been times when I could see anger boiling in you but your outer appearance is as calm as a glassy lake."

Da'Leth was silent, unsure of how to respond. In her heart of hearts, she knew he was right and it touched her that he had noticed it about her when no one else had. "I have been this way for more years than I care to admit. When you live as a serf in Pirtonshire you learn very quickly to hide what you truly feel or it will be used against you."

"You did what you had to in order to survive," he concluded.

Thinking back over the many things she'd been forced to do Da'Leth nodded. "Yes."

Her voice held a small hint of pain and Nicholas wondered what events were running through her mind. Wishing he hadn't gotten on the topic, not liking the way she withdrew herself from him, he decided it was time to know a happier Da'Leth. "Tell me about your childhood," he said. "Tell me about the little girl before she became a serf."

Eyes wide she turned to look at him shocked that he had remembered that conversation. "What does milord wish to know?"

"Anything, everything," Nicholas smiled, leaning back onto the grass, splashing the water a little with his feet. "Tell me about your childhood, back when life was still uncomplicated."

Fixing her stare on her feet she didn't know where to begin. "My favorite time of day was the morning," she said after some time, pulling at the first memory that came to her mind. "My father would take me out to the orchard and we would pick apples for Mother, she used to like eating them with her breakfast when they were in season."

Staring out across the river, seeing nothing that was before her, Da'Leth's mind saw those mornings vividly. "It was just us. He would come and get me from my room in the morning, help me to get dressed in a pair of pants and shirt from when he was a child, and we would slip out of the house before anyone else was awake. It was a long walk to the orchard but I never seemed to mind. He would tell me stories about his childhood, or tales of faraway places he hoped I would see one day."

"What I loved to hear the most though were his stories. Now I realize that they were lessons to learn from but when I was little they were fantastical stories that would seep into my dreams and fill them with wonderful adventures." Blinking she looked back down at her feet. "I think I miss those the most."

Nicholas smiled. "Which was your favorite?"

She smiled. "The one about the little girl who lived in the forest; I use to imagine that I were that little girl. In my dreams I saw myself living her story."

"Tell me," Nicholas encouraged, poking her arm gently. "Tell me about the little girl in the forest."

Looking down at him, seeing that he was in earnest about wanting to hear the story, she gave in, repeating the story from memory having memorized it so many years ago.

"In the forest by the lake there was a small cottage where a little girl lived all by herself. Her heart was pure, untainted by the evil and greed of the world beyond the edge of the forest. Every morning she would go to the lake and take a drink of water. One day she hid at the edge of the forest, surprised to see a young man sitting by the water's edge. She had never seen a man before and didn't know what to do."

"The man saw her and tried to call out to her but he couldn't for he had been hurt and didn't have the strength to move or speak. Unable to bear the sadness of seeing a living creature in pain the little girl she helped him to her cottage and healed his wounds. When the man was better he tied to talk to her but began to notice that the girl would never answer him. Before he left, healed by her care, he asked her why she never spoke to him and she showed him a scar on her neck. Promising to help her if she ever needed it the young man left, giving her a small necklace as thanks for saving his life."

"Many years passed, the little girl had grown up into a beautiful woman. One day a hunter came to the forest to try and kill the animals she knew as her friends. When he saw the beautiful young woman, he wanted her as his wife but she refused to leave her home. Later that night he snuck back and kidnapped her from her home in the forest. Terrified the woman tried to get away but he tied her tightly and she couldn't escape."

"When they got to the city the hunter untied her so she could walk into the church and she took the only chance she could to get away, running through the large city toward the gated entrance. The gates were shut and when she tried to climb over them the guards pulled her off roughly, thinking she was a criminal running from the sheriff."

"They brought her to the courts to stand trial and when it was her turn she stood before the judge, unable to explain why she had been running through the city. Watching the young woman standing before him the judge frowned. She looked familiar to him but could not think of why."

"The judge stood up, limping towards her to get a better look at the beautiful young woman, and the woman recognized him. Reaching out to him with one hand, pleading for his help, she pulled the necklace he had given her out from underneath her shirt with the other and held it up for him to see. The judge recognized the necklace and ordered the guards to release her."

"Taking the woman home to his family he made sure she was all right, letting her sleep through the night before taking her home to the forest she had missed so dearly. It was too late for him to go home, the roads too dark and dangerous for him to travel alone, so the judge spent the night in the small cottage in the woods."

"When the time came to leave the next morning, the man found that he couldn't leave. Though he had left many years ago it had taken him several years to forget about the young girl that had helped him. If he were to leave now he knew that he would never be able to forget the beautiful young woman that loving girl had become."

"The judge asked her to marry him, to come back to his home and live with him as his wife for he had fallen in love with her. Her eyes filled with tears but the woman shook her head no. This was her home; she had to stay here no matter how much she wanted to be his wife. Saddened the man left, his heart sinking with every step he took away from the cottage. The young woman watched him go, her heart breaking for she had loved him from the moment she had seen him wounded by the lake."

"Winter came and went and when spring was making its way into the forest the young woman went out to the lake as she did every morning to get a drink of water. Stopping at the water's edge tears came to her eyes. There, standing across the lake, was the judge, a strap crossed over his chest that held the bag at his side. Walking to her as fast as he could the judge held her close and promised he would never leave her side again. Together, they lived in that little cottage in the forest, happily in love for the rest of their lives."

Lying on the grass, listening to her tell the story, Nicholas was in awe of this woman sitting next to him. The story seemed nothing more than a childhood fairy tale and yet in her voice he sensed so much more. "And the lesson to be learned?" he asked softly.

Smiling down at him Da'Leth answered, "The season will always change. When good people suffer ill times, they need only wait for spring to come again."

"A good lesson," he acknowledged. "Tell me, what season are you in?"

"Winter; milord," Da'Leth answered honestly, thinking over her life as a serf, separated from her mother. "But," she continued, looking back across the river, "I can feel spring just around the corner."

~~*~*~*~*~*~*~*

Standing near the fence around the stables, Da'Leth held Tome in her arms while Giselle stood next to her watching the horses as Brian was trained by the riding master. "Pretty," she whispered when the horse cantered past them. "Pretty horses."

"Yes," Da'Leth agreed with Giselle. Seeing her reaching out to the horse as it was about to come around again Da'Leth quickly pulled her hand back outside the fence. "No, no Giselle," she warned. "Keep your hands on this side of the fence, all right?"

The little girl nodded and Da'Leth breathed a sigh of relief. When Brian's lessons were done the foursome went back to the manor, the noon meal ready to be served. Leaving the two girls with the maids Da'Leth went with Brian to make sure he didn't give his maids a hard time about bathing and dressing before joining the family for the meal. Satisfied that he was clean and dressed she followed him back to the dining hall, maintaining a proper distance behind him as he had instructed her to upon first finding out that she would be this guardian for the trip.

Sitting down at her place with the children Da'Leth hadn't the time to take a bite before she was called from the room by the Princess. Glancing at the food, wishing she'd taken the time to eat breakfast that morning, she left the hall, following the servant to Rianne's chamber and curtsied the moment she entered the room. "You wished to see me, milady?"

"Da'Leth, do come in!" Rianne's grinned broadly, her good mood floating around her like a cloud. "I wanted your opinion on this gown before the ball tonight."

Looking at the gown Da'Leth nodded. "It is very beautiful," she advised. "The color matches your hair very well."

"Isn't it just divine?" Rianne was practically glowing as she stood before the mirror, holding the frock in front of her. "Mother ordered it for me from Paris; it's the height of fashion. No one there tonight will have anything like it!"

"You are looking forward to the ball then?" Da'Leth asked as she took the gown Rianne handed to her, hanging it back in its place.

"Oh yes! Lord Forint gives one every year for his wife, Lady Agnes. The music is divine and the food is perfection but they always introduce a new dance for us to enjoy. Last year it was a joy to dance."

Taking Da'Leth's hand in her own Rianne danced them around the room, Da'Leth struggling to catch on to the steps she didn't know. By the time they stopped both women were slightly out of breath, collapsing into chairs to rest.

"Just wait until you see it, Da'Leth," Rianne continued when she could talk normally again. "The flowers everywhere, candles lighting every last bit of the room." She sighed, "It's simply too beautiful to describe."

"You will have to tell me all about it when you return."

Raising her head to look at Da'Leth Rianne frowned. "You won't be coming? But why?"

"Princess," Da'Leth said softly. "I am only a serf. It is not a serf's place to attend a ball with the royal family. I shall stay here and be content to watch over the children while they sleep."

"Well I shall just have to speak to my father about that!"

Adamant that Da'Leth comes with her Rianne stood up and left the room, Da'Leth following her, trying to reason with the young woman. "Milady, please! It simply is not done. You must accept that."

"I certainly will not," she protested, entering her father study. "Father, might I claim a moment of your time?"

Looking up, surprised to see such a look of anger on Rianne's face Liam nodded. "What is it girl?"

Explaining why she had come to see him Rianne asked her father to allow Da'Leth to go to the ball with them. Looking over at the young woman Liam asked, "And what have you to say about this request, Da'Leth?"

"I am a serf, Majesty. It is not the place of a serf to attend a ball in the presence of Lords and Ladies. The guests would be offended."

"She makes a valid point, Rianne," Liam told his daughter. "I do not think that she wants to go."

"Who wants to go where?" Nicholas asked as he and Richard walked into the room. "What's going on?"

"I want Da'Leth to come to the ball but she is refusing!"

"I don't blame her."

Rianne glared at her brother. "Just because you don't like these things doesn't mean that Da'Leth wouldn't."

"That's not what I meant," he defended himself, sitting down on the desks edge. "I only meant that she would not be made welcome by the other guests. Given her station I have no doubt they would make her feel inferior. Well" he amended, "They would try."

Looking at him Da'Leth shook her head, a small smile tugging at her lips for a moment before she turned her attention back to Rianne. "Princess, the knowledge that you wish for me to attend such a grand event with you is more than I could have asked for. You have given me your friendship and that is something that I will treasure forever. However, I cannot allow you to bear the disapproval and disdain that such an action would bring upon you."

"I don't care what anyone else thinks of me!" Rianne began to protest.

"But I do!" Da'Leth finished, daring to interrupt her this one time. "I will do whatever I must to protect the crown when it is needed, even if it entails protecting it from itself."

"Well said, Da'Leth," the King nodded. "I believe the decision is final, Rianne. Da'Leth is free to spend the night here at her own leisure. The children will be cared for by the maids and Da'Leth may have the night to do with as she pleases."

"Thank you, Majesty," Da'Leth smiled.

~~*~*~*~*~*~*~*

Sitting in the courtyard Da'Leth sipped at her glass of wine, smiling at the peaceful night she was enjoying. Though Rianne had acquiesced she had decided to give Da'Leth her own ball; a small string quartet played music and a feast for one was laid out on the table before her along with a bottle of wine. The children were asleep, the maids having tucked them in some time ago, and she was content to simply sit, enjoy the music, and watch the night sky unfold above her.

"You look like a cat with a dish of cream."

Smiling she looked over to see Richard approaching. "I feel like one. Help yourself," she invited, motioning for him to join her. "What brings you out here tonight?"

"Boredom mostly," he admitted with a smile. Helping himself to some of the food before him he sat down in a chair across from Da'Leth. "I've finished my reports and have nothing else to do tonight. What about you? Have you any special plans for your night of freedom?"

She shook her head. "I've nothing to do but sit and enjoy the peace."

"Would you rather be alone?"

"No," Da'Leth assured him. "Your company is welcome. I don't recall that we've had the chance to truly get to know one another."

"I believe you are correct in that assumption," Richard smiled. "Shall you go first, or shall I?"

"You first," Da'Leth smiled. "How did you come to be the Captain of the Guard?"

"It was my father who encouraged me. You see I had always wanted to be a knight but you must be of noble blood to be so. The next best thing was a guard so that was where I set my sights. I wanted only to serve the crown but when I joined the guard I quickly discovered there was more deception and trickery than honor among the guard."

"What do you mean?"

"The old Captain was a greedy man. He extorted money from shopkeepers for his own pockets to protect them from the destructiveness of his own men. There were but a handful of trustworthy men in the guard and they were forced to keep their heads low so as to stay alive. At first, I tried to stop what was happening but it almost cost me my life. That was when I began to learn the art of deception. Though I pretended to be one of his men I was quickly putting together a plan to provide proof of what was happening."

"What happened?" Da'Leth asked when he paused, curious about how it had turned out.

Richard smiled. "Let's just say it was a long hard battle but the good men were victorious. A guard named Pierre was named the new Captain of the guard. He quickly cleaned out all of the men that had been destroying the name of the guard and those who had been keeping their heads low were suddenly free to do their job the right way."

"If he was named Captain how did the honor come to be yours?"

"You like this story, eh?" Da'Leth smiled at him but said nothing, waiting for him to finish. "Pierre knew what I had done to help get rid of the old Captain. He took me under his wing, training me as an apprentice and just before he died he asked the King to grant him the decision of who was to be the next Captain of the Guard."

"He chose you," she finished.

Richard nodded. "I was the youngest Captain anyone had ever seen and it took me several years to prove myself to them but, in the end, they respected Pierre's choice."

"What about your relationship with Prince Nicholas? You two seem very close."

"Not at first," he admitted, pausing to drink some wine and wet his throat. Knowing the Prince had already told her his past he spoke freely. "When I first became the Captain, he was still very much a rabble-rouser, always getting into trouble that I needed to get him out of."

Da'Leth grinned at the look of disgust on his face.

Smiling he continued. "When he began to change he turned to me, asking for help to make sure his family would be safe. We worked closely on a few different plans should anything happen to him or if harm should come to his family. After a while we became close," he said with a shrug. "Of course, when he began jousting in the tournaments I insisted on accompanying him as his herald to make sure he was protected. While he was within the palace walls he was safe but when he was outside he was unprotected and I had vowed to make sure he was kept safe."

"You've done your duties well," she praised. "From what I have seen it has been a full-time occupation to keep him safe from that man."

"I almost wish I could simply arrest the man for murdering the other young men from that night," Richard admitted. "But the Prince won't hear of it and we have no definitive proof of his guilt."

Thinking about what he had said Da'Leth could only nod, there was nothing to say in response to such a truthful statement.

"What about you? Is your family still at Pirtonshire?"

Da'Leth shook her head; giving him the same answer she had anyone else who asked her that question. "My father is dead and I have not seen my mother since I was a child." She could see the pity in his eyes and hated it. "What of your family? You said your father encouraged you to join the guard?"

Nodding he replied, "Yes. They still live in my home town of Wernersville. It's a small town to the south of here. Mostly it is a farming community though there are a few skilled craftsmen. I try to visit them a few times a year."

"Do you have any siblings?"

Richard smiled proudly. "A younger brother and two younger sisters. My brother, Charles, helps our father to maintain the farm. One of my sisters, Bette, is married with a beautiful little girl. The other, Jean, is still too young to marry, though she is rumored to be in love with the blacksmiths son."

She smiled. "A good match."

"If he loves her," he shrugged. "The boy is honest but I would rather she wait a few more years before she marries."

Sensing something in his voice she wondered about it. "And you?" Da'Leth asked hesitantly, unsure of his reaction.

"Me?"

Not sensing any irritation, she asked, "Have you found someone to love?"

Staring at her in silence Richard made no reply. Wondering if she had pressed where she did not belong Da'Leth was about to retract her question when he sighed. "Nicholas said you could see things in other people," he said with a small shake of his head. "There is someone, but it can never be."

"Why?"

"Her father would never allow it."

Da'Leth could feel the sadness and frustration in his voice and let the subject drop, not wishing to cause him further pain. Listening to him her own heart tried to speak but she forced it to stay silent, not allowing herself to consider what could never be. They sat in silence for some time, each one lost in their own thoughts. In the silence Da'Leth heard footsteps and turned to see Nicholas approaching them.

Her mind still dwelling on what her heart wasn't allowed to consider she had to remind herself to breathe at the sight of him walking towards them. His clothing a shimmering silver and rich blue under the light of the moon he seemed to sparkle as brightly as the stars shining overhead. With slow easy strides he approached them, his left hand swinging freely while his right held a goblet of wine.

"Milord," she greeted softly when he was close enough. Hearing the altered state of her voice Da'Leth rebuked herself in her mind. Clearing her throat, she watched him sit down next to Richard. "You left the ball?"

"I don't care for them anymore," he groused. "I am tired of people who are trying to befriend me simply to elevate themselves in society."

"The troubles of being royalty," Richard replied, a small teasing tone in his voice. Seeing the Prince's glare, he smiled back, his mood lifting as he was pulled from his own thoughts. "Pardon me, milord, it must be the wine."

"Of course, it is," Nicholas said with a wry grin, looking over at his friend.

"Is the Princess enjoying herself?"

Turning his gaze to Da'Leth he nodded. "I dare say she is. My sister loves to dance; she looks forward to the ball every year."

"I'm glad," Da'Leth smiled. Looking down at her hands she fell silent again, unsure of how to act until she had managed to regain control of the heart hammering in her chest. Angry with herself that she hadn't been able to quell the emotions in her heart before she had spoken she didn't hear Nicholas speaking until she heard Richard reply.

"It's been a pleasant evening," he answered. "Da'Leth and I have been getting to know one another."

"And have you found any answers to the mystery that is Da'Leth?"

"A few." Seeing Nicholas waiting for him to continue Richard smiled. "For example, did you know that Da'Leth had a love for music and a yearning to dance?"

Glancing up at him in surprise Da'Leth asked, "How could you possibly have known that? We never touched on that subject at all!"

"It was your foot, madam, which gave you away. It has not yet stopped moving in time to the music."

Glancing down at her feet she realized he was right. She had been completely unaware that her foot was moving, surprised that he had noticed. A smile spread over her face and she shook her head. "You amaze me, Captain Krausley."

"I have asked you several times now to call me Richard."

"And I have advised you just as many times that it is not my place to do so."

Nicholas watched the interchange with a smile, his previous mood beginning to lift. "Tell me, Richard," he asked suddenly. "What are you going to do with this newfound knowledge?"

"I intend to put it to good use, milord," his friend grinned. Getting to his feet he called out to the musicians, "Musicians play a rousing tune so that we may cure this woman of her need to dance!"

While the musicians conferred with each other Richard took hold of Da'Leth's hands and pulled her to her feet, setting the goblet of wine on the table. "Now tell me, what do you know of dancing?"

"Nothing," she admitted with a shrug. "Other than the peasant dances we would dance at Pirtonshire."

"Then we'll agree on a pact. I shall teach you one courtly dance and you shall teach me one peasant dance. A fair trade I would say."

When the music began to play Richard told her where to stand, which foot to put where and how the dance was done. Watching them Nicholas could see that Da'Leth was a fast learner, picking up the moves quicker than he had thought she would. However, the grace with which she moved caught him by surprise. By the time they began the dance for a second time she danced the steps as if she had been practicing them her entire life.

"And now it is my turn to learn," Richard said as they completed it a third time. "What dance shall you teach me?"

Thinking for a moment Da'Leth decided on a dance and asked the musicians to play something a little faster than the previous song selections but to wait until she gave the signal to begin. Intrigued, Richard paid close attention to the dance she was teaching him. The steps were simple enough and he was confident that he could keep up.

"We'll see," she smirked, motioning for the musicians to begin.

Waiting for the right beat Da'Leth began to move in the steps she had just finished showing Richard. Able to keep up he grinned triumphantly but as the music began to speed up he grin slowly slipped off his face. By the end of the song he had stopped, watching as Da'Leth finished the dance on her own, Nicholas laughing from his seat at Richards's failure.

"Don't feel bad," she smiled, touching his shoulder gently. "It is a difficult dance to learn. I could teach you a simpler one."

Doubling over with laughter Nicholas had no pity for his friend's plight. "You think this is easy?"

Richard groused. "Come on over here and try it for yourself."

Still laughing Nicholas stood and crossed the small space between them, standing to Da'Leth's right while Richard stood at her left. "Okay," he said, wiping his eyes. "Show me the steps again."

Demonstrating the dance at a slower pace Da'Leth went over it twice with the two men before motioning for the music to begin again. As Richard had the first time they were able to keep pace in the beginning but as the music began to speed up they lost their rhythm and fumbled through the steps. Out of breath Da'Leth laughed at them, watching the two men who were trying to keep up with her.

Giving up on the dance Nicholas stood still, watching Da'Leth, listening as she laughed at them. It was the first time he had heard her laugh and he was struck by the beauty of it, light and happy; it made him think of a trickling brook or stream. Smiling, glad that he was finally able to hear the solemn woman laugh, Nicholas asked the musicians to play again, trying the dance several more times before he was able to get through the whole thing.

Chapter Twelve

"I said no, highness," she repeated herself, trying to keep the irritation with the young man out of her voice. Though he was only eight years old the son of Prince Philip was more like his father than Da'Leth cared for.

"I am a Prince, you are a serf," he informed her. "You do as I say."

"Yes," she confirmed. "You are a Prince, and that is why it is important that you do what you can to stay safe. A dead Prince is of no use to his kingdom. The river is too dangerous to swim in right now."

Glaring at her, a glare she knew all too well from his father, Brian waited until she had turned to face Tome to run toward the river. "Brian Nathan!" Stopping in his tracks, feet away from the river bank, the young Prince turned around to face his uncle. "What did Da'Leth just finish telling you?"

"She is a serf!" he countered, not answering the question.

"That is not what I asked." Folding his arms in front of his chest Nicholas waited for an answer. When he heard the mumbled reply from his nephew Nicholas motioned for him to come closer. Taking his arm, he spoke firmly. "You have been put in her care while your own teacher is not here. If I find that you have disobeyed her again you will answer to me. Do you understand what I have just told you?"

"Yes Uncle," he answered crossly.

Letting him go Nicholas watched Brian run away, toward the tent that had been set up a good distance from the river. "He needs a lesson in obedience," he said.

"He is his father's son," Da'Leth muttered to herself.

Chuckling, hearing her comment, Nicholas turned to face her. "Yes, he is."

"Highness," she began, her face reddening at being heard.

"It's all right," he smiled. "I am the only one that heard you and we are in agreement on the matter."

Shaking her head Da'Leth took the worm out of Tome's hands. "No, no, sweetheart. You can't eat that. Come with me, I'll get you a piece of fruit." Taking Tome by the hand she led the little girl towards the tent where the rest of the royal family was sitting, making sure their pace was slow enough for her to walk on her own. "It still was not right of me to say it," she said to Nicholas. "He is a Prince."

"He is a spoiled little boy," he frowned. "He needs to be disciplined or he will turn out like his father."

Not wanting to touch that subject Da'Leth turned the conversation in a different direction. "This area is beautiful."

"Yes, it is," he smiled, knowing what she was doing. "We come here every summer for a few weeks. Very few people know about it which makes this a nice retreat."

"Indeed," Elizabeth said, smiling as Tome ran to her. "Hello darling, did you have fun with Da'Leth?" Nodding Tome reached for one of the apple slices on her mother's plate. Handing it to her she smiled up at Da'Leth. "I can feed her if you'd like. Why don't you get yourself some lunch while there is still food left?"

Smiling back at the Princess Da'Leth said she would and took a step towards the table only to stop still. Unsure of what it was that had caught her attention she looked around, a frown pulling at her face. "What is it?" Nicholas asked, seeing the frown on her face.

Shaking her head, she continued to look around silently. Shrugging her shoulders, unable to find anything out of place she smiled briefly at Nicholas. "I suppose it was nothing," she said. "Just a feeling." Nicholas looked around quickly to see if anything was out of place but saw nothing. "It was just my imagination," she said. "May I fix you some food, highness?"

Heading towards the table laden with food again Nicholas took the plate Da'Leth handed to him, insistent that he could make his own plate of food, and turned to reach for a leg of meat when he heard her gasp. Before he could turn back to ask what was wrong he heard the screams coming from the direction of the river. Dropping her own plate Da'Leth ran out of the tent, skirting around the servant standing at the edge of the tents opening. She was halfway to the river when she heard another scream coming from the tent, a mother only just being told that her child was in danger.

Without stopping she ran to the bank and, spotting Brian in the water being pulled downstream, dove in after him. With long hard stokes she swam with the current to get to the terrified little boy. Reaching out for him she grabbed his shirt just as the water pulled him under again. Pulled under the water with him Da'Leth's feet touched the bottom of the river bed and she pushed herself back up to the surface, dragging the young boy with her.

On the shore she could see Nicholas running along the land, trying to get ahead of them to help pull them out of the water. Holding on to Brian with a firm grip Da'Leth scanned ahead, trying to keep them both above water, for something to grab onto. Her eyes widened when she saw a large boulder in the middle of the river. Struggling to swim with only one arm she managed to maneuver them around the boulder, her shoulder hitting it as they passed.

"Grab my hand!"

Nicholas had found an outcropping on the shore and was stretched out on it, extending himself as far as he could to try and reach her. Reaching out with her free hand, Da'Leth grabbed his as she got closer, holding on tightly as the current pulled at her skirt trying to drag her along. Grabbing a fistful of the boy's shirt she pulled him as high up out of the water as she could, ignoring his terrified screams, pushing him toward Nicholas.

"Take him!" she cried.

Letting go of her wrist with his right hand he grabbed his nephew, still holding onto Da'Leth's arm with his left hand. Holding onto both of them with all his strength Nicholas could ignore the pain of overstretching his muscles but couldn't ignore the feeling of being pulled into the water. Meeting Da'Leth's eyes he could see that she knew what was happening. "Don't!" he yelled a moment before she released her grip on his arm.

"Let go!" she yelled back when he didn't release his grip. "You can't hold us both, save him!"

Wrenching her arm out of his grasp Da'Leth felt the river drag her away though she kept watching to make sure Brian was safely removed from the river before turning to focus on getting herself out. Scanning the river shore, fighting with the current, Da'Leth saw a tree limb hanging low over the river. With every bit of strength in her she reached up, grabbing hold of the limb and pulling herself up onto it. Her chest heaving, she stayed there, trying to catch her breath, exhausted from the exertion.

"Give me your hand," she heard a man call to her. Opening one of her eyes Da'Leth saw Captain Krausley holding his hand out to her. "I'll help you to shore Da'Leth." Reaching out she felt him grab her hand and pulled her off the branch to the safety of shore. Her legs giving way beneath her she crumpled into him. Supporting her as best he could Richard gently sat her on the ground, kneeling next to her.

"Da'Leth!" she heard Rianne cry as the Princess hurried toward them. "Oh Da'Leth, are you all right?"

Unable to speak just yet she nodded.

"Captain, please, bring Da'Leth back to the tent, she must lie down and be cared for."

Helping her to her feet Krausley supported Da'Leth as they began a slow walk towards the tent only to be stopped by Nicholas. "Give her here, Krausley," he commanded.

"Your shoulder," she protested.

Ignoring her comment, he put his arms behind her back and under her knees, picking Da'Leth up, carrying the soaked woman back to the tent. Lying her down on the small reclining chair that his mother had vacated Nicholas stepped back to allow the doctor to look her over. Seeing the wince when he pressed on her shoulder Nicholas realized she had hurt it, no doubt when she had put herself between the boy and the boulder.

"I believe she will be well, given time and rest," the doctor announced.

"Then time and rest she shall have," Liam announced, watching her lay still. "Take her to her room," he commanded two of the guards, "Gently," he added as they approached.

Watching the two men lead Da'Leth to the manor to rest he turned to Brian when they were out of sight. "Tell me how this happened, boy."

"I was playing by the river and slipped," he answered with a guilty look on his tearstained face.

"The serf slacked in her duties to watch my son!" Philip growled. "She must be punished; my son could have died!"

"Yes," Nicholas interjected. "He could very well have died had it not been for Da'Leth." Meeting his nephew's eyes, he commanded the young boy, "Now tell them what you had been told several times by your guardian."

"Da'Leth told me to stay away from the river," he confessed, fresh tears in his eyes.

"Why didn't you listen?" Brian simply shrugged. "Perhaps if you had listened this would not have happened," Liam advised. "Go to your chamber, young man, you will not leave it until I have decided upon a suitable punishment for your actions."

"I am his father," Philip reminded as his son left the tent, his head hung low. "It is not your place to punish him."

"You are his father but I am his King. How am I to control my subjects if I cannot even control my own grandson?" Liam stared at his son for a moment to let the thought sink in. "However, as you are his father, I shall leave his punishment to you."

Philip nodded. "It shall be handled."

"Remember this when you think about his punishment," Liam finished. "Your son would have died today had it not been for that serf you dislike so much."

~~*~*~*~*~*~*~*

Knocking softly on the doorframe Da'Leth waited until she was granted an entrance. "Come," she heard called.

"You wished to see me, my King," she said, bowing low to the floor. Straightening herself she stood respectfully, waiting for him to speak.

From his chair by the fire Liam stared at the young woman standing before him. He had thought about her many times since the day she had saved his grandson from the river. "Sit down, Da'Leth," he said, motioning to a chair near the fire. "We must speak."

Hesitating for a moment she did as she was told, folding her hands in her lap and waiting for him to speak again. Though her exterior was calm a million thoughts raced through her mind. Had the King discovered who she truly was as well? Had she displeased his with her service in some way?

"Don't fear," he smiled gently. "You've done nothing wrong. I simply have a few questions I need to ask, things that have roused my curiosity and I wish to have answered."

"I will answer you truthfully, my King."

"You were a serf under Lord Byron, is that correct?" Da'Leth nodded. "Nicholas had told me as much. My son has high praise for you, as do my wife and daughters. It seems Philip is the only one who does not share their views. My eldest son is a brilliant strategist; I trust his input impeccably when it comes to defending this kingdom. However, he is not the easiest man to get along with as I assume you have already figured out."

Not wanting to say anything negative about the Crown Prince Da'Leth said nothing.

Liam smiled at her. "You don't want to speak ill of a member of the royal family," he chuckled. "Very wise. But you do not need to agree or disagree with me; I know his disposition well enough. My first question is this. Why do you believe that my son dislikes you so much?"

Remembering her promise to speak honestly, she sighed. "It is because I refused to allow him to take the only thing a virgin has to offer her husband."

Liam's smile slipped from his face. "Did he try to force himself on you?" Seeing the redness fill her cheeks he shook his head. "I knew he was too attentive with the maids but I had hoped it was always consensual. For what it is worth, Da'Leth, I am sorry for his actions."

"His goal was prevented, Majesty."

"I am glad to hear it." Pausing for a moment he asked his second question. "How is it that you are so skilled with a blade?"

"My father taught me, my King," she answered. "When I was a little girl he wanted me to know how to defend myself."

"Is your family still at Pirtonshire?"

Da'Leth shook her head. "No, my King, my father died in service to his King during the war."

"One more question, child, and you shall be free to go. Several days ago, you saved the life of my grandson at great risk to your own. I do not allow courage of that nature to go un-rewarded. Ask me anything and if it is in my power I will grant it to you."

"Majesty?" she said, confusion filling her face.

"Do I need to repeat myself?" he smiled. "I am asking what you would like as reward for your brave deed. Would you wish for your freedom?"

Sitting still Da'Leth didn't respond. 'Freedom,' she thought to herself. 'A chance to go home and right the wrongs that have been done to my family.' The desire pulled at her but a feeling fought for the choice from the back of her mind. There was a matter, an important matter, that she could settle now, a chance for her to alleviate the worry in her new friends' mind and heart. 'My freedom will one day come,' she thought to herself with finality.

"May I have your word that what I ask for will be given to me, my King, no matter what it is?"

"Within reason, yes," he nodded, "if you do not ask for more than I can allow you to have."

"What I ask for is a freedom of sorts," she told him. "I ask for the freedom of choice. In exchange for the life I gave back to your grandson I would ask for you to grant the choice of marriage to whomever the woman loves, no matter his station or place in life."

"You wish to marry a man who is not a serf?"

She shook her head. "This request is not for me, Majesty. I will tell you who it is for if you will give me your word as an honorable man that you shall grant it when the time comes."

Sitting back in his seat Liam studied Da'Leth for a moment. "Very well, you have my word of honor and my promise as King."

"Thank you," smiling at him with a grin of relief. "I ask this in behalf of your daughter, the Princess Rianne."

Shocked he raised his eyebrows. "You are in collaboration with Nicholas," he accused.

"I do admit that it was he who brought the matter to my attention however I feel strongly that no one, be she serf or Princess, should be forced to marry a man they do not love or respect."

"Are you saying my daughter is in love with someone?"

Shaking her head, she put him at ease. "No, as of yet I have seen nothing to indicate that she is in love. I only speak of the future when it is possible she will fall in love with a man who is not of the proper station for a Princess."

"Then there is no need to worry for the time being. She may very well fall in love with a Prince!"

"She may yet, my King," Da'Leth smiled. "But I pray you; speak of this arrangement to no one. I fear that if a dishonorable man should hear of it he may try to take advantage of the arrangement and seduce Rianne into marriage."

"You have my word; this shall stay within the walls of this room until such a time arises."

Silence fell as Liam thought over what he had just done. Shaking his head after some time he raised his gaze back to Da'Leth. "I can see that I cannot open myself to such an unspecific reward should this happen again," he admitted with a slight nod of his head. "You are a shrewd woman, Da'Leth, but I must ask why did you not request your freedom? I would think as a serf it would be something you would desire."

"I do, Majesty," Da'Leth admitted. "More than I can ever describe."

"Then why?"

"The Princess has been good to me," she answered, giving the question a moment of thought. "She has given me friendship when most others simply offer kindness. Her happiness matters more to me than many things. Besides," Da'Leth finished with a stiff shrug, her shoulder still tender. "Whether I am a serf, a freewoman, or a lady, I serve my King."

~~*~*~*~*~*~*~*

"Tome, it is time to sleep!"

Their first night back at the palace after the two weeks in the manor by the river, Tome was too tired from the journey to fall asleep. Fighting with the small Princess to get her in the bed Da'Leth finally picked her up, the child becoming a dead weight in her arms, and placed her in the bed. "No!" she screamed the moment she felt the bed beneath her. "Want 'tory!"

"You want what?" she asked, forcing her to stay on the bed.

"A story, miss," one of the maids said, holding the bath bowl that Tome had been washed in. "Times like this she refuses to sleep until Prince Nicholas agrees to come and read to her."

"Then please," Da'Leth gave in. "Go and find the Prince so that he may come and read to her. The child needs to sleep." Nodding the young woman left the room to find Nicholas. Promising that her favorite uncle was going to come and read to her Da'Leth was able to keep Tome in the bed.

"What's this I hear about you not going to sleep?" Looking up Da'Leth saw Nicholas standing in the doorway, a teasing smile on his face. Coming closer he reached out to tug on one of her curls. "Which story will it be tonight?"

Struggling down from the bed Tome ran to her shelf of books and picked one, bringing it back to him. Picking his niece up Nicholas settled her under the blanket and lay down next to her, opening the book to read. His soft voice filled the room and Da'Leth smiled. The Prince had a way with children and she had no doubts he would one day be a good father.

Sitting in the chair next to the bed, Da'Leth watched Nicholas reading to Tome, the little girl fighting her tiredness with every bit of will power she had in her body. When at last her eyes drooped shut and stayed shut Nicholas closed the book and, smiling at his niece, got up from the bed, slowly stretching the kinks out of his back. "Good night Little Lady," he whispered to her, placing a soft kiss on her forehead. Walking around the bed he smiled down at Da'Leth. "Sleep well, Da'Leth," he whispered softly.

"Thank you, highness; you as well." When the door was shut behind him Da'Leth blew out the candles before she sat down again in her chair, staring at the sleeping child.

'Little Lady.'

His words rang in hear ears with another man's voice. Raul had been her father's steward while he still lived, the man was faithful to the family and she knew he would have stayed to care for her mother so long he had been able. He and his wife Mara had lived in a small cabin near the garden that she had tended for the family with several of the other servants. The couple was childless and had always looked after her as if she had been their own child.

For as long as she could remember Raul had called her his 'Little Lady'. When she had been a good girl he would say it sweetly but when she had done wrong, whether she knew she had done wrong or was naïve to it, his tone conveyed his disappointment in her actions. 'Little Lady' was her nickname, her praise and her punishment all rolled into one in a way that only Raul had the ability to do.

Smiling at the memory she stood from her chair and left the room, leaving the little girl to her slumber. Shutting the door softly Da'Leth was walking down the corridor when she saw Philip approaching from around the corner. Glancing around, realizing there was no way to avoid any interaction with him, she braced herself for the verbal beating that was to come.

Since the day she had saved Brian from the river the boy had been tolerable, and his mother, while she had always been nice enough to her, had become friendlier to her, neither one able to forget how close the boy had come to dying. Philip, on the other hand, had simply ignored her since that day and she hoped he would continue to do so now.

"Come with me," he commanded as he walked past her, not even bothering to slow his pace or meet her eyes.

Closing her eyes for a brief moment she turned on her heel and followed him down the corridor, through the palace until they were at his personal chamber. Standing in the doorway she didn't enter any farther, unpleasant memories of the last time she had been in this room swimming to the surface of her mind. If it had not been for the interruption of the maids coming to clean the chamber she would not have been able to escape that night.

"Shut the door and come over here."

With a heavy heart Da'Leth did as she was instructed, though not shutting the door all the way, a small crack left should she need it, and moved farther into the room. "You wanted to see me, highness?"

"My son could have died in that river and I am holding you responsible for it." Philip stood from his seat and began walking around the room. When she couldn't see him anymore Da'Leth tensed, expecting him to grab her at any moment. She breathed a silent sigh of relief when he came back into view. "Tell me why you let it happen."

"Your Highness," she began, frustration bubbling under her skin. "I had told your son not to play near the river but he had refused to heed my warning."

"You were in the tent stuffing your face with food while my son was drowning in the river." Philips tone was harsh. "However, I am not an unreasonable man," he said, his tone suddenly changing. It put her senses on alert, her skin crawling. "Your error can be repaid and as my son has recovered your punishment does not need to be as harsh."

"Highness," Da'Leth began, sensing that this visit was beginning to head along the same route as the previous one had. "I beg of you, please, leave me be. I will do whatever you ask of me but I cannot give you that."

"Oh, but you will."

Seeing him reach for her Da'Leth darted out of his reach. "Please!" she begged. "Do not do this!"

Ignoring her he reached for her again, grabbing her before she could get away. Struggling against him, trying not to hurt the Crown Prince, Da'Leth fought to get away. The feel of his hands where they did not belong burned her skin and tears of shame filled her eyes. When his lips touched her neck she wept, begging him to leave her alone.

A strong hand grasped her upper arm and Da'Leth felt herself being pulled loose from Philip's sickening grip. Looking up she saw Nicholas standing before her, gently wrapping a comforting arm around her, pulling her into his safe embrace. Relief flooded her and Da'Leth wrapped her arms around him, weeping into his chest.

"I warned you to leave her alone!" he yelled at Philip. "You will pay for what you've done Philip, mark my word."

Not staying to hear his reply, Nicholas led Da'Leth out into the corridor, slamming the door shut behind him. "Do not let him leave his chamber," he instructed the guard standing in the hall. "I don't care what he says or does, do you understand?"

The man nodded and took up a position in front of the door. Leading Da'Leth away, his arms still wrapped around her, Nicholas headed toward the main hall. Trying to pull herself together Da'Leth realized where they were going and stopped still, refusing to go any farther, the door to the main hall only a few feet away. "No," she said, shaking her head.

"Yes," Nicholas insisted. Still shaking her head, she started to back away but he stopped her. "You've done nothing wrong; no one will believe anything he tries to say about you, Da'Leth."

Not wanting to go in Da'Leth shook her head but he insisted, telling her it would be all right, asking her to trust him. Giving in she wiped her face, trying to look as normal as she could. Entering the room Da'Leth saw Rianne look up, smiling when she saw who it was. Her smiled slipped from her face a moment later when she saw Da'Leth's tearstained face and Nicholas's scowl.

"What's happened?" she cried, getting up and hurrying to Da'Leth's side.

Letting Rianne take Da'Leth from him Nicholas turned to face his father. "Captain Krausley and I are leaving for the next jousting tournament tomorrow morning. I shall be taking both Rianne and Da'Leth with me."

His tone was final. Looking past his son to the woman Rianne was hugging Liam began to understand the scowl on Nicholas's face. On Da'Leth's wrist he could see a red mark, a bruise beginning to form beneath it. "Philip," he frowned. Nicholas nodded. "Very well. Take them with you, keep them both safe."

Giving his promise Nicholas turned on his heel, telling Edward to make the necessary arrangements, leading Da'Leth out of the room, telling Rianne to get her things ready to travel. He led Da'Leth up to the tower, sitting her down against the wall before sitting down next to her. Comfortingly rubbing her shoulder, he looked down at her face to see her eyes closed, her hands clenched tightly in her lap as she tried to control the emotions running around her mind and heart.

In his mind he could still hear her plea's as he had walked past his brother's chamber door, on his way to his own chamber.

'Please!' Her cry had cut into his heart and when he opened the door Nicholas had been enraged. He still was but now it had been taken over by concern for his friend. "Da'Leth?"

Taking a deep breath, she opened her eyes, raising them to meet his. Though she had tried to school her features Nicholas could see the shame and sadness in her eyes and it hurt him to realize he had not been able to stop it.

"I'm sorry," he said after a moment. "I wasn't able to stop Philip."

She shook her head. "No one could have stopped him. He knew what he was doing; timing it just right to make sure I would be alone and no one was around. How you happened to be there," she shrugged. "I don't know. All I can say is thank you for being there when you were."

Shaking his head Nicholas replied, "I am the one who put you in this situation and couldn't protect you from it and yet you are the one thanking me."

"Milord, you did not put me in this situation," she refuted.

"Yes, I did. I brought you here, I saw that he had his eyes on you, I saw the way he was treating you and yet I did nothing."

"You told him to leave me alone, you told the men and James to leave me alone. You have done so much already!"

"Well it will be over, I promise you. My father will speak with him and though he may think nothing of going against my wishes he would not dare to ignore a command from my father."

Chapter Thirteen

Waking to the feel of someone shaking her Da'Leth opened her eyes to see Richard standing over her. He smiled. "Lord Timothy said to let you sleep as long as you could but it's time to go now."

Sitting up she looked over to see Rianne still sleeping. "I will get milady ready," she said, wiping the sleep from her eyes. "Thank you for waking me."

"I'm surprised you're still asleep," he teased. "Usually you're awake before any of us."

Nodding she climbed out of the bed, reaching for her brush. "I did not get to sleep until very late last night. We'll be out momentarily."

"I heard you were helping the inn-keeper's wife."

"She needed it desperately."

Telling her he would wait outside for their trunks Richard left the room and headed back out to the table he and Nicholas had been sharing. "She says they will be out soon."

Nodding he took a bite of the bread in his hands. "I'm surprised she wasn't already awake."

"The inn keeper's wife told me she was a big help to her last night."

"Da'Leth?"

Richard nodded. "She washed dishes and served the crowd even after the rest of us had retired to bed."

Shaking his head Nicholas frowned. "She is not supposed to be working like that while we are touring."

"You tell her to stop," Richard grinned.

Chuckling Nicholas didn't reply; they both knew there was no convincing Da'Leth not to work. Since they had left the palace she had spent every waking moment working, taking care of the needs of the entire group. He'd asked her to relax once and she had simply shaken her head with a smile. "'I prefer to be busy'," he said, repeating her words.

"Yes, that sounds like Da'Leth."

"A sweet woman if ever I met one, Milord," the inn keeper said as he refilled their tankards. "I'd like to thank you for all her help last night. I'll accept no money for your rooms; it's the least I can do."

Called away the man gave a slight bow and left, leaving Nicholas and Richard to sit in silence and watch his back disappear into the crowd. "Milord?"

Seeing Da'Leth standing before them, finishing tying the lacing to the edge of her braid Nicholas shook his head, telling her what had just happened. Smiling she turned to try and see him. "That was very kind of him!" Turning back to face Nicholas she advised him they would be ready to leave in a few moments. "The trunks however are ready to be taken out."

"I'll come and get them."

Getting to his feet Richard quickly drained his tankard before moving to get the trunk. "I'll come with you," Nicholas said, doing the same thing Richard had.

Walking behind them Da'Leth couldn't help but reflect on the changes she had seen since coming on the tournament tour with the Prince. As he jousted under an assumed name she had to be very careful how she addressed him, simply calling him 'Milord' so as not to attach a name to his identity. Da'Leth had yet to see him in the arena so she could not speak as to his skill but from the way Richard talked about his previous winnings she had a feeling he was skilled.

Working quickly, they were back in the carriage, traveling to their first stop in the tour, the tournament in Bluefield. At the edge of their border it was the closest one to them and therefore the first one Nicholas had chosen to attend. As it was within his own country Nicholas knew he had to be careful and keep himself locked away in their tent whenever he wasn't jousting.

He had told Rianne to do the same, allowing only Da'Leth and Richard to roam freely through the camps, though they too knew to be careful. They would oversee taking care of any needs that might arise and he was confident they would be able to go undetected.

After a few hours the carriage pulled to a stop and Nicholas and Rianne waited in the carriage while Richard and Da'Leth set everything up with the help of two trusted squires he had brought with them, Edward directing them in their duties. "I must tell you, brother, I am excited to finally be here!"

Looking over at Rianne Nicholas smiled. "One would never have known," teasing her about the ever-present smile that graced her face. It was not her courtly smile, nor was it a reserved smile for the masses. Rianne was grinning like a fool and it made him laugh.

"Oh, do be nice to me," she replied. "Or else I shall report to mother every indiscretion and ungentlemanly thing you do."

Gasping in playful horror he smiled. "Then I suppose I shall have to behave."

Grinning at him she looked out the window past him and saw Richard approaching the carriage. "We are ready for you, milord, milady," he said with a nod to them both. Opening the door to the carriage he helped Rianne down and led her to the tent, Nicholas not far behind. "I hope you find the arrangements comfortable enough," he said. "Da'Leth has set you a place by the fire so you may keep warm if the nights get too chilly."

"Why this is quaint!" Rianne exclaimed with a smile as she examined the large tent. "Are there enough beds for everyone?" she asked, seeing only two beds.

"Your brother and I shall sleep over here, milady," Richard answered, pulling what she had thought was a tent wall back so she could see beyond it. "Yourself and Da'Leth shall sleep on this side."

"Pin that back for now," Nicholas said. "Leave the space open, so we may sit together."

Doing as was asked of him Richard pulled the material back, looping a rope around it to keep it in place. Passing by him Da'Leth looked back with a smile. "It does seem roomier now." Turning to face Nicholas she said, "Your bed is ready, milord, as is your desk per your wish."

"Thank you, Da'Leth," he replied. Crossing the room to the desk he sat down. "Richard, try to find us some dinner, would you? Rianne, work with Da'Leth to finish setting up our new home, I know how strict you are about certain things."

Smiling at his teasing Rianne looked at Da'Leth, "My brother has decided I must be teased this entire trip. You have done an excellent job Da'Leth. Is there anything more that needs to be done?"

"No, milady," she said with a shake of her head. "I need only unpack your trunk and we are finished. Perhaps you would like to work on your stitching?"

Sitting down at her work, happy that Da'Leth had convinced her to bring it, Rianne worked on her stitching, listening as Da'Leth finished her task. Glancing up she saw that she was still working even though the trunk had been unpacked and asked what she was doing.

"I was only attending to my own things, milady. Did you need something?"

"No, I was simply curious."

"Da'Leth has an inherent need to work, it would seem," Nicholas said. Looking over at him Da'Leth saw him leaning back in his chair watching her. "She cannot sit still. To do, so I fear, might kill her."

Rianne laughed but Da'Leth only shook her head. Picking up her basket she sat down on the bed, setting that basket in her lap and looking up at him defiantly before she began to organize the herbs she had gathered during their trip. They had dried in the supply wagon and were ready to be included with the rest in her basket.

"Just because you are sitting does not mean you are not working," he insisted. "My statement holds true."

Closing her eyes, she paused, a small smile curving her lips, before continuing her work. "Then I shall have to admit defeat," she said. "For now."

Laughing Nicholas stood and moved to stand in front of her. "Do you plan on stopping your work anytime soon?"

"Perhaps, one day in the future," she said, thinking about the days she would finally be reunited with her mother and reclaim her place in society.

Nicholas could see the seriousness in Da'Leth's eyes and he didn't press her, moving away to look at his sister stitch work. Standing behind Rianne he complimented her on the details and then raised his eyes back to Da'Leth. Though he felt he knew her better now, their time spent together at the river helping him to answer some of the many questions he had about this woman, Nicholas knew there was a part of Da'Leth that no one was given access to. She still held many secrets and he hoped to come to know them during their tour.

~~*~*~*~*~*~*~*

Sitting on the ground near the fence around the arena Da'Leth watched the men practice their jousting, getting ready for the tournament to be held later that day. Nicholas and Richard had already come and gone, practicing while there had been no one else around, and now the other knights filled the arena, taking turns charging down the lane, aiming for a painted mark on their squire's shield.

Watching them a smile came to Da'Leth's face as she thought back to her childhood days, watching her father and Fredric practicing in the yard. Though he had stopped jousting in the tournaments when her mother had demanded it, her father had refused to give up the sport entirely. When the weather was right he and the servants would work together to get the far field ready to hold their own private joust. As a child she would sit there for hours, watching as two men charged towards each other with their lances in the ready position.

Once she had asked her father to ride with him and after thinking about it for a long time he had agreed. Well protected she had ridden with her father on his horse, helping him to hold the lance while Fredric had come charging toward them, his shield ready for the blow. Though her father had used a lighter touch than usual the wooden shield the young squire had been using to protect himself was old. The lance split the board in two, hitting Fredric in the shoulder and, although it was a lighter impact, it was hard enough to knock him off his horse to the ground.

Terrified she had screamed out his name, struggling against her father to get down from the horse. Finally dropping free she had run to his side, the dazed young man still lying on the ground clutching his shoulder. Kneeling next to him she had wept, apologizing for hurting him, begging for his forgiveness. Raul had pulled her away, handing her to Mara who held her safely until Fredric could be helped, his dislocated shoulder put back into its place.

After that day she had sworn never to ride in the jousting arena again.

Seeing the area begin to clear Da'Leth realized it would soon be time for the joust to begin. Getting up from her seat on the ground she left the arena, heading back to their tent to gather Rianne. They had arranged to watch the joust as peasants, able to slip in and out of the crowd unnoticed. Even with that precaution though Da'Leth had insisted they go only for those jousts in which Nicholas would be riding. Though disappointed that she would not get to see much Rianne had agreed, for the safety of their identity.

Entering the tent, she saw Nicholas standing in his full suit of armor and smiled. "You look comfortable," she teased.

"Better to be uncomfortable than dead," he smiled back, craning his head to see her while Edward finished locking the armor in place. "Where will you two be?"

"On the far side of the arena, out of the sight of the nobles seating area so they could not accidentally see us."

He nodded. "Good thinking." Nicholas saw Rianne emerge from behind the curtain and a grin broke out. "Why sister, you look positively radiant."

Laughing Rianne curtsied. "Thank you, milord, I feel well hidden."

"Almost," Da'Leth said, crossing to her side. "We must change your hair."

"Why? It is braided just as yours is."

"It is too neat," she explained. "You must look tired from your work." Undoing the braid, she braided it gain, messily, and pulled a few wisps of hair out to frame her face giving her a windblown look. "There. Oh, wait one moment."

Bending over Da'Leth rubbed her hand in the dirt for a moment and smudged it over Rianne's cheeks and jaw. "We must hide that fair complexion."

"I must say, you do look like a different person all together," Richard said, looking up from his work when Da'Leth announced she was finished. "Just be careful that you do not catch the eye of a single peasant man or he'll want to steal you away to be his wife."

Rianne smiled at him. "Never fear, Da'Leth shall protect me."

"Of that I have no doubt."

Not bothering to reply Da'Leth stepped behind the curtain to change her clothes, doing to herself as she had done to Rianne. When she stepped back into view Nicholas stared, reminded all too clearly of the first time he had seen her in Pirtonshire. Not noticing his staring eyes Da'Leth bent down to remove her shoes.

"Do I need to do that as well?" Rianne asked when she saw what Da'Leth was doing.

"No," shaking her head. "Your feet would hurt too much, mine are used to it."

Setting her shoes down next to her bed Da'Leth reached for a small pile of red cloth on the corner of the bed. Unfolding one of them she motioned for Rianne to come closer, wrapping it around her waist and tying it in a knot. Doing the same to herself she glanced up to see the curious looks from the other three.

"Many masters will make their servants wear something to identify them as his. These scarves have the same symbol as your banner." She shrugged. "One more thing to help us blend in."

Not surprised at how well she had thought this through Nicholas nodded his agreement. "We must go but I shall look for you in the stands."

"Be careful, milord" Da'Leth said, walking him to the entrance of the tent.

"I will be," he smiled to reassure her. "I don't want to have to drink that tea again!"

Smiling she shook her head, saying goodbye to Richard as he followed Nicholas out. "Are you ready, milady?"

"Da'Leth," she smiled teasingly. "You're not following the rules."

"So long as we are inside this tent I will call you as I should," she replied, her tone friendly but sincere.

Rianne sighed, "Very well. Shall we go?"

Leaving the tent Da'Leth led the way to the arena, making sure Rianne stayed by her side the whole way. Letting her stop at a few of the booths to examine the wares they eventually made it to the arena, taking up a spot near the rail for a good view of the joust. Listening as the herald for the opposing knight introduced his master Da'Leth looked to the other end of the arena to see Nicholas sitting on his horse. Her heart quickened at the sight, recalling the way Fredric had been hurt, praying that he be kept safe.

When the first herald was done Richard stepped before the nobles and smiled, bowing low. In his simple tunic and pants he looked nothing like the captain she knew him to be, playing the part of a herald very well. Listening to him go on and on about the fake names of Lord Timothy's ancestors she couldn't stop a smile from slipping onto her face.

"Is something funny, Da'Leth?" Rianne asked.

"No, Jacqueline," she replied, using the fake name Rianne had decided on. "I was simply listening to the heralds."

Nodding both women turned their attention back to the field below, watching as the flag was readied and then dropped. Instantly the horses on both side of the arena were spurred into action, the knights charging toward each other with their lances held at the ready position. Watching as they collided with each other Da'Leth smiled when she saw Nicholas's lance collide and break on the other knight's helmet while he had only managed to hit Nicholas in the shoulder.

Placing the points on either side the crowd cheered. "What has happened?"

"Lord Timothy is in the lead."

Cheering for her brother Rianne watched as his horse was led back to first position. Watching as well Da'Leth waited to see if he would be attended to by the squires for any injury. When she saw that he was well enough she began to breathe again, closing her eyes to thank God and pray that he be safe in the next charge as well.

Scanning the crowd Nicholas looked to see if he could find Rianne and Da'Leth. Finding them near the rail in the corner he smiled beneath his helmet. Rianne was cheering, her face filled with joy. When his eyes found Da'Leth he saw that her eyes were closed, her lips moving in a silent prayer. When she opened her eyes, he saw her look at him, smiling in encouragement and support.

He knew that she had been praying for his safety, she had told him as much when they had talked during their travel to get to the tournament. She worried about him and it warmed his heart to know she was watching out for him. Watching her for another moment Nicholas turned his attention back to the joust. Making another pass when the flag was lowered he smiled as he trotted back to first position. He had broken a lance on his chest; it was now three points to one, the other knight's lance unbroken. All he needed to do was stay on his horse and he had won.

Watching from the stands as the final charge was made towards each other Da'Leth let out a shout of triumph when she saw Lord Timothy's lance knock his competitor off his horse. "What's happened?"

"He's won!"

Cheering together with the rest of the crowd Da'Leth knew they would have a few hours break until the next joust as all the other knights competed to move on to the next round. Pulling Rianne away from the crowd they slipped out of the arena and back to the tent in time to see Nicholas and Richard entering it just ahead of them. Helping Richard to remove the armor Da'Leth congratulated Nicholas on his win.

"Thank you," he smiled. "I guess it helped having someone watching out for me."

Smiling at him she touched his shoulder to see if it hurt him to do so. "Does your shoulder bother you?"

"A little stiff but no real pain."

"Would it help for me to massage some oil into it?"

Nicholas nodded. "I believe it might." Stripping off his shirt he looked up to his friend. "See if you can find some food and wine for us, would you?"

"Of course," Richard replied. "Anything in particular?"

"Bread," Rianne answered.

"Cheese," Nicholas replied at the same time.

Grinning Richard looked up at Da'Leth, "And you?"

"Some fruit would be nice," she shrugged, reaching down for her basket to find the right oil to use.

Richard left to gather the food and Da'Leth rubbed the oil onto her hands before turning her attention to Nicholas's shoulder. Sitting at her stitch work Rianne asked, "I'm confused about how the game works, Da'Leth. How did you know that Nicholas had won?"

"It's easy enough to remember," she replied, glancing at Rianne before looking back down at her own work. "Whoever has the most point's wins. Each time a lance is broken on the chest it is one point. If a knight breaks it on his opponent's helmet then he is awarded two points since it is a smaller, moveable target. However, when one knight knocks the other from his horse he is awarded three points and he wins the riders horse as well."

"You won that knights horse?" she asked, looking to her brother.

"Yes."

Da'Leth heard the pain in his voice and frowned. "This hurts more than you are telling me." He nodded, unable to speak through his clenched teeth.

Sighing Da'Leth continued to work, massaging out the tenseness in his shoulder. When she knew he couldn't take the pain anymore she stopped working on that shoulder and turned her attention elsewhere, massaging the tenseness out of his neck and shoulder. When the pain was under control again she returned to working on the bad shoulder.

"All right," she said after a while. "Enough for now. I'll wrap it with some herbs to help it heal but you'll need to stay still."

"You have my word," he promised. "I don't think I could move it I wanted to." Da'Leth saw the sheen of sweat on his forehead and offered some of the tea. "No, I need to be able to joust later."

"You need to try and avoid getting hit by the lance on that shoulder," she corrected.

"I'll make sure to tell them so." Nicholas grinned.

Before she could reply Richard entered the tent again, a small sack in his hands from which he produced everything they had asked for. Telling Nicholas to stay where he was Da'Leth cut him a small piece of cheese and poured a goblet of wine. Letting him have a moment to eat and drink she readied an herb paste to smear on his shoulder before wrapping it.

"That smells vile," he complained as she rubbed it on his shoulder.

"Be glad I'm not making you eat it."

Laughing he sipped his wine again. "I'm grateful for the reprieve."

"How did you come to know so much about herbs Da'Leth?" Richard asked as he sat with Rianne to eat his own meal.

"The old woman who took me under her wing at Pirtonshire," she answered, tying the bandage in a knot behind Nicholas's shoulder. "She taught me what herb would do what and how to best use them."

"Is she still at Pirtonshire?"

"No," she replied, sadly shaking her head. "She died several years ago. She was a good woman, I'm glad she finally found her freedom."

Rianne frowned. "I don't understand. She died."

"Yes. There are only two ways for a serf to find their freedom," Da'Leth explained. "One way is for the King to grant it. The other is for the serf to die."

"Oh," she whispered, sinking back in her chair. "I didn't realize…" her voice fading with uncertainty of what to say. Looking up at Da'Leth she frowned. "I must say I'm somewhat surprised that my father has not granted you your freedom. Especially when you take into consideration all that you have done for this family."

Da'Leth didn't respond immediately and Nicholas looked over to see her thinking. "He has offered it, milady," she said at last.

"You didn't take it?" Nicholas asked incredulously. "Why?"

"There was something more important at the time that needed to be tended to."

"Da'Leth you value freedom so highly," Richard interjected to the conversation. "What could possibly be of more importance to you?"

Silent, Da'Leth didn't reply, looking down at her hands for a moment to consider what to say. "I am not at liberty to say right now," she finally decided on. "Perhaps one day I might, but not now."

Frowning, curious, the three of them glanced at one another but when it was clear Da'Leth would not give any more information they let the subject drop. Finishing the meal Nicholas lay down on his bed for some rest before the next jousting match. Leaving Richard to watch over them Da'Leth left the tent, heading out to get some fresh air. Walking aimlessly, she stopped when she found herself in the middle of the square. Sitting down by the well she watched the people around her go about their business.

Shop owners made and sold their wares in the square, their voices calling out to potential customers to come and buy from them. Ignoring them Da'Leth's attention was caught by a small child walking in the square with his mother. They were peasants and Da'Leth watched as the mother helped the little boy carry his load, adjusting the pack that was on his back. The boy said something with a grin and the mother laughed. Smiling as she watched them Da'Leth thought back to her own mother, allowing herself to dwell on the past for a few moments.

What she remembered most about her mother was her touch. It was as soft as a kitten's fur and as comforting as a warm blanket on a cold day. Closing her eyes, she could feel the memory as if she were really there with her. Sighing Da'Leth forced herself back to the present, getting up from her seat to head back to the tent, not wanting them to worry about her.

~~*~*~*~*~*~*~*

Sitting in the stands, the knights below racing towards each other, Rianne and Da'Leth watched as Nicholas unseated another rider. They had been on the tour for a month now and neither of them had grown tired of watching him joust, enjoying the thrill of the sport. Now, in Ivanhar, they were far enough away from their own country to walk about freely, though they still needed to be careful.

"Did he win?" Rianne asked.

"Yes, milady, Lord Timothy of Falcone has won the match, he will move on to the next round."

"Good," she said with a smile.

The jousting tournament over for the day the crowds began to disperse. Taking their time to get back to the tents Rianne and Da'Leth walked leisurely through the square. As they were passing an herbalists shop Da'Leth stopped to see if there was anything she needed. Standing at a small shelf of herbs she couldn't help but overhear the conversation between the shop owner and one of his patrons.

"Lord Edwin is in need of a doctor; have you any in this town?"

"Yes, good sir, but he's is out in the country right now, he won't be back for many days."

"A jousting tournament in town, and he leaves to go to the country?" the man repeated, outraged. "Who will help my Lord now?"

Disgusted the man left the shop. Watching to see which way he was heading Da'Leth purchased some herbs and followed him, asking Rianne to wait for her in the shop. Hurrying down the street she caught the man by his sleeve and pushed the herbs into his hands.
"Boil these in a tea for your Lord. Tell him the taste is vile but it will help with the pain until the doctor can return or another can be found."

Confused the man looked down at the herbs and then back up to Da'Leth. "Who are you?"

"Someone who knows Lord Edwin to be a good man," she replied. "Now go, boil the tea and see to it that he drinks it."

Turning she left, going back to the shop to gather Rianne before heading to the safety of the tent. Nicholas and Richard already there and resting, she went about preparing a meal for them to eat, knowing they would prefer to avoid the places the knights would usually feast at.

As she worked Da'Leth looked up to examine Nicholas, trying to discern if he needed her to attend his shoulder. "I'm fine," he said with a smile when he caught her eye. "There is no pain right now."

"Miss Da'Leth?"

Looking toward the tent entrance, she saw Edward entering and smiled at him before returning to her work. "Hello Edward, what can I do for you?"

"I had hoped you might be able to help me with a small problem."

"Of course, what is it?" When he didn't answer Da'Leth looked up from her task. Seeing that he looked somewhat embarrassed she stepped closer allowing him to whisper in her ear. She nodded and reached for her basket, handing him a small pinch of herbs and telling him to mix it with some water. Knowing the reaction that would happen when he did so, "Stay where you can easily access the needed place," she warned.

Thanking her he left.

"What was that all about?" Richard asked.

"Just a small personal problem," she answered, not wanting to embarrass the poor man by telling them about his constipation problem. "The food will be ready momentarily."

Sitting down to eat the four friends talked until the night stars had begun to shine. Declaring that she needed to walk and stretch her legs Rianne asked Da'Leth to go for a walk with her. Liking the idea Richard decided to go with them, Nicholas joining them as well. As the foursome walked through the nearly deserted square, Rianne stopping occasionally to look in the windows at the items for sale, Da'Leth raised her eyes to the stars.

"They're beautiful tonight."

Lowering her gaze, she saw Nicholas standing beside her, his eyes on the heavens above. "Yes, they are."

"My father used to tease me and say that the moon was made of cheese and that if the sun didn't go away at night that when the moon would come out it would melt."

"Maybe he's right," she said with a straight face. Feeling him look at her she met his gaze, unable to keep the smile from pulling at her lips.

Nicholas shook his head. "I hope not, melted cheese can be very difficult to clean up."

"But it is delicious."

Staring at each other they both laughed at the absurdity of their conversation. Up ahead, Richard and Rianne stopped to look back at them, shaking their heads before continuing their walk. Falling back into an easy pace Nicholas looked at Da'Leth. "Do you know the constellations?"

Shaking her head Da'Leth stopped in surprise when Nicholas grabbed her hand and led her over to the jousting field where they could clearly see the stars without the rooftops interrupting the expanse above them. Lifting Da'Leth onto the railing he leaned against it and began pointing out the constellations above them. Able to see each one Da'Leth was amazed, wanting to hear the story behind each one, fascinated by them.

When he finished pointing out all the constellations that could be seen he began to describe the ones they couldn't see at that time of the year. Watching Da'Leth listening to him with rapt attention Nicholas felt a sense of peace washing over him that he rarely felt anymore. For a few hours he could forget the man that was haunting his every step.

"There they are!"

Looking down to the entrance of the arena Nicholas saw Richard and Rianne walking towards them. "Were you looking for us?"

"We thought you were behind us, brother," she answered. "I thought perhaps you had gotten lost."

Nicholas laughed. "Not likely. Have you finished looking at all the shop windows?"

"For now," she smiled, knowing how he hated to window shop with her. Richard had made the experience enjoyable though and Rianne had easily forgotten that Nicholas and Da'Leth had been with them until Richard wondered aloud where they had gone. "I may need to stop in at one of them before we leave; I found some beautiful material that would make a lovely gown."

"Make sure to have it sent to Victoria so they don't realize who you are," he warned. "You cannot have it sent to the palace."

"I will."

Heading back toward the tent to retire for the night Nicholas watched Da'Leth help Rianne to ready for bed, drawing the curtain for privacy while she changed. Once the young Princess was settled into her bed Da'Leth peeked around the curtain.

"Is there anything you need before you retire?" she asked, addressing her question to both men.

"Thank you, no," Nicholas said, Richard also shaking his head.

"Good night then, sleep well."

Letting the curtain drop behind her Da'Leth left the two men alone. Turning his attention back to getting ready to sleep Nicholas caught sight of Richard from the corner of his eyes, his foot tapping silently against the bed. "Is something wrong?"

"Wrong?" Richard repeated with a frown. "No, nothing is wrong."

"Richard," Nicholas said, his tone implying his disbelief. "What is it?"

Unsure of how he would take the thought flying about in his head he shook it slowly. "Just my own thought's milord," he said after a moment.

"About Rianne?" he asked softly so the women could not hear. Shocked Richard met Nicholas's even gaze, nodding slightly. "I thought as much. You've cared for her for quite some time now."

"Milord, I..." he started.

"It's all right, Richard, I'm not angry. Philip might be if he was to find out, but thankfully I'm nothing like him. Have you told her how you feel?"

He shook his head. "I haven't dared to; she is a Princess and I am only a Captain of the Guard. The King would never allow it."

Nicholas nodded; he had to agree on that point. "Yet it hasn't stopped you from loving her?"

"There was nothing that could have stopped that," he admitted.

Feeling for his friend Nicholas didn't reply. He liked Richard; he was a good man and a good friend who had been there for him every time Nicholas had needed him. Wanting to give him some sort of hope he kept his mouth shut, knowing there was nothing he could say to help the situation at the moment. Slipping under the blanket he snuffed out the candle and left Richard to his own thoughts, wishing there was something he could do for his friend.

Chapter Fourteen

Walking toward the arena Nicholas was dressed in his full armor, not wanting to take the chance that anyone would recognize him. Ahead of him Richard carried his shield and led his horse while the squires were already in the arena setting up his lances. Rianne was still back in the tent, needing a few more moments to finish getting ready, Da'Leth with her.

"Milord!"

Hearing Da'Leth call him Nicholas stopped and turned around. Watching her run towards him he smiled beneath his helmet. Da'Leth closed the distance between them, bowing quickly when she had reached him. "Lord Timothy, your sister has asked that you take this is you should need it for good fortune."

Holding out a small pendant to him she smiled. "Though I must say I don't know where you'll put it."

"My sister is kind hearted," he replied, chuckling at Da'Leth's comment, "But she has the tendency to not think things through. Perhaps you could hold it for me; I shall entrust my good fortune to you."

Meeting his eyes, her face suddenly serious, she answered, "I shall guard it with my life."

Needing to get ready for the joust Nicholas was called away. Once he was settled onto the back of his mount he scanned the peasant's area for Rianne and Da'Leth, spotting them as they stood at the railing. Straining his eyes, he looked to see if Da'Leth was still carrying the pendant Rianne had offered to him. When he saw that she clutched both hands to her chest he knew she had kept it with her and the thought warmed his heart.

This tournament tour had gone well for him so far and Nicholas couldn't help but wonder if Da'Leth's presence had any effect on that. One of the squires caught his attention for a moment and he looked away from the stands. Waiting for a few final adjustments to his armor he listened as Richard began to announce him as Sir Timothy of Falcone. He only needed to win this match and he would win the tournament.

Nicholas was confident.

The helmet was hot and stuffy and Nicholas could feel the sweat dripping down the back of his neck. More than ready for this tournament to be over he was looking forward to the long ride to Paris for the next one, a relaxing break between the bone jarring jousting tournaments.

It was Da'Leth that had been tending to his minor scrapes since they had started this year's tournament, mending his scrapes and bruises with a tender touch. She would tell him what he had done well and what he could expect from the other jousters. He'd asked her once how she had come to know so much about jousting but she had evaded the question with her usual skill. Watching her now Nicholas suddenly realized how much it meant to him to have her in the stands, watching him joust, worrying about his health. It was a good feeling to have, much different than the pain of having Rianne worry about him.

Sitting still for a moment, the men already finished adjusting his armor, he stared at Da'Leth. Nicholas was more than a little surprised by the feelings that washed over him at the sight of her. From the moment he talked with her by the fire Nicholas had known her to be a good person, trusting, honest, capable, honorable, but looking at her now he pushed those thoughts aside in favor of the new ones creeping into his heart. Seeing the bright red hair that flowed down her back in a single braid, the smooth complexion of her creamy skin, made him long to sit next to her. The grace with which she moved was as womanly as most of the ladies or courtier's he knew and yet when the need arose she was as strong and as fierce as any of his men in battle.

'A woman of such contradictions,' he thought to himself yet again. Only this time, with no small amount of shock, Nicholas realized one very important detail. At some point in their travels together she had managed to capture his heart. When it happened, he wasn't sure, nor how. All the Prince knew for certain was that she had taken hold of his heart and he had no desire to take it back from her.

Smiling he saw Rianne whisper to Da'Leth and she whisper back, no doubt wondering how long it would be until the joust began. The thought reminded him of his current task and he looked down to see one of the men holding his lance for him to take. Taking it, settling it into its place, he waited for the signal, tensing himself to spur his horse into action.

The flag dropped and both women turned their full attention to the arena before them to watch the two men on horses charge at each other. Both held their lances held in the ready position as they drew closer to their target. Wincing when she saw both lances make contact Da'Leth calculated the points in her mind, knowing what Rianne's next question was going to be.

"What happened?"

"Sir Timothy has scored two points for a breaking his lance on the head and Sir Ethan has scored one for a breaking his lance on the chest," she answered, explaining the match to the Princess. "Sir Timothy needs only one more point to win the match."

"Will he win do you think?"

Da'Leth nodded. "I believe he will."

Back to their starting points the two knights prepared to charge again. Da'Leth frowned when she saw Nicholas's lance wavering, dipping up and down as he rode toward Sir Ethan. At the last moment he pulled it up, breaking it on Sir Ethan's chest while his opponent missed him altogether. Breathing a sigh of relief, she smiled. "Sir Timothy has won."

Cheering for her brother, Rianne clapped with a bright smile. Next to her, worried about the lack of movement on the horse, Da'Leth watched Nicholas carefully as he rode back to his starting point. Meeting him halfway Richard placed a hand on his knee, looking up at him worriedly. When the man suddenly called out for the squires to come and lead the horse away she knew her worry was well founded.

"Milady, come," she said quickly, moving away from her place at the rail and tugging on Rianne's sleeve. "We must go."

Knowing better than to question Da'Leth when she issued a command Rianne followed Da'Leth. Her smile slipping from her face she hurried out of the stands behind Da'Leth. Through the streets they hurried until they reached the tent. Looking inside she saw that it was empty and turned to look around her, searching for a sign that Richard and Nicholas were on their way to the tent.

Beside her she heard Rianne gasp and turned to see where she was looking. A little way away three men carried Nicholas, still in his full armor, through the crowd towards their tent. Instructing the Princess to hold open the flaps Da'Leth hurried inside to ready the stool for him to sit on so they could remove the armor. When he was seated, a low groan escaping from under the helmet, she looked up at Richard, glancing at Rianne before looking back at him. Nodding, understanding her meaning, Richard stepped away from the Prince and placed a hand on Rianne's shoulder.

"Come with me, milady," he said gently. "Let Da'Leth care for your brother."

Resisting him she looked at Da'Leth and saw her nod, her face solemn. Da'Leth watched Richard lead Rianne away, promising that her brother was in good hands, and motioned for the men to lower the tent flaps. Working quickly, they removed Nicholas's armor, tossing it aside to be dealt with later. When his armor was off Da'Leth saw the blood on his side and knew this was more serious than the other injuries he had suffered.

"Go and get my basket," she ordered one of the men.

While one of the squires hurried to get the basket the other stayed to help Da'Leth finish settling Nicholas onto the bed, removing his shirt so she could see the wound. "Get me some clean cloth and boil some water," she instructed the second man once the Prince was settled on the bed. "Go now!" she ordered when he didn't move, staring at the wound on his master's side.

"Will he be all right?" the young man asked.

"I will take care of the master," she said, softening her tone when she saw the worry in his eyes. "Go now so that I can help him to begin healing."

With a nod he ran from the tent to do as she had instructed him. "He's a good boy," she heard rasped from the bed.

Turning her full attention back to Nicholas Da'Leth frowned when she saw his pinched face. "Rest," she told him in no uncertain terms. "Stay still and let me do my work."

Lying back, unable to move if he had wanted to, Nicholas could feel her rubbing the blood away from around the wound as gently as she could. Opening his eyes, he looked up and saw her concentrating on his wound; she didn't see him watching her. Her eyes were filled with worry, tears shimmering in them as she worked, blinking them away as often as she could. One of them escaped and he reached up to brush it away, his finger lingering on her cheek just a moment longer than needed. "You're crying," he whispered.

Meeting his gaze Da'Leth's heart stopped in her chest for a single beat before resuming its frantic rhythm. "Milord, please," she whispered. "I must concentrate or you will suffer."

"Your basket, Da'Leth!"

Turning away to accept the basket Da'Leth examined its contents before asking him to find an herbalist and gather some herbs she would need to wrap the wound with. When she turned her attention back to the Prince she saw that he had passed out and was grateful. It would be easier to do her work without having to worry about causing him too much pain. Bending over him to work she cleaned away the blood to examine the wound. Nothing appeared to be broken, there were no bones protruding from the wound. However, a piece of the lance had become stuck in his side

Working quickly, she removed the chunk of wood that had embedded itself in his side and cleared out all the splinters she could see. When the younger squire returned with the hot water she lathered some soap to clean the wound before preparing an herbal paste to help keep away an infection. Her task complete, she covered him with a blanket and sat down on the stool next to the bed, taking Nicholas's hand in her own to gently kiss his palm.

"Sleep well, highness," she whispered, settling in to wait for him to wake.

~~*~*~*~*~*~*~*

Slowly the pain began to creep into his sleep, rousing him to the world around him. Blinking he looked around to see his friends gathered around. Richard sat at the foot of the bed, his feet propped up as he slept. To his left Rianne sat on a chair, leaning her head on her fist, also asleep.

"How do you feel?"

Hearing her whisper Nicholas looked over to see Da'Leth watching him. Feeling her soft touch holding his right hand he squeezed her hands gently. "Sore."

"Is the pain too much?"

"Not yet, but I fear it will be soon."

"When it is, I have an herb that will help. The taste is awful but it helps with the pain."

"What time is it?"

"Well after midnight, milord," Richard answered, woken by their whispering. "Do you remember what happened?"

"The joust," he nodded. "Who won?"

"You did," Da'Leth smiled. "Three points to one."

"When do I need to be up for the ceremony?" Seeing Richard and Da'Leth glance at each other he asked, "How much time have I missed?"

"Six days, milord," Da'Leth answered. "We are in Paris."

His eyes wide Nicholas repeated her answer. "Six days? How did we travel?"

"We used a wagon. Da'Leth lined it with furs to make is softer for you. The Princess traveled in the carriage with Edward while I drove the wagon. Da'Leth stayed with you to see to it that you were well during the journey."

"Nicholas!"

Looking over at his sister Nicholas smiled. "Hello Rianne."

"Oh, you had me so worried!"

"I'm well enough, Rianne," he assured her. "From what I hear, Da'Leth has taken good care of me."

"Indeed, she has," she agreed. "Da'Leth has been taking care of all of us I dare say."

"She has run this camp as well as any general," Richard teased. Seeing the look on Da'Leth's face he smirked. "A word to the wise," he told Nicholas. "Do not cross her."

"I have never heard a cross word from the woman," Nicholas complained. "The one time she does speak crossly I don't get to hear it."
"It is fearsome. Beware an angry Da'Leth."

"Enough," Da'Leth interrupted, rolling her eyes. "You two are incorrigible." Letting go of Nicholas's hand she stood and walked across the tent, listening as Rianne and Richard caught Nicholas up on what had happened while he was sleeping. Returning to his side she handed him a cup of steaming tea. "Here, this will help with the pain."

Taking it, he smelled the aroma of the tea and, recognizing it, made a face. "It doesn't hurt that bad yet," handing the cup back to her.

"Better to catch it before the pain begins than to wait until it is too much to handle." Pushing the cup toward him again she refused to allow him to give it back. "Drink the tea, highness."

Making a face he gagged it down as fast as he could. "That is still the vilest most disgusting thing I have ever tasted."

"You'll be thanking me in a few moments," she replied, taking the empty cup. "Make sure he lays still, please, Captain. I will be back as soon as I can."

"Where is she going?" Da'Leth heard Nicholas ask.

Out of the tent before she could hear their reply Da'Leth began to walk away, taking deep breaths to control the emotions roiling inside. Hooking her basket over her arm she set out to gather the supplies they would need. Walking through the square she picked her supplies, paying for them with a small bag of coin Richard had given to her, haggling with the vendors for a better price. Approaching an herb vendor, she took her time looking over his selection, mentally reviewing which herbs she was out of and which she did not need just yet.

"Da'Leth?"

Looking around, startled that anyone would know her in this foreign place, she saw a familiar face smiling at her. "Beatrice!" Setting her basket down Da'Leth hugged her old friend, tears of joy stinging at her eyes. "What are you doing here? How are you?"

"Pregnant," she smiled, patting her swollen stomach. "I live here in Paris with my husband now."

"Husband!"

Beatrice nodded. "The master who bought me that day lives here in Paris. He was traveling through and needed a serf to replace one that had run away. When I got to Paris I met one of my masters' other serfs and we just fell in love! The master gave us permission to marry and now I'm pregnant."

"I can see that!" Da'Leth laughed, touching her stomach gently. "Where is your husband now?"

"Working in the stables right now. The master is jousting in the tournament this year so he has to take especially good care of the horses."

Smiling, the two women talked about Beatrice's new life in Paris and how different it was from life in Pirtonshire. Having told her all about her own life Beatrice changed the topic to Da'Leth. "What about you? What happened to you that day?"

"I travel with Sir Timothy of Falcone now. His sister needed a woman to wait on her," she said, sticking as close to the truth as she could. "We're here for the jousting tournament."

"Petri has mentioned Sir Timothy to me before. He says he's a good jouster."

Da'Leth nodded. "He is."

"So, you're happy then?"

"As happy as I can be right now," Da'Leth smiled. "I serve good people, Beatrice."

Needing to get back to her work the two women hugged one more time, promising to find each other again before the joust was over, and Beatrice left to go back to her chores. Picking up her basket again Da'Leth turned back to the herbs and picked the ones she needed before she too headed back to her own work. Entering the tent, she saw Nicholas lying on the bed asleep, Richard gone and Rianne writing on a piece of parchment.

"Oh good, your back," Rianne smiled when Da'Leth entered. "I was just sending a letter to mother and wanted to tell her how Nicholas is doing."

"Tell her he is recovering nicely. The wound has already begun to heal itself."

"Will he be jousting in Paris?"

Shaking her head, she set her basket down. "No, the wound is still too fresh. The pain would be too great."

"You will burn that letter in the fire and begin again," Nicholas called from the bed. "Do not mention the wound and you may tell her that yes, I will be jousting in this tournament."

Sighing Da'Leth turned to look at the man she had thought was sleeping. "You are not healed enough yet to joust, milord. If you aggravate the wound now it will never heal properly."

"I do not need a second mother, Da'Leth."

Moving to the bed she sat on the stool next to him, feeling his eyes on her as she approached. "I am not nor would I wish to be a mother to you," she began. "I am simply someone who cares." Nicholas raised his eyebrow at her and Da'Leth suddenly realized what she had said. Speaking quickly, she added, "I bandaged that wound and I do not desire to do it again should you aggravate it."

Nicholas was silent for a moment, simply watching her. Da'Leth's mask had slipped back onto her face but, for just a moment, before she realized what she had said, he had seen the concern and worry in her eyes. "I will take it under advisement."

"A bargain," she offered. "If you can mount your horse and handle the pain I agree to keep silent on the matter."

"Done," he smiled at her. "Richard," he called out to the man that had just entered the tent. "Saddle my horse; I must prove myself to Da'Leth today."

Glancing at Da'Leth for confirmation Richard nodded his head and left the tent again. Rising from the bed, slowly and stiffly, Nicholas dressed himself in simple clothing and left with Da'Leth and Rianne to meet Richard in the stable. Standing back Da'Leth watched as he took hold of the reins and pulled himself up onto the horse, his face blanching though he managed to stay upright. Her face screaming her displeasure Da'Leth held up her hands in defeat.

"I gave my word, milord, I will say nothing."

"But you want to, don't you?" Seeing her glare, he smiled. "Very well Da'Leth, let me hear what is burning your tongue."

"You will not last one round," she said bluntly.

"I fear," he admitted with a grimace. "That you are right."

Leaning on Richard Nicholas knew better than to try and joust in the Paris tournament. His side burned, the world dipped in and out of an inky blackness. Leaning on his friend he made it back to their tent, collapsing into the bed once more. Without a word Da'Leth removed his shirt, and the bandaging, to examine the wound. Satisfied that it was all right she re-bandaged it and helped him to put his shirt back on.

"Are you going to scold me?" he asked with a grin, relieved that the pain had begun to subside.

"No."

"Not even an 'I told you so'?"

"No."

Sensing her foul mood, he stopped teasing and asked her to sit for a moment. "You were right," he admitted. "I was wrong. When I am wrong I admit it."

"I'm glad to hear it."

Silence filled the tent, Richard and Rianne wisely keeping silent as they slipped out of the tent, not wanting to get involved. Watching her get back to work he frowned. Her censure was one thing, he had expected it, but her silence was deafening and Nicholas discovered that he hated it. Suffering for as long as he could he said, "Speak."

Turning to face the Prince Da'Leth raised her eyebrows in silence at his command.

"I do not enjoy your silence when I know there are words you wish to say."

Meeting his gaze, she spoke evenly. "And I do not enjoy seeing you hurt when I know that common sense would have prevented it."

"Then you are mad at me," he concluded. Knowing she would evade the question if she could, he clarified, "Yes or no?"

"Yes."

"What can I do to apologize for making you mad?"

"Behave and do as I say when it comes to that wound."

Nicholas smiled. "If you give your word that you will speak your mind to me no matter what the subject then I give my word that I shall heed your every command so far as my health is concerned."

"Agreed," holding her hand out to him. Taking her hand, he shook it gently, lingering until she pulled her hand away to reach for the whistling kettle. Taking the boiling kettle off the fire Da'Leth closed her eyes for a moment, her back to Nicholas. Her hand was tingling from the contact and she scolded herself for being foolish enough to feel anything, reminding herself forcefully that he was a Prince and she was still only a serf. Preparing another cup of tea for him Da'Leth handed it to him and sat down on the stool.

"Drink that for the pain."

"Talk to me and I'll drink it," he smiled, holding the cup just away from his lips.

"What do you want me to say?"

"Tell me something I don't know about you."

Thinking for a moment she motioned for him to drink. With her repair work in hand she said, "My favorite color is green."

"Why?" he grinned in surprise.

"Because it reminds me of spring; it's my favorite season. Everything is starting over again, a fresh start to wipe out the past mistakes and start over again. I am hard pressed to find something negative to say about nature."

"What about it do you like most?"

"The forest. When I was a little girl my father and I would go for walks in the forest. He would show me all the different trees and flowers, tell me each of their names and what each one meant. We would go swimming in the river and if the night was warm enough we would sleep out under the stars." Da'Leth fell silent for a few moments. "I miss those times very much."

"Tell me more."

Looking at him she frowned. "Why so curious all of the sudden?"

"This is hardly sudden," he replied. "You have raised questions in my mind from the moment I first saw you." He saw the confusion on her face and smiled. "You didn't see me that day but I saw you standing up to Lord Byron the day before he sold you in the market. Even then you intrigued me, humble yet proud at the same time."

"Was that why you...?" Da'Leth trailed off, unable to say the word.

Nicholas nodded, another question coming to his mind. "Why do you never say the word 'bought'? Nor do you ever say you were sold, or that you are considered to be owned." He saw the hesitation in her eyes and added, "And speak plainly."

"They are vile words," Da'Leth replied after a few moments. "No human has the right to own another."

The vehemence in her voice shocked Nicholas. He knew no one wished to be a serf, 'Who would choose to be owned?', but the anger and disgust in Da'Leth's voice made him realize she felt more strongly about it than he had thought. "I'm sorry," he said after some time.

"You didn't do this," she said, her voice softening again. "If anything, you saved me from a nightmare. I can never thank you enough for what you and your family have done. You gave me hope again."

"Hope?"

Closing her eyes for a moment Da'Leth knew she had said too much. "Hope that life would get better. Kindness to a serf is rare; you showed me that there are people who do care for serf as though they are human."

Silence fell again but this time it was comfortable, mutual. Her mending done Da'Leth stood and, seeing that Nicholas had fallen victim to the sleepy effects of the tea, went outside to stretch her legs and back, both of them aching from being still for so long. Bending and twisting she worked the kinks out of her body until she felt good again. About to head back in Da'Leth stopped and stared at a man standing a good distance away at the pub entrance.

"Lord Edgar," she whispered in shock.

Suddenly realizing she was standing in full view Da'Leth hurried back into the safety of the tent, daring to peak out from behind the flaps. The man had aged since she had seen him last. His hair had fallen out and his gut protruded like a man who liked to eat rich foods. Staring at him Da'Leth could feel her anger boiling up and knew she needed to release it before she did something stupid.

Making sure Nicholas was still asleep she stepped out of the tent, skirting along the edge of the buildings until she could disappear into the stable. Once inside she began to work, moving grain sacks from one side of the stable to the other as she had seen some men doing earlier that day. Working to vent her anger and frustration she moved the grain back and forth until she was too exhausted to move, her energy gone. Dragging herself back to the tent, the night sky filled with stars and the moon high overhead, she fell into her bed, never seeing the worried or confused look of the three people waiting for her return.

~~*~*~*~*~*~*~*

Waking the next morning Da'Leth was surprised to find the tent already packed up and the wagon already loaded except for the bed she had been sleeping on. Sitting up she looked around in confusion. Edward entered the tent and smiled at her. "Good morning Miss Da'Leth," he greeted. "The family is dining in the pub and has asked that you join them when you wake."

"What's going on Edward?" she asked standing up from the bed. "Why is the tent packed?"

Simply urging her to go and meet the other three for breakfast Edward didn't reply. Confused and still half asleep she walked out of the tent, going to the pub as instructed. Entering it she saw Rianne, Richard, and Nicholas sitting by the fire and moved closer to join them. Seeing her Richard smiled and stood, pulling out another chair for her to join them.

"Milord, you should not be out of bed," Da'Leth said as she sat down, checking his face for any hint of pain.

"I am well enough to travel," he replied. Motioning for someone to bring some more bread and cheese he turned his attention to Da'Leth. "Did you sleep well?"

Sensing that something was wrong she answered him briefly, "Well enough, milord. What is the matter?"

"Da'Leth?"

Looking up she saw Beatrice holding a tray of food. "Hello," she smiled distractedly, her mind still on Nicholas's tone. "Is this the pub you work in now?"

Nodding she looked back, calling for a man to come over. "This is my husband," she smiled. "Petri, this is Da'Leth, the woman I was telling you about."

"It's a pleasure to finally meet you," the man smiled. He was a good-looking man, not too handsome but not plain either. His eyes were kind and Da'Leth was glad Beatrice had found herself a good husband. "Bea has told me so much about your time together at Pirtonshire."

Da'Leth smiled at him. "Beatrice is a good woman."

Nodding a greeting to the others at the table the husband and wife left them alone but Da'Leth could see the questions in Beatrice's eyes and hoped she could find a way to avoid them. Her friend gone she turned her attention back to Nicholas, still trying to find out what was wrong.

"Where did you go last night?" Nicholas asked before she could say a word.

"Last night?" she frowned. "I was in the barn."

"What were you doing?"

"Moving grain sacks," she answered honestly, still trying to catch up with what was going on, why he was asking these questions. "You were sleeping, I needed to..." She stopped, her mind suddenly becoming clear.

"You needed to what?" he pressed. Nicholas could see in her face that she wasn't telling him everything. Something had happened, something she didn't want to share with them but he didn't care.

When he'd woken the day before to see Richard and Rianne but not Da'Leth he'd wondered where she was and as the day had turned to night he had begun to worry about her. The stars were shining brightly and the moon was high in the sky before she had finally returned to their tent, collapsing into her bed without even noticing that the three of them were up, worried about her.

"I needed to work, milord," she said after a moment, trying to avoid answering the question but knowing that it would be impossible.

Telling her what had happened last night Nicholas frowned. "That is not like you at all Da'Leth" he finished. "What is wrong? What happened yesterday?"

Closing her eyes Da'Leth said nothing for a few moments. When she opened them, Nicholas could see resignation in them and he hated that he had been forced to use her unwillingness to lie to him against her. "I saw my uncle, milord."

"Your uncle!" Rianne repeated. "Da'Leth I didn't know you have an uncle in Paris! Did you spend time with him?"

"Rianne," Nicholas interjected quickly. "Would you and Richard please go check on the men after you have finished your meal? Da'Leth and I will meet you at the tent in a little while."

Getting to his feet Nicholas looked down at Da'Leth. Unsure of what was going to happen, but knowing he would not leave things alone until he was satisfied, Da'Leth stood and followed him out of the pub. They walked down the streets in silence until they had reached a small park area that was relatively deserted. Stopping he lowered himself down onto a crude wooden bench, his movements stiff.

The bench was too small to comfortably fit two so Da'Leth sat down on the ground, laying her hands in her lap and staring at his boots. She did not want to discuss last night with anyone but especially not the Prince. It was becoming harder for her to keep her feelings separate from her daily interactions with him. With the recent injury, tending to him closely over the last week, Da'Leth had caught herself focusing on him not only with her mind but her heart as well.

"Tell me what happened, Da'Leth. How did you see your Uncle?"

Watching her sit before him Nicholas could see the sadness in her and the resolve to keep her emotions under control, hidden as best she could. Though he hadn't understood at first Nicholas had quickly remembered why the sight of her uncle would have bothered her so much.

"He was walking past the tent," she said at last, her voice low. "He didn't see me."

"Then he's here in Paris now. Where is he?"

She shook her head. "I don't know and I don't care to know."

There was bitterness in her voice and he didn't like it. "This is the man who sold you into serfdom, the one who took you from your family. It was an undeserved action and he should be confronted for it!"

Surprised by the vehemence in his tone Da'Leth looked up at him. He was angry, not at her but at what had been done to her. Warmth rushed through her and Da'Leth could feel her face flushing and she looked away. She didn't know what to say, simply shaking her head.

"Tell me his name and I shall find him," Nicholas said when Da'Leth was silent.

"No!" she started, raising her eyes to meet his. "Milord, please, I am not ready to confront him yet. There are other things that must be done before I can find justice."

"Da'Leth!" Nicholas began, ready to refute her request.

"Please!" she said quickly, moving to kneel before him, grabbing his hand in her urgency. "Please, I beg of you, do not do this. There is more to lose than you realize."

He wanted to ask what but Nicholas knew she would never answer the question. She would not lie, that much he was certain of, but she would find a way to avoid answering the question. Wanting to do something to help her Nicholas realized he would need to do as she requested, not willing to risk the friendship they had developed.

"I don't agree with you," he began firmly. Sighing he finished, "But I will do as you ask."

"Thank you," she breathed, her eyes showing how grateful she was.

Sitting on the bench, staring down at her, he could feel the softness of her hand on his, and the feelings he remembered from earlier came flooding back to him. Watching the change that came over Nicholas Da'Leth's breath caught in her throat. 'Am I seeing things? Is my heart imagining this?' she wondered to herself. Wondering at the possibility Da'Leth forgot herself and dropped her guard allowing Nicholas to see what she kept tightly hidden away in the deepest part of her heart. Within her eyes he could see his own feelings reflected back at him. Reaching out with his free hand he cupped her cheek, her eyes closing against the feel of his hand on her face.

In the next instant she tensed, realizing how far, too far, she had let herself go and jumped away from his touch, standing several feet away from him. Before his eyes he saw her guard come up again, her eyes blank as she stood respectfully before him. Confused, 'Hadn't she felt the same way he did?' he stared at her.

"Milord," she said; her voice carefully even. "We should go."

Watching her for a moment Nicholas frowned, hurt that she had turned away from him. Nodding he got to his feet and they walked back towards their traveling party. Passing through the square they were almost to the carriage when Da'Leth felt a hand tugging on her arm. Turning to look she saw that a woman she didn't know was trying to get her attention.

"Are you Da'Leth?" she asked hurriedly.

"Yes."

"Beatrice sent me to find you. Petri has been hurt, please, can you come?"

The woman's voice was filled with urgency and Da'Leth took a step towards her before turning to look at Nicholas. He nodded and she left his side to tend to her friend's husband. Continuing to the carriage Nicholas advised that they would not be able to leave right away. After several hours had passed, a serf already come and gone for Da'Leth's basket, Da'Leth herself joined them.

"Petri has been hurt very badly. A horse kicked him in the chest and he is in a great deal of pain."

Sitting on a bench by the edge of the square Nicholas watched Da'Leth carefully. On the surface nothing appeared different but he knew something had changed between them. Da'Leth could not hold his gaze for more than a few moments before looking away to one of the others.

"Do they need your services still?" Richard asked.

"I would like to see him through the night if I may," she answered. "But the decision is yours."

"We are not expected at the next tournament so we shall skip ahead to the next one in Petithome. Take the time you need Da'Leth, we shall stay here for the night."

With a small curtsy, glancing at him for a moment, Da'Leth left again to tend to Petri. Watching her walk away Nicholas felt a heavy weight settle over his heart.

~~*~*~*~*~*~*~*

Walking out into the street, stretching her back and breathing in the fresh air Da'Leth took a few moments to refresh herself. Petri was asleep and Beatrice had been called to work in the pub, a rowdy crowd of drunken men demanding food and ale, leaving Da'Leth alone with her own thoughts. As hard as she had fought it her mind kept recalling the look she had seen in Nicholas's eyes, the feel of his hand on her face. Closing her eyes, she could almost hear his voice in the wind.

With a rough shake of her head Da'Leth forced her eyes open, staring at her reflection in the glass window she stood in front of. "Stop it!" she ordered herself vehemently. "It cannot be and you know it!"

"Da'Leth?"

Turning she saw Richard, Rianne, and Nicholas standing a few feet away. Two looked confused but the third simply stared at her, his eyes telling her that he had heard what she'd said. Slowly she faced them, clasping her hands in front of her in a stoic position, forced but effective in helping her to maintain control over her emotions. "Milady?"

"Are you all right? You seemed upset."

"I am well enough," she replied, meeting only Rianne's eyes. "Are you enjoying the night?"

"Yes," she smiled. "How is your friend's husband?"

"In pain I am afraid, but he will recover. I have instructed Beatrice how to use the herbs and she will be able to tend to him after tonight. I shall be ready to leave in the morning."

Stepping away briefly Nicholas pulled Richard towards him, the two men whispering amongst themselves while Rianne and Da'Leth were talking. Her attention was called away when one of the serfs told her Petri had woken in pain again. Going into the house to help him Da'Leth emerged back into the street a few moments later to see Nicholas and Richard looking around in confusion.

"Milord?"

"Where is she?" Richard asked, hoping Da'Leth would know.

"Jacqueline?" she replied, trying to confirm they were talking about the same person, unable to say her true name aloud.

Richard nodded. Frowning as she looked around, Da'Leth wondered where the Princess would have gone. From the corner of her eyes she saw a worried Beatrice approaching her. "Da'Leth you need to come."

"I just left, Petri," she said. "He's asleep. Have you seen my lady?"

"That is why you need to come," Beatrice said. "She is in trouble."

Something in her tone caught Da'Leth's attention and she looked at her old friend. Seeing her holding a tankard in her hands Da'Leth's heart sank. "No," she whispered, her mind recalling the times at Pirtonshire when she had been called upon to save a woman in trouble at the pub.

"I'm sorry, but the crowd is too large to do it any other way. Your master would lose if he were to try and fight his way in."

Confused Nicholas and Richard moved closer in time to see Da'Leth take the tankard of ale and drink from it until it was empty. Handing it back to Beatrice she took a deep breath, closing her eyes to try and build the courage needed to do what she had to do. With a frustrated sigh she began to walk towards the pub.

"What is going on?" Nicholas called after her.

Stopping in her tracks she turned around and he could see in her eyes that she had forgotten they were still there. "Richard, come with me, I'll need your help when the moment is right. Milord, please, I beg of you, stay out of sight, I don't want you to get hurt."

Promising Nicholas he would help Da'Leth Richard moved to follow the woman, missing the look that crossed the Prince's face at being left behind. "What do you need me to do?"

"Get as close to her as you can. When the time is right take her, and get her out of there."

Da'Leth's instructions seemed clear and Richard nodded but when they entered the over-crowded pub he saw it was not going to be as easy as he had thought. His anger blazed when he saw that Rianne was surrounded by a group of men, each one drunker than the next. The Princess was terrified and Richard knew he had to get her out of there as fast as he could. Hurrying over to the counter

Da'Leth motioned for Richard to get closer and climbed up to stand on the counter.

Standing in the doorway, understanding what Beatrice had meant about the crowd, Nicholas looked into the pub and saw Da'Leth standing on the counter towering above the crowd. Frowning he watched as she got the crowd's attention, pulling them into a string of raunchy drinking songs as she danced on the counter before them. He saw that she kept looking back to Rianne and wondered what was going on. When she saw the moment was right, the drunken crowd focused on her alone, Da'Leth motioned for Richard to steal Rianne away.

As his sister neared him Nicholas saw the fear and the tears in her eyes and his heart went out to her, the poor girl naïve about how rowdy a pub could become. Ordering Richard to take her back to the inn they had decided to stay at for the night Nicholas turned his attention back to Da'Leth, not letting her out of his sight until she was off the bar and making her way through the crowd toward the door. More than once she was stopped and had to force her way past the man that had grabbed her. By the time she reached the door Da'Leth had had enough and forcibly shoved the next man that grabbed her.

Walking past Nicholas in silence Da'Leth turned towards the area their tent had been set up. Touching her shoulder gently he motioned in the other direction towards the inn. Without a sound she turned and headed in that direction. Walking side by side, neither one speaking, Nicholas looked over to see tears on Da'Leth's face. Stopping her he reached out gently to wipe them away.

"I had hoped I'd never have to do that again," she said at last, her voice tired and ashamed. Refusing to meet his eyes Da'Leth shook her head. "I'm sorry."

"You don't need to apologize," Nicholas told her. "You were trying to rescue my sister. I'm not happy that it had to be done, but it's over now."

Raising her eyes to his Da'Leth closed them suddenly, swaying on her feet. "Oh no!" she whispered.

Reaching out to catch her Nicholas frowned with concern. "What's wrong, are you hurt?"

"Not yet, I will be in the morning though," she answered honestly.

"I don't understand."

"Beatrice forgot to cut the ale with water." Still frowning he shook his head in confusion. "I don't drink ale, milord. That tankard was full."

Staring down at her a smile began to pull at his lips. "You're drunk," he grinned.

"Not yet," she sighed. "But I will be soon."

Laughing at the hopelessness in her voice Nicholas put an arm over her shoulder and squeezed her gently, leading her to the inn. Once they were safely in their room he explained the situation to Richard, the captain smiling when he heard about a drunken Da'Leth, before checking on his sister.

"Oh Nicholas!" she cried, running to him. "I don't ever want to go through that again!"

"Then stay away from pub's," he said firmly. "There was a reason I said we wouldn't go in there."

"I'm sorry," she said softly. Looking over at Da'Leth she left her own shame alone for a moment to focus on the woman that had rescued her. "What's wrong with Da'Leth?"

Turning Nicholas saw Da'Leth lying on the bed, her arms flung over her head as she stared at the ceiling with a glazed look on her face. "She'll be all right in the morning. Richard, why don't you and Rianne go for a walk and get some food for us?"

Nodding he helped the Princess to her feet, escorting her out the door. Glancing at Da'Leth one more time before he left he smiled. He was in her debt for what she had done for him tonight.

Waiting until the door was shut behind them Nicholas sat down on the bed next to Da'Leth, smiling down at her. "How do you feel?"

"Da'Leth is numb," she smiled, her eyes glassy. They were beginning to droop shut as she fell asleep. "You?"

"I'm well enough," he chuckled. Realizing now might be the only time he could get a straight answer from Da'Leth Nicholas asked the question that had been burning in his mind all day long. "Da'Leth," he said softly, leaning closer. "Do you love me?"

"No," she said after a moment of silence. "Da'Leth isn't allowed to love the Prince." Nicholas' heart sank at her words but he wondered if that meant she didn't love him or had simply stopped herself from admitting that she loved him. "But," she said, speaking again after a long period of silence, "Josephine loves Nicholas very much."

Confused he prodded, "What do you mean? Aren't you Josephine?" She nodded sleepily, her eyes almost shut. "Why is there a difference? Why can Josephine love me but Da'Leth can't?"

"Da'Leth lives but she's not allowed to love," she yawned, her words slurred and she was nearly asleep. "Josephine loves, but she's not allowed to live."

"What are you talking about? Why can't you allow yourself to love me?"

"Josephine is dead," she mumbled before falling asleep.

Sitting on the bed, frustrated and confused, Nicholas watched her sleeping, her words running through his head like a herd of stampeding horses. Da'Leth didn't love him but Josephine did. It didn't make any sense; Da'Leth and Josephine was the same person. Reaching out he brushed his fingers over her hair leaning down to gently kiss her cheek before getting up. After covering her with a blanket he sat down in a chair across the room to think over what she had said, watching as she slept.

Chapter Fifteen

Pain.

It was the first things she knew as she began to wake. Her head felt thick, filled with cotton, and the tips of her hair hurt. Something had happened last night, she could remember that much. She had been in the street talking, Beatrice had approached and ... 'What happened then?' she thought, trying to recall the next event. Talking, Beatrice, Rianne...

"Milady!" she gasped, sitting upright and regretting it instantly. Moaning with pain she put her hands on her head, trying to stop the pain from pounding behind her eyes and ringing in her ears.

"She's all right."

"Please don't yell," Da'Leth groaned, frowning as she tried to open her eyes, shutting them quickly when she saw the light streaming in through the window that was spinning around the room.

"My apologies," Nicholas whispered. Smiling, struggling not to laugh, he got up from his chair and, picking up a small teacup, approached Da'Leth. "Here, Beatrice said it would help." Sitting on the bed he handed her the teacup and waited for her to drink. "Better?"

"No," she admitted. "It takes time to go away."

Sitting next to her, watching her put her head back in her hands, Nicholas sympathized with her pain. He'd woken the next morning with a bad headache a time or two. Her hands covered her face, obscuring Da'Leth from his view and he reached out, pulling on them a little so he could see her.

"Is there anything you need?"

"Only to be blind and deaf until the pain has passed."

At that he did laugh, stopping when he saw her wince. "I'm sorry," he whispered. "Stay up here and rest, when you are ready to leave we shall be downstairs."

"I can be ready now, milord," she replied, not wanting to be the reason they were still there.

"Don't be silly, you're in too much pain to travel. Besides, Rianne is still looking over the local merchants' wares. I doubt she'll be back before the morning is over. Rest, Da'Leth, you need it."

Without a sound she finished the tea Beatrice had made for her and sank back into the pillows. She felt Nicholas lay the blanket back over her before falling back to sleep to escape the pounding in her head. Spending the next few hours in a dreamless sleep Da'Leth awoke, her headache almost gone and the room standing still, to find the room empty. Getting out of the bed, dressing quickly, she went downstairs to see Nicholas sitting by the fire, Richard and Rianne nowhere to be seen.

"Milord?"

Lifting his gaze from the fire Nicholas smiled as she approached. "How do you feel?"

"Much better now, thank you." Sitting down in a chair opposite him she asked, "Where is your sister?"

"Out walking with Richard. Those two are getting closer with every passing day."

"Is that bad?" she asked, unable to tell his feelings on the matter from the tone of his voice.

Frowning he replied, "Bad? No, but it is going to cause some difficulties as far as my father is concerned. He wants her to marry a man of proper station. Richard is not one of them."

"Love will win out in the end," she said confidently. "If they truly love each other everything will find a way to work out."

"You sound as if you are certain of that."

"I am."

Regarding her for a moment Nicholas decided not to press the issue, he had something more important on his mind. "Josephine," he began, watching as she froze in her place, reaching for a piece of bread one of the serfs had placed by her chair. "You made an interesting comment last night that I cannot seem to figure out."

Bringing an empty hand back to her lap Da'Leth sat still, tense in her chair. "Milord?"

"You said that Da'Leth can live but not love whereas Josephine can love but not live. What did you mean by that?"

Wide eyes rose up to meet his and Nicholas could see that he had scared her with his comment. "Did I say anything else, milord?"

"Only that Josephine is dead. I don't understand. Your name is Josephine but you speak of yourself as if Josephine and Da'Leth were two different people. Why?"

"Milord," she said with a small forced laugh, shrugging her shoulders. "I was drunk."

She offered no further explanation and Nicholas doubted she would give him a firm reason even if he pressed her for it. "Da'Leth, I want to know you, all of you, but I don't want to force you to tell me what you are not ready to reveal." Relief filled her face and he frowned. "I don't understand why you keep a part of yourself a secret but you must have a reason for it. All I ask is that you be honest with me. If there is another man then you need to..."

"No," she said quickly. "There is no one else, milord. There never has been," she paused for a brief moment before continuing, "And there never will be."

Meeting her eyes with his own Nicholas could see that she was telling the truth and his heart soared with hope. Opening his mouth to ask why then she would not allow herself to love him he never got the chance to speak. Her voice was soft and he could hear the effort she was taking to keep it under control.

"You ask that I be honest with you and I shall. My life is not all that it seems, that much you have already deduced. The part of myself that I hide I do so not out of spite but out of necessity. There are five other people in this world who know my secret and all of them are bound to keep it a secret. Three were responsible for what was done to me, one was an innocent bystander, and one recognized me because I look like my mother. Until I can find a way to fix what was done I cannot allow any more to know the secret I have carried with me for the last fifteen years. As much as I wish it could be otherwise that includes you."

Silence fell as he tried to take in what she had said. Finally, he sat forward, reaching out to take her hand in his. "However long it takes, I shall wait, Da'Leth."

Tears filled her eyes at his promise. "I cannot ask that of you," she choked, shaking her head. "You have a responsibility to marry and continue the family line. I do not know how long it will take to..."

Nicholas cut her off, placing a hand over her mouth as he knelt in front of her. "I don't care how long it takes Da'Leth. 'Love will win out in the end', remember?" Wiping away the tears that had fallen from her eyes he kissed the hands that he held in his own. "Let me help you, let me talk to my father about setting you free."

"No," she said, clearing her throat and wiping her eyes. "No, I must earn it or I will never be able to prove that was done was undeserved."

"You mean being sold as a serf," he realized. "Nothing you could have done would have deserved that, Da'Leth."

"Perhaps not, but I will not allow my father's memory to be tarnished with the knowledge that his daughter was sold as a serf. His memory is all I have left, it matters more to me than anything."

"Even me?" Nicholas asked.

She was silent for a moment, searching his face. "Please do not make me chose between my father's honor and you."

"I'm sorry," he sighed. "That was unfair of me." Closing his eyes for a moment he stood, pulling Da'Leth to her feet. "We need to get underway. Perhaps you could find my sister for me? I need to attend to some business with Edward."

"Of course, milord," she said, sensing that they both needed some space to absorb all that had happened.

Asking one of the serfs which way Rianne had gone she headed off in that direction. As she walked her heart varied between soaring with happiness at the knowledge that he loved her and plummeting with despair over the same fact. So long as she was a serf nothing could ever happen between them and the pain of that knowledge was getting harder to deal with every day.

Caught up in her own thoughts Da'Leth didn't hear Richard calling her until he put a hand on her shoulder. Turning she blinked in surprise to see him standing before her. "Are you all right?" he asked, concern tingeing his voice.

"I am well," she nodded. "Milord has sent me to find you; he says it is time to leave."

Richard nodded. "She is in that shop," pointing to the doorway a few paces away. "Will you wait for her so I may go help him?"

"Of course," Da'Leth agreed. Watching him leave for a moment Da'Leth moved into the shop to find Rianne. Telling her it was time to go she waited while the Princess finished her business, paying the shopkeeper and picking up a small package before leaving with Da'Leth to walk back to the inn.

Rianne purposefully kept their pace slow, wanting to talk with Da'Leth while they were alone. "Are you feeling better?" she asked, seeing the red eyes she was trying to keep hidden.

"I am, milady, thank you. The tea I was given earlier has done its work."

"I'm glad to hear it. I didn't have a chance to thank you for what you did last night."

"I am glad you were not harmed but milady, I beg of you, please stay away from such places."

Rianne nodded. "I have no desire to ever go into another pub for as long as I live."

"That is good to hear," she smiled, hearing the disgust in Rianne's voice.

"I feel as though it has been a long time since we last spoke," she said. "So much has been going on lately."

"It does seem to have been a long time." Sensing there was something on her mind Da'Leth asked, "Is there something you wished to discuss?"

"Have you ever been in love, Da'Leth?" Thinking about Nicholas Da'Leth nodded. "I think I may be falling in love but I can't be sure."

"Why do you believe you are?"

Rianne sighed. "I enjoy spending time with him, he is so very kind, a perfect gentleman." Smiling as she thought about him

Rianne continued, "His eyes are beautiful, he's a handsome man to be sure, but I feel as though his eyes can see to the very core of my heart."

"How long have you felt this way about Richard?"

"How did you know?" she asked, stopping still in shock. "I've never spoke a word of this to anyone!"

"Milady," Da'Leth smiled, "You have been spending so much time with him, preferring his company over anyone else's. It was he that you turned to for comfort after last night and he that you take all of your meals with now. I have seen this coming for quite some time now."

"And what do you think of it?" Rianne asked, wondering what she thought.

"I believe that he loves you as much as you love him. You are a good match to each other."

A broad smile filled Rianne's face as she listened to Da'Leth's opinion. "I'm so glad!"

Reaching the inn, they saw the carriage waiting, Nicholas and Richard standing outside watching for them. Letting the Princess step inside first Da'Leth was about to join her when she heard Beatrice calling her name.

"Thank you for everything," she cried, hugging her friend goodbye. "Here, I have written down the master's address. He says it will be all right if you were to write to me. Please, stay in touch. I don't want to worry about you."

Promising she would write soon Da'Leth hugged her friend again before turning back to the carriage to see Nicholas waiting for her. Smiling at him she stepped into the carriage. Taking her seat across from Rianne she couldn't help but smile sadly as the carriage got underway. Two women, two men, each one in love with the one they weren't supposed to love and yet unable to stop themselves.

~~*~*~*~*~*~*~*

In the stables Da'Leth watched the squires as they saddled a horse for the joust. Off to the side Nicholas stood with Richard, putting the finishing touches on his armor while Rianne waited nearby with his helmet. She could feel him watching her and wondered what was going through his mind. The journey to Petithome had been uneventful, leisurely almost, and when they arrived they had been the first to do so, the other knights still traveling from the previous joust.

Standing still while Richard finished adjusting his armor Nicholas smiled when he realized something about Da'Leth he'd never noticed before. "She doesn't like horses," he whispered to Richard. "Look at the way she keeps away from them."

Watching the squire lead the horse down the aisle he saw Da'Leth step well out of the way. "I never noticed that before," he admitted. "I wonder why?"

Unable to finish their conversation, Lord Timothy being called to the jousting arena, Nicholas put the question to the back of his mind. Sitting on his horse, waiting for the flag to drop, Nicholas found her in the stands. She was watching him carefully as she always did and he smiled inside of his helmet, a thought coming into his mind. When he had won the joust, three lances to two, Nicholas returned to the stables with his horse, telling the squires to make sure there was a horse available for use tonight after the evening meal.

Making his way to their tent he found Da'Leth alone, Richard and Rianne off walking through the square. Sitting down in a chair he smiled when she began to gather her basket without being asked. His shirt in a pile on the ground by his feet Nicholas felt her approach him from behind. Without a word he felt the warm oil drip onto his shoulders, her gentle fingers massaging it into his skin. Putting his head on the back of the chair he closed his eyes content to enjoy the soothing touch of her hands.

When she was finished with his shoulders Da'Leth moved to his back, careful to avoid the wound on his side. Though it was almost healed she knew it still caused pain and wrapped it every night with an herbal paste. 'At least I don't have to drink it,' he thought to himself with a smile.

"Do you find something funny, milord?" she asked softly, seeing the smile on his face.

"Only thankful for the little blessings," he answered. Opening his eyes, he looked back to see her watching him. "And the big ones."

A blush rose to her cheeks as she turned her attention back to her work. Still watching her he saw a smile pull at her lips and he grinned. Closing his eyes Nicholas sat contentedly until she was done, listening as she moved away, picking up his shirt to dust the dirt off before holding it out to him. Getting to his feet he took the shirt from her, pulling it on. Standing still, silently staring at her Nicholas smiled when she was forced to look away, unable to hold his gaze for more than a few moments.

"Would you like to take a walk?" he asked.

Her eyes met his once more and she nodded, quietly following him out of the tent. Through the town toward the open fields they had passed on the way into town a few days ago. The grasses had grown tall in the field, brushing against them past their knees as they walked through the fields. Nicholas stopped in the middle of one of the fields and sat down, motioning for Da'Leth to do the same.

Waiting for a few moments to see if she would speak he did when it became clear she wasn't going to. "Tell me something if you wish," he began, making it clear that it was an optional question. "Why don't you like horses?"

She frowned. "Why do you think I don't like horses?"

"You make sure to steer clear of them when they are near you. I've never seen you touch one of your own will. At times you seem almost skittish around them. I'm curious as to why."

"They're such large creatures," she shrugged. "They can kill people."

"Is that why you don't like them?"

"It's not that I don't like them, milord, it's just that I have never had much exposure to them since I was a little girl."

"When you were a child? Did you feel differently then?"

Da'Leth nodded. "My father used to take me riding through the fields after dinner when the sun was setting. Sometimes we would go when the moon was bright as day. Mother would watch from the window and wave when we turned to face her."

Nicholas could see the happiness in the memory and it furthered his resolve to break Da'Leth of her concern about horses. Spending the rest of the day in the fields, talking, sharing stories about their childhood, the pair walked back toward the tents in time to meet Richard and Rianne for the evening meal. When the night stars had emerged, the moon high in the sky, Nicholas looked across the tent to see Da'Leth working on some mending. Asking her to put it down and come with him he could see the questions in her eyes.

He didn't say anything to her, sensing her curiosity as they approached the stables. When one of the squires emerged with a horse in tow she finally asked what was going on. "You'll see," he said with a smile, enjoying the fact that she had no idea what was going on. "Come here."

Raising an eyebrow at him Da'Leth moved closer, gasping with surprise when he suddenly grabbed her, lifting her up to sit on the horse. Clinging to the saddle Da'Leth didn't relax her grip until Nicholas had climbed up to sit behind her, wrapping his arms around her as he took the reins. Encased in his arms Da'Leth had begun to relax a little when he spurred the horse into action. Grabbing the saddle again she clung to it, unsure of the movement all around her.

"Relax, Da'Leth, you're safe."

Her heart hammering in her chest Da'Leth did as she was told, relaxing her grip on the saddle. Trotting through the square she could see that they were heading towards the fields they had spent the afternoon in and she realized what he was doing. A smile pulled at her lips and Da'Leth turned back to look at him. Meeting her gaze Nicholas grinned back and when they reached the edge of town he spurred the horse into a faster gait until they were galloping through the fields.

Holding her arms out at her sides, secure in the knowledge that she was safe in Nicholas's arms, Da'Leth closed her eyes and felt the wind whipping past her. Feeling as though she were flying she smiled, laughing when he suddenly changed direction, heading along the outskirts of a small forest at the edge of the fields. Racing past the trees they ran as long and as far as they could, stopping to give the horse a break when they reached the end of the forest.

"That was fun!" she laughed breathlessly.

Laughing Nicholas turned the horse back towards the town, letting the horse walk at an easy pace. "You see, not so scary when you ride them."

Da'Leth smiled, turning to look back at him. "Thank you," she whispered.

Sitting as close as they were she could see the flecks of color in his eyes and feel his breath of her face. Her heart stopped in her chest and Da'Leth held her breath, knowing she should turn back around but unable and unwilling to do so.

Nicholas stared down at her, feeling her chest rise and fall with each breath between his arms, seeing the laughter in her eyes and he fought the urge to kiss her, unsure of how she would react, not wanting to ruin the peace of the moment. Smiling at her he took her hands in his, placing the reigns in them. "Your turn," he grinned.

Her eyes widened for a moment before she turned to face front again. "I can't do this!" she claimed, trying to hand the reigns back to him.

"Yes, you can," refusing to let her give them back. "Just do as I say and he'll take us back to the town. Now hold them like this," putting her hands in the proper position, "And if you want him to stop simply pull back on them to let him know what you want."

Terrified at first, she soon picked up on the knack of holding the reigns and began to calm down. 'This isn't so bad,' she thought to herself. Going along she looked out ahead of them and saw a bush looming a little way away. "How do I make him turn?"

"No horse is going to walk into something if it can avoid it, but if you want to make him turn pull on the reigns in the direction you want him to go."

Doing as she was instructed Da'Leth smiled when she successfully averted hitting the bush. Making it back to town under Nicholas's guidance she pulled on the reigns just outside of the stables and they came to a stop. Sitting still Da'Leth was silent in wonder. "I just rode a horse," she said at last, her voice filled with awe.

"And you did very well," he praised. Swinging down from the horse he reached up and helped Da'Leth to get down, his hands lingering on her sides a little longer than needed. Instructing the squire to put the horse away he took Da'Leth's hand in his and led her into the stable. "Pick one."

"What?" she asked in shock.

Nicholas repeated himself. "Pick a horse that you like."

Looking over all of them she saw one in the far corner that was watching her. While the rest of the horses were moving about or whinnying this one stood still, simply watching her with its big brown eyes. "I like that one," she said, pointing to it.

Curious, "Why that one?" he frowned.

"It looks like it has a big heart," she explained. "And it's quiet."

"Her name is Nadia," he said, walking towards the stall. "Starting tomorrow you will be learning to ride her. We'll have lessons every night until you are comfortable to ride her on your own, without anyone else around."

"Milord, you don't need to," she began, cut off when he held up a hand.

"I know I don't need to," Nicholas told her. "I want to."

Thanking him Da'Leth gave Nadia one last look before they walked out of the stables. Walking towards their tent at a leisurely pace neither spoke, each one aware of the fact that their hands were still joined together, not wanting to break the contact. When they reached the tent Nicholas stopped, holding Da'Leth's hand to prevent her from going in.

"I had fun tonight," he told her.

"As did I," meeting his tender gaze. She could see the love in his eyes and it made her heart hurt with a bittersweet pain. "Thank you, milord."

"Do you think, perhaps when it is just you and I, you might call me Nicholas?"

She was silent for some time and he wondered if she was going to reply at all. When Da'Leth finally spoke, he could hear the longing in her voice. "I want to, very much," she admitted. "But so long as I am a serf I cannot."

Before she turned away he saw the tears shimmering in her eyes and he let her go. With a frustrated sigh Nicholas ran a hand through his hair and glanced around him. With Da'Leth gone his senses became aware of what was around him. Scrutinizing the area, he couldn't find anything out of place but a bad feeling began to creep over him. He had suspected something in Paris but hadn't been sure. Now though he knew without a doubt, the feeling hitting him deep in his gut. It was the same thing he had felt when the barn had collapsed at the palace, the same feeling that had frozen his heart when he saw the carriage attacked in the road.

They'd found him again.

~~*~*~*~*~*~*~*

Da'Leth woke to see Richard and Nicholas deep in discussion on their side of the tent. From the seriousness on their faces she knew something was wrong and sat up. The movement caught Nicholas's attention and he looked over. She was a beautiful sight in the morning, her face still somewhat sleepy as she tried to wake to the world around her. This morning though he could see that she was wide awake and concerned. He motioned for her to come over to them.

"We will be leaving this morning while the rest of the city is at the joust."

Frowning she was about to ask why when the reason became clear. "They've found you, haven't they?"

Nicholas nodded. "I had hoped we could make it through this joust before heading to the manor but it has become clear that we can't."

"Will they be able to follow us to the manor?" she asked, mentally reviewing their options.

"No, we'll create a diversion and slip out a different way. No one knows about the manor, it is a closely guarded secret."

"What do you need me to do?"

"Take care that Rianne does not suspect anything. Both of you will need to dress in breeches so you can travel on a horse. We'll send the carriage one way and slip out the other to circle around to the manor. We should be able to reach the manor in a few days. Edward and the squires will go with the carriage so it will only be the four of us."

Nodding Da'Leth left them to finish their planning and hurried to do what she would need to have everything ready for travel. Pulling two pairs of breeches from the men's trunk she altered them so they would fit Rianne and herself, fixing two of the shirts as well. By the time Rianne woke an hour later the clothes were ready, the necessities packed for travel.

"Milady, please trust me," Da'Leth said, asking her to dress in the shirt and breeches.

Unsure of what was going on, but knowing better than to doubt Da'Leth, Rianne dressed quickly, allowing Da'Leth to do her hair in a tight bun before placing a hat on her head. When she was done Rianne saw Richard waiting in the entrance of the tent, Nicholas nowhere to be seen. She could sense that something was wrong. "What is it, Richard?" she asked. "What's going on?"

"We'll be leaving in a few moments, milady. You shall ride with me," turning to Da'Leth he continued, "Nicholas has asked that you ride with him, he has a small task he needs you to help him with."

Nodding, curious, Da'Leth went with Rianne and Richard to the stables. Nicholas was already there, Nadia loaded with supplies while his own horse waited nearby ready to be ridden. Pulling his sister close Nicholas hugged her for a moment. "Go with Richard, and do exactly as he says," he told her. "We shall meet again at the manor in a few days."

"You're scaring me," she said, her eyes wide.

"I promise, I shall explain when I am sure we are safe. Until then do as your told."

Kissing her forehead Nicholas helped her into the saddle, Richard climbing up behind her, and they left, heading out the back of town. Watching them go Nicholas hoped he was doing the right thing. Forcing himself to get back to work he turned to see Da'Leth watching him. Her face was serious, concern in her eyes, yet she was calm and he was grateful for it.

"I need your help, Da'Leth, and I hope that this ruse of mine will work."

"What do you need me to do?"

"Put these on so you look like a serf."

Taking the skirt from him she put it on and placed the dirty tunic over her shirt to hide the good condition of the material. Facing him again she waited for more instruction.

"Here, take this," handing her a small pouch. "Go into town and buy a large bottle of wine, make sure it is known that you are buying it for your master, Lord Timothy. When you return to the tent give the bottle to the squire, remove your costume, and slip out the back; meet me in the fields where we were riding last night. Make sure no one sees you leave the tent."

Confused she did as he asked, buying the bottle of wine and returning to the tent. Giving the bottle to the squire her eyes widened when she saw four people lying in each of their beds, dead. Slipping out the back she hurried to the fields, dropping the tunic and skirt as she ran. As she reached Nicholas, the Prince waiting with the horses, she looked back toward the town to see a large black cloud of smoke rising up into the sky.

"Let's go."

Helping her onto the horse Nicholas climbed into the saddle behind her and they left, hurrying away as fast as they could. When they were a good deal away from the town Da'Leth turned to look at him, a question burning in her eyes. "Milord," she began, unsure how to phrase her question.

"They died from a fever the night before. Their families had not yet had time to bury them."

"I don't understand."

"They knew the name I was jousting under," he explained. "Every tournament I use a different name so no one will recognize the name from the previous year. Somehow, he found me as he did when I was jousting as Lord Richmond. I am hoping that if I can convince him we died in the fire it will give us enough of a head start to get away."

"All he need do is inquire if the Prince and Princess have been declared dead and he will know the truth," she reasoned.

"I know. It is not a permanent solution but it is enough to get us away to the manor." Nicholas sighed. "I should not have let Rianne come along."

"Why did you?"

"She wouldn't let the subject drop. I was afraid that if I did not allow her to travel with me she would travel without me, unprotected."

"She would be safer with you than without you."

He nodded, "Exactly."

They fell silent for a little while before Da'Leth asked a question she had thought about a few times before. "What are you going to do?"

"What do you mean?"

"You cannot run from him forever."

Nicholas didn't reply. Turning to look at him she saw the seriousness in his eyes and knew it was something he had given thought to before. "I don't know. He's reacting out of pain, vengeance, but he has a right to it; his daughter was killed."

"Not by you!"

"I know that, but he doesn't."

"Have you ever tried to tell him?"

"Once," he nodded. "He refused to listen."

"What happened?"

"It was back when he almost killed me. I tried to tell him what happened that morning, what I had seen. But," he sighed with frustration. "It was no use; he refused to hear anything I said."

Still facing him Da'Leth wished there was something she could say, something, anything that would take the pain away, lift the burden from his shoulders. Deep down she knew there was nothing she could do, no way to help. She could do many things, had many skills, many answers, but this was not one of them. Turning back around Da'Leth watched the horizon approach, placing her hands around his arm, knowing that holding him that way was the only comfort she could give.

They rode in silence for many hours, making a turn off the road, disappearing deep into the forest, until Nicholas finally pulled the horses to a stop at a good-sized clearing, the sun nearly set in the horizon. Getting down he lifted Da'Leth to the ground, unsaddling the horses and setting them on a line to graze in the field. When he turned back he saw that she had already gathered a stone ring, filling it with wood for a small fire and was working two sticks together to make a flame.

Kneeling down next to her he put his hands over hers, stilling them. "No fire," meeting her eyes. "I don't want to run the risk he'd be able to find us."

"The night will get cool."

"We should get to sleep, it's a long ride to the manor tomorrow," Nicholas whispered.

Setting the sticks down he sat back against a log she had pulled toward the stone ring. Bringing Da'Leth with him he silently wrapped his arms around her, shifting until they were both comfortable. As the day dissolved into night and the chill began to set into the air around them they felt none of it, warmed by the person they shared the night with. Both knew they should separate, sleep apart in the cool night air, but both were unwilling to break the forbidden contact.

Her head resting on his chest, the sound of his hearts steady beat beneath her ears, Da'Leth fell asleep.

~~*~*~*~*~*~*~*

They were almost to the manor.

Da'Leth had no idea specifically where they were, the scenery around her was unfamiliar, but she could feel the tenseness begin to seep out of Nicholas and knew they had to be close. The sun was just starting to set when she saw the tips of the roof peeking through the trees. With a relieved sigh she watched it come closer, growing in size as they approached. By the time they had entered the courtyard the sun was almost set and torches had been lit by the front door to guide them to it.

"Home at last," Nicholas smiled as he dismounted from the horse.

Reaching up he set Da'Leth on her feet and heard, "Safe and sound."

Smiling at Nicholas she followed him inside the manor, searching out Richard and Rianne, finding them in the main room by the fire. Glad that they were both safe Nicholas sat down while the servants piled more food on the table. When he'd had a chance to eat and drink he turned to his sister, seeing her impatience growing with each passing minute.

"How much were you able to get out of Richard?" he asked. "I know you tried."

"Tried and failed!" Rianne groused. Demanding, "Tell me now, Nicholas, what is going on?" she waited for him to begin his story.

From the beginning Nicholas told his sister what had happened, leaving out many of the details but allowing her to gather the full extent of the situation. Watching Rianne from her seat Da'Leth could see her worry begin to grow, not for herself but for her brother. "He's going to kill you!"

"Not if I have a say in the matter," Nicholas replied.

"Nor I," Richard and Da'Leth announced at the same time, conviction in their voices. Richard continued, "Milady, we shall do all that we can to see to it that your brother is kept safe."

Looking up at him she nodded. "I know, but everything that has been happening, is it because of this man? The stables, the attack on the road?"

"Yes," Nicholas admitted. "That is why I did not want you to come for the tournament; you are safer if you are not around me."

"Your brother puts the safety of his family above his own, milady," Da'Leth said gently. "It is why he spends so little time at the palace and so much traveling the roads, never staying in one place for too long a period of time."

Silence fell as Rianne tried to absorb everything she had been told. Seeing that she was trying to come to terms with the fact that she could very well lose her brother Da'Leth reached over to take her hand, squeezing it gently to help assure her everything would be all right in the end. A small smile flitted across her face as she met Da'Leth's eyes but Rianne couldn't hold it and it slipped away again.

"I think I need to go for a walk," she announced, getting to her feet.

"I'll come with you," Nicholas said, standing with her.

Walking out of the room, his arm around her shoulders, they left Richard and Da'Leth to watch them leave. With a small sigh Richard leaned back in his chair, staring out at nothing, his hands templed in front of his face. Drawing her knees up to her chin Da'Leth stared at the fire, thinking over everything that had happened in the last few days.

It shamed her to admit it but she had forgotten about the father that was trying to kill the Prince. It had been so many months since the incident at the stables that it had slipped out of her mind, neither the Prince nor Richard ever mentioning it. She was worried about Nicholas, worried that this would keep on going forever, him running and the father chasing. "He deserves better."

"Pardon?"

Glancing up, realizing she must have spoken out loud, Da'Leth shook her head. "Just thinking to myself."

Nodding he met her gaze. "Myself as well," he admitted. "I'm worried about Rianne. This is going to be hard for her to bear."

"You'll be there to support her," Da'Leth assured him. "She trusts you."

Frowning he stared at Da'Leth. "You know, I assume?"

"That you love her? Yes, I've known for a while now."

"When did you realize it?"

"The last time we were here," she explained. "I knew there was a woman but it wasn't until a few days after the ball that I realized who it was."

"What gave me away?"

"Nothing in particular," shrugging as she recalled the moment she realized. "I suppose it was just seeing the care and concern with which you treated the Princess."

Richard said nothing, simply nodding his head as he stared at nothing. She could sense his helplessness at the situation and sympathized. "Don't give up, Richard. If you truly love her then tell her so and see what..."

"I already have."

"And?" she prompted.

"She says she loves me as well." Richard met her smile sadly. "But what is the use? She is a Princess; I am a Captain of the Guard. Nothing will ever be allowed to come of it."

"You mustn't give up so easily," Da'Leth admonished. "My father used to say that honor will return to itself. Do the honorable thing, Richard, and the honor will be given to you in return."

Confused Richard frowned at her but Da'Leth said nothing more, afraid she had already said too much. Wishing her a good night's sleep he left the room, heading up to his chamber to think.

Watching him leave she hoped he would ask the King for Rianne's hand, knowing it would work out for them if they were truly in love.

Sitting before the fire Da'Leth's mind drifted back to that morning, the feeling of waking in Nicholas's arms. Closing her eyes, she could still feel the warm strength wrapped around her, protecting her from the chill in the early morning air. She had known she should move, free herself from the prison of pain her heart was trapped in, but she didn't, she had closed her eyes again and stayed where she was lying.

Dropping her head to her knees she closed her eyes, her mind willing the feeling to go away but her heart not wanting to let go. Her heart longed to love him but her mind refused, knowing it would only cause more pain than joy. There were other things to focus on, more important matters to be taken care of.

With a resigned sigh she stood, dousing the fire and leaving the room to get some sleep. As Da'Leth laid her head on the pillow, pulling the blankets over her, she blinked away a tear, missing the sound of his heart beating in her ear.

~~*~*~*~*~*~*~*

Under the shade of a large tree, fanning herself with a small fan Rianne had given her, Da'Leth heard someone approaching. "Enjoying the heat?"

"I never do," she admitted.

"I prefer the cold myself, winter is my favorite season."

"And yet you choose the hottest season of the year to get dressed in a metal suit of armor and joust under a blaring sun."

Nicholas laughed. "True. I must be daft."

"Your choice of words, milord, not mine."

Grinning Nicholas reclined on the shaded grass next to Da'Leth. "Then may I assume you don't want your next lesson?"

"Perhaps it can wait until the sun has set and the temperature has cooled somewhat?"

"Agreed."

They fell into a comfortable silence, too hot to talk, enjoying each other's company. Dozing in the summer shade Nicholas was startled awake by moans to his left. Opening his eyes, he looked over to see that Da'Leth too had fallen asleep but was having a nightmare, her face scrunched with pain as she moved her head from side to side. Her hands clutched the fan she had been holding and before he could move to wake her the wooden handle snapped under the pressure of her grip.

"Da'Leth," he called out to her, getting to his knees to take hold of her. "Da'Leth, wake up."

Giving her a gentle shake, Nicholas watched her jump in her skin, waking from her nightmare, chest heaving from it. Startled she grabbed at his arms, stopping when she saw who was holding her in place. "Milord?"

"You were having a nightmare," Nicholas explained. Sitting down he took her hands in his, placing the broken fan on the ground next to her. "What was it?"

"I don't remember," she shook her head. "I'm sorry."

"Nothing to be sorry for; you've done nothing wrong."

Closing her eyes, she took a few deep breaths to calm her nerves and catch her breath. Da'Leth could feel his hands covering hers and though her heart screamed at her not to do it, pulled them from his grasp. "Thank you for waking me."

Wanting to take her hands back in his Nicholas only nodded. "I'm glad you don't remember it. I hate remembering my nightmares."

"Why?"

"Being scared is not something I enjoy."

"I prefer to know what it was."

Nicholas frowned. "Really?"

"Yes," nodding. "I prefer to know so that I can conquer whatever it is that frightens me. There are too many things I cannot control but I refuse to allow fear to be one of them."

"Then the question begs to be asked, what frightens Da'Leth?"

She smiled. "You."

"Me?" he repeated in shock. "How do I frighten you?"

Da'Leth regarded him for some time in silence, trying to form in her mind the right words to say. "You make it too easy for me to forget. To forget what I am, where I am, why I am in such a place. I am afraid that one day I will forget the thing I have been fighting for my entire life."

"What have you been fighting for?"

"To go home," she answered honestly. "To find my family again; to attain justice for what has been done to us."

Before Nicholas could reply Da'Leth closed her eyes, putting her hand to her temple with a frown.

"And I am terrified of the way you are able to get answers from me that no one else can."

Nicholas wanted to smile at the frustration in her voice but he couldn't. "You could tell me the truth," he said after a moment. "Whatever it is I can help you."

Dropping her hand to her lap she looked at him. "I have never lied to you."

He heard the offense in her voice and shook his head. "I know that, but you do not tell me everything either. How can I help you if you will not tell me everything?"

"No one can help me," she said with a sigh. "Not yet. But I give you my word," reaching out to take his hand in hers. "When the time has come, when Da'Leth is dead and Josephine is free to live again, you shall be the first to know the secret I keep."

Wanting more, knowing he wouldn't get it, Nicholas nodded, forced to accept that he could not have the answers he wanted. Bringing her hand to his lips he kissed it, pleased at the blush that spread over Da'Leth's cheeks. "If I must wait I shall," he said. "But do not expect me to like it."

Chapter Sixteen

Sitting in the carriage as it bounced along the road Da'Leth looked down at her lap with a smile, Rianne's feet resting in her lap as she slept in the seat across from her. They had been traveling back to the palace for a few days now, they would arrive by the end of the day and she was glad. On the road there were far too many opportunities for an enemy to capture them. At the palace, though there was still some danger, it was far less with the guard all around the royal family.

The two weeks they had spent at the manor, hidden away from the rest of the world, had been relaxing. The four friends had spent their days lounging and their nights talking, passing the time quickly. Each day before the sun could rise to its peak, Nicholas had schooled her to ride Nadia without fear. But when a letter had arrived from the palace asking them to come home Nicholas realized it was time to go, no doubt the word of Lord Timothy's death had reached his parents.

The carriage was silent, Richard staring out the window lost in his own thoughts while Rianne slept on his shoulder. Next to her Nicholas was also silent; though his eyes were closed she could tell he was awake, his thumb circling the inside of her palm. She had tried to take her hand away when he had taken it the first time but Nicholas had refused to release it.

Since their talk under the tree he had kept his word, never pressing her for information about her past, and for that she was glad. However, Nicholas had also taken to touching her whenever he could. Holding her hand to help her up, leading her in and out of a room with his hand on the small of her back; he was always careful to make sure no one could see, not wanting to cause any trouble for Da'Leth. Though she had fought it at first Da'Leth soon fell under his spell, allowing, and even enjoying, the contact.

As she saw the palace looming before them she wondered how much things were going to change when they returned.

Rubbing a finger over the top of Rianne's foot to wake her up Da'Leth told her they were almost home. By the time the carriage had pulled up to the front door the four riders were ready to disembark. Out of the carriage, up the stairs and down the hall they entered the main room to see Winifred waiting for them alone. When she saw her children alive and well the Queen breathed a sigh of relief.

"What happened?" she demanded when they had said their greetings.

"There was a small situation mother," Nicholas explained. "But I have taken care of it."

Narrowing her eyes, she said nothing for a moment, trying to decide if she was being lied to or not. "Da'Leth," looking towards the one person she knew would not lie. "Is my son telling the truth?"

All eyes turned to her, waiting for her to speak. Frowning at her predicament she chose her words carefully. "In as much as the situation could have been taken care of, it was."

"Then whatever happened may happen again?" she pressed.

"I cannot see the future, my Queen. I can only pray that it does not."

Satisfied for the moment she let the subject drop, promising herself she would speak to Da'Leth again. "Dinner shall be ready soon; perhaps you would all like some time to refresh yourselves before then?"

Thanking her they left the room. Going with Rianne to help her Da'Leth had almost reached the door when she felt someone pull at her arm. "Richard?"

"You have a gift of knowing things that others cannot Da'Leth," he said in a hushed voice. "Tell me please; will I succeed if I ask for Rianne's hand?"

"Tell me why you love her."

Confused he shook his head. "Her innocence," he answered. "Rianne has an inner light that makes her natural beauty glow. If she were she the ugliest woman in the world that light, her love of the world and everyone in it, would make her the most beautiful woman alive."

She listened carefully, hearing more than the words he was saying. "Ask, Richard. If Rianne truly loves you, she will become your bride."

Excitement filled him and Richards face split open with a grin. A moment later it was tempered by logic as he asked, "How can you be so sure?"

Da'Leth smiled. "As you say, I have a gift."

Letting go of her arm, thanking her again, Richard hurried away. In Rianne's chamber Da'Leth worked with the maids to help Rianne bathe and dress, choosing the gown herself. When the Princess was dressed Da'Leth hurried to her own room to bathe and dress, finishing just in time to see Rianne emerging from her chamber. "You look lovely, milady."

"Thank you Da'Leth," she said.

"Milady," Da'Leth pressed, sensing her sadness. "What bothers you?"

Rianne sent the maids away, making sure they were alone in the hallway before speaking. "These last few months have been wonderful, Da'Leth, but now they are over and I must go back to the way things were." She paused for a moment, double checking to make sure they were alone. "How will I stand to see him every day knowing that I can never again be with him the way we were during the tournament?"

"Princess you didn't...?" Da'Leth stopped, finishing the question with her eyes.

"No!" she answered quickly, blushing furiously. "That is not what I meant. We were together every day, talking, laughing. Now though there are too many people about, too many eyes that would see."

Relieved Da'Leth smiled. "As I told your brother, 'Love will win out in the end'. Have faith milady, you shall see."

Not giving her a chance to reply Da'Leth turned them toward the dining hall. Almost past the threshold she stopped when she heard the King calling her. Turning Da'Leth saw Richard walking towards them, King Liam waiting a few feet away, his gaze fixed on Da'Leth. "The King wishes to see you," Richard told her as he neared them. Confusion was written on his face.

Curtsying to Rianne and Richard Da'Leth walked toward the King, her face carefully blank. "Yes, my King?" she said, bowing low when she stopped before him.

"Did you know about this?" he asked, not needing to say what he was talking about. "Is this why you made that request?"

"Not solely," she replied honestly. "My main concern was the Princess's happiness. However, I was aware that he had feelings buried deep for her. That was one of the reasons I wished for it to be maintained as a secret, so as not to force Rianne into any decision she was not yet ready to make."

"And you believe she is ready now?"

Meeting his gaze, she answered honestly. "She loves him."

Matching her gaze Liam sighed. "He is the Captain of the Guard and she is a Princess! There will be much backlash for this decision."

"She is a Princess in love with the Captain of the Guard, yes," Da'Leth nodded. "But who would dare go against your word when you are the King who rules over them all."

Raising an eyebrow at her Liam smirked. "And you are a witch who would seem to have all the answers."

"Only to the problems that are not my own," she smiled.

Telling her to go to the dining hall Liam waved her away, needing a few moments to think over what had been asked of him. With a sigh he entered the dining hall and stood at his place at the head of the table. Capturing the attention of everyone, his family as well as the few members of the court who were dining with them, he spoke.

"Many of you have been wondering when I will find a husband for my youngest daughter, the Princess Rianne. I myself was uncertain of when it would happen, however just today a man has asked for my daughters' hand in marriage. Rianne, come here," motioning for her to stand next to him. When she reached his side, he smiled down at her, "I leave the decision in your hands."

"I don't understand," she frowned, her eyes shimmering with tears at the thought of being married off as her sisters had. "Father, who is the Lord?"

Liam glanced at Da'Leth for a moment before looking at Richard. "He is no Lord," he answered. "Captain, come here."

Getting up from his seat Richard walked over to the father and daughter standing at the head of the tables, his heart pounding in his chest. "Majesty?"

"Rianne, Captain Krausley has acted as a man of honor and has asked me for your hand in marriage. I have given my word that the decision would be yours to make. If you love this man you have my blessing and my permission to marry him."

Rianne's eyes grew wide. "Do you mean...? I am allowed to choose my own husband?" Liam nodded. "No matter whom he is?"

Taking a deep breath, he nodded. "So long as you truly love him" he said, "It does not matter who he is."

The tears that had rested in her eyes began to slide down her cheeks. Throwing her arms around her father she hugged him close. "Thank you, father," she cried. "Thank you!"

Hugging her back he said nothing, praying he had done what was right for his little girl. Over her father's shoulder Rianne saw Richard watching her, an unspoken question in his eyes. Nodding she smiled through her tears. Unable to contain his own joy Richard smiled broadly, reaching out to hold her when Liam had released his daughter.

"You cannot be serious!"

Liam sighed as he looked up at his oldest son. "Philip, I have given my word in good faith and made my decision. It is done."

"Who could you possibly have promised so as to allow such an inconceivable match?" he demanded to know.

"Da'Leth!" Rianne gasped, suddenly remembering their earlier conversation. "You knew, didn't you? Somehow you knew."

Getting to her feet, hearing Liam's chuckle, Da'Leth nodded. "Yes, Princess I knew."

"How?" Richard asked. His arm around Rianne's waist he was unwilling to let her go. "How could you have known this?"

Opening her mouth as if to speak Da'Leth shut it again without saying anything, offering a small shrug as her only reply.

"Tell them," Liam said as he sat down in his chair. "Tell them what you did."

Glancing at Nicholas Da'Leth looked over to Rianne and Richard. "His Majesty the King granted me a reward for saving young Prince Brian's life from the river that day. He asked what I would wish for, anything within reason, and I asked that the Princess be free to choose her own husband."

"More importantly she asked that the promise be kept secret from everyone so that no man might hear of it and take advantage of my daughter's innocence to seduce her into believing she was in love." Liam looked approvingly at Da'Leth. "She has proven to be a shrewd and understanding woman as well as a good friend to my youngest child."

"A serf!" Philip yelled; getting to his feet as his fists pounded the table before him. "You gave your word to a serf!"

Sitting in his seat, his hands folded under his chin, Nicholas smiled. When Da'Leth took a moment to glance his way he met her gaze, nodding his head in thanks for what she had done. He understood now what she had meant that day in the tent about choosing something that was more important and he only loved her more for it. Although he was happy for his sister and his friend Nicholas couldn't help the pang of jealously. They were now free to love each other openly.

"Do be serious, father!" Philip cried, waving his hand as if to dismiss what had just been announced. "This marriage will do nothing for the kingdom."

"Perhaps not," Liam admitted. "But I have given my word none the less."

"It is our responsibility to protect the kingdom," Philip reasoned sarcastically. "When our enemies hear that you have given your daughters' hand in marriage to a Captain," he laughed. "They will attack us in our weakness!"

"Or perhaps they will see his actions as an expression of a fathers' love for his daughter! A kind King is a good King!"

All eyes turned to Da'Leth, wide with surprise at her outburst. Her own face open with shock Da'Leth stared at King Liam with wide eyes. "My King, forgive me! I did not mean to speak so boldly," she started, her voice drowned out by the roar of Philips outrage.

"How dare you, serf!" he roared, stepping towards her, his face red with anger.

Philip was halfway to Da'Leth when Nicholas suddenly appeared by her side, pushing her behind him. "Leave her be Philip!" he warned. "She was only doing as I commanded."

Stopping in front of his brother Philip glared at him. "You commanded her to speak out of place to me?"

"I commanded that she be free to speak her mind."

Starting to object Philip stopped when they heard Liam yell out, "Enough of this!" When he had everyone's attention he continued, "My decision has been made and as I am still King it cannot be contested. Krausley and Rianne will be married on a date of their choosing. There will be no more discussion on the subject."

Disgusted Philip stalked from the room. Taking a deep breath Da'Leth shook her head, turning to reclaim her seat. "Are you all right?" Nicholas asked, touching her elbow briefly as they walked.

"I should have kept silent," shaking her head. "It's not my place to speak out of turn."

"You defended my father; I doubt anyone would fault you for that."

She smiled softly but kept her eyes cast downward. "Thank you, for coming to my defense."

"I don't want him anywhere near you," Nicholas scowled, his skin crawling at the memory of her cries that day. "I am commanding you to stay away from him."

Though her cheeks blushed at the memory she smiled. "Have no fear of that. I have no desire to be anywhere near him."

From the corner of her eyes she saw Tome toddling toward them and frowned, the little girl's cheeks flushed and her eyes glassy. "Tome?" she called, reaching out to pull the little girl into her lap. "You have a fever!" feeling the warmth of her skin. "Pardon me, milord, I must take her to bed, she is sick."

"Is it serious?" he asked, concern filling his voice as he reached out to touch Tomes forehead.

"I don't know yet," she said, gathering Tome close. Getting to her feet she left the main hall without another word, hurrying to gather her herbs so she could tend to Tome.

From her seat at the head table Winifred watched Da'Leth leave with Tome. She had seen the interaction between Da'Leth and her son, the concern in his eyes. She couldn't recall ever seeing Nicholas move as quickly as he had when he'd seen Philip heading towards Da'Leth. "Is it possible?" she wondered softly to herself. Had her son fallen in love with the young woman?

"Is what possible my dear?" Liam asked, leaning towards her. "Is something wrong?"

"I believe Tome may not be well," she said to her husband. He'd had a hard time coming to terms with a Captain marrying his daughter. Liam was not ready to hear that his son had fallen in love with a woman who was, technically, a serf.

No sooner had she spoken than one of the maids came into the dining hall, approaching Elizabeth. "Highness," she said with a bow. "Miss Da'Leth has asked me to come and fetch you. The little Princess is unwell."

"Send for the doctor at once," Liam motioned to his steward.

~~*~*~*~*~*~*~*

Sitting in the hallway, worried about his niece, Nicholas turned the pages of a book he wasn't reading. The door was shut, as it had been for the last week. Everyone was worried for her, the doctor and Da'Leth working side by side to keep the little girl with them one day at a time. He hadn't seen Da'Leth since the night of their return, she hadn't left the room and he wasn't allowed to enter the room lest he also became sick with what had befallen Tome.

Victoria had left to return home, not wanting to catch the ailment while she was pregnant, and Rianne had been sent with her, a dual reason to keep her safe as well as keep her sister company. Richard traveled with Victoria and Rianne to make sure they arrived safely and had already sent word they he was on his way back, the two Princesses safely within the walls of his sister's home. Philip and Elizabeth were also forbidden to enter the room. Though Elizabeth was sitting in the hallway with him Philip steered clear of the wing as a whole.

Sighing with frustration he stood, pacing the corridor. Nicholas had lost count of the number of times he'd passed by the door when it opened, one of the maids slipping out with a bundle of rags in her arms, tears in her eyes. His heart sank at the sight of the young woman hurrying away. "Tome," he whispered, falling back against the wall, putting his hands to his face

"Da'Leth?"

Hearing Elizabeth's teary voice he looked up to see an exhausted Da'Leth standing in the doorway, tears in her eyes as had been in the maids. Crossing the corridor to Elizabeth's side Da'Leth knelt before her, taking the young mothers hands into her own. "Highness, her fever has broken," she said. "Tome will live."

Sobbing, Elizabeth threw her arms around Da'Leth, hugging her before disappearing into the child's room. Peeking in through the doorway Nicholas watched his sister gather her daughter into her arms; Tome was awake though still tired and weak. Taking a deep breath, assured that the little one was going to be okay, he turned his attention to Da'Leth, seeing her sit down where Elizabeth had been sitting. Her face was drawn, dark shadows under her eyes, and he remembered she had been working nonstop to save Tome's life, suddenly realizing she must not have taken any time to rest during the last week.

Without a word he gathered her in his arms, carrying her to her own room that joined with Tome's. Protesting at first, he silenced her, insisting that she needed sleep. Laying Da'Leth on the bed Nicholas pulled the covers up over her, tucking the edges in as he had seen her do to Tome many times before. Her closed eyes opened when she felt the bed dip down on the one side and she saw him sitting next to her, leaning down to kiss her forehead. "Sleep now," he whispered. "Your work is done."

Too tired to say anything she only nodded, her eyes drooping shut against her will. Gathering himself to leave her in peace Nicholas stopped when he felt her hand on his arm. "Just stay until I'm asleep," she asked, her voice slurred by exhaustion.

No sooner had she asked him to stay did she fall asleep, her hand falling away from his arm. Sitting back down on the bed he put her hand under the covers, tucking them in again. Sitting by her side he stared down at her, seeing her beauty through the damage the last week had inflicted on her face. Wisps of red curls escaped around her face and one had come to rest over her eye. Brushing it aside his fingers lingered on her temple.

"I don't care what anyone says," he told the sleeping woman. "I love you. No matter what it takes I will find a way for us to be together. Richard and Rianne can have their happiness, thanks to you, and as God is my witness so shall we."

Leaning down once more he kissed her lips, never seeing his father disappear from the doorway behind him.

Liam had hurried to the nursery wing when he had heard the little girl had finally pulled through and had seen Nicholas carrying Da'Leth into her room. He had stopped in the doorway to ask if his granddaughter was truly going to be all right but silenced the question when he saw Nicholas putting Da'Leth to bed. Hearing the vow his son had made he stepped away. After checking on Tome, assured by the doctor that she was going to be all right, the silent King slipped back down to his study. Shutting the door for privacy with his own thoughts he crossed the room, instinct leading him to his chair.

Sitting in a chair by the fire, his feet propped up on a stool; Liam stared at the fire as he sorted through his thoughts. Da'Leth was a good woman; he had no doubts of that. Although Philip was in line to inherit the throne when he died should anything happen to him Nicholas would need to step up and rule the kingdom until Brian was of age to assume the throne. And, God forbid, anything should happen to the boy it would fall to Nicholas to produce an heir. How would the kingdom react if they were to learn that the Prince had fallen in love with, and married, a serf?

The easiest solution would be to grant Da'Leth her freedom but the fact still remained that she had been a serf at one time. A Princess could marry a Captain easily enough; she wasn't in line to rule and the Captain could easily be knighted. But for a Prince to marry a Serf? Could Liam bend his own rules that far? Still thinking about it he heard the door open and looked up to see Winifred approaching him, tears of joy in her eyes.

"She will be all right," she smiled, not realizing he had already been up to see her. "Tome has come through the illness!"

Gathering her in his arms Liam hugged his wife. "I know."

"What is it, Liam? What bothers you?"

Sighing he sat down again, Winifred in his lap. "Our daughter is going to marry a Captain," he said. "And our son has fallen in love with a serf."

"When did you realize?" she asked, smiling at him gently.

"Just now. I overheard him telling her. Da'Leth was asleep though so I don't think she heard him."

"This bothers you?"

"There might come a time, should something happen to Philip and Brian, when he would need to rule," Liam started, stopping when Winifred put her hand over his mouth. "I don't want that of course," he continued, taking her hand in his. "But it is always a possibility."

"You said yourself," she reminded him. "Da'Leth is a good woman."

"Yes, she is. But that doesn't alter the fact that she is still a serf."

"Then set her free."

Nodding he turned his stare back to the fire, a sign Winifred knew all too well, his mind caught up again with the many facts to be taken into consideration. She wanted to tell him who Da'Leth really was but couldn't, her vow to the young woman too serious to be broken. Kissing him softly she stood, leaving him to his contemplation. Shutting the door softly behind her she motioned for one of the guards to come stand watch. "See to it that the King is not disturbed by anyone."

Climbing the stairs, she made her way back to the nursery wing. Stopping at Da'Leth's door she looked in to see Nicholas gone, Da'Leth sleeping in the bed while the doctor stood by the window drying his hands. When he saw her the old man motioned for her to go out into the hallway so they could talk without disturbing the sleeper.

"That girl is your granddaughter's miracle," he said. "If she had not begun to work with her herbs the child would have been dead by the time I got to the palace." Thinking back to the previous week Winifred nodded, recalling how delayed the doctor had been, arriving several days after Tome had fallen sick. "We will need to watch her carefully. Miss Da'Leth has spent too much time with the child, there is a very good chance she will fall ill as well."

"Do we need to worry?" Winifred asked, glancing at the door that blocked her view of Da'Leth.

"Not yet," he said shaking his head. "Let her sleep for now; that is what she needs most."

Agreeing to do as she'd been advised Winifred ordered two maids to watch over Da'Leth. It wasn't until well into the next day, taking lunch with her soon to be son-in-law, that they told her Da'Leth had awoken. Ordered by the doctor to stay in bed and rest Da'Leth was contemplating escaping from her bed to check on Tome when Winifred entered her room. Sitting in a chair that Nicholas had left by the side of the bed she smiled at Da'Leth.

"Had I not known who your parents were, I would have sworn you were an angel sent by God to watch over my family."

Da'Leth blushed. "My Queen," she began, stopping when Winifred held up her hand.

"Say nothing," she commanded. "Rest now and we shall talk when you have done so."

Getting to her feet she leaned down to kiss Da'Leth cheek. "Thank you, child," she whispered. "Thank you."

Chapter Seventeen

The bells chimed merrily around her as the acrobats jumped and stretched through the room, dancing and performing to entertain the audience. Watching one of the men jump through the air Da'Leth saw Tome's eyes wide open in awe. A smile tugged on her face as she watched the child sitting silently on her grandfather's lap. She could still feel what it was like to sit on a father's lap, the strength of his arms surrounding her was as strong as if he were holding her at that moment.

Her attention was caught by one of the guards stopping behind Captain Krausley to lean down and whisper in his ear. Da'Leth frowned when the captains face paled slightly before he nodded, taking a piece of paper from the young man. Looking it over briefly he stood and moved to stand next to the King. Leaning down he whispered in the man's ear. Curious about what was going on Da'Leth's eyes widened when the King suddenly stood, barely catching Tome before she tumbled to the ground and ordered the room cleared.

Though her curiosity was overflowing Da'Leth stood to leave with the rest of the people filing out of the room until she heard the Queen call out, "Da'Leth, please stay." Turning around she saw the older woman holding the parchment in her hands, her face pale, lips quivering, and her eyes wide in both shock and fear. Raising her face to Da'Leth, her face stricken and her eyes pleading she held the note out to the young woman as she walked towards her. Her curiosity quickly turned to worry and fear as she quickened her steps toward the Queens side.

"What is going on?" Philip demanded.

"Rianne is being held for ransom," Krausley replied.

Shocked Da'Leth's steps faltered and she reached out to steady herself. A hand caught her from falling, pulling her back upright. Standing again she let go of the hand but it continued to hold her. Looking up she saw Nicholas, his eyes filled with worry as they met hers. Squeezing his hand for a brief moment she separated herself, moving toward the Queen again. Taking the parchment from her Da'Leth read it quickly, recognizing that this was a serious threat. They would kill Rianne if they didn't get the money. Her heart sinking Da'Leth sat on the step near the throne, barely listening to the conversation going on around her.

"We'll have to gather the gold," Nicholas said after reading the note over Da'Leth's shoulder.

"De be serious, Nicholas! One hundred thousand gold pieces? Even if we had it in the treasury it would bankrupt the entire nation. We'd be open to attack on all our borders."

"She's our sister!"

"Let me go after her, my King," Richard announced. "I shall bring her home to safety or die trying!"

King Liam shook his head, taking the note from Da'Leth's hands. "It says if we send any man to attempt to rescue her they will kill her without hesitation."

"I will succeed!" Richard declared.

"No," Da'Leth said suddenly. Getting to her feet she faced the King. "If you send any man to rescue her they will kill the Princess."

"We have already established that, serf!" Philip degraded.

Raising her eyes to him for a moment Da'Leth forced herself not to respond to his anger, turning her attention back to the King. "Majesty, you cannot send any of your men, they will be watching for them no matter how well hidden they would be," she added for Richard's benefit. Drawing herself up to her full height she fixed her eyes on the King. "Send me, Majesty. They will not expect a woman and I fight as well as any man here. I will bring the Princess home safely."

"You?" Philip scoffed.

"Yes her!" Richard exclaimed, understanding Da'Leth's view. "She is the best, the only, solution to this problem. Da'Leth knows how to pass herself as a serf; no one would suspect her of being anything else."

"Naturally she can pass for a serf, she is a serf," Philip reminded them with a scowl.

Da'Leth ignored the Crown Price, watching as King Liam weighed the decision. "This is a large risk for you Da'Leth. You could very well be killed."

Meeting his eyes with her own Da'Leth answered from her heart. "Better she lives than I, Majesty."

Nodding his head Liam advised, "Give her whatever she desires." Bowing to the King Da'Leth turned to leave, wanting to get underway as soon as she could. "Da'Leth," the King called to her. When she faced him again he promised her, "When my daughter is safely within the palace walls again you will be a free woman."

Da'Leth stood still, unable to move. After several moments, her eyes misty with tears, she bowed low to the floor and said the only thing that came into her mind. "Serf, Freewoman, or Lady, I serve my King."

Nodding his head Liam watched her leave. "If anyone can succeed it will be her."

"Of course, she will; you just gave her freedom!" Philip spat, disgusted by the fondness his father seemed to have for this serf.

"Da'Leth will succeed because she has a love for this family that I cannot help but wonder if you could ever possess!" Nicholas growled to his brother.

Hurrying out of the room Nicholas followed Da'Leth to her chambers, watching as she gathered the few supplies she would need. Helping her to carry them down to the stable he saw that Krausley had already saddled Nadia for her. Handing Richard the items to be added to the saddle he turned to face Da'Leth.

"You won't need to bother with any of the large cities, I doubt they would have taken Rianne there, her face is too recognizable. Stay on the main road and check with the keeper of every inn that you find. Ask questions but be subtle," he advised. Placing his hands on her shoulders Nicholas squeezed them gently.

"I will find her, milord, I promise."

"I know you will." Pausing he lowered his voice, "Be careful, Da'Leth. They won't hesitate to kill you once they realize that you've come for the Princess. Come back to me alive."

From the corner of her eye Da'Leth saw Richard approaching, Nadia's reins in his hands. Taking a deep breath, she nodded to him before turning her attention back to Nicholas. Looking up into his eyes she saw his love, his worry, his fear staring back down at her. Before she knew what she was doing, Da'Leth reached up, her heart screaming for her to kiss him and her head yelling at her to stop. Giving into her heart, kissing him gently, she stepped away.

"Just in case," she whispered before turning to climb into the saddle.

Without another word she turned Nadia toward the gates, racing off to begin her search for Rianne. Watching her go Nicholas stared, his lips burning from her single kiss. Though she had promised to return he couldn't shake the bad feeling that was settling over him, her kiss telling him goodbye.

"Will we see her again?" Richard asked aloud, his fear for her safety outweighing his confidence in her ability.

"I hope so," Nicholas answered. "Dear God above I hope so."

~~*~*~*~*~*~*~*

Slowing the horse Da'Leth stopped to examine the area she was in. For nine days she had been traveling the roads, hunting for clues as to where the Princess was being kept. Yesterday she had finally found one that she hoped would make a difference in finding Rianne.

An innkeeper's wife had told her about four men traveling with a woman that had appeared to be ill. She never left the room, except to leave in the morning when the group had left the inn. Even then she had been carried out to the carriage, covered by a cloak to keep the chill away. The carriage had been heading east when it had left the inn. Now, stopping for a brief moment to rest both herself and her horse, she could only hope and pray that she was heading in the right direction still. The description she had been given of the carriage was commonplace at best but the people she spoke with had stopped recognizing it at all in the town she'd just left.

Sitting down on a fallen tree Da'Leth watched Nadia drink from small puddle that had formed from last night's rain. The thought brought a shiver to her bones as she recalled sleeping, trying to sleep, in the rain. She'd woken up soaked to the skin and it had taken all morning for her clothes to dry though she still felt chilled to the bones. Da'Leth craved the warmth of a fire but refused to delay long enough in her search to build one. 'Tonight,' she promised herself. With a sigh she stood again and took the reins in her hands, reaching for the saddle to mount again. The sound of a passing carriage on the road stopped her in her tracks. Heading deeper into the woods she hid from sight, watching, praying, that the carriage was the one she was searching for.

A triumphant smile tugged at her lips when she saw the carriage pass by. Brown with silver handles, pulled by two horses, it matched the description the wife had given her. The color of the horses was wrong but enough of the details matched to be relatively sure it was the one she was searching for. Letting it pass by Da'Leth headed out onto the road, staying far enough behind to stay out of sight. The rain last night had washed away all the tracks so that only one set was there, making it easy to follow them.

After some time, a down pour of rain began again, soaking Da'Leth through all over again. Ignoring the cold and wet surrounding her she realized that the tracks were beginning to wash away. Quickening her pace Da'Leth was sure she had lost them again when she saw the small glow of a light farther down the road. When she was closer she saw the carriage parked, the horses already stabled, the light glowing out from the inn she had come to.

Sighing with relief Da'Leth approached the inn and, stabling her horse, entered the inn to search out the innkeeper's wife. "Pardon me ma'am," she asked, lowering her eyes to the floor. "May I beg a meal and bed in exchange for a good night's labor? I can clean quickly; I've worked in a pub kitchen all my life, ma'am."

Looking up the older woman shook her head, her eyes softening at the sight of the shivering young woman. "Sorry dear, I've got no work for you to do but come and warm yourself by the fire. I've a small bowl of stew you can help yourself to if you like. Guests have all eaten already, no sense in letting it go to waste."

Sitting down in the chair near the fire Da'Leth accepted the bowl of food with a smile. The smell of it turned her stomach but she forced herself to eat, knowing she needed the nourishment. "Thank you," she said to the woman.

"No harm done. It'll be nice to have a woman to talk to while I do the chores. What's your name, dear?"

"I'm called Da'Leth," she replied. "May I ask yours?"

"Sylvia's my name. My man owns this inn, has for the last twenty-six years. We've had all sorts come through here. Why we've even had a Lord and Lady spend a few nights here a year or so ago. They were of a place called Whispering Winds and were the ..."

The woman continued talking but her words were lost to Da'Leth, her ears ringing with the words she had just heard. 'A year or so ago,' she thought to herself. 'My mother is still alive! But, a Lady and a Lord? Did she re-marry?'

"Ma'am please," she interrupted. "The lady of Whispering Winds, what was her name?"

"T'was Chelaine. A beautiful name, don't you agree?"

"Yes, it is. What was she like? Beautiful? Healthy?" Da'Leth knew she was taking a risk asking so many questions but she had to know.

"Oh, most beautiful! She was a lovely, kind woman, always polite, even to the servants. But it seemed to me she was sad. The Lord too. Now I ain't one to gossip but I overheard them talking about their child. The area had just suffered a terrible sickness, lots of people died. I almost lost my own son to that dreadful plague."

Silence fell for a moment when the woman stepped out of the kitchen to wait on the customers. Sitting next to the fire Da'Leth set the bowl down and dropped her pounding head into her hands. Her mother had married and lost a child to a plague all while she had been simply trying to stay alive. Who was this man her mother had married? Was he a good man? Did he love her as much as her father had? Would he accept her as the daughter her mother had lost?

Still pondering the questions in her mind, she heard the older woman enter the kitchen again. "Such a shame, that poor girl."

Lifting her head, she looked at her with confusion in her eyes. "I'm sorry?"

"There's a girl who's not feeling well at all. Her man says she just needs to sleep but I'm a little worried. She hasn't had anything to eat yet today. Sick or not a woman needs to keep up her strength with some weak broth."

The mission came back to her mind with a sudden jolt. "Have you spoken with her?"

"No," Sylvia shook her head. "She was carried in and put to bed right away. I gave them the warmest room in the center of the inn so she could stay as warm as possible. Poor dear."

Making idle chit chat with Sylvia for a little while, hoping for some more details while she tried to will her headache away, Da'Leth planned on how to make their escape from the inn to freedom. Without knowing what state the Princess was in, she had to form a plan that would accommodate an unconscious woman. After some time Da'Leth rose from her chair and, thanking the woman for her kindness, slipped from the kitchen into the main room.

The inn was filled with people but Da'Leth spotted the three men sitting in the corner of the room by the fire. Keeping to the edge of the room she slowly made her way to the door on the far side. Checking the first door she found it unlocked and opened it to peer inside the room. A man was sitting by the fire, asleep in his chair from the effects of the empty tankard, but, on the bed, lay a small figure tangled up in a cloak. Slipping into the room she quietly shut and locked the door behind her.

Cautiously Da'Leth approached the bed, pulling the cloak back to see Rianne's terrified face staring up at her. A filthy cloth covered her mouth preventing her from saying anything though a low moan escaped from the Princess. Putting a finger to her mouth Da'Leth motioned for the Princess to stay quiet. With a quick glance over her shoulder to make sure the man was still sleeping she removed the cloak from around Rianne's' legs. Taking a small knife from the table she made quick work of the ropes on her wrists and ankles. Helping the Princess to her feet, seeing that she was too unsteady to walk alone, Da'Leth sat her back down for a moment.

With the hilt of her sword she hit the sleeping man on the back of the head to ensure he didn't get up. Working quickly to bind and gag the unconscious guard Da'Leth helped Rianne to her feet again and together they crept out of the room, down the hall to a door at the back of the inn. Moments later Rianne was settled on the back of a horse Da'Leth was leading out of the stable.

Under the cover of night, staying hidden in the forest to avoid being detected on the road, Da'Leth led the horse and rider away from the inn. Walking until she was sure she would pass out Da'Leth finally stopped the horse under the protection of a large tree. Gathering some sticks together she started a small fire before helping Rianne down from her perch atop the horse, sitting her on the ground, propped up against the tree. Collapsing against a fallen log a few feet away Da'Leth closed her eyes to try and stop the world from spinning for a moment.

"Da'Leth?"

Lifting her head, forcing her eyes to open, Da'Leth looked over at Rianne, her scared eyes wide. "Princess?"

"What's going on? How did you find me? Where is my brother, where are his men or Richard?"

Her hands raised Da'Leth tried to stem the barrage of questions that were tearing into her head like a cannon. "Milady, please!" she cried. "I shall tell you." Da'Leth detailed the events that had led up to her rescue. "Now we must focus on staying safe until you are back within the walls of the palace with your family." Closing her eyes again Da'Leth wrapped her arms around herself in a vain attempt to stop the shaking and warm herself against the chill of the night air.

"Da'Leth?" she heard as a cool hand pressed against her forehead. "You don't look well!"

"I will be fine, milady. Rest yourself by the fire, we cannot stay here long."

"No," Rianne insisted. "We must rest here until you are well."

Forcing her eyes open Da'Leth met the young woman's eyes with a firm gaze. "We cannot allow any delay until you are safe. One hour's rest and then we shall move on."

~~*~*~*~*~*~*~*

Staying in the early morning shadows the two women waited for the right time to move from one shadow to the next, slowly making their way through the city to its heart. After some time Da'Leth approached a door, knocking on it softly. Listening to the sound of the feet on the other side of the door she waited for the door to open, speaking when it did. "I need your help."

The man on the inside stared at her in shock. "Da'Leth?" he whispered in surprise. "Come in, come in!"

Motioning for Rianne to come closer Da'Leth let her enter the house first before shutting the door behind them. Falling into the chair Da'Leth looked up at her old friend. "Thank you Pith, I cannot tell you what this means to me."

"You know you will always have a place in my home, Da'Leth."

"I'm afraid I must ask for much more than that, Pith."

The man sat down at the small table and motioned for her to continue. Glancing at Rianne as she sat down as well Da'Leth told her friend how they had come to be at his door. "This woman was kidnapped while traveling on her way home. Her father sent me to rescue her and bring her home safely. That is why I need your help. No one knows that she has been kidnapped so she must return home as though nothing has happened."

"You want the use of my coach," Pith surmised.

"And you as a driver. I will pay you of course."

Pith nodded. "I do not want to take your money Da'Leth but times are hard so I must. When shall we leave?"

"Give us a few moments to rest and then we shall leave," Rianne spoke up before Da'Leth could speak. "I am tired and must rest."

"By the time the horses and carriage are ready we shall be rested enough, Pith. Thank you, my friend."

Nodding Pith left the small house to ready the carriage for use. "Milady I cannot allow any delay in returning you to your family," Da'Leth admonished.

"You are unwell. You cannot stop shaking, your skin burns with fever, and your eyes are glassy as well; truly, you need to rest!"

"I shall, milady, when you are safe." Getting up from her chair Da'Leth adjusted the cloak around Rianne's shoulders, pulling the hood up to cast a shadow on the Princess's face. Opening the door, she checked the street before leaving the safety of the house. Hurrying to the stable she opened the carriage door, ushering Rianne in before turning to look at Pith. "Head out of the city to the north, I will tell you more once we are safely out of the city."

Nodding Pith shut the door behind Da'Leth, watching as she shut the curtains to block themselves from the view of the world. The inside of the carriage plunged into darkness and Da'Leth squeezed Rianne's hand to reassure her as the carriage began to move. The horses slowed as they reached the gate of the city, Pith's voice advising the guards that he had been hired to transport two women to see their families in the next township. A moment later they were moving again and Da'Leth breathed a sigh of relief. Closing her eyes, she felt the world around her slipping away from her, her head landing on something soft just before her world went black.

Leaning her head against Da'Leth's hair Rianne pressed a hand against the sweaty, burning forehead near her chin. Worry filled her when Da'Leth didn't push her hand away. Lifting her head, she looked down at her friend and saw the ashen face leaning on her shoulder. The sight of her sleeping face impressed on Rianne how sick Da'Leth really was. Thinking back over the past few days she had seen her friend grow steadily worse, her health deteriorating with each passing hour. Covering Da'Leth with the cloak she had tossed on the other seat Rianne wrapped her arms around the sleeping woman and held her close.

With nothing else to do but think Rianne thoughts turned to the past week's events. She had spent a week with Victoria before traveling home. Her ladies' maid had fallen asleep and Rianne was almost asleep herself when it happened. Their carriage had come to a sudden stop, both women tossed to the floor. Outside she heard the sound of a small battle but silence soon fell over the area. Fear filling her veins she screamed when a man's face filled the window of the carriage, his face pulled back into a sneer.

'Y'all right, girl?' he'd asked.

Shocked, confused by his concern Rianne didn't know what to say.

'I'm all right, father,' she heard the young woman sitting next to her reply.

With wide eyes she had turned to her ladies' maid. Betrayed by someone she had thought she could trust; Rianne hadn't been given any time to respond, the man ripping the door open and pulling her from the carriage. Ordering the girl to go home he had pushed Rianne toward a trio of men a few yards away. 'Take her away, keep on the move, head towards Belding. I'll meet you after I send the demand.'

She hadn't seen it coming, the pain knocking into her head, the world growing dark all around her. Wincing at the memory Rianne closed her eyes, thankful that it was almost over; she was on her way home. The carriage slowed and stopped, shaking for a moment before the door opened and Pith looked inside.

"Is she all right?" he asked, worriedly look at his friend.

"She's very ill, I believe. We should hurry."

Pith nodded. "If anyone stops us I will say the lady is ill. Where am I to drive, milady?"

"The palace."

Rianne could see the shock and questions in his eyes as he glanced back and forth from Rianne to Da'Leth and back again. Clearing his throat, he nodded, "The palace, yes milady."

~~*~*~*~*~*~*~*

Hurrying down the lane Pith saw a small group of men on the side of the road and tightened his grip on the reins. One of the men stopped the horses, standing in the middle of the road to make them stop. Inside the carriage Rianne recognized the voices of the men speaking to Pith and knew she had precious little time to act. Pulling her cloak from her shoulders she draped it over Da'Leth, covering all of her clothes. With quick jerks she pulled the jeweled clips out of her hair, placing them in Da'Leth's braid. Removing her necklace and rings she put them on Da'Leth as well, making sure to place one of her hands in view on the seat. Scrunching down as low as she could go Rianne climbed under Da'Leth's skirts, hiding as best she could, her own gown peeking out from under the hem of the cloak.

"My lady is very ill!" she heard Pith cry out, his voice carrying into the woods.

"We'll see about that!" another man replied.

Yanking open the door he peered into the carriage. Seeing the ghastly pallor of the woman sleeping inside as well as the jewels on her hands and neck the man examined the rest of the carriage for a moment before shutting the door.

"She's not here. Be on your way."

"Thank you, sir," Pith replied. Getting back into his seat he spurred the horses into motion, moving away from the men. Traveling down the lane Pith drove the horses as far away from the men as he could, the man's words ringing in his ears. 'He could be the one that bound up Jeffers,' one of the men had said.

'Check the carriage. Find her!'

His heart had risen to his throat when he saw the man reaching for the handle of the door. 'My lady is very ill!' he had cried, trying desperately to make them stop. He had almost fallen off his perch when they'd told him he was free to go. Realizing they were far enough away from the men to stop Pith pulled the horses to a stop and jumped down to the ground, hurrying to open the door and peer inside. Seeing only Da'Leth he frowned. "Majesty?" he whispered.

The skirt at Da'Leth's feet began to move and Pith watched Rianne appear from underneath. "Is it safe?" she asked worriedly.

Pith nodded, holding his hand out to help her up. "Yes, Majesty. The men let us go."

Nodding Rianne checked on Da'Leth. "We should hurry. How long will it take us to reach the palace?"

"By nightfall if we rush."

"Then, please, Mr. Pith, make this carriage fly!"

Smiling he nodded, shutting the door and pulling himself up into the drivers' seat. Grabbing the reins, he urged the horses into motion, hurrying down the road as fast as they could fly. Anxiously waiting to get home, worried about Da'Leth, Rianne found it nearly impossible to stop fidgeting with everything around her.

"You are going to wear a hole in this cloak, milady."

Looking down Rianne saw Da'Leth watching her with glassy fever-ridden eyes. "Then I will replace it when we get home," she smiled, relieved that her friend had woken and seemed to be in good spirits.

'Home.'

The word echoed in Da'Leth's mind. Home was the only place she wanted to go. The warmth of the palace didn't appeal to her right now, she wanted to go home. "Whispering Winds."

"Da'Leth!" Rianne cried, her joy covering over Da'Leth's whisper. "Look! We're home!"

Raising herself up Da'Leth looked out the window and smiled at the sight of the palace getting closer and closer to them. Sinking back into the cushion she closed her eyes and smiled with relief. "Safe and sound," Da'Leth breathed.

When the carriage pulled up to the palace gate Pith mentioned Da'Leth's name and he was ushered in. Stopping in front of the main entrance he jumped down to open the door even as Rianne was reaching for the handle. Helping her down he smiled as she ran for the stairs, hurrying in to see her family. Looking into the carriage he locked gazes with Da'Leth, the young woman looking as tired as an old woman.

"Take me to Whispering Winds, Pith," she whispered. "Take me home."

Unsure of what she was talking about Pith frowned. He knew of the land called Whispering Winds but she had said to go home. "Surely you don't mean Pirtonshire?"

Shaking her head once she closed her eyes; the effort of talking was taking its toll. "Whispering Winds, Pith, take me to Whispering Winds."

"Very well," he relented, closing the door and climbing back into his seat.

Opening her eyes for a moment Da'Leth looked out the window just in time to see Rianne disappear into the place entrance. Running down the corridor, hurrying towards the main hall, she pulled open the door and stopped still, soaking in the sight before her. The entire time she'd been held by those men she had wished she could see her family, feel the warmth of the large fire. Her father was standing with Philip near the map spread out on the table. On the floor near the fire Nicholas was spread out letting Tome crawl all over him.

Sitting off to the side in one of the chairs was Richard, staring at the floor with a worried expression filling his face. Rianne's heart went out to him, knowing in the bottom of her heart that it had taken every ounce of self-control not to go with Da'Leth to find her. The door closed behind her and Rianne took a step forward, the movement catching Richards's attention.

His eyes wide Richard stood up from his chair, crossing the space between them in three long strides, placing his hands on Rianne's shoulders, needing to touch her to make sure she was real. "Rianne," he breathed, relief filling his eyes, flooding his heart. Pulling her into his arms he held the Princess tightly feeling her arms wrapping around his back. "Are you harmed?" he asked.

Holding him tightly Rianne shook her head. "I am well enough."

Richard closed his eyes for a moment, trying to reign in the relief that was coursing through his body at her reply. "Thanks be to God," he replied, opening his eyes to meet with hers. "Your family is anxious to see you again."

"Wait!" she whispered, pulling on his arm. "Please, go and gather Da'Leth from the carriage. She is very ill!"

Frowning he nodded. "Majesties," he called out, turning Rianne toward the family before heading out of the main hall.

Pausing just outside the door he leaned against the wall, closing his eyes as he thanked God that Rianne had been brought home safely, swearing to both the Lord and himself that he would never let anything happen to her again. Pushing himself away from the wall he glanced into the main room to see Rianne walking towards her family, the cries of relief echoing out into the halls as he headed out to get Da'Leth.

"Rianne!" Winifred cried, standing up from her seat and holding out her arms for Rianne to come to her. "Oh darling, are you hurt?" the Queen asked as she folded her youngest child into her arms, tears forming in her eyes.

"Mother," Rianne whispered, burying her face in her mother's shoulder when her tears finally broke through, the ordeal beginning to catch up with her.

"Oh, my little sweetheart," she crooned. "It's all right now, you're safe now."

Walking towards his daughter Liam laid a gentle hand on her shoulder. "I'm glad you are safely home again, Rianne," he said, gently kissing her hair.

Lifting her head to look at her father Rianne smiled a watery smile. "Thank you, father," she cried; her voice thick with tears.

"It's a good thing that serf brought you back," Philip said as he approached. "We would have been hard pressed otherwise."

Glaring at his brother Nicholas pulled Rianne into his arms, holding his sister close, the reality of how close he had come to losing her nearly overwhelming him. Pressing tighter Nicholas held her for a few moments longer before releasing her, planting a brotherly kiss on her forehead. "You're safe Rianne; that is what matters more than anything else."

"Nicholas," she said, lowering her voice so only he could hear her. "I recognized the men."

Closing his eyes with the realization that his fears had come true Nicholas pulled Rianne to him again. His eyes closed he didn't see Richard enter the room again, a perplexed look on his face.

"Captain," Liam called out to him. "What is it?"

"My King," he said with a small nod before turning his eyes to Rianne. "Da'Leth is nowhere to be found."

"What?" Rianne cried, pushing herself away from Nicholas. "Where is she?"

Richard shrugged but it was Philip who answered. "Run off most likely, that ungrateful serf."

"Silence that thought, Philip," Nicholas cried, his eyes blazing at his brother. "It is we who owe our lives to Da'Leth." Turning to Rianne he asked in a gentler tone, "Rianne, why do you worry about Da'Leth? She is more than capable of taking care of herself."

Shaking her head, the Princess gripped her brothers' arm. "No, she is ill, very ill. Did no one see where she went?"

"The guards said the carriage pulled away the instant you passed through the doors of the palace."

"She dumped the Princess and ran!" Philip sneered.

"No," Liam declared. "She fulfilled her end of the bargain and now I will fulfill mine." Going out into the hall he called for the secretary, directing the man to enter his words into the records. "For her service to the crown let it be known that from this day forth Da'Leth has been freed of her servitude as a serf, never to be a serf again so long as she lives."

Chapter Eighteen

The sky was an early morning gray when the carriage pulled into the yard of the Whispering Winds. Stopping some little ways from the front door pith climbed down from his seat, exhausted after driving for too many hours, and opened the door to the carriage. Inside Josephine stirred when the morning light poured into the carriage. Blinking she looked up at Pith. "Are we home?" she asked softly.

Nodding he replied, "We're at Whispering Winds. Should I get one of the servants?"

Josephine nodded, watching Pith walk away to get someone. Her gaze fell on the small family cemetery in the distance and she pushed herself up from the cushion with a strength she didn't think she had left. Stumbling from the carriage she shuffled through the distance between her and her destination, falling to her knees before the headstones. Scanning them quickly she saw one that had been toppled over, brush and grass overgrowing it. Reading the name tears sprang to her eyes.

'Here lies Lord Charles of the Whispering Winds survived by his loving wife and daughter. His legacy lies in the heart of his child.'

Tears fell from her eyes as she frantically ripped at the grass growing over her father's headstone, horrified that anyone had let it grow so unkempt. From somewhere far away she heard someone calling her, ignoring them until her father's grave could be restored. A strong hand pulled her shoulder, pulling her away from her work.

"Da'Leth, stop!" Pith yelled at her.

Unbalanced she fell backward, staring up into a face she could barely remember. Shock registered on the old man's face followed quickly by an overwhelming concern. "Fetch the Lady," he commanded to someone behind him. "Find the Master!" Turning his attention to Josephine he reached out gently, stroking her cheek with a father's caress. "Don't fret now, all will be well. Rest now."

"How could you?" she despaired. "How could you forget?"

The old man frowned. "Forget what, little lady?"

"You turned your back on his memory," she accused, struggling to get to her feet. "How could you?"

Trying to get to her feet, wanting to get away from a man she had thought was a friend, Josephine staggered a few steps before falling to her knees at the edge of the grass. From within the house she saw a woman emerge, her clothes fine, her creamy skin paling a few shades when she saw the young woman kneeling before her. Staring up at the older woman, seeing herself in thirty years, Josephine couldn't move as the woman began to run towards her. Servants flooded out of the house but she couldn't see any of them, her eyes focused solely on the woman who had fallen to her knees before her, reaching out with a shaking hand to touch her face.

"My daughter," she wept, placing a cool hand against her burning cheek. Her eyes widened at the searing temperature of the skin she was touching. "You're ill!" she cried. "Hurry, send a man for a doctor!"

"Mother," Josephine whispered, unable to draw out any strength for her voice. "Why did you forget?"

Confusion filled her mother's eyes but Josephine couldn't see it as the world around her went black. Feeling herself falling she was unconscious before she could realize that she had been caught, cradled in the arms of a man who held her as gently as a child.

~~*~*~*~*~*~*~*

There was a feeling of warmth that enveloped her like a blanket covering her from head to toe. It was comforting, welcoming her to stay as long as she wished. Sighing in contentment she snuggled in a little lower under the cover, smiling with satisfaction, glad she was able to sleep in. Suddenly that warmth was ripped away with an icy blast taking its place. A pair of strong arms lifted her from the bed as though she were as light as a child, stripping her of her beautiful nightclothes and forcing tattered rags over her shoulders. The dark figure that had pulled her from her bed suddenly grabbed her beautiful red braid, shearing it off with a knife he pulled from his belt. Screaming she bit the hand that he clamped over her mouth, running to get away from her attacker.

The door to her room began to shake, a violent pounding from the other side causing the hinges to give way. A large man burst into the room, grabbing the attacker and hauling him out of her room. Moments later, huddled in the darkest corner of her room she saw the man enter her room again, calling out to her, searching for her. She wanted to go to him, she wanted to tell him she was there but she was stuck. Unable to move she opened her mouth to call out to him but her voice was gone.

Seeing and hearing nothing the man turned and left the room, his red hair flowing out behind him, never seeing the tears that fell from her eyes.

~~*~*~*~*~*~*~*

Laying still, her entire body both numb and aching at the same time, she felt a heaviness covering her, crushing her. A small moan escaped her lips from the pressure on her chest and suddenly a cool hand gripped hers, stroking it comfortingly.

"Go get him!" she heard a voice say. Softening in its tone the voice called out to her, "Josephine, sweetheart, can you hear me?"

"Mother?" she rasped, struggling to open her eyes.

Finally succeeding she looked up into the teary eyes of a woman she saw in her dreams. She was older now, gray tufts of hair at her temples where it used to be a rich brown color. The once smooth skin had wrinkled slightly around her eyes and the corners of her mouth. Her beauty was undiminished though; the kindness and grace she had always remembered from her youth still filled her eyes.

Hearing her daughter's voice, seeing her eyes staring up at her with recognition was too much for Chelaine, the older woman bursting into tears even as her daughter slipped back into a dreamless sleep. Laying her head on the bed she sobbed, clutching her hand as if her daughter would disappear again at any moment if she let go. A pair of strong arms enveloped her and Chelaine looked up into the eyes of her husband.

"She woke!" she sobbed happily. "And she spoke as well! She called me mother."

Smiling he held his wife closely, gently rubbing her back as she wept tears of joy into his chest. Staring at the young woman his mind drifted back to the day Raul had told him what had happened that terrible night so many years ago.

'The night had been quiet, milord," he'd told him. 'Sir Edgar had taken to locking the servants in their quarters, he claimed that if he didn't we would desert our post if he didn't. But we would never have done any such thing, milord; you know we wouldn't desert the family like that.' He'd been forced to assure Raul that he knew the servants were loyal before the man would continue with his tale.

'I had heard the sound of a wagon approaching but couldn't see who it was. All was quiet for some time after that. I was almost asleep when I heard the Little Lady begin screaming. I tried to get to her milord, I swear to you I did, but the door was locked. As soon as it had started it ended. I thought perhaps she'd had a nightmare about her father's death and the Lady or one of the maids had quieted her.'

Raul had closed his eyes for a moment, reliving the nightmare of that night with perfect recollection.

'I thought all was well until the next morning when I heard Lady Chelaine trying to open the door to my home. She was frantic with worry. That was when I found out that Josephine had been taken from her bed the night before. The child's room was in shambles, her nightclothes in a heap on the floor, and her braid shorn off and lying on the bed. I left then and there to search for her, milord. I traveled the entire kingdom looking for her, beyond our borders as far as I could go to find her. There was simply no trail for me to follow. It was as though she had vanished!'

Lady Chelaine had been forced to suffer through that ordeal alone, his heart pained at the thought of her suffering at all. For years he had made the attempt to find Josephine himself, searching the land far into the surrounding nations, using his status as a Lord in a hope to gain information that Raul could not about the missing girl. As years passed despair set into the family though no one would dare give up hope. The name of Josephine had become a prayer to Lady and servant alike.

There was no headstone raised in the family cemetery for the girl, Lady Chelaine refusing to even entertain the notion. After his own search he had come home to Whispering Winds to stay by his wife's side. Though he himself was not out searching he employed several of the best trackers in the kingdom to do the searching for him, men he paid well to hunt down any clue no matter how small it was. Each month they would report in to him that there was simply nothing to report.

'Now,' he thought to himself with a smile. 'I have something to report to them.'

"Darling," he whispered softly, pulling his wife to her feet. "Let her rest. You need to rest as well."

Chelaine shook her head. "I can't leave her!"

"I promise you she will not go away again. Two of the servants will tend to her and alert you the moment she wakes. Of what use will you be to her if you fail to rest?"

Giving in she allowed him to lead her away, stopping in the doorway to watch her sleep for one moment more.

~~*~*~*~*~*~*~*

Slowly the world around her began to creep into her senses, sounds echoing in her ears, light filtering in through her eyelashes as she blinked her eyes. The heavy weight of many blankets covering her reminded her of how sick she had been, forced to stay in bed, unable to do anything more than sleep. Opening her eyes, she looked around in confusion. This was not the room she had been given at the palace.

It was slightly larger and though she didn't recognize it the room had a familiar feel to her somehow. A large canopy hung overhead and a tapestry of the same color hung near the wall across from her. Near the fire was a table, three chairs surrounding it of the same design. A small doll sat on the top of the table and she smiled at the resemblance, fiery red hair flowing down in curls around a smiling pink cheeked face.

Pushing the blanket away Josephine slowly swung her legs off the bed. Sitting on the edge of it she saw and older woman sitting in a chair by the window, sleeping in the warmth of the sun. Hesitantly, silently, she stood up from the bed, reaching for the robe draped at the foot of it. Once the robe was tied tightly she walked toward the door of the room, peeking into the corridor.

Unsure of where she was Josephine wandered through the halls until she came to a set of stairs, one leading up the other way down. Descending the stairs, she collapsed into a chair at the bottom of them, exhausted from the effort, needing to catch her breath. Looking around she spotted a tapestry hanging on the wall that took away what little breath she had recovered.

Grateful for the chair she was sitting in she stared at her reflection in the tapestry. Though the hair was brown the face that stared back at her was impossible to mistake. The woman was dressed in the finest gown she'd ever seen, a handsome man standing behind her and a red haired little girl stood before them. With a realization so clear that it made her heart hurt she knew without a doubt where she was and who the people in the tapestry were. Tears sprang to her eyes and she stood, moving toward the tapestry. Reaching out with a shaking hand she ran her fingers against the woven face of the man, her father, standing behind the mother and child.

"Father," she whispered. "I miss you so much!"

Hearing a noise behind her she turned to see Raul standing in the archway, his face smiling though his eyes shone with unshed tears as he watched her. "You should not be out of bed, Little Lady," he chastised gently.

"Raul," she smiled at him. Crossing to his side she wrapped her arms around him, hugging her old friend. "It is good to see you again."

"And you," he replied, hugging her carefully. "You have been much missed."

"I've missed you as well. Tell me, how is Mara?"

Closing his eyes for a moment he released her to see her face. "My wife passed on three years ago."

Fresh tears sprang to her eyes. "Raul, I'm so sorry, I didn't know!"

"It is well, Little Lady. No more tears now. The Master and Lady will want to know you are up, come, I will take you to them."

"Wait," she said, pulling on Raul's arm to make him stop. "Raul, tell me, what is my mother's husband like? Is he a good man?"

Frowning he searched her face. "What do you mean?"

"My mothers' husband, the new Lord of Whispering Winds, is he a good man?" she repeated, desperate to know what kind of man had taken her father's place.

Daring to touch her he felt for a fever on her cheek. "Did the illness affect your memory?"

"What are you talking about? Raul, just answer me!"

Confused he shrugged his shoulders. "Lord Charles is a good, kind, and honorable man."

Sighing she closed her eyes. "Please, Raul, why won't you tell me about this man? I know what kind of man my father was but this man who took his place, please Raul, who is he?"

Realization dawned in the old man's eyes and his mouth dropped open with shock. "Oh child," he whispered. Leading Josephine back to the chair she had been resting in he sat her down, kneeling slowly before her. "There is something you need to hear." Taking a deep breath, he held her hand gently. "When your father was fighting in the King's war he was stationed in one of the villages near the battle with the other knights. Our King's enemies found out and attacked the village killing many."

"Raul stop!" she cried, closing her eyes. "I don't want to hear about his death, I have shed too many tears already."

"Please," he pleaded. "You must listen to understand."

Not wanting to she shook her head, pulling away from him but he held firm making her stay still. Giving in, too weak to pull away, she finally nodded for him to continue. "Many loyal men died that day; one of them was our friend Fredric, your father's squire. Lord Charles laid his cloak over the boy in honor of his friendship and in respect of loyalty. While his back was turned one of the enemy plunged his sword into your father's side to kill him."

"Raul stop!" Josephine sobbed.

"But he did not die!" Raul cried, raising his voice be heard over her cries. From behind him he heard the sound of feet running through the corridors and knew the others had heard them. "Your father lives!"

Wide eyes overflowing with tears stared up at her father's old servant, her shock silencing the words that had been on the tip of her tongue. Staring at him in silence she waited for him to continue. "A fellow knight saw your father be wounded and fall. When he went to check on him he saw your father's cloak lying on the ground and assumed the body underneath it was Lord Charles. That night he sent a letter of condolence back to Whispering Winds to inform us of his death. It wasn't until three months after your disappearance that we were informed that your father lived."

Feeling as though she were going to faint Josephine stared at the man who had just uttered the very words she had dreamed of every night for fourteen years. "My father lives?" she whispered in disbelief.

"Yes pumpkin," she heard. Looking past Raul Josephine saw her mother standing in the arch that led to the main sitting room, tears in her eyes. Next to her stood an image from her dreams; his once vibrant red hair was dulled now, speckled with gray and cropped just below his chin. The mouth that had always been curved in a smile now trembled as water misted over his eyes. "Your father is alive."

Leaning on Raul Josephine rose from her seat and took a few steps toward her father but stopped, unable to move. Seeing that she couldn't come any farther he moved to meet her, reaching out to take his daughter in his arms, the fifteen years between them melting away. Pressing his lips to her hair with a fatherly kiss he tightened his hold on her.

"Josephine," he breathed, a prayer and a sigh combined together as only a father could. Removing one arm from her he held out his hand to Chelaine, the Lady quickly moving into the embrace.

Standing back, watching the three people embrace; Raul wiped an old man's tear from his eyes. A family separated for too long, reunited at last.

~~*~*~*~*~*~*~*

The pillows propping her up Josephine waited, silently, as she watched her parents try to accept where, and what, she had been for the last fourteen years. They had made her return to her bed, her mother joining her on the bed while her father sat next to her in a chair, both of them flanking their daughter. Glancing at her mother, her face filled with shock and horror, Josephine looked at her father. His pose hadn't changed, feet propped on the bed and hands folded gently in his lap, but his eyes belied the calm he was projecting. Deep in his eyes she could see anger, rage, hate and pain. The sadness that she had caused him with her story made her heart hurt.

"You were a serf?" he said at last. Josephine nodded. Charles fingertips tightened slightly as he fought to keep control. "Tell me what happened the night you were taken from Whispering Winds. I want to know everything."

"I don't remember every detail, it was too long ago, but what I can remember is that my uncle had sent me to bed before locking up the servants. I was sleeping when someone picked me up from my bed. He changed my clothes and cut off all my hair. I was screaming and he kept yelling at me to shut up but I was too scared. Finally, he hit me and that's all I remember until I woke up at the pub in Pirtonshire."

"I'm sure Lord Byron will tell me who brought you to his land."

Josephine shook her head. "No, father, he won't. Lord Byron's silence was bought for a chest of gold and jewels stolen from Whispering Winds. The necklace I wear is all there was remaining when I left Pirtonshire." Charles clenched his fist and Josephine knew she needed to tell him the rest. "Father there is more."

"Tell me," he growled, angry by what he had heard and scared by what he hadn't.

"Before I left Pirtonshire, Lady Jane confessed to me what she knew. Her silence had been bought by the jewelry but what her husband had done had never sat well with her. She told me that I had been brought to Pirtonshire to be hidden away. The man who had sold me couldn't bring himself to kill me so he bought their silence and hid me where no one would ever think to look."

"You know who did this?" She nodded mutely. "Tell me," he demanded.

His voice was soft but Josephine shuddered at the venom she heard in it. Taking a deep breath, she told him. "It was Sir Edgar, my uncle."

Lord Charles shot to his feet, storming out of the room. Sighing she leaned her head back against the pillow and closed her eyes, knowing that her father was going to fight his brother over what he had done to her. Lifting the blankets, she stood up from the bed and reached for the robe again. Moving as quickly as her aching body would let her, assuring her shaken mother that she would be all right; she left the room to find her father, following the sounds of activity that echoed in the hall. Entering her father's study, she saw him standing at the window while servant bustled around getting his things ready for travel.

Silently she motioned for them to leave the room. Waiting until they had done so she approached him; gently linking her arm through his. Folding his large hand over hers they were both silent, watching the sun set in the distant horizon. "I won't let you go," she said when the sun had dipped out of sight.

"He tried to destroy my family," Charles replied. "I will not let that go unanswered."

"Nor will I, but for fifteen years I have lived with the thought that my father was dead. I refuse to allow any instance to occur where that event might actually come true just when I have found out that it is not true."

Turning to look up at him she waited for her father to meet her eyes.

"My family was wronged by my uncle and as soon as I am well I will fight for every last drop of justice that is to be had."

~~*~*~*~*~*~*~*

Standing in the doorway to his of his daughter's room Charles watched her sleeping in the early morning light as he had every morning since she arrived home a few weeks ago. This morning though, he smiled, it was time to remind her of their special time. Entering the room, he reached out to gently shake her shoulders, waking her. "Time to wake up, Pumpkin," he whispered.

Waking, blinking the sleep from her eyes, Josephine looked up at her father. Confused at first her mind cleared and she smiled. "Give me one moment to dress," smiling back at him.

Several moments later she was standing on the steps leading out of the manor. Charles stood at the base of the hill and she hurried to meet him, falling in step together without a word. Walking away from their home Josephine took his hand in hers until he brought them both to a stop. Looking around she saw a small stone bench circling around a large oak tree.

"What is this?" she asked, glancing up at her father.

"I built this when I returned home from searching for you," he explained, sitting down with her on the bench. "This was what I kept thinking about when I wondered where you were, what you were doing. I couldn't stop thinking about why you hadn't come home."

Looking at the stone backrest she saw that some words had been etched into it. Reading them aloud she couldn't stop the tears from forming in her eyes.

"Little one wherever you may be,

I write these words for all the world to see,
That I'll wait each day until I am free,
To hold my little one that has returned to me."

Holding a hand over her heart Josephine let her tears fall. "Oh father!" she whispered, moving to wrap her arms around him.

Charles held his only child tightly to him, his own pain dripping down his cheeks. "I love you, Pumpkin," he whispered to her.

Sitting next to him on the bench Josephine held his hand in her lap, her head on his shoulder and was content to stay there. After a long time of silence Charles moved his shoulder a little bit to get her attention. "Tell me what you have done with your life since you left Pirtonshire," he asked, reminding her that she had stopped her story at Pirtonshire. "How did you come to be freed by the King?"

Settling in for a long story Josephine told him about Nicholas and Rianne, Richard and Edward, Tome, Brian, and Giselle, the jousting tournaments, summarizing her life over the last two years. She left out some of the details to try and protect him but Charles pressed her for it, wanting to know what she was hiding from him.

"Father," she sighed. "I don't want to cause you any more pain than I already have."

"Then do not ever lie to me," he replied, his face stern. "Tell me what you have left out of your story."

Closing her eyes, she sighed again, leaning against him as she told him about the few instances with James and Philip. Josephine could feel him tensing beneath her cheek. By the time she had finished he was furious.

"The Crown Prince!" he yelled, getting to his feet. His face was as red as his hair and she frowned. "The guard can be dealt with easily enough, one word to the King and he will be dismissed, but the Prince!"

"Father please!" she cried, trying to soothe his anger. "Prince Philip has already been taken care of, both King Liam and Prince Nicholas have seen to that!"

Turning to look at his daughter Charles asked, "Have either of them...?"

"No!" she replied quickly, cutting him off before he could finish his thought. "No, both King Liam and Prince Nicholas have been kind to me; no one could have treated me better than they did."

Hearing something in her tone Charles watched his daughter for a moment. "Tell me about your time with the young Prince," he asked, sitting back down again. "You traveled with him?"

"Yes," she smiled. "That was a good time for all of us."

"All of us?"

"Richard, Rianne, Nicholas and I; we traveled together."

"Josephine," Charles asked quietly. "Have you found love with one of these men?"

About to refute it she stopped, realizing that she was finally free to speak the truth that had been hidden away for so long. "Yes, I have," she said, smiling at her father. "I have!"

"Which man?"

"Prince Nicholas," she admitted. "I have fallen in love with Nicholas." She laughed, shaking her head. "I have been fighting it for so long I forgot that I am now free to say how I feel."

"Does he love you?"

Josephine said nothing, smiling as she thought back over their time together at the manor. Watching the light in her eyes, her skin seeming to glow, Charles didn't need to hear the words to know the truth. He was happy that his little girl had come to know love but at the same time his heart was pained that there was a young man wanting to take his daughter away after he had only just gotten her back.

Taking her hands in his, kissing them gently, he led the way back toward the manor. Letting Josephine spend the morning with her mother Charles stayed in his study, thinking over everything he had learned that morning. He could feel his anger at the Crown Prince simmering beneath his skin but it was outweighed at the moment by the sense of dread at losing his daughter all over again. Still dwelling on his thoughts and feelings he looked up when Chelaine entered the room, a paper in her hands. "What is it?"

"A wedding invitation," she smiled. "The Princess Rianne is marrying Lord Richard Krausley."

"I thought he was a Captain of the Guard? Isn't that what Josephine said?"

"Perhaps Liam knighted him when he gave permission for them to marry," she shrugged. "Our daughter wishes to go; she feels that she needs to be there to see them wed."

"From what I heard it is she who was responsible for their betrothal in the first place." Chelaine only smiled. "Very well, we needed to go to the palace at any rate."

He didn't say why but Chelaine's smile slipped from her face, understanding what he wasn't saying. "What are you going to do?"

Charles smiled sarcastically. "I have been forbidden from doing anything."

"I don't understand," she frowned. "Why would you do nothing?"

"If I were to have my way I would take my revenge against that brother of mine but Josephine has forbidden it. She says she will seek justice in my place."

"No!" Lady Chelaine gripped her husband's hand. "She could be killed!"

Grinning Charles got to his feet, crossing the room to his desk to pull open one of the drawers and remove a letter. "Liam sent me this many months ago," he said. "I quote, 'This young serf has one of the best eyes for a blade I have seen since you my friend. Captain Krausley tells me she is well trained and has been working with him to brush the cobwebs off her skill. Were she to meet you in battle I do not hesitate to believe that she would give you a good fight.'"

"Is he describing Josephine?"

Charles nodded. "When she was little I taught her to use a long blade," he explained. "I knew you would not approve and therefore we never told you but she picked up the skill very quickly. When I left for the war I asked Raul to continue her lessons if she wanted to. I must admit though I never expected her to retain the skill after so many years."

"I practiced," he heard from the doorway. Looking up Charles saw Josephine entering the study. "As often as I could."

"This does not make me happy," Chelaine frowned, her tone scolding to both her husband and her child. "You are supposed to be a Lady, not a knight!"

"Mother, I have no wish to be a knight," she soothed, crossing the room to hug her mother. "Had it not been for father teaching me to use the long blade I would never have been able to protect the royal family as I have."

"I still do not like it."

Charles pulled his wife into his arms. "Josephine has your beauty, your heart, your grace, your manners and my strength of body and mind. What more could we have asked for?"

Giving in Chelaine hugged him back, smiling at Josephine as she watched.

"Perhaps you could have asked for two?" Josephine teased.

Laughing, Charles opened his arms to his daughter, hugging both of his beautiful women and thanking God that he was able to do so one more time.

~~*~*~*~*~*~*~*

Sitting in the ballroom, the entire court gathered together with many of the knights and ladies from around the kingdom, Nicholas was bored. Even the silly antics of Tome weren't enough to pull him from his foul mood. He knew he had no right to feel this way. Rianne was safe, she and Richard were to be happily wed in a large ceremony tomorrow, and those who were closest to the royal family had already arrived at the palace to celebrate their union. Though most of them had been shocked to that the Princess was allowed to marry a Captain of the Guard they were mollified by the fact that King Liam had made Richard a Lord earlier that day, doing so before the wedding would actually take place.

"Stop brooding."

Looking up he saw the happy couple standing before him. "I'm not brooding," he replied. "I'm contemplating the joy I am going to have watching the people that have always looked down on Richard suddenly try to be his friend."

Clapping a hand on his shoulder Richard laughed. "A brave attempt to lie but it was useless. We know you miss her."

Sighing he leaned his head back, staring at the ceiling. "It is that obvious?"

"Only to us, Nicholas," Rianne soothed, sitting down next to her brother. "We miss her too. I only wish I knew where she is, if she's well or not."

"Da'Leth is a survivor, she'll be fine."

"But why did she leave?" Rianne despaired.

No one could answer. They'd had this conversation before, not long after Rianne had returned home. Through the night Rianne had told them exactly what had happened and what both she and Da'Leth had done to get back safely. They had all asked the same question. 'Why?' Why had she left, why didn't she tell anyone where she was going? Was she safe? Was she well? Why didn't she write to them or send word that she was all right?

They didn't know.

Called away to say hello to one of the many Lords Richard and Rianne left Nicholas to himself but before he could fall back into his own thoughts a young serf approached him timidly. "Milord?" she whispered. "I am to give you this."

Confused he took a small note from the girl and thanked her as she fled from before him. Frowning he unfolded it, reading the words that were written inside.

'My Dearest Nicholas,

I wish I could have taken the time to say this to you in person, a promise made by Da'Leth not so long ago. I gave my word you would be the first to know my secret and here it is. I ask only that you remember one fact. I never lied to you, not once.
With all the love in my heart,
Josephine of the Whispering Winds'

His confusion doubled when he read the signature but recognizing both the writing and the promise he stood, scanning the room for her. Before he could take a step in any direction the sound of the herald's cane tapping on the floor announced the arrival of another guest and all eyes turned towards the doorway. The celebration had been underway for several hours now; the new arrivals were unfashionably late. Looking towards the door Nicholas smiled a gentle smile and turned to look at his father before looking back towards the new arrivals.

"Charles!" the King cried with joy at seeing his old friend.

"Lord Charles and the Lady Chelaine of Whispering Winds," the herald announced with a bow.

Walking towards the King and Queen Lord Charles and Lady Chelaine bowed low, smiling at their old friends.

Standing off to one side Nicholas frowned. "Whispering Winds," he said to himself. "Da'Leth?"

"You have been too long gone from our side," Winifred smiled as she saw her good friends. "We are glad you are here!"

"We are happy to be with good friends," Chelaine smiled back.

"My King, I come to you today with joyous news," Charles announced with a bright smile. "For fifteen years my wife and I have been searching for what was stolen from us. After so many years I am pleased to present to his Majesty my daughter."

"Your daughter?" Liam repeated as his eyes widened with surprise. "You've found her?"

"No, My King," Charles corrected. "It was she who has found us."

"Bring her to me my friend; this truly is a joyous day!"

The cane tapped on the floor again as the herald announced, "Presenting to the crown Josephine of the Whispering Winds, the daughter of Lord Charles and the Lady Chelaine."

All eyes turned to the door, staring at the beautiful young Lady who entered the ballroom. Her fiery red hair was put up in the latest fashion and her gown reflected the most current style, her mother insisting she be introduced in the most popular fashion. For her part Josephine felt like an over-stuffed peacock and she would be glad when this was over so she could wear a simpler dress.

Watching the crowd as she stood in the doorway she could see that a few of the faces were confused, no doubt wondering who she was. Those were the ones that didn't matter. With a confident step she began to move away from the entrance, through the crowd towards her father's side. As she walked her eyes sought out those people whose opinion did matter to her.

Sitting on her throne the Queen watched Josephine approach with a smile, glad that the time of truth had finally come. Beside her stood Liam, his face a mixture of sudden understanding and confusion. She ignored the glare on Philips face and the confusion on Elizabeth's to seek out the Princess. Seeing Rianne standing next with Richard, 'Lord Richard' she reminded herself, she hoped they would forgive her for the deception once she explained in full what had happened.

When her eyes fell on Nicholas Josephine's breath caught in her chest. His face was emotionless but his eyes screamed out to her of the pain in his heart at being misled away from the truth, a truth he knew more of than nearly anyone else had.

Stopping by her father's side she smiled at him before taking a few more steps toward the King. Bowing low she stood to her full height and faced the King. "Your Majesty, my name is Josephine of the Whispering Winds. I am the daughter of Lord Charles and Lady Chelaine."

Waiting silently, she watched as he stepped down from the small platform and approached her. Standing in front of her he regarded her silently for a long moment. With a gentle hand he reached out, laying it on her shoulder. "You have a long story to tell tonight, woman," he said so only she could hear.

"Yes, my King," she whispered back.

"The crown welcomes Lady Josephine and rejoices with the family of the Whispering Winds at her safe return."

His small speech announcing his acceptance of her into the court she was soon surrounded by well-wishers and the curious stares of the elite. Unable to get away from the people it wasn't until late into the night that she was finally free to speak to any of the people that mattered most. Slipping away from the crowd she saw Rianne sitting alone in the hall, her hands pressed to her temples. Her face filled with concern Josephine approached the Princess. "Milady?"

"Da'Leth," she smiled, dropping her hands into her lap. Smiling back at her Josephine knelt before her friend, taking Rianne's hands in her own. "I'm sorry; it's not really Da'Leth, is it?"

"My name is Josephine," she replied.

"Why?" Rianne asked after a moment. "Why would you lie to me, to all of us?"

Closing her eyes for a moment Josephine leaned her head against their joined hands. "I did not lie to you, Milady," she said. "But I did not tell the whole truth either and for that I can only beg your forgiveness and hope that you can understand why I did the things that I did."

"Will you tell me now? Tell me the truth about what is going on?"

Raising her head Josephine nodded solemnly. "I will tell you whatever you ask."

Before Rianne could think to ask her first question, her mind jumbled with them, the King appeared in the hall and motioned for Josephine to come with him. Without a word she stood and followed him to his personal study. It was a room she had been in only once before but she smiled at the memory of what had happened on that occasion and what it had brought about for Rianne and Richard. Standing just inside the door, watching Liam settle himself into his chair by the fire before sending the servants away with a silent nod, she approached once the door had been shut.

"Before the rest of them get here answer one question, child," he said. "Did you befriend the royal family in order to one day seek revenge against whoever did this to you?"

Josephine was silent for a moment. "If I were to tell you the thought had never entered my mind, I would be a liar. However, I am my fathers' daughter and even when I thought he was dead I carried his lessons with me. My father had always told me stories of his good friend, King Liam. When I was told that my father had been killed I wanted to hate you for sending him to war and when I was sold as a serf I tried to hate you. I would hate you for a few moments but then my father's love for you would return to my mind."

"No matter how many times I tried I could never bring myself to truly hate you. Then, one day, Prince Nicholas rescued me from a life I thought I would never escape from. He was kind to me, Rianne was friendly to me, and most of the family has been nothing less than kind and loving toward me." Josephine paused for a moment. "That is why I have acted as I have toward the royal family."

Nodding, his face unreadable, Liam said nothing more until the rest of the people he had sent for had gathered in the study. His family, including his soon to be son in law, as well as Charles and Chelaine were seated around the room waiting for Liam to say something. Without saying a word, he motioned for Josephine to begin her story, sitting back to listen to the story behind the reasons she had briefly touched on before.

Across the room Charles, forcing himself to stay in control of his emotions as he listened to her story again, focused his attention on the people hearing it for the first time. The women were horrified, Queen Winifred's temper beginning to glimmer in her eyes. The Kings face was unemotional, years of training helping him to keep it that way, able to hide his emotions like a stone. Charles frowned with anger when he saw Philips glare but stopped to watch Nicholas' reaction to his daughter's tale.

The young man was trying to keep his face as straight as his fathers but he was failing miserably, his emotions too strong to be held in. The Prince's eyes never left Josephine as she told her tale. Though his daughter made it a point to meet the eyes of everyone in the room she could not hold his gaze for more than a few moments, her ears tingeing as she shifted her gaze away. Josephine showed no embarrassment about her history with anyone else and Charles wondered why she would with the Prince, the one she was supposedly closest to. Switching his attention back to Nicholas he remembered why, the memory hitting him like an arrow in his heart.

They were in love.

The Prince was in love with his daughter and she, the fact reinforced by her inability to meet his eye, was in love with him.

A familiar pang of jealousy swept over him as Charles watched Nicholas watch his daughter. He had only just gotten his daughter back and this young man was going to ask to take her away again. Dwelling on his jealousy for a moment another thought began to creep into his mind. His natural curiosity took over and the knowledge that this young man had fallen in love with her even though Josephine had been a serf at the time intrigued him. The love was more than an infatuation with her beauty, of that much he was certain. Nicholas' reaction to her story was too strong to be simply an infatuation with his daughter. That fact endeared the young Prince to him a little more. Charles had heard stories about the way the young man had acted in his growing years but Liam had told him the young man had gone through a sudden change of heart and attitude. He didn't know why but Nicholas hadn't reverted back since.

Josephine's words intruded upon his thoughts and Charles looked up at his daughter as she spoke. "... He is my father's brother. Law would dictate that it be left to the man in the family to exact revenge. But I beg of you, Majesty, give the right of justice to me. My father is a skilled knight but he is not as young as he once was. My uncle, though not a young man either, is many years younger than Lord Charles. My King, I beg of you, allow me to serve the justice my family is owed."

The room fell silent as Josephine stopped talking and stood still to wait for the King's decision. She tried to ignore the tears in Rianne's eyes and the anger in Winifred's. Josephine ignored the skepticism on Philips face and focused on the Kings reaction to her tale. Though the desire to see Nicholas's reaction was strong her fear of it kept her from meeting his eyes.

"Why did you never lay a claim to your place until now?" Liam asked after a moment of silence. "Did you not trust us to help you?"

"That was never my reason, Majesty," she explained quickly. "So long as I was a serf I could not be Josephine. That is why I answered to the name of Da'Leth. I refused to allow the honor of Whispering Winds to be associated with that of a serf. My father has never owned a serf; he has always found the concept of owning a human being revolting, as do I. He is known to the entire Kingdom for this attitude. No amount of freedom would justify dishonoring his memory. I would have rather died a serf than lived free with the knowledge that I had destroyed everything my father stood for."

Chapter Nineteen

Standing in his room Nicholas stared out at the moonlit grounds below his window. His body was tired but his mind refused to sleep, going over and over the story Da'Leth had told. "Josephine," he corrected himself aloud. Despite himself he smiled at the sound of it. Da'Leth had never seemed like the right name for her. Sighing, tired, he was about to turn away from the window when he saw a light pass by the window in the tower across the grounds. Knowing it was her he slipped on a shirt, forgoing the proper attire in his rush to get to her before anyone else did, and hurried out the door.

After their family gathering, her full history finally laid bare, Josephine and Lord Charles had been kept behind while everyone else had been ordered to leave the room. He had tried to wait but the private meeting had gone on late into the evening. Promising himself he was going to wait by the door Nicholas was called away to help put Tome to sleep. By the time he had returned to the room it was empty, the fire put out.

Opening the door to the tower Nicholas climbed up the stairs, taking them two at a time, and emerged at the top to see Josephine huddled in the corner, hiding from the stiff wind. The intricate gown she had been wearing had been exchanged for a simple green one he recognized immediately as the one he liked most. As he shut the door behind him he couldn't help but wonder if she had purposefully chosen that gown to soften him. 'It worked,' he thought to himself with a small laugh as he felt his heart softening toward her. Seeing her waiting for him to arrive, huddled in the corner, cold and scared, made his urge to protect her surge to the surface, stronger than he had ever felt before.

Sitting down next to Josephine he looked at her to see that she was watching him carefully. Her eyes reminded him of Philips dogs and the thought disgusted him, the poor animals ready for a beating they expected to come at any moment. "What are you doing out here?"

"I felt I needed to be here tonight," she answered with a shrug.

Seeing her shiver in the cold Nicholas wished he had brought a cloak with him for her. Moving closer he put an arm around her to try and warm her against the chill. Startled by the move Josephine jumped in her skin, stiff for several moments, before relaxing into his side, soaking in the warmth he was sharing with her. Silence surrounded them for several more moments before she finally spoke, her voice so low he almost missed her comment. "I never meant to deceive you."

"Why didn't you tell me the truth?" he asked; the pain still evident in his voice.

"There was a time when I did," she reminded the Prince. "That night in the inn you knew more than anyone had ever known."

"After you saved Rianne," Nicholas remembered. "You did tell me some of the truth but left out many of the details."

"I had to milord."

"Why?" Josephine didn't reply and Nicholas realized she didn't have to, his mind recalling the reason she had given to them all in his father's chamber. "Your father," he remembered. "You were protecting his honor."

"And my mothers."

"Your family's honor is very important to you."

"It was all I had."

"You had me."

Silence fell again as Josephine smiled gently at the warmth spreading through her with his words.

"What about that day in the park in Paris?" he asked after a moment, leaning his head onto hers.

"I was scared," she admitted, remembering that day when she had clearly seen how he felt about her. "The only man whose love I had ever known was my father's and he had died when I was a child.

I had been fighting what I felt for you for so long and I was scared that if I allowed myself to admit what was in my heart that I would betray the vow I had made to seek justice for my family."

Her words stopped his heart. "How did you feel at that time?" he asked, hope rising up in his chest so fast he could barely contain it.

"I was in love with you," she whispered.

Nicholas noted the past tense and his heart began to sink. "And now?"

"Da'Leth is dead so that Josephine may live," she said, reminding him of the night she had riddled her true feelings for him. "My feelings have not changed but it does not matter. You are a Prince; you have an obligation to the people to marry a certain kind of woman that I simply am not. I was never..."

"Better suited to serve the people in such a role," he finished for her. "You have lived among them, as one of them. Who better to help bring about the changes that will benefit the people?"

Josephine could feel tears stinging in her eyes. She had expected anger, disappointment, hurt; never had she thought he would praise her. "You're not upset? Not angry that I deceived you?"

Sighing Nicholas took her hand in his. "I was. Furious, hurt, upset; but I thought about it and I began to understand. You were protecting your family the same way I am, by staying away."

The tears that had stung at her eyes now began to fall from them when she heard his words, realizing that he truly did understand her actions. A smile tugged at his lips when felt her tears soaking into his shirt. Looking down he wiped them away with a gentle hand. "Such a contradiction," he teased. "Strong as a man in body, tough as a knight in character, and yet inside beats the heart of an innocent woman."

Josephine could feel the heat of a blush burning in her cheeks. Unsure of what to say she said nothing, dropping her gaze to the hands that held her. Hooking a finger under her chin Nicholas forced her to look at him. "When you were a serf you said that it was not your place to love a Prince. I didn't believe you then and I still don't even now."

Josephine was silent for some time, staring at him. Her tone wavering only slightly she spoke quietly. "My place cannot be at your side."

"That is not what I wanted to know," knowing he had to make her tell the truth. "Do you love me now, as a free woman and a Lady? Yes or no?"

There was no way for her to escape the question. "Yes."

Nicholas smiled and leaned forward, placing a chaste kiss on her lips. "I already know that you would never lie to me so if you say that you love me it must be true." In spite of her trepidation Josephine smiled at his suddenly playful mood. "Therefore, it is only proper for me to do tell you that I will do whatever I have to in order to keep you by my side forever. This last month has proven to me how much I need you in my life." Reaching out to cup her cheek he leaned in closer to whisper in her ear, "You see, I love you too, Josephine of the Whispering Winds."

~~*~*~*~*~*~*~*

Leaning against the railing of the upper balcony Josephine watched as Rianne walked down the long aisle below her toward the man she had pledged her love to. Dressed all in white she was radiant, a glow shining out that even Josephine could see from so far away. When she reached the halfway point of the aisle King Liam met her, taking her hand to lead her the rest of the way to her groom. Kissing his daughter gently Liam gave her hand to Richard, shaking his firmly, a few whispered words in his ear. 'Take care of my daughter,' Josephine imagined he had probably said to the new Lord.

Smiling she watched, listened, as the priest married the man and the woman, each of them repeating in turn their vow to love, honor, and obey - till death do they part. A part of her ached to be down there now, celebrating with her friends instead of stuck, hidden away, watching from a distance. Glancing at the audience, though, she knew she had to be where she was. Both Lord Byron and Sir Edgar were in attendance at the wedding and she could not take the chance of being seen before it was time to make her presence known.

Refusing to dwell on unhappy thoughts she looked back at Rianne, smiling when she saw her wipe a tear from her eyes. Watching them kiss their first kiss as husband and wife she wiped away a tear of her own. "One day," she promised herself. "One day I will find that happiness as well."

~~*~*~*~*~*~*~*

Standing by the fire Nicholas waited for his guest to arrive, a small breakfast for two waiting a few feet away. His eyes stared at the flames calmly but his mind was flying over the possible outcomes of the next few moments.

"Prince Nicholas?"

Turning he saw Lord Charles standing in the doorway to his study, waiting for permission to enter the room. Nodding to the servant that had led the man to the study Nicholas asked Charles to come and join him, the door shutting to give the men privacy. The knight sat down in one of the chair, crossed his legs, folded his arms and looked up at the young Prince, waiting for what he knew was coming.

"Thank you for agreeing to meet with me for a meal," Nicholas said as he took his seat across the small table from Lord Charles. "I hope you were not interrupted in any way."

Charles shrugged. "I serve the crown, Prince Nicholas."

Despite his nervousness Nicholas chuckled. "Josephine always says the same thing."

Seeing the grin, hearing the chuckle, and pleased that he had called his daughter by her name of Josephine, Charles relaxed his position a little bit. The rest of the family still called her Da'Leth, a name that he had come to detest. Nicholas, however, had called her Josephine and not Da'Leth. "Tell me of the first time you met my daughter."

Realizing he was going to be talking for a while Nicholas made himself comfortable, leaning back in his chair. "It was in Pirtonshire," he began. "I was traveling with my men and had stopped to get some rest. The crowd in the marketplace had caught my attention so I walked about in them for a little while. The first time I saw her was at the pub. She had slipped a scrap of food to a hungry child but didn't escape attention of Lord Byron. What stood out to me was the way she stood before him. Most serfs shrink back from people that are not one of their own class but Josephine didn't. She stood before Lord Byron with respect but maintained her own dignity as well. It confused and intrigued me. She was punished but slipped away before I could get any answers."

Charles nodded; she had told him how she had come to be sold that day. "Why highness?" he asked. "Why did you buy my daughter?"

"I'm afraid," he said with a small shake of his head, "That it was for purely selfish reasons."

"Explain."

"My sister had joined us unexpectedly without any of her ladies' maids. She was to travel home with us but would be alone with my men and me. I was on my way to see Lady Jane when we passed by the auction. I saw her there and knew I would never get the chance to gather my answers if I didn't get them now. I was simply going to speak to her at first but then I saw her standing up to the crowd. Josephine refused to be humiliated by the crowd; she held her head high and met each man's eyes. That was when I knew I wanted her to travel with us to serve my sister."

Charles wondered. "You trusted her to protect the Princess without even knowing her?"

"No," Nicholas shook his head. "Not at first. I had Edward keeping an eye on her."

"Then when did you trust her? Why?"

"While we were traveling the party was attacked. Josephine defended my sister, making sure she was safe before attacking the men that had attacked. She did all that at the risk of her own life and it almost came to that. We found her hurt, unconscious, on the path."

Watching Nicholas recount what had happened Charles heard the admiration in his voice and saw it in his eyes.

"That was when I knew she could be trusted. It was also when I knew there was more to her than met the eyes."

Silence fell as Charles studied the young Prince for a moment.

"For fifteen years I have been searching, hunting, for any sign or clue that my daughter was alive. Hope was slipping away with each passing year. You helped return her to me and for that I owe you more than can ever be repaid. However, asking me to let my daughter go when I have only just gotten her back is too much. No, I cannot allow my blessing."

Nicholas was surprised by his insight on their meeting and his denial stung deeply. "My father has always told me you were never one to say no to the royal family."

"I have never and will never say no to the crown," Charles frowned. "You are a mere Prince; I serve only the interest of my King."

Nicholas nodded in understanding. "I have heard that many times from your daughter. Now I know where her devotion comes from." Sitting forward Nicholas met Charles eyes. "You have been searching for Josephine for fifteen years and for fifteen years Josephine has lived with the knowledge that her father was dead. I cannot begin to imagine the kind of nightmare your family has been living with. I have seen the pain and sadness in Josephine's eyes and now I have seen it in yours as well. You can rest assured that I will never allow anything to hurt Josephine, including myself. You are already aware that I love your daughter; that much I can see."

Charles nodded. "I knew as much the night we came to the palace. You were angered by her story but more than that you were offended. Her pain hurt you. That told me more than any words could have."

"As a man who loves your daughter I cannot accept no as an answer," Nicholas told him honestly. Seeing the hard look that came into Charles eyes he held up his hands to stop whatever anger was building. "However, as a man of honor who loves your daughter I would never try to separate Josephine from you."

"So, what do you propose?" he inquired, curious as to the Prince's line of thinking.

"My brother is to become King when the time comes, his son Brian to do so after Philip has died. I am left to make my own way in the world, a way that I have made quite well in the jousting arena. My herd of horses is one of the finest in the kingdom and the money to be made from the breeding and selling of them ensures you will never need to worry about Josephine being provided for. All I ask is this," he finished. "Promise me a blessing to take your daughters hand in marriage and I give you my word as a Prince, a gentleman, and a future son-in-law, we will make our home at Whispering Winds."

Charles looked at the Prince, saw the determination in his eyes and sighed. "If my daughter loves you enough to agree to marry you, without coercion, then you may have my blessing." He added with a pointed finger, "So long as you honor your word."

~~*~*~*~*~*~*~*

Liam resisted the urge to roll his eyes when he heard his son's request. "Do you think me a blind old man, boy?" he demanded. "I have seen the way you look at her, even when we thought she was a serf. Your brother has spoken to me multiple times about the indecency of it."

Nicholas frowned at the mention of his brother. "What did he say?"

Waving his hand, he dismissed the question. "That is unimportant. You love her and she loves you; were she only a free-woman I would need time to consider your request. As it stands, she is a Lady and the daughter of a man who is as close to me as if he was my brother."

Liam got up from his chair and lovingly slapped Nicholas on the back. "Go on son, you have my permission and my blessing. Josephine could not be more welcome in my family if she were my own daughter."

Thanking his father, promising to announce their engagement to the court later that night at dinner, Nicholas left to find his mother. Kneeling before her he asked for the ring she had promised him for his wife when he was a child. "For Josephine?" she asked with a smile. Getting up from her seat she walked to the bureau and pulled a small velvet bag from the top drawer. Handing it to her son Winifred kissed his cheek, brushing a tear from her eye. "You've chosen a good woman, Nicholas. Make her happy, you both deserve it."

Returning her kiss Nicholas hugged his mother tight before leaving the room. He wanted to find Josephine right away, his heart bubbling over, but there was one more person he needed to see before he could start his life with her. Hunting down his brother he found him in his study ogling one of the maids as she reached to dust the top shelf of books. 'Per his command no doubt,' Nicholas thought to himself with a frown. "Get out," he told the maid, shutting the door behind her. Turning to face his brother he saw him start to stand and pointed at him. "Sit down!"

"What is the meaning of this?" Philip demanded. "What has gotten into you, Nicholas?" Ignoring the warning he stood.

"What did she ever do to you?"

"What are you talking about?"

"Josephine," he growled, getting angry at Philip's oblivions. "I am talking about Josephine."

"Who?"

"Do not belittle me, Philip!" Nicholas seethed. "Josephine has saved this family many times over; even your son owes her his life."

A light dawned in Philips eyes and he frowned. "She is a serf. No serf should be stationed above their place."

"She is a Lady," he replied, forcing himself to resist the ever-growing urge to hit his brother. "And soon she will be my wife. You would do well to remember..."

Before he could finish warning his brother to treat Josephine with the respect and dignity that she deserved Philip stormed out of his study, yelling for the servants to find his father. "First a Captain and now a serf!" he yelled, storming down the hall. "It will be a hot January before I will allow a serf's blood to pollute this family line!"

Rounding the corner with the newlyweds Josephine stopped still at the Prince's words. Before she could think to react, Nicholas grabbed his older brother's shirt and pushed him into one of the tapestries hanging from the wall. Fighting back Philip punched Nicholas' side, struggling to get away. Josephine and Richard rushed forward to separate the two men.

"Stop it!" Rianne cried out, anger and worry mixing in her voice.

"Enough of this!" Richard cried. Pulling Philip away from Nicholas at the same time as Josephine pulled Nicholas away from Philip, Richard stumbled back, catching the Prince before he could stumble into one of the statues.

"Do not touch me!" the Crown Prince ordered, pulling himself from Richards grasp. "This marriage will not happen, I will not allow it!"

Turning Philip stalked down the hallways, servants scattering from before him in a hurried attempt to get away from his anger. Reaching for Josephine's hand Nicholas followed his brother to the find their father and put an end to this once and for all. Entering the room, he saw that Philip was speaking abusively of Josephine before a small crowd of people including his parents, Josephine's parents and a few influential members of the court.

"Prince Nicholas," Lord Thomas spoke. "Is this true? Have you asked a serf to marry you?"

"No," he refuted immediately, his face hard with anger. "I have asked Lady Josephine of the Whispering Winds, daughter of Lord Charles and Lady Chelaine to be my wife." Hearing a small gasp from beside him he turned to face Josephine, tightening his hold on her hand and smiling as best he could through his anger. "I have already asked for her father's permission and he has given it. If Josephine agrees to marry me we shall be wed on any date of her choosing."

Slipping the ring from its velvet home he gently placed it on her finger, watching her eyes. Staring down at her, waiting for some sort of response, his heart soared when she raised her face to his, a smile shining up at him brightly. With a small laugh he reached down, wrapping his arms around Josephine and holding her tightly, feeling her own arms around him, her smile on his neck. Across the room from each other the four parents smiled at each other, glad that things had worked out so well even without their involvement.

"Prince Philip," one of the older courtiers asked with a confused look. "I do not understand the objection. Prince Nicholas and Lady Josephine were betrothed when they were children. Why do you object to the match now?"

Pulling apart, glancing at each other briefly, the two lovers looked to their parents for confirmation. Nodding Charles said, "Our families have always been close. It was a good match. When you were old enough we had planned to make it known to you. Sadly, that did not happen as we had planned."

"But," Winifred added. "It has all worked out in the end. Our son and your daughter have come together for the best reason of all."

"Love," Lady Chelaine smiled at her friend. "You have both made us very happy," turning to look at her daughter.

"She is a serf!" Philip cried, pointing accusingly at Josephine.

Charles shot to his feet, anger filling his eyes but Nicholas spoke before he could defend his daughter. "I warned you brother," he ground out between clenched teeth. "Speak ill of her again and you will regret your words."

Opening his mouth to retort Philip was silenced by his father. "Enough of this!" Liam declared. "The match has been made and it has been blessed by both fathers. Josephine shall choose her date and on that day, they shall wed."

Knowing his father's decree was final Philip could only show his displeasure by storming out of the room, a glare on his face as he passed his brother, purposefully hitting his shoulder to Nicholas' roughly. Turning to reach out and grab Philips arm Nicholas stopped when he felt Josephine pulling on him. "Just let him go," she said, her calm voice belying the anger in her eyes. "It's not worth it."

Turning to face her Nicholas forced a small smile onto his face. "Already the voice of reason?"

"I always have been," she replied, her smile just as forced as his, still upset by Philips reaction.

Putting an arm around her Nicholas held her, his thumb gently stroking her shoulder. Allowing herself to lean into him for a moment Josephine recalled there were other people in the room and stood up straight, taking a step toward the King.

"Thank you, Majesty," she said with a small bow. "You have always been too kind to me."

Chuckling, Liam stepped down from his chair and took Josephine's shoulders in his hands, placing a fatherly kiss on her cheek. "You have only ever received from me that which you earned for yourself." His smile fell away for a moment as Liam lowered his voice. "Be ready child, in one week's time you shall have your justice. Tonight," he announced, raising his voice again for everyone to hear. "We shall celebrate, for my son has chosen his bride."

Escaping away from the well-wishers Nicholas and Josephine escaped up to their tower, alone to bask in the love they were finally able to admit to themselves and each other.

"Betrothed."

Nicholas smiled. "Apparently so." Looking down at her he asked, "Does it matter to you?"

"No," she answered right away. A smiled tugged at her lips. "Though I do find it interesting that we still fell in love."

"God must have wanted our hearts together, no matter what."

Nodding Josephine looked up at him. "When did you fall in love with me? Was it that night in Paris?"

Leaning his head against hers, wrapping his arm around her tightly, he laughed. "It was during the joust in Ivanhar. You had always intrigued me. I knew that I trusted you, valued your honest opinion and your friendship. But during the joust, when I saw you sitting with Rianne, watching and worrying, I realized that having you there meant more to me than having Rianne there. Knowing that you were watching, worried about me, made me feel good and when you were tending to my wounds that night," he shrugged. "I just knew that I needed you to stay with me, by my side forever."

Josephine was silent; soaking in the information he had just laid out for her, his love from the very beginning.

"When did you know?" he asked, turning her own question against her. "More importantly when did you let yourself admit it?"

In spite of herself she laughed. "They were two very separate moments," she acknowledged. Thinking for a moment she sat still. "I believe I began to love you defending me from James after he..." she couldn't finish the thought, shaking her head a little to dismiss it. "Until then I thought of you as a rescuer, a knight in gleaming armor, the man who woke me from my nightmare. As time passed I knew you were a good man and I respected you for it. When I saw you playing with Tome though I knew I had found a friend and kindred spirit."

Smiling at the praise he pressed her. "And when did you allow yourself to admit it?"

"It was while I was lying in bed, recovering my health at Whispering Winds. I began to think about the life that I had been missing for the last fifteen years. I was a free woman again; I was finally home with my family where I belonged and my father was alive. It was more than I had ever dared to hope for and yet I felt incomplete, as though something were missing. Everything that I had ever wanted I had, yet it wasn't enough."

"I missed you. I missed seeing you, talking to you. It was only a matter of time until I came back to the palace to seek justice. I knew I would see you again but as much as I wanted to see you I was scared, terrified really, that you wouldn't forgive me."

Nicholas gently kissed her. Sitting in silence for some time, content to simply be together, it wasn't until the sun had sunk into the horizon and the stars were shining brightly in the sky that they touched on a subject neither one wanted to bring up.

"What do you think he will do?" she asked quietly.

"Philip is full of himself. He blows off steam like a kettle and then simmers down." Nicholas forced Josephine to look at him. "Stay away from him until this is over. I don't want you near him without me."

"You don't believe I can protect myself?" she frowned.

Meeting her eyes, "You know I would lay my life in your hands," he reassured. "That is not in question. My brother is a subversive man, he will whittle away at your confidence until you no longer trust your skills or yourself. Then he will attack you with ten men before putting the final blade in your back himself."

"You truly do not like him," Josephine said after a moment. "I knew you didn't care for him but..."

"I learned the hard way not to trust my brother."

"What do you mean?"

"It started back when I was a little boy. There are many years between us and I used to look up to him as an older brother. Philip knew that and took advantage of it. He used me to smuggle things into the palace and get things he would have gotten in trouble for having. After a while I stopped wanting to be near him but I still thought of him as my older brother, someone to be looked up to."

Nicholas paused for a moment, collecting his thoughts from that awful day eleven years ago. "When I was young there was a family that lived in the servants' quarters, they had served us since before I was born. They had a daughter and a son, twins, that were the same age as me and we would play together whenever we could.

As we got older the daughter, Sienna, became a beautiful young woman."

"Oh no," Josephine moaned, suddenly understanding where the story was heading, what had happened to put hate between two brothers.

Nodding he wrapped his arm tighter around Josephine. "I'm afraid so. Philip was never sorry for it. Sienna was destroyed, her family disgraced. Her brother, Stephen, tried to avenge her by challenging Philip to a duel but he lost and was killed in the process. I sent the family to serve another Lord in the southern tip of the kingdom so they could start over. A few years later I received notice that Sienna had taken her own life."

"Oh Nicholas," she cried. "How awful!"

He fell silent for a few moments, remembering his long-gone friends. "I've never been able to forgive Philip for what he did and I doubt I ever will. He knows that I never told father what had happened and it is the only reason that he will keep away from certain things if I press the issue hard enough. As the years pass though it gets harder and harder to keep him in line."

"Nicholas, this man is to be King one day! How can he be trusted to rule a kingdom?"

"He is the firstborn son of the King, Josephine, heir to the throne."

"If he becomes King he will destroy this kingdom, you have to realize that."

"What can I do about it?" he replied. "I have thought about this for many years. He is a good strategist; he'll keep the kingdom, as a whole, safe. All I can do is to try and help the people in every way that I can. Please understand this Josephine," looking down at her. "It's the only thing that can be done until Philip shows his true colors to my father."

~~*~*~*~*~*~*~*

"No."

"Sweetheart," Chelaine tried to reason. "This is a beautiful design."

"No."

"It sounds as though her mind is made up, Chelaine," Winifred smiled.

Sighing in frustration Chelaine sat down in her chair. "Why do you keep rejecting every design that is brought to you?"

"Because they are too much," Josephine tried to explain. "I will gladly do whatever you ask on every aspect of the wedding, except this one. I am the one who has to wear the dress, mother, please do not make me wear something I do not like!"

"I believe I may have just the design for you," one of the seamstresses said, getting up from her seat in the corner, a new sketch in her hand. "Does the Lady like this one perhaps?"

Looking down at the paper in her hand Josephine saw a very basic design, a scooping neckline that was decent, sleeves the flared a little at the end and a simple belt to tie around the waist. There was only one flaw.

"If you remove the gathering at the elbow this will be perfect," she smiled at the woman. "Thank you."

Nodding with a smile the woman left to get to work after showing the design to Winifred and Chelaine. Smiling at them Josephine sat down again and looked over the various bouquets of flowers that had been left for her to choose from. Picking one that she liked she asked, "Is there anything else I need to tend to?"

"I have never seen a bride with so little interest in her own wedding," Chelaine said with a small shake of her head.

"I do not care to concern myself with details that will most likely be forgotten in a few years. The only thing that matters to me is that Nicholas and I will be wed. What else need I be concerned with?"

"You may go, Josephine," Winifred smiled. As she was leaving she heard the Queen continue to her mother, "She knows her mind as well as you do your own, Chelaine," she said with a small laugh. "You cannot fault her for that."

Smiling Josephine escaped into the hallway, leaving them to sort out the details of the wedding. Walking down the hallway she didn't have a direction in mind, simply happy to wander wherever the next turn led her. As she took in the sight around her Josephine was flooded with memories from her time in the palace as a serf. Chasing Tome through the halls, talking with Rianne near the fire in her chamber, practicing with Richard in the courtyard; they assaulted her as she wandered.

"Da'Leth?"

Turning at the sound of her old name Josephine saw Philip standing in the doorway, hidden in the shadows until he stepped forward. "Milord?" she said, watching him carefully.

"You're all alone? My brother must have more confidence in your skill than I do. After all I know how easy it can be to get past your defenses."

"Did you need something in particular, milord?" she asked, not allowing him to get under her skin. Keeping her tone even and her face blank she asked, "Or did you simply wish to bother me?"

"You would dare to address me in such a tone? It's not befitting a serf," he told her.

"I am no serf, milord, as you have been told on countless occasions."

"You will always be a serf, Da'Leth," he whispered to her, stepping closer even as she stepped away.

"Milady?" Hearing the sound of another person approaching Philip winked at her before disappearing around the corner of the next hallway. "Is everything all right?"

Looking up to see Edward walking towards her Josephine smiled, her hands trembling as she folded them. "It is now, Edward, thank you."

He looked at her carefully before nodding. "Very well then. His Majesty, the King, has asked that you join him in his study. He awaits you there."

"Thank you, Edward," she nodded, turning to move in the proper direction.

Before she rounded the corner, Josephine took one final look backwards and saw Edward disappearing down the same hall Philip had only moments ago. Continuing down the corridors to the King's study she thought back over the last few days since Nicholas had announced to the family that they were going to marry. Edward had been scarce, difficult to find but when he did appear it was usually before or after Philip. Pausing outside the door she wondered if Nicholas had ordered Edward to follow Philip, to keep track of him.

Entering the room, she put the thought to the back of her mind and smiled at the King. "You wished to see me, Majesty?"

Liam motioned for her to sit down across from him. "I have received replies from Sir Edgar and Lord Byron. Both will be in attendance tomorrow."

Her heart stilled in her chest for a moment and Josephine forgot how to breathe. It had finally come. Forcing herself to take in a breath of air she looked at Liam. "What shall be done, my King?"

"I wanted to discuss that with you." Leaning back in his chair Liam folded his hands over his chest and stared at his daughter in law to be. "You say that you want to be the one to claim revenge for what they did to you and I can understand that. Would you have them killed?"

Josephine shook her head. "No," she said softly. "I have had fifteen years to think about this. As much as they have hurt my family, as much as they have hurt me, I cannot in good conscious demand that they be killed."

"I disagree," he countered. "If you allow them to live they will simply try to get revenge for whatever it is that you are going to do to them."

"I know."

"Why don't you want them dead?"

Josephine sighed. "Sir Edgar is my uncle. Like it or not we share a little bit of the same blood. I cannot kill my own family."

"And Lord Byron?"

"I do not want to see Lady Jane hurt. She did what she could to help me. Though I may not understand why, she does love her husband. If I were to kill him it would hurt her and that I could not bear."

Liam was quiet for several moments as the thought over her logic. "Very well," he said at last. "Tell me what you have in mind for them."

"An eye for an eye."

Liam raised an eyebrow and motioned for her to continue, curious about what she meant.

"I was sold into serfdom against my will. For six years I slaved for Lord Byron until one night I was able to escape. I had an entire day of freedom before his guards found me again. When I was brought back to Pirtonshire I was whipped for escaping and sent back to work. I slaved from then on until Nicholas took me away. After that, as you know, I served for about two years here at the palace before I was free to return to my home."

Liam noticed the difference of her choice of words, 'slaving' for Lord Byron but 'serving' here at the palace, and he appreciated it. "That is what you want their punishment to be?"

"Yes. There are a few more minor details however." Listening as she detailed out the rest of their punishment he was amazed at her thoroughness, telling her so. "As I said, my King, I have had a very long time to think about this moment."

~~*~*~*~*~*~*~*

Standing in the shadows Josephine could see that the main hall was filling quickly, the upper class gathering to celebrate the Prince's engagement to Lady Josephine, a woman that most were eager to meet as they had never heard of her before. She doubted they truly wanted to know her; they only wanted to know about her so they could talk about her when they were away from the palace. Scanning her eyes over the crowd she saw Lord Edwin passing by and she watched him closely. Josephine could see that he was in well enough health, the wound from the joust had obviously healed, and she was glad. Her cousin had always been a good man and she doubted he'd had any involvement with her kidnapping.

When Edwin was out of sight she scanned back over the crowd and stopped in shock. "Lady Jane?" she whispered to herself. Frowning she saw that Lord Byron was with her as well. The King had told her that her uncle and Lord Byron would be there but hadn't mentioned the Lady of Pirtonshire would be as well. Josephine realized it was going to be tricky now. She wanted Lord Byron to pay for what he had done but not Lady Jane; she had been a friend to her and Josephine didn't want to see her hurt.

"Are you ready?"

She felt a strong pair of arms encase her from behind and Josephine sank into their embrace. "I must admit I'm a little nervous."

"Why?" Nicholas asked.

"I've wanted to confront them for sixteen years. Now that the moment has finally come I don't know if I'll be able to control my temper."

He smiled. "You will do fine."

"There's more to it now. Lady Jane is here."

"I don't understand why that should matter?" She explained her reasoning but Nicholas shook her head.

"She should have done something. She let you live in that nightmare for nigh on fifteen years, Josephine. Lady Jane shouldn't go unpunished."

"No, Nicholas. She didn't ask for it to happen and when the time came she did what she could to help me. When Lord Byron is exposed she will be humiliated, I don't want her hurt any farther than she has to be."

Nicholas didn't agree but he said nothing, knowing her mind was made up on the matter. He had made sure that the guards in the room were armed and alert, in case something should happen. Both he and Richard wore their swords, ready to come to Josephine's aide should she need it, and he had seen Lord Charles with his as well. He was anxious for justice to be delivered. If he could have had his way the ones responsible for this would be dead already but Josephine had been adamant.

No killing.

From the head of the room he saw his father take his place after escorting Winifred to her throne and knew the time had finally come. Listening to Liam begin his speech he led Josephine out one of the hidden doors and they made their way to the main entrance to wait for Liam's command to enter. Standing together in silence Nicholas raised their joined hands to his lips, kissing her knuckles.

"Just remember, no matter what happens in there today, I will always be there for you," he said as the doors began to open.

"I love you," she smiled gently.

When the large doors came to a stop the musicians began to play a fanfare to announce their arrival. Leading the way, her hand held high atop his, Nicholas and Josephine entered the room, walking down the long carpet that led to the throne.

As they passed by the people Josephine kept her face turned to the front but her eyes scanned the crowds. She saw various Lords and Ladies that she recognized from her time at the palace but paid them little attention. As they reached the midpoint of the room she saw Lady Jane, her eyes widening in shock when she recognized her. Nodding at the older woman she offered a small smile before fixing her eyes on Lord Byron standing next to his wife. Nodding to him as well she schooled her face, the smile disappearing from his view as quickly as it had appeared for his wife.

Refusing to waste his time on the Pirtonshire couple Nicholas looked ahead to Sir Edgar. Picking him out of the crowd he could see the older man watching them approach, his face pulled down in confusion. Meeting his eyes as they passed by he smiled at the shock and fear the crept onto his face. From the corner of his eye he saw Josephine nod at her uncle, her face carefully blank though her eyes were filled with a mixture of emotions.

Continuing on they stopped in front of the throne. "Father, Mother," Nicholas said with a formal bow while Josephine curtsied. "I wish for you to meet Lady Josephine of the Whispering Winds. In two weeks' time we will wed and wish for your blessing to do so."

When his ceremonial request was made Nicholas waited for his father to reply so the crowd could hear his answer. He listened as Liam gave his blessing, welcoming Josephine to his family. Then, when Liam's speech was over, Nicholas kissed Josephine's hand and stepped away, letting her face the King on her own. "My King, I stand before you now, thankful for everything the royal family has given me in the few short years that I have had the privilege to have known you. But I must ask now, nay, I demand that justice be given to my family, and to myself, for what has been done to us."

Liam nodded and motioned to the guards. Several men suddenly stepped out of their line, moving towards the people they were ordered to bring forwards. Keeping her back to them Josephine heard the cries of surprise that echoed through the crowd. She could hear movement from behind her and wanted to look back but kept her eyes forward until Liam spoke.

"Lady Josephine, please do examine these people behind you and tell me which of them are responsible for the wrong that was done to you and your family."

Nodding once she turned around. Gathered in a group she could see that her uncle's entire family had been pulled forward, including Sir Edwin and his own family. Moving forward she arranged the group into two, directing the women to stand in a separate group from the men. When the split was complete she approached her cousin.

"Answer me honestly, cousin," she said looking up into Sir Edwin's eyes. "Do you know why you have been brought to stand with this group?"

"On my honor," he said, his head shaking from side to side, "I do not know."

Watching his eyes for a moment Josephine nodded, motioning for him to stand with the women. Turning to look at the only two remaining men she met each of their eyes for a moment before turning back to the King. "It is these two men, My King, that have wronged me. There is a third but as I was too young to know him I cannot give you his name."

Stepping down from his throne Liam approached the two men. Pausing before the second, larger group he glanced at them before speaking, "You may all go, save for Lady Jane. Lady, you must stay." Hesitating only for a moment the group slipped back into the crowd.

Liam turned his attention back to the two Lords standing before him. "Until this moment I had considered you both to be good men," he said to them with a venomous tone. "To hear what you have done to the daughter of my most trusted friend sickens me and were I to do as I please I would hang you by the neck so the vultures may feast on your carcasses."

The hall was silent, every eye riveted on the scene unfolding before them. The Kings anger was palpable, and it filled the room with a dark cloud.

"As it is I have given my word that your punishment shall be decided by the one to whom the wrong was done. Send a prayer of thanks to God alone that she does not wish your blood to be spilled for I would see you both killed this very moment."

Liam turned to Josephine and nodded, stepping back so that she could face her uncle and captor. "Tell me the name of the man who took me from my bed," she demanded, looking at her uncle with a cold stare.

"Niece, I do not understand the meaning of all this!" he cried, reaching out to touch her elbow. "Only just now have I discovered you to be alive, how could I possibly know what else has been happening to you these last sixteen years?"

"Do not play games with me Uncle," she warned him. "I have hated you for sixteen years and the only thing preventing me from taking your life is the fact that you are my father's brother."

Sir Edgar dropped his hand to his side and stared at her.

"I know why you did what you had done that night uncle, now tell me the name of the man you hired to do it."

"My niece," he began, trying to convince her of his innocence.

"Tell her!" Liam roared, his anger echoing off the walls.

"Roche," Lord Byron answered, hoping to gain favor in their eyes by giving them what they wanted. "His name is Arnos Roche, a petty thief who lives on the border."

"Then if he has a friend in this room let that friend warn him to flee for his life," Josephine advised, raising her voice so they could all hear. "If Arnos Roche is found he will suffer the same fate as these two."

"And what fate might that be, milady?" Byron asked, his voice begging forgiveness. "Would your mercy prove to be as bounteous as your beauty?"

Nicholas took a step forward in disgust but stopped when he saw Josephine wither him with her stare.

"No, Lord Byron, it would not." Looking at both of the men she told them their punishment. Looking directly at Sir Edgar she said, "Uncle, an eye for an eye and a tooth for a tooth."

"I lived as a serf for fifteen years because of your greed and now so shall you. Your title will be taken away from you and you will be sold to a Lord as a serf. In the sixth year of your punishment you shall be given one day of freedom to do with as you please. The next day you will be found and whipped before resuming your time as a serf."

Listening to her Nicholas frowned. He knew she was going to make them live the nightmare she had lived through but this was the first he'd ever heard of a whipping. Glancing over at Lord Charles he could see that this was a new fact for him as well, the father's hands balled into fists by his side.

"If, when your fifteen years have come and gone, you are still alive then you shall be given your title back and all that goes with it. However, if you do not live to see the end of your fifteen years as a serf, any land currently un-owned by your eldest son shall be given to your eldest daughter to do with as she pleases until she is married. It will then be given under the control of her husband."

Staring at her uncle in silence for a moment Josephine could see the anger in his eyes and matched it with her own. Without saying anything else to him she turned her attention to Lord Byron. "You accepted two chests filled with gold and jewels stolen from my family in return for your silence. That same amount shall be taken from you now and given to all the serfs and servants in Pirtonshire."

"Should any of your servants wish to leave your employ they are free to do so. If any of your serfs wish to buy their freedom with the gold and jewels they are given they too shall be free to do so. The price of their freedom shall be half of what they are to be given. The payment for their freedom shall be given to Lady Jane and shall be hers to keep or sell as she pleases."

"As for you, Lord Byron, you too shall be stripped of your title and forced to live as a serf for fifteen years," she said, repeating to him the same punishment she had detailed out to her uncle. As she had with her uncle Josephine met his eyes, letting him see her anger at him, and anger she had never been free to express to him before. Lord Byron however could not meet her eyes, having the decency to be ashamed for what he had done.

"Where shall their time as a serf be carried out?" Liam asked.

"At a land of the King's choosing. The Lord who takes them on as serfs will be compensated for their incompetence in their duties for the first three years. All I ask is that their time be spent well away from both the palace and Whispering Winds. I will not have the stench of their shame and dishonor polluting my home."

Nodding his head Liam motioned for the two men to be taken away. "They will spend the night in the dungeon until I have decided which Lord they will be sold to. Come the new morning a band of guards shall be sent out to find Arnos Roche and if he be found he too shall suffer the same fate as these two men."

Josephine watched as her uncle and her captor were taken away, her eyes never leaving them until the doors were shut behind them. Turning to face their families intermixed with the crowd her face softened. "You are all innocent parties to what has happened here and I for my part am sorry to see you suffer in your innocence. Rest assured there are no bad feelings, no ill will, on my behalf towards any of you. I hope you will find the strength to face the problems that lay before you."

Taking a few steps toward Lady Jane she touched her shoulder gently. "You had given me what help you could while I was at Pirtonshire. When I left your land, you sent me away with a token of hope that has carried me through these last few years and I thank you for it. No matter what happens in the future, Lady Jane, you will always have a welcome place in my home."

With tears in her eyes she nodded silently before disappearing into the crowd.

"Justice has been served, My King," Josephine said when she turned to face him again. "On behalf of my family, I thank you."

"Forget all that has been done to you, Lady Josephine," Liam said, placing a fatherly hand on her cheek. "Live on for the future and find happiness with my son."

Chapter Twenty

The moon was high in the sky when he slipped through the doors and down into the dungeon. Silently making his way to the end of the hall he found the cell he was looking for and knelt down by the door. Peering inside, disgusted by the filth he saw within, the man called out to the prisoner inside the cell.

"What do you want?" Edgar growled, opening his eyes to see who was calling him.

"I want revenge," the man advised him. "So, you see you and I are in a position to help each other."

Slowly he grinned. "Speak on friend."

~~*~*~*~*~*~*~*

Lying in her bed, staring at the ceiling, Josephine couldn't sleep, her mind going over and over everything that had happened the night before. The sun was just beginning to peek into the sky when she finally got out of the bed, unable to stay still any longer. Dressing she went down to the kitchen to work out her energy. Seeing Jenni working at one of the counters she stood by the girl, smiling down at her as she helped her to finish her work.

"Milady, you should not be down here," one of the cooks declared.

"I have worked side by side with all of you before," she replied. "Why do you refuse me now?"

"Because then you were a serf and now you are a lady."

Looking around Josephine saw the same look in many of the faces watched her. "I am the same woman now that I was then. Title or slavery does not change who I am. While I was Da'Leth I counted you as my friends, are you going to refuse me now that I am Josephine?"

"No!" Jenni cried, taking her hand. "I'm still your friend."

"As am I," one of the other cooks called out from across the kitchen.

Slowly several more of the kitchen serfs called out to Josephine to tell her their friendship was still hers and she smiled. "Thank you," she replied.

"Be that as it may," the head chef declared unwaveringly, "I will not have a Lady working in my kitchen. I must ask you to leave."

Stung by their rejection Josephine nodded once and turned to leave but stopped when she felt something grab her arm. Turning back her heavy heart lifted when Jenni wrapped her arms around her, hugging her friend tightly. Josephine returned the hug and smiled at her, kissing her hair gently before turning to leave.

Not sure where to go, not wanting to disturb the sleeping castle, she decided to wander up to the tower and enjoy the fresh air. Opening the door, she was surprised to find her mother sitting on the edge, smiling at her as she approached. "Mother?"

"Good morning, Josephine," Chelaine said with a tired smile. "I'm surprised you're up this early."

"I couldn't sleep anymore. Why are you up here?" she asked, curiosity filling her voice. "Are you well?"

"Not to worry, I am well enough. Like you, I simply couldn't sleep. I came up here to watch the sunrise. Looking back out to the sky she finished, "It was beautiful this morning."

"Mother," Josephine said, moving closer to take her hand. "Tell me what's wrong."

Shaking her head, she looked down to the ground. "I keep thinking about the night you went missing. Edgar had told me he would find you no matter what it took to do so. All along..." she shook her head. "I had thought I could trust him. If I had known then what kind of man he is..."

"You could not have known," Josephine interrupted. "I did not know until a few years ago. Do not blame yourself for what you had no control over. I am simply content to be thankful that the nightmare is over and justice has been served."

"Here, here," a voice said from behind them. Turning to look both women saw Nicholas standing behind them, his face solemn but a small twinkle in his eye. "I am sorry, Lady Chelaine, but I have come to steal your daughter away for the day."

"I understand," she smiled. Getting up from her seat on the ledge she kissed her daughter and moved toward the door. Pausing by his side she smiled as she touched his arm, "Enjoy your time."

"We shall," he winked at her, a grin appearing on his face.

Rolling her eyes Josephine schooled her face as he moved closer. "And what shall be done if I have already made plans of my own?"

"Then you'll break them," he smiled, moving closer with every step. When Nicholas stopped, his arms wrapped around her, pining her arms to her side, he was a hairsbreadth away. "Because you yourself have admitted that you cannot say no to the crown."

"Ah, but Milord, you forget," she whispered, teasingly pulling her head back as he moved closer to kiss her. "You do not wear the crown, your father does."

"You still won't say no," Nicholas smiled, placing a hand on the back of her head so she couldn't move away. "You couldn't... not even if you wanted to."

Cutting off her reply Nicholas kissed her, stealing the breath from her chest as his lips touched hers. Unsure of what to do, her lips virgin, Josephine was overwhelmed by the feelings coursing through her body, from head to toe a tingling sensation tickling every bit of her.

"I have wanted to do that for a very long time," he breathed, finally pulling his lips from hers.

Unsure of what to say, unable to breathe without thinking about it, she could only stare at him with wide eyes. Looking down at her Nicholas saw the world reflecting back at him and realized he had given Josephine her first true kiss; the thought burning through him like wildfire. He wanted to kiss her again but hesitated, unsure of how she would react. Taking a deep breath Nicholas stepped back, taking her hand in his as he led her to one corner of the tower.

"Milord," Josephine began, unsure of what he was doing.

Stopping mid-stride Nicholas turned to face her, a frown pulling at his features. "Stop that!" he commanded, his tone suddenly severe.

"Stop what?" she asked, confusion in her voice, her eyebrows drawn together. "What's wrong?"

Closing his eyes for a moment he opened them and took a deep breath. "Stop calling me 'Milord'," he said at last. "I don't ever want to hear that from you again."

"You are the Prince," she tried to reason.

"I don't care!"

Knowing his voice had risen again Nicholas stepped away from her, trying to calm down so he could explain why that title angered him. Pacing for a moment, his fist clenching and unclenching by his side, Nicholas forced himself to soothe his anger before turning to face Josephine. When he saw the confusion in her eyes he sighed. Pulling her down into the corner of the wall Nicholas wrapped his arms around her but made sure he could see her face, and she his.

"Hearing that word from your lips reminds me of the nightmare that you have lived through and I hate it. You can remember how many times I asked you to call me Nicholas while we were touring the tournament. Every time I asked you always responded the same way, 'It is not my place.' You are no longer a serf, Josephine, and hearing you call me by my title only reminds me of how much you suffered and how little I was able to help you."

She was silent as she listened to him explain his request and when he had finished Josephine could only smile, too moved by his emotions, his love and his protection, to speak. Reaching out she placed a hand on his face, gently brushing her thumb over his cheekbone. "I give you my word," she said at last. "I will never again call you by your title."

Nicholas took her hand from his face, kissing the palm tenderly. "From a woman who has never broken her word that means more to me than you will ever know."

Laying her head on his shoulder Josephine felt his arm around her waist tighten, drawing her closer to him. Content to simply sit together in silence neither one moved until they could hear the castle coming to life below them. Wanting to get away before anyone could stop them Nicholas stood, pulling Josephine to her feet.

"Come," he said, leading her toward the door. "It's time for us to leave."

"Where are we going?"

Looking over his shoulder Nicholas only smiled, his good mood returning as he contemplated having a day alone with the woman he loved. "You will have to wait and see."

~~*~*~*~*~*~*~*

Josephine looked around her in confusion. When he had led her to his bed chamber she had frowned slightly but watching him pull a large chair away from the wall made her question his mental health. She had obeyed, however, when Nicholas had motioned for her to come closer and her confusion had begun to melt away when she saw him reach for a hidden handle, the wood worn though it was barely visible from a distance. A secret door had opened and Nicholas had hurriedly ushered Josephine inside, eager to shut the door lest someone walk by.

Now, standing in an archway of a small tunnel that led from his chamber to another chamber, a hidden one, she stared at the room he had brought her to. The room was had a dark interior but once he began to light the candles it was well lit. Off to one side there was a large bed and in the corner sat a desk piled high with books of all sizes. Across the room were two comfortable looking chairs, one covered by a large fur the other empty. On the floor, centered in the room, lay a large rug, the animals head facing away from her.

Only when he moved to light it did she realize there was a fireplace on the far corner and as the firelight filled the room she saw tapestries lining the walls. They were old but their design was unique, she had never seen anything like it before. Moving closer she noticed two sets of initial intertwined in the corner and wondered whose they were.

"So, what do you think of this place?"

Turning to face him she smiled. "I like it very much."

"Good," he grinned. "I'm glad. I plan on spending much of our time in the palace in this very room. This is my private getaway; you are only the third person to ever set foot inside this room since I discovered it."

"Who was the second?"

"Edward of course, someone has to know where to find me should I be needed for anything."

"How very wise," Josephine smiled, moving around the room to examine it in detail. "Why did you bring me here?"

"Several reasons actually," he shrugged. "Mostly though, it was so we could have some time to ourselves. The wedding has been taking all of your time and I feel as though we haven't spent more than a few moments together since you came to the palace."

"That is not by my doing," she frowned.

Nicholas chuckled. "I know. I've heard your mother complaining to mine about how uncooperative you are being."

"I have been very cooperative!" she countered. "I've told them many times to do as they please. All I ask is that Jenni be allowed to stand as my flower girl and that my dress be simple.

"And your hair be down," Nicholas interrupted, moving closer to her. "I like it better that way."

"You've never seen it down," she replied, watching him approach.

"Once," he admitted, reaching for the braid hanging down her back. "I did see it once. You and Rianne were bathing in the tent while Richard and I had gone out to give you privacy. I happened to be walking by on my way to see Edward about one of the knights and passed by the tent."

As he spoke Nicholas pulled the string from the tip of her braid, unraveling the interwoven locks of hair. "You were sitting on the ground by the parted opening, blocking the view so my sister could bathe without stifling in the tent. The long braid I knew so well was gone and your hair was wavy as it fell down your back, free from the prison you always keep it in."

Her braid undone Nicholas gently ran his fingers through her hair, pulling it around her shoulder to rest in front. "Bright as a roaring fire but soft as a kitten's fur coat," he whispered, letting one lock glide over his finger. "Down. You must wear it down."

"Then down it shall be."

Nodding he stared down at her. "Good."

Her heart was hammering in her chest and Josephine knew she had to do something or she would fall prey to the burning desire she felt from head to toe. Clearing her throat, she nodded toward the tapestry she had noticed earlier.

"My great-grandparents," Nicholas told her when she asked him about it. "They were in love from the moment they met, even though it was an arranged marriage. She had this tapestry made for their fifth year of marriage and it hung in the main hall until the day she died. The King couldn't bear to see it every day and be reminded of her so he had it put in here and when he missed her too much to go on he would come to this room to spend time with her."

"Oh Nicholas, how sweet!"

Nodding, "I thought so. When I was a very little boy, one of the old servants told me that story and I went hunting for the room. I found it when I was seven years old; it had taken me several years to finally locate the hidden room. Right away I asked my father to give me this room instead of my other one and he agreed. I never told anyone about this room until one day the palace went mad trying to find me."

"I had fallen asleep in the chair and forgotten to come down to dinner. The entire palace was searching for me and when I finally woke it was to hear Edward calling for me in the main chamber. When I opened the door, he scolded me for disappearing. Edward promised not to tell anyone about the room so long as I allowed him to check and make sure it was safe. Since then he has been the only one to know about it. Until you," he smiled.

"Did all of this belong to your great-grandfather?"

"Not all." Turning he pointed to the chairs and the desk, "Those I had brought in several years back. The books have slowly accumulated through the years." Facing the bed, he smiled. "The bed however has been here since my grandfather had it brought in before their wedding. He wanted a special place for their wedding night and had this room furnished so they could spend their first night together here, hidden away from the prying eyes of the palace servants."

Wrapping one arm around his back Josephine smiled up at her husband to be. "Then so shall we."

~~*~*~*~*~*~*~*

Sitting at the window of her room Josephine could hear the revelry from the main square and she smiled. The city was celebrating the Prince's engagement that had been announced earlier that day in an official proclamation. Getting to her feet, unable to resist the pull of the music and laughter she could hear in the distance, Josephine went to find the only ones she thought would be interested in slipping out of the palace. Finding Rianne and Richard first she explained her plan and they both nodded, going off to quietly get a carriage while she went to find Nicholas.

Opening the door to his chamber she saw that it was empty, the chair moved farther down the wall and smiled. Entering through the hidden door she stopped in the archway, watching Nicholas reading by the fire, his feet propped up on the opposite chair. Josephine paused, her mind drifting back to the previous week, their day spent hidden away together. There had been no plan, no schedule to adhere to, and they had spent the entire day doing as they pleased, reading, talking, eating when they were hungry and drinking when they were thirsty. She had been a little worried that Nicholas might want more but he had been a gentleman and she had forgotten to worry after a little while.

"Do you wish to misbehave and have some fun?" she said, approaching his chair.

"That sounds like an intriguing offer," he grinned, looking up at her. "What did you have in mind?"

"The main square."

"And difficult at that," he whistled, getting to his feet. "How do you plan to get there?"

"It's being taken care of," Josephine smiled. Kissing his cheek, she took his hand, pulling him out of the room. "Come on."

Slipping out of his chamber they hurried down the corridors, avoiding the guards and servants as they made their way to the courtyard. There, waiting, was a plain carriage, Richard and Rianne already in it. With the door shut behind them Nicholas told the driver to go and they were off, past the gate and on their way to freedom.

"Take off all of your jewelry, anything that would make you stand out," Josephine advised. "We'll need to blend with the crowd."

As the carriage pulled to a stop the four people inside had changed their appearance enough to pass as a lower Lord or Lady and decided to call each other as they had while touring for the joust. "Shall we start with a pint of ale, Lord Timothy?" Richard grinned, using the names from the last tournament. "I do believe that I see a tavern nearby."

"Perhaps we shall," he nodded, "Milady?" holding out an arm for Josephine to come with him.

"Thank you but no," she said, shaking her head. "You go with your herald while Jacqueline and I will head toward the square where there is sure to be some music and dancing."

Smiling at her Nicholas nodded. "Very well, be sure to stay with the crowd."

"Yes, mi… my good sir," she switched, barely catching herself in time from using the title he detested.

Nicholas raised an eyebrow but let it go, not wanting to spoil the good mood. Catching her eye before they parted he winked to let her know it was all right, not wanting her to worry that she had upset him. Smiling back Josephine was pulled away, Rianne eager to get to the dancing she had heard talk of. Heading into the tavern neither Nicholas nor Richard saw the man slip from the shadows and follow the two women into the square.

Squeezing their way through the crowds Rianne and Josephine heard the music before they could see the dancing. Finding it they stood on the sidelines for a little while, Rianne watching to learn the steps before joining in with the rest of the dancers. Caught up in the merriment neither of them noticed how much time had passed until they saw Nicholas and Richard standing at the edge of the crowd.

"Join us!" Rianne cried as she skipped past her husband, pulling him into the ring of dancers.

Stepping out of the line Josephine stopped next to Nicholas, putting her arm through his. "She learns the steps very quickly!"

"My sister has a natural gift for dance."

"I can see that," Josephine nodded. "Did you enjoy your ale?"

Smiling he nodded, watching Richard try to keep up with his wife. Laughing at his failure he saw his friend glare at him, a challenge to do better. With Josephine's hand in his Nicholas moved into the group of dancers, making their way closer to Richard and Rianne. "Do you need some help?" he teased.

"I'd like to see you try this one," Richard groused playfully. "This one is worse than the one she tried to teach us."

"It's not so bad," Rianne laughed, barely avoiding Richards foot on hers. "You just need to find the right rhythm."

"Come," Josephine said, switching Nicholas's hand for Richards. "Follow me."

Leading him through the steps, breaking the steps into smaller movements, Josephine applauded him when he was able to keep up on his own. "Huzzah!" she laughed.

Laughing along with her the crowd of dancers congratulated Richard on his success. Smiling at them, proud that he had finished the dance, he took a small bow much to the delight of those present. The musicians struck up another song and the dancing resumed, this time at a slightly slower pace, and Josephine returned to Nicholas's side, Richard taking his wife back from her brother.

Well into the night the two couples enjoyed the festival, eating and drinking while they rested from the dancing, listening as the musicians played on. Sitting at a table, not quite ready to dance again, Nicholas and Richard drank ale as they watched the two women dancing. A peaceful feeling filled him and he relaxed into his chair, glad that Josephine had thought to come out among the people tonight.

Next to him Richard suddenly tensed, sitting upright in his chair, and Nicholas frowned. "What is it?" he asked, knowing Richard's instincts were nearly perfect.

"I thought I saw..." he began, his voice dropping off as he scanned the crowd.

Seeing his sudden alertness Nicholas's senses began to come alive, his eyes roving over the crowd. As his scan passed by Josephine and Rianne he frowned when he saw that Josephine wasn't dancing, her face pulled into a look of concentration, she too looking around at the crowd. He saw it a moment before it happened, too far away to stop the man from attacking. Jumping to his feet, Richard moving at the same time, he hurried toward them, pushing the people aside to try and protect the unarmed women that were about to fall under attack.

"Milady!" Josephine cried out, hurrying back to her friends' side.

Rianne's scream filled the air at the sight of the blade coming towards them. She felt Josephine pushing her behind, trying to protect the Princess as she had on so many occasions. Meeting the eyes of the man attacking them Josephine suddenly realized it wasn't the Princess the man had come for. From the corner of her eye she saw Richard and pushed Rianne towards him, out of harm's way. "Take her!"

Catching his wife in his arms Richard held her close, keeping an eye out for any others that were coming towards them to aid their attacker. Nicholas rushed past them towards Josephine but he knew he was too late, the blade arcing down and cutting at her. She tried to move out of harm's way but wasn't fast enough, the tip of the blade slicing through her sleeve and skin, blood quickly staining the material.

"Josephine!" Nicholas cried out, fear filling his voice at the same time as she cried out in pain. "Leave her be, she's done nothing to you!" Rushing toward the man who had attacked her Nicholas didn't see the second man until Richard cried out a warning, Josephine already moving to intercept the three men to stop them from meeting.

"Stop all of you!" she cried. Putting a hand on Nicholas to stop him she looked at the other two, her own self between them and the Prince. "There are innocent people about that will get hurt if this continues. Leave now!" she commanded, her voice hard. "Go!"

"You will pay Prince!" the older man cried as he and his friend disappeared into the crowd.

Watching them leave Nicholas reached out to steady Josephine when she suddenly leaned against him. Turning his attention to her his eyes widened at the amount of blood covering her sleeve. "Josephine!" he cried, lifting the wounded woman into his arms. "Richard, take Rianne and get the carriage," he commanded. "Hurry, Josephine is wounded."

Around him the crowd parted, word spreading about who was in their presence, making him a path to leave the square. Ahead of him men ran to help Richard get the carriage ready, doing what they could to help their Prince and future Princess get away to safety. When he was near the carriage one of the men opened the door, helping Nicholas to put Josephine inside, the Prince climbing in after her. The door slammed shut and the carriage took off, careening down the streets as men ran ahead to part the crowds.

Faster than he thought possible, though it seemed to take an eternity, they approached the palace, the gates opening and the carriage passing through, stopping at the main entrance in the courtyard. Nicholas opened the door and told one of the guards running towards them to fetch the doctor. Turning back to the carriage he saw Josephine watching him, her hand pressed to her arm to try and stop the bleeding. Her face was pale and his heart stopped.

"Josephine?" he called out, reaching out to lift her out of the carriage.

"I am well enough," she replied, her voice low. "I believe it is only a scratch."

"There is too much blood to be a scratch," he argued.

"A deep scratch then," shaking her head at his concern. "There's no cause for alarm. A small dressing and all will be well."

Snorting in disbelief he took her in his arms. "Not until that man is dead. As God is my witness, he'll pay for this."

"Nicholas no," stopping him from walking any farther. "You know you cannot do that. If you kill him then you become the very thing he thinks you are."

"He tried to kill you!"

"And he failed. Be the better man, Nicholas, be the man I know you are." Josephine pleaded with him. "Let him go."

"We'll talk about this later," he evaded, pushing her towards the door again.

Refusing to move she looked up at him, her face set in a stubborn scowl. "No, we'll talk about this now."

"You're bleeding!"

"All the more reason to finish this discussion quickly," she reasoned. "You are not a killer, Nicholas. The man I fell in love with would never kill someone out of pure revenge. If you can kill him for this, then you are not the man I thought you were."

Nicholas stared at her in shock. "Are you refusing to marry me?"

Josephine sighed, fighting to keep a wave of dizziness from overwhelming her. "No, that is not what I am saying. Nicholas, I..." swaying on her feet she reached out to hang onto his arm for support. Trying again she said, "I love you, that won't change, but if you kill him I don't know if I can believe in you as the man I thought you were."

Watching her he saw her eyes roll back into her head and reached out to catch her before she could fall to the ground. "Josephine?" he said, worriedly calling her name. When she didn't respond Nicholas picked her up, carrying her into the palace. The doctor, having already been alerted, met him in the hallway and directed him to lay her in her chamber.

Dismissed while the doctor worked to help Josephine, Nicholas crouched down in the hallway, her words echoing in his head. 'If you kill him I don't know if I can believe in you as the man I thought you were.' From the bottom of his heart a sense of shame crept over him. Since that day so many years ago he had fought to keep himself alive, knowing the man was simply a father trying to avenge the death of his daughter. The man thought he was a murderer and, if Nicholas were to take that father's life, he would be proven right in that assumption about the Prince.

With his head in his hands Nicholas didn't see Lord Charles standing over him until the Lord touched his shoulder. "Prince Nicholas?"

Nicholas jumped to his feet. "Lord Charles," he said, trying to school his face. "I'm certain Josephine will be well soon. She said it was only a scratch."

Charles saw the blood on Nicholas's shirt and didn't believe him. "Where is my daughter?"

"The Lady will be well," the doctor said as he emerged from the room before Nicholas could reply. "She was right to say it was only a scratch. A deep one if I have ever seen one but a scratch and nothing more."

Thanking the doctor Lord Charles waited until he was out of hearing range before turning his attention
to Nicholas. "I had your word as a Prince and a gentleman, milord," he scolded. "My daughter was to be safe and protected with you!"

He didn't know what to say. "You're correct, Lord Charles," he said, shame filling his voice. "I swore to protect her and I failed. I failed them all," he said more to himself, his thoughts falling on the men that had died to keep him safe.

Wondering what he meant by his last words Charles opened his mouth to ask but stopped when he felt a soft hand on his arm. "Father, please," Josephine said, moving to stand by Nicholas. "You cannot blame him for what happened tonight. It was my idea to go into the square, mine alone."

"How did you end up hurt?" he demanded, looking from Nicholas to Josephine and back again.

"The fault is mine, sir," Nicholas admitted, holding out a hand to stop Josephine from replying. "I was not completely honest with you the night we talked."

Charles frowned, "You had better explain everything to me right now or this wedding will not happen."

"Father! Please, you cannot," Josephine began.

"No," Nicholas cut her off, taking her hand in his. "He's right; I cannot marry you if I cannot be man enough to tell your father the truth."

"That is hardly fair! Even your own father does not know the entire truth!"

"Josephine, please." Leaning his head against hers he kissed her gently before turning to walk her back
into her chamber. "Lie down and rest, I'll come and see you when we are finished."

"Nicholas," pulling at his arm when he tried to leave her. "Please, do not let him separate us. I do not wish to lose you."

"No matter what happens after tonight," he promised her. "My heart will always belong to you."

Charles watched from the door, forcing his heart to be immune to the pain in his daughter's eyes and in her voice. The boy had lied to him and he would not let his daughter marry a liar, even if he was a Prince and the son of his best friend. He watched as Nicholas forced Josephine to lie down, covering her with a blanket and kissing her one last time before turning to face him. With a nod he led the way down the hall to his own study in the next wing. Easing down into his chair, he stared at the fire for some time before turning his attention to Charles.

"No doubt my father has told you that several years ago I was a much different person."

"Yes," Charles nodded. "He could not seem to find a reason for the change though," he admitted, wondering what this had to do with Josephine's attack.

"I was a drunk and a reveler who's only mission in life was to win the joust and spend the rest of my time in every pub and tavern in the kingdom."

Charles frowned. "Milord, if this is how you plead your case…" letting the rest of the thought hang between them like a storm cloud.

"No," he shook his head. "I only want you to understand the type of man I was before I tell you the rest."

With a heavy heart Nicholas detailed to Lord Charles the events of that night and the years since, leaving nothing out, filling in the details he had spared Josephine when she'd heard the story. When he finished the sun was readying to make its way into the sky, the sky filled with an early morning gray. Silence fell between the two men, one contemplating all he had heard and the other dreading the moment he spoke in reply to what he had said.

"Is that everything I need to know?" Charles asked. "Is there anything else?"

"The only other thing I would wish for you to remember is that I love your daughter with everything I am. I will do whatever you ask in order to keep her safe."

"What if I tell you to stay away from her?"

Nicholas closed his eyes, his heart cringing. "Yes," he said painfully, "Even if you ask me to stay away from her. But," he said, opening his eyes to meet Charles. "You cannot ask me nor would I ever agree to stop loving her."

Charles met his stare unblinking for several moments before he nodded. "Come and see me tonight at sunset, you shall have my answer."

"Yes, sir," Nicholas answered, watching his future leave with a heavy heart.

~~*~*~*~*~*~*~*

His arms folded over his chest Nicholas stared at the door in front of him trying to find the courage to open it and enter the room.

All day he had sat in his hidden room, keeping away from the rest of the world as he waited to find out whether his heart was going to live or die. Edward had come to advise his mother was requesting his presence but upon seeing his master's state of being he left again without a word uttered between them. A short time later Josephine had come to his side, knelt at his feet and took his hands in hers. Neither one had said a word; Nicholas sinking down to the ground next to her as they sat in silence, each one afraid of what her father's reply was going to be.

Now the time had come to find out. Taking a deep breath, he raised one hand to knock on the door, opening it when he heard to command to enter. When the door was shut behind him, closing with a thud that echoed in the silent room, he turned to face Lord Charles. He wanted to speak but found his throat was too dry to say anything.

"I will not stop the wedding," Charles said, a feeling on discontent filling him. Watching the young prince carefully he saw his hands tremble as he reached for the back of the nearest chair to steady himself, swaying a little bit on his feet from sheer relief. "There is a caveat I'm afraid. You had better sit down."

Doing as he was told Nicholas said nothing, waiting for Charles to detail his rules.

"The man whose daughter was killed, I want to meet with him. This issue must be settled once and for all. Once you are married and Josephine is settled safely at Whispering Winds you and I shall go find him to sort this problem out. Are we in agreement?" Nicholas nodded, still trying to recover his voice. "From what I have seen and heard you are a good man that has made some very bad choices. However, my daughter loves you as much as you love her and for that reason I will help you to correct what has gone wrong."

"Thank you," he said at last, his recovered voice thick with emotion. "Lord Charles I do not know how to thank you for what you have done."

"Love my daughter; keep her safe and happy while you clean up the mess you have created."

Nicholas stood, offering his hand to Charles. "You have my word."

Charles walked him to the door, watching his future son-in-law head down the hall. Before the Prince reached the end of the corridor Charles started to shut the door, stopping in alarm when he suddenly saw Nicholas stagger, falling into the wall and sliding to the ground. He took a step toward the young Prince but stopped when he saw him drop his head into his hands, his broad shoulders shuddering. Hearing the whispered prayer "Thank you God!" Charles turned and shut the door, finally content with the choice he had made.

Pacing in the corridor Josephine was unable to wait any longer and turned to head toward her fathers' chamber when she heard something thud to the ground around the corner. Hurrying her step, she rounded the corner into the next corridor and stopped still, staring at Nicholas sitting on the ground. Tears filled her eyes and a strangled "No!" escaped from her throat.

Nicholas looked up at the sound in time to see Josephine closing the distance between them, tears falling from her eyes as she fell to her knees next to him, her eyes searching his face. "It is okay," he whispered, pulling her into his arms. "We are to be married."

Chapter Twenty-One

A loud jangling noise told them their jailer was around, his ring of keys chiming against one another signaling a freedom they were not allowed to enjoy. The noise grew louder as he approached the lower level of the prison, looking for one man in particular. The first had been dispatched a week ago, the day after he had been sentenced, but the King had instructed him to leave Lord Edgar to rot for a few days in the filthiest cell the prison held.

Now though it was time for him to be shipped off, a Lord in the southernmost tip of the kingdom having been chosen to house the new serf for his punishment. "On your feet, serf," the jailer called out, fingering through the multitude of keys to find the right one. When he reached the cell door the rough soldier stopped, staring into the cell for a moment before shaking his head with a heavy sigh. "This is not good," he said to himself.

Hurrying out of the prison he rand to find the new Captain of the Guard, telling him what he had seen. Swearing profusely, the Captain turned and went in search of the King. Less than a month on the job and already he was going to lose his head for this. Finding the person he sought, the man knelt low, delivering the message.

"How did this happen?"

"I do not know, Majesty," he answered honestly.

Ordering him to find the prisoner immediately Liam sent for the family; asking them to join him in his study. When she was sitting in front of the fire he told her what he had been told only a short time ago. Josephine stared up at Liam, her mind trying to absorb what he had just told her. "He's escaped?"

"Yes."

"When?"

"I don't know. It is my own fault I'm afraid. Byron was sent off to begin his punishment almost immediately but I ordered Edgar to be keep in the prison for a few days to give him time to think on what he had done."

"He certainly used the time to think," Philip said, "To think about how to escape from under the ever-watchful eye of our new Captain of the Guard."

His contempt was tangible but Josephine ignored him, looking to Liam instead. "Can he be found?"

"I have my best men out looking for him," Liam assured her. "You have my word we will find him."

Nodding she fell silent. The joy she had been swimming in was beginning to drain away. Her wedding was in two days, there should be nothing to mar the occasion and yet here it was. Her uncle had escaped from prison and it was unclear as to whether he would ever be caught to serve his punishment.

"Look at me." Raising her eyes Josephine saw Nicholas kneeling before her. "Edgar will pay for what he has done if I have to hunt him down myself. Do not let him steal the joy you have found. In two days we will marry and no one will be allowed to take that from us."

The room fell silent, waiting for her to reply. Finally, she nodded. "No one."

The family dispersed with a somber mood, each one going their own way to digest the news. In a far corner of an isolated section of the palace three men met in secret, their moods buoyant given the family's reaction to the news of Edgar's disappearance. "The time is coming," one man said. "We shall have the revenge that has been denied us."

"The wedding is still two days away," the leader reminded them. "Do not make any mistakes between now and then."

"Just do your part of this arrangement and let us worry about the rest."

~~*~*~*~*~*~*~*~*

Standing in front of a mirror Josephine looked at her reflection, examining it closely. The dress was beautiful, the seamstress working long and hard to get it done in time for the wedding. As she smoothed an imaginary wrinkle from the material Josephine's hands trembled, excitement and nervousness filling her from head to foot. A small knock sounded on the door and she turned in time to see her mother entering the room, tears in her eyes when she saw her daughter.

"You look beautiful," she cried, reaching out to hug her. Pulling back in a vain attempt to regain control over her emotions she smiled. "Have you decided what you want done with your hair?"

"Nicholas wants me to wear it down."

"Down?" she frowned. "But there are so many beautiful styles to be used."

"I know, mother," she smiled. "Nicholas has asked this of me and I have no reason to deny him."

Realizing it was useless to argue with her Chelaine shrugged. "It is your wedding day, I suppose."

"Thank you," kissing her cheek. "Is father coming soon?"

Chelaine nodded. "Yes, he was with the King when I left but he promised to be here momentarily.

"And here I am," Charles smiled, "As promised."

Watching her father approach Josephine was filled with pride. "You look so handsome," she praised. Reaching out to touch him when he stopped next to her she looked at both of her parents. "This is the moment I have dreamt of for so many years," she told them, "the day that I could stand with my family and simply be happy that all was as it should be for us. Only now, this day is far better than my dream because not only do I have my mother to rejoice with me but I have my father as well."

"I am proud of the woman you have become," Charles told her, reaching out to hug his daughter. "While you were gone I prayed that the lessons we had taught you would guide you in everything you did and I can see now that they have. We could not have asked for a better daughter."

"I love you both," she whispered, hugging her parents tightly.

Drinking in the bittersweet happiness of the moment Charles cleared his throat. "The chapel is filled," he said. "We should go now."

Nodding, taking one last look in the mirror to wipe the tears from her face, Josephine stepped off the stool she had been standing on and took her place at her father's side. While Chelaine slipped on ahead to take her seat they stood at the entrance of the chapel, the door shut. Smiling at Jenni Josephine motioned for her to begin her walk down the aisle, glad that the girl was able to be a part of her wedding day.

"This is it, Pumpkin," Charles smiled, squeezing the hand that was wrapped through his arm. "Are you ready?"

"Father," she said, pausing before they walked into the chapel. "Thank you, for everything. I know you aren't pleased with some things, but I know Nicholas will take care of me. He will prove to be a good son, you shall see."

Charles sighed. "He has made bad choices," he said. "But if he has earned the love and respect I see in your eyes then I know I've made the right decision."

Smiling she kissed his cheek and turned to face front, taking their first steps into the chapel. Up ahead she could see Nicholas standing, waiting for her to meet him before they walked up to the priest. As they drew closer she could see his smile grow and when he took her hand in his, taking her place by his side she couldn't stop the tears that stung at her eyes.

"Keep your word, Prince," Charles said as he relinquished his hold on his daughter. "I love you, Pumpkin."

Kissing her father's cheek, watching as Nicholas shook his hand, she turned her attention to Nicholas as her father stepped away to take his seat. Walking together toward the priest Josephine could feel Nicholas rubbing his thumb over the top of her knuckles, his eyes glancing down at her. "I've loved you as Da'Leth and I've loved you as Josephine," he said softly so only she could hear him. "I will love you until the day I die."

A tear slipped from her eyes, sliding down her cheek as she listened to his words. "I promise I will love you until the last breath is drawn from my chest and it will be to say the name of the man who has given me everything I could ever want in this world."

Closing his eyes Nicholas took a deep breath, his chest suddenly tight w/ emotion. A smile tugged at his lips as they continued toward the priest. When they reached the foot of the stairs they climbed them together, eager to reach the top and begin the rest of their life together. His eyes only on Josephine, and hers locked with his, they stopped at the top of the stairs, waiting for the priest to begin his marriage sermon.

Curious about his silence when the priest didn't begin speaking right away Josephine looked away from Nicholas and up to the man they stood before. Her eyes widened in recognition and before she could draw in breath to gasp she saw the flash of steel and felt the burn as it was plunged into her body. The chapel echoed with her scream of pain, falling against Nicholas as he staggered under the sudden weight of her collapse.

"Josephine?" Nicholas cried out in confusion and fear, catching her when she fell against him. "Josephine?"

"Nicholas," she breathed, her eyes fluttering shut.

Lowering her to the ground he looked down and saw the hilt of a dagger sticking out of her body. His face blanched at the sight of it and Nicholas looked up to see Charles kneeling before him, his eyes glued to his daughter pale face. "Get the doctor!" he roared, the cry of alarm echoing off the walls as her scream had seconds ago. "What happened?" he demanded of Nicholas.

"I don't know! We were standing there in front of the priest," looking up to the priest for confirmation. Seeing the man backing away Nicholas's eyes widened even as they filled with rage. "Stop him!"

Two guards jumped forward to grab the priest. Nicholas stood, reaching for the sword from the nearest guard. Pulling from its sheath he pointed the tip of the sword at the man's neck, a small dot of blood rolling down his throat from the pressure. "The last words you will ever hear are the ones I have told you from the beginning. I did not touch your daughter!"

"A life for a life, Prince," he said with satisfaction in his eyes. "You took from me what I loved and now I have taken it from you. No matter what you do to me we both die today.

Unable to speak Nicholas could only stare at the man in front of him. Every inch of his being urged him to push the sword forward; killing the man who had buried a dagger in his brides' body. The memory of Josephine's words was the only thing holding his hand from striking.

'If you kill him then you become the very thing he thinks you are.'

Shaking his head, he gripped the handle tighter, glaring at the father who stood before him. "You have put a dagger into my bride," he growled, pressing the sword a little tighter into his throat. "You should be killed."

'The man I fell in love with would never kill someone out of pure revenge. If you can kill him for this, then you are not the man I thought you were.'

Turning his head away, closing his eyes against her voice playing over and over in his mind, Nicholas fought with himself, his mind telling him to kill the man but his heart dwelling on the words she had told him only a little while ago.

'If you kill him I don't know if I can believe in you as the man I thought you were.'

A yell of frustration, pain and guilt erupted from him and Nicholas dropped the sword, the metal clanging against the stone steps as it skittered down to the ground. Kneeling down next to Josephine he leaned down to kiss her forehead, tears filling his eyes. Looking down at her pale face he took her hand in his.

"Let him go," Nicholas said, never raising his eyes from her face. "Leave this place sir, and don't ever come back."

"Nicholas!" Liam said; his voice filled with shock at his son's choice. "He has tried to kill your bride and the kingdom's future Princess; that cannot go unpunished!"

"If I kill him now then I become the very monster he believes me to be, father. Should Josephine survive I could not live with what I would see in her eyes when she looked at me." He shook his head. "Let him go and leave him unharmed."

Listening to them Charles knew Nicholas was right. "She would never forgive him," he said to Liam. "Let the man go, my King. Nicholas is right in his decision."

Liam looked down at the group huddled on the stairs, Josephine unconscious, Nicholas staring down at her, and Charles, holding his daughters hand staring up at him with a knowing look. Not liking what he was about to do Liam nodded at the guards and they released the man dressed as a priest. "Leave now before I change my mind."

The man glanced down at Nicholas, questions ringing in his eyes before turning to flee, running past the doctor as he hurried to the front of the chapel. Taking one look at the situation he did what little he could to stop the bleeding before he ordered someone to pick her up and carry Josephine to her chambers. Nicholas put his arms under Josephine to lift her but couldn't stand, his muscles suddenly forgetting how to work.

Coming to his aid Richard touched his friends shoulder, picking the unconscious woman up off the ground and carrying her, following the doctor to her chamber. Watching them walk away Nicholas could only stare, his feet unable to move, oblivious to the gaping stares of the audience witnessing the entire scene.

"Come son," Liam said, putting a gentle hand on his shoulder. "She rests in God's hands now. Trust in him to take care of your woman."

"So long as he does not keep her," Nicholas replied after a long silence, his fathers' words slowly sinking past his shock, letting the King lead him from the chapel.

~~*~*~*~*~*~*~*

"What do you mean he failed?"

"She's still alive," the leader said, a frown filling his face.

"He should be killed," the man sneered. "We had an arrangement."

"It doesn't matter now, he is inconsequential to me. Nicholas has been hurt far worse than if he had been killed."

"But she lives!"

He looked at his companion with an exasperated look. "Her injury is severe; she will not survive the night."

"You are certain?" The leader nodded in reply. "Then perhaps all is not lost."

"We must be sure they both die."

"Leave it to me," he grinned. "I have a man I can send for. For the right amount of coin, he will do whatever is ordered with no questions asked."

~~*~*~*~*~*~*~*

The room was dark, moonlight barely daring to enter through the window. On the bed Nicholas lay next to Josephine, his one arm under her neck, the other laying gently over her hips below the wound so as not to cause her pain. The doctor had done all he could, washing the wound, stitching it closed as best he could, and bandaging it with the herbs Josephine swore by.

'All we can do now is to wait, milord,' he'd said as he slipped from the room to inform the rest of the family.

And so, he had waited.

Three days had come and gone, the kingdom waiting anxiously for word that the Lady had lived or died, praying that she lived. Nicholas had yet to leave the room, alternating between lying next to her and watching her from a seat by the window. Anyone who entered the room could hear him, whispering to her over and over again, begging her not to leave him. The family came and went, each one stopping in to sit with them several times a day. Each time they asked the same question, over and over, as if they hoped the answer would change if it were asked enough times.

'How is she?'

'Not well.'

His reply was the same every time, responding automatically without ever looking up at the person asking the question. Nicholas's entire being was focused on Josephine and that would not change until she opened her eyes to promise him she would not leave him on this earth alone. As Liam stepped into the room he glanced at his son lying by her side, his back to the door, and asked the question again, "How is she?"

He waited to hear the monotone reply they had all come to expect when he answered but this time Liam's blood ran cold when he heard his son speak. "She has a fever that burns hotter than Hades," Nicholas said, his voice catching in his throat. "The doctor doesn't hold out much hope if this continues like it has."

Liam closed his eyes for a moment, swallowing the lump that had doubled its size in his throat. Nothing he could say would make the slightest difference to his son. He reached out to gently squeeze his shoulder before leaving them alone in the room. Out in the corridor he sat heavily on one of the benches, leaning forward to place his head in his hands. "Dear God in heaven, please!" he prayed, "Please let this girl live."

~~*~*~*~*~*~*~*

Sitting in the corner of a crowded inn a man sat alone, silently nursing a tankard of ale. Though he appeared calm his mind raced, thinking over the chain of events that had led him to the seat he held now. A sword had been at his throat, ready to strike him dead as he fully expected for his actions. But instead he walked out of the palace alive and unharmed save for a small prick on his neck. William shook his head in confusion.

Closing his eyes, he put his hands to his face, replaying that moment in his mind, searching for something to explain why he was still alive. He'd stabbed the woman; though he'd wanted to kill the Prince first it had been her that had recognized him first. She had fallen, Nicholas taken to the ground with her. The guards had seized him and Nicholas had put a sword to his throat before he could think to try and get away. The eyes that had stared down at him were murderous, but then he had closed his eyes, turning his face away before letting him go free.

"Why?"

"Why what, love?"

Looking up William saw a wench standing over him. "Nothing."

"I'd be asking 'why' myself if I'd had time to think. Why anyone would want to hurt a good Lady like Lady Josephine."

"What?"

"The Lady that was to marry the Prince, she's been stabbed, ain't you heard?"

"Yes, I heard. I heard that she was a bad woman who…"

"Bad!" the wench cried. "I don't know who you heard that from but they're wrong! My sister is a servant in the palace and she's told me about this woman, Lady Josephine."

"Tell me," he demanded. "Tell me what you know about her."

Shrugging the wench sat down across from him, glad for the brief break from her duties.

~~*~*~*~*~*~*~*

He slipped into the room, shutting and locking the door behind him as he did so. On the bed he saw Nicholas lying on his side, his back to the door and his arms wrapped around the wounded woman. "How is she?"

Nicholas didn't reply. Raising his hand from her hip he reached for the wet rag on the table and brushed it over her face as he had throughout the last week. Her skin burned with fever, sweat dripping from everywhere as her body fought to recover from the infection that had set into her wound. When the doctor changed the dressing, Nicholas had seen the white skin surrounding the ugly wound, red streaks snaking out from it. The grim look on the doctor's face had told him all he needed to know.

Josephine was dying.

Continuing his ministrations Nicholas never looked up, "Her fever still burns hotter than Hades."

"She doesn't deserve this," he said. "I never meant for someone innocent to get hurt, you were the only one I wanted."

The words sank into Nicholas's ears and he turned to look over his shoulder. Seeing who it was his face turned into a stony glare, rising from the bed gently to make sure Josephine wasn't affected by his movements. Watching him step away Nicholas moved forward a few steps and stopped still, crossing his arms over his chest. "Why are you here?"

Shifting where he stood he looked down and Nicholas could see the shame on his face. "You let me go even after what I did to her. Why?" he asked, looking up to meet the Prince's eyes.

"Because I refuse to become the monster you think I am."

"I saw you running from the barn and a moment later I found my daughter, raped and beaten to death by you and your friends."

"I have told you on every occasion that we have met," he said, his tone cold. "I did not touch your daughter. I was passed out drunk in the barn and when I came to she was dead and buried in the hay."

William pulled his hat off his head, twisting it in his hands for a moment before he spoke. "I don't know whether to believe you or not," he began. "But you had the opportunity to kill me and didn't take it, which says to me that there is a possibility I might be wrong. If there is that chance then I will not be a man who kills an innocent being."

"Why are you here?" he asked again.

"I know that you didn't kill me because of her. The people in the square say she's a good woman, fair, honest, strong, and loyal to the crown. They also say she was a serf. Is that true?"

"What she was or was not is no concern of yours."

"Prince, tell me," he demanded. "Is it true?"

"Why should it matter?"

"Just tell me!"

He stared at him silently before he answered. "Yes, she was."

"Always?" Sighing Nicholas turned his back to William, irritated by the questions that served no purpose. "Prince I have given you no reason to trust me, I know this, but if you want me to tell you why I have returned, risking my own life to do so," he pointed out, "You must answer my question."

"She was sold by her uncle." Turning to face him he growled, "I have answered your questions now answer mine. Why are you here?"

William's eyes fell to the sleeping woman. "She was sold by her uncle Sir Edgar," he said with a shake of his head. "And yet it was he who claimed to be wronged."

"How do you know of Sir Edgar?" Nicholas asked; frowning when he heard the escaped man's name.

"There is a truth you need to hear. Were it your life only then I would not have come back. As her life is in danger as well I cannot stay silent."

"What are you talking about?"

Sitting down in an empty chair William tossed his hat to the floor and looked up at the Prince. "I will tell you what I know."

~~*~*~*~*~*~*~*

Three men sat locked away in the Kings study silent with shock. A fourth stood before them nervously, waiting for some kind of reaction. He didn't have to wait long.

"What proof do you have of this outrageous claim?" Liam asked, trying to think clearly without letting his emotion get the best of him.

"It was a hidden entrance that led into the palace, Majesty, on the south wall near the stables."

"And you say it was these two men, no one else?"

"Yes," William nodded. "We met on several occasions. I was instructed to kill the Lady after I had killed the Prince."

Charles had been silent up until now, listening to what was being said, trying to keep in mind that the man was here to help them. He fought to keep the rage that was searing in his mind and heart from escaping before they could determine whether he was telling the truth or simply trying to get closer to them to finish the job he had begun.

"Then why did you strike my daughter first?"

"She recognized me, milord, and I acted without thinking, trying only to attain my goal."

"Which was to kill my son," Liam scowled.

"I will not lie, majesty, I have been trying to kill Prince Nicholas for many years now. If I'd have had the chance I would have put my blade through his heart.

"Then why should we trust you now?"

"He came back to help find the men who are behind the attack father," Nicholas said in Williams defense. "What was between this man and I will never go away but I am willing to trust him now to make sure no one ever plans an attack on Josephine again."

Staring at his son Liam frowned. He was too calm, too level headed, and it made him wonder what Nicholas could be thinking. "I cannot help but wonder if perhaps you are only grasping at straws, trying to seek a way to make someone pay for what has been done," he said, forcing himself to play the devil's advocate.

Nicholas sighed. "You think I'm seeking revenge." Liam nodded. Getting to his feet Nicholas paced the small study. "From the day she was wrongly informed of her father death Josephine's life has been one beating after another, some mental, some emotional and too many of them physical. Now, I have found out that there was a planned attack on her life that may yet still succeed."

Stopping still he faced his father with a look of determination fueled by anger, pain, and worry. "A part of it is revenge, I do not deny that, but it is not revenge alone. Revenge told me to put a sword through that mans' neck," he said pointing at William. "But it was Josephine that made me hesitate. Now I find out that this man did not act alone in what was done but rather there was a master plan behind the attack from within these very walls. I will not let this go unpunished and if it means that I must act without the sanction of the King then so be it."

Liam held up his hands to stem his son's rising anger. "I want this matter resolved as well but we must locate them in order to punish them. I promise you, I will see to it they are both..." His words were drowned out by a pounding on the door, Richard hurrying in with a frown on his concerned face. "What is it?"

Entering the room Richard stopped in shock at the sight of William standing freely with the Prince, the King, and Lord Charles in the room. His frown deepened but he maintained his original purpose for bursting to the room. "There's an intruder in the palace, Majesty. We've gotten the rest of the family safely tucked away but you need to join them for your own protection."

"Do we know why he's here?"

"No, majesty, now please, come with me!"

Moving toward his friend Nicholas asked, "Richard where was he last seen?" hoping his instincts were wrong.

Reaching for the Kings arm Richard answered hurriedly, "He entered through the southern wing and was heading upwards."

"Wandering?"

"No," he said, his eyes meeting Nicholas's. "Wherever he was going he knew exactly where it was located and how to get there."

Nicholas's eyes widened. "Josephine!" he cried, running from the room.

"I will go with the Prince," Charles assured Liam. "Go to your family and stay with them in safety. Make sure the whole family stays with you."

Richard saw the meaningful glance between the two friends and wondered what was going on. "What of him?" he asked, jutting his chin in William's direction.

"He will come with me," Charles said, meeting his eyes. "If he proves to be a liar I will kill him myself."

William nodded and left the room behind Charles, watching for a moment as Richard led Liam to safety. Running through the corridors, up several flights of stairs, they rounded the corner in time to see Nicholas duck into Josephine's chamber. Glad that he was there to protect her Charles slowed his steps a little, knowing she was okay. When he heard the yell and crash that rang out from inside the room however he ran with all he had in him.

The moment Nicholas had entered the room his eyes had fallen upon Josephine, lying where he had left her, and he breathed a sigh of relief that she was safe. No sooner had the thought crossed his mind, though, a movement in the shadows caught his attention and he raised his eyes to see a man emerging from the dark corner of the room, a dagger in his hands. With a loud cry he lunged at the man, blocking his access to Josephine.

"I can kill you first, if you like, Prince," the man said with a grin when he saw Nicholas coming for him. "It makes no never mind to me."

"You can try," Nicholas growled.

Lunging at the attacker Nicholas caught his wrist that held the dagger, preventing him from swinging it towards his body. The two men fought for several moments until the attacker pinned Nicholas beneath him, one arm pinned to his neck preventing the young man from breathing. Raising the dagger to plunge it into his heart the attacker grinned in evil triumph. His movements exposed the man and he had no way to protect himself against the long blade the buried itself into his chest, emerging from his back with a death dealing blow.

Lord Charles pulled the sword out with a sickening slurp and the dead body fell, covering Nicholas with its blood. Pushing it off of him Nicholas got to his feet, and immediately moved to check that Josephine had been unharmed by their attacker. Behind him he heard Charles talking to William.

"Do you recognize this man?" he demanded.

"No, milord, I've never seen him before." Charles challenged him again, staring him down with a look that could wither a stone. "I give you my word, Lord Charles; I do not know this man!"

"We know who will," Nicholas said as he rose to his feet. "Josephine is unharmed," he advised, "Let us settle this once and for all."

Bending over to kiss Josephine gently Nicholas turned and left the chambers. Stopping to gather his own sword Nicholas led the way through the palace the three men hurried, winding around corners, making their way to the wing that William had entered through. When they reached it William took the lead, retracing his steps to the room they had always met in. Stopping in front of a door he turned to look back at Nicholas and Charles, motioning to them that this was the room.

Nicholas suddenly realized how the men had managed to stay hidden away from the rest of the palace, this wing was old and crumbling; Liam had ordered everyone to stay away from it until the builders could fix the structure. Setting his face into a stony mask he reached out to open the door. Stalking into the room he looked around and saw one of the men sitting by the fire, a satisfied grin on his face that slid off when he saw the three men enter the room, each one armed.

"You," he glared when his eyes fell on William. "I knew I should have had you killed when you failed."

"Then it was your mistake, brother," Charles said, moving towards Sir Edgar. "You're going to come with us and you are going to do it quietly, if you do not I will slice your head from your shoulders, do you understand me?"

Edgar nodded, setting his goblet on the table next to his chair and getting to his feet. Without a word he left with them, making their way back through the castle to the room Nicholas knew his family would be hidden away in. Richard, standing guard outside the door, saw them approaching and relief filled his face. When his eyes fell on Sir Edgar though his face changed, glaring at the man and reaching for the hilt of his sword.

"What is he doing here?" he demanded.

"Just take care of him for the moment. When you hear me call out bring him in," Nicholas replied. "William, stay out here."

Charles and Nicholas entered the room to find their families within; the women huddled together while the men stood by the fire, Liam maintaining a frosty distance from everyone. At the sight of the blood all over Nicholas Rianne cried out, Winifred's face paling as she looked him over to find the wound. "Were you hurt?" she asked with a shaky voice when the Queen found no evidence of a wound.

"No, I am unharmed," he answered. Seeing the questions in Lady Chelaine's eyes he continued, "As is Josephine."

"Who did this?" Philip demanded. "Who would dare to attack the royal family in such a manner?"

"Don't you know dear brother?"

Philip stood straight and met his younger brother's cool eye. "What are you saying Nicholas?"

"You failed Philip," Liam answered. "You tried, and very nearly succeeded, but in the end, you still failed."

"What is going on here?" Winifred asked, not liking the turn of events she was witnessing.

Calling out to Richard it was Nicholas who answered. "Philip conspired with Sir Edgar and William to kill Josephine and myself. That is how William was able to stand in as the priest and why the man from tonight knew exactly which chamber to go to. No doubt it was also Philip who helped Edgar to escape from his prison cell."

Behind him he heard the door open and the three men walk in, Edgar at the tip of Richard's sword. Gasps flew into the air, Chelaine fighting to keep from fainting when she realized they had been betrayed yet again. "Oh Charles!" she cried, reaching out for her husband.

Taking her hand Charles looked to his old friend. "I know that my daughter had detailed out a punishment for my brother," he said. "But I cannot live in peace knowing he is out there and could strike out at her again."

Liam nodded. "I agree. Take Edgar back to the prison cell, I want a guard posted outside of his cell at all times. He will be executed after an appropriate trial can be held."

Turning to face his eldest son Liam shook his head. "I do not know where I have failed you," he said, disappointment and anger battling for control of his voice. "You will stand trial as well. Whatever the outcome I want you to know that you and your line will never sit on this throne. I will not entrust my kingdom to a man that would betray his own brother and kill a Lady simply because of what her station had wrongly been."

~~*~*~*~*~*~*~*

Sitting in the window of her chamber Nicholas watched Josephine sleep. His arms were crossed in front of him, his head leaning against the frame. His mind over everything that had been happening since the day they were supposed to get married. He'd run through every emotion in him and it had left him spent; anger to sadness, hope to despair, and everything in between. Now, watching his love lie there in the bed, not knowing if she was going to live or die, he felt his hope beginning to slip away.

Closing his eyes, he sighed, fighting with himself not to give up and admit defeat. He heard a maid enter the room and set a pail of cool water down on the ground and the splashing as she dunked a rag into it to wipe down the feverish forehead. The maids soft voice called out to her as she worked, gently talking to Josephine as if she were a little child sick with a fever. All these were sounds that he recognized.

It was the gasp that caught his attention.

Opening his eyes Nicholas saw the maid standing next to the bed, her hand over her mouth, eyes wide. Following her line of sight to see what had made her gasp his heart jumped into his throat even as it stopped beating. There, lying on the bed where she had been for the last two weeks, Josephine blinked her eyes, her face filling with pain. "Josephine," he whispered, moving to her side.

Climbing onto the bed with her Nicholas wrapped his arms around the woman he loved, holding her as gently as he could. Oblivious to either of them the maid fled from the room, running to tell the family that Josephine had awoke at last.

"Nicholas?"

"I'm right here," he whispered, kissing her forehead. "It's all right, my love. Everything is going to be all right."

"The priest?"

Nicholas hushed her sweetly. "Rest now. You need to rest so you can gain your strength back."

Sighing she closed her eyes, her face slackening a little and he assumed she had fallen asleep again. Cradling her in his arms Nicholas leaned down to kiss her temple, thanking God that her skin wasn't as warm as before, the fever beginning to break.

"I wasn't going to leave," she whispered suddenly. "I can't promise you that I never will, but I will do everything I can to hold it off as long as possible."

Her words were slurred with sleep and so soft he had to strain to hear them but when she was finished tears had filled his eyes, falling when he closed them to lean down and whisper back, "I love you."

Epilogue

The couple lay in their bed, spooned together under the covers. Drifting in and out of consciousness they tried to hold the day at bay as long as they could. Her husband at her back, one arm under her head while the other curled over her waist; she could feel his fingers running over the scar on her hip. Since the moment the wound was healed enough to touch without any pain he had done that, tracing and retracing the scar that had almost cost him everything he cared about.

Time had taken its toll on the couple, exacting a tax for allowing them to live life and enjoy it. Josephine's hair had dimmed from its once brilliant red color while Nicholas's had begun to gray at the temples and fall out, a small patch of skin at the back of his head already showing through. Her figure had rounded out somewhat, partially due to the three children she had given birth to, and he had grown a small paunch in his middle. Neither of them noticed though, their eyes still seeing each other through the rose-colored hue of love.

Dozing in the early morning sunlight, content to stay there until the world forced them out of bed; both were startled awake when their door was thrown open, a young man rushing in to stand at the foot of their bed. "Father? Mother?" he called out to them. "I have something to tell you, are you awake?"

"No," Nicholas grumbled, burying his face in his wife's hair. "Go away we're still sleeping."

"Do be serious father, I have wonderful news!"

"Let me guess, you passed your exams," Josephine smiled sleepily, opening her eyes to look at her son.

He smiled at her, his grin a mirror image of the man she lay next to. Charles looked like his father in every way but for his hair, a bright red mop that was almost never where it was supposed to be, flying about in the wind as he raced through the day. "No mother, the exams aren't until next month. It's better news!"

Next to her Josephine heard Nicholas grumbling about the early time of day and she swatted him to get his attention. "Your son has something he wishes to tell us, Nicholas, pay attention."

With a long sigh Nicholas lifted his head to look at the eldest of his three boys. "Well?" he waited. "Are you going to tell us or simply stand there grinning like a fool?"

"Father, Mother," he began, his smile widening. "I've decided to get married!"

Josephine winced when Nicholas's hand suddenly tightened on her hip. Under the covers she tapped him to tell him he was hurting her and his hand loosened its pressure. "Who is the girl, Charles?" she asked, giving Nicholas time to adjust to his announcement. "Do we know the family?"

Charles shook his head, his smile dimming a little bit. "She lives in the village."

"What is her name?"

"Patrice," he answered. Knowing he would have to tell them eventually the young Prince decided to get the truth out of the way. "She's the daughter of an innkeeper."

"A peasant?" Nicholas asked, his head coming off the pillow again to look at his son.

Josephine looked over her shoulder at him, surprised that he would respond like that. Ignoring her husband for the moment she smiled at her son. "We will want to know the girl, Charles. Bring her to dinner tonight and we will meet with her. Take her to a dressmaker right away so she may have an appropriate gown to wear, I would not want the court looking down on her before they have a chance to know her."

His smile brightening again Charles nodded, rushing to her side to kiss his mother gently before hurrying out of the room, telling them how much they would enjoy her company as he left. Josephine paused for a moment before turning around to face her husband. "What was that?"

"What?" he frowned; looking down in confusion at her question.

"'A peasant?'" she mimicked. "Why should that matter? You fell in love with a serf, why can your son not love a peasant?"

"I did not mean it like that, Josephine," he reasoned. "It's only... what will happen when the court hears of this?" He sighed.

"Besides the boy promised me he would not marry until he was finished with his studies."

"And you promised my father we would live out our days at Whispering Winds," she reminded him of his own broken promise. "Yet look at where we live now."

"I did not have a choice in that and you know it."

"Regardless," she dismissed his reply. "His exams are in one month and then his studies are finished. As for the court, you have never been bothered by what their opinion is. Why should you begin to now? You are the King, you may command as you please."

Nicholas grumbled, rolling his eyes as he sunk his head back into the pillow, pulling his wife tighter to him. "Must you always be the voice of reason?" he groused.

Josephine smiled. "It does grow tiresome at times," she teased. "But I suppose I must yes." Reaching out she brushed his hair away from his face with a loving gesture. "Consider this; you may still be able to convince Liam or Edward to fall in love with a Lady. Then perhaps they would not follow in their older brothers' footsteps."

Opening his eyes, he stared at her, a small smile tugging at his lips. "I suppose if they must marry it is best if they marry for love. Fighting it would do me no good," he admitted, moving forward to kiss his wife. "After all a very wise woman once told me something very important about love."

Though she began to answer him he quickly silenced her with a kiss. "Love will always win out in…"

The End